The
TUSCAN
HOUSE

BOOKS BY ANGELA PETCH

The Tuscan Secret
The Tuscan Girl
A Tuscan Memory

ANGELA PETCH

The

TUSCAN HOUSE

bookouture

Published by Bookouture in 2021

An imprint of Storyfire Ltd.
Carmelite House
50 Victoria Embankment
London EC4Y 0DZ

www.bookouture.com

ISBN: 978-1-80019-390-1
eBook ISBN: 978-1-80019-389-5

To my soulmate: Fagiolino xx

'Without women, resistance would have failed.'
Anon.

PROLOGUE

Corbello, Tuscany

1944

I follow the young woman into the little church of San Martino. She makes her way to the side altar where a statue of the Madonna stares down over a row of candle stubs. I sit in the shadows against a pillar and listen to the strike of a match, a coin pushed into a metal box. My eyes scan the building, checking for the best escape route, my senses on alert. On the other side of the aisle, somebody blows their nose and I turn to see an old woman dressed in black, kneeling, her fingers running through wooden rosary beads that clank against the pew as she mouths her prayers. It's musty-cold and my breath mists the air as I wait for the young woman to finish. After a while, she makes the sign of the cross, genuflects before the altar in a half curtsey and hurries towards the open door. I catch a scent of rose water as she passes. Tears glisten on her cheeks.

I trail her across the piazza where an old man is selling withered potatoes. I pull my scarf over my face and adjust the spectacles I use as one of my disguises. Soon the German soldiers will be crowding into Da Bruno, the little *osteria* opposite the church. It won't do to be recognised. Not after last night. I will be the main suspect. But the theft of the revolver in the fuggy atmosphere of the hostelry was worth it. It's time to make myself scarce in the little town of Corbello. Before disappearing, I need more information about this girl from the *osteria*.

I'd watched her yesterday as she worked and I mingled with the *tedeschi*, my ears and eyes ready for anything I could pick up.

The one who plays the piano was drunker than usual. Impossible to engage him in useful conversation when all he wanted was to sing and make love. 'Come for a walk with me, pretty *ragazza*,' he'd whispered in his strange Italian, his words spitting in my ears. I'd fluttered my eyelashes and pinched his cheek and promised to meet him later, but of course I didn't. And I don't plan to meet him ever again, if I can help it. The stupid oaf should not have left his revolver hanging in its holster on the back of the chair for me.

Bruno's *osteria* offers easy pickings and this new girl might be of help to us in the future. I've never seen her in there before. She kept herself busy behind the bar, drying glasses, glancing at the crowd of noisy men from time to time, her expression dispassionate, cold. When one of the soldiers leant against the bar to chat her up, she moved away, turning her back on him to wash a pile of espresso cups in the sink, rolling up her sleeves before plunging her pretty arms in the water. It's obvious she wants no truck with these men, unlike some local women I have watched, flirting for a hot meal, sitting on the enemy's knees, whispering in their ears, not stopping the brutes' wandering hands. And I have seen more than one of these miserable females leave at the end of the evening to wander into the back alley with one of the pigs. I understand hunger drives to desperation but I have seen too much to prostitute myself with the enemy. I hate them. I will live for the rest of my life with what men like them did to me.

The young woman makes for the track leading away from the town centre and I keep close to the walls of the houses, stooping like an old woman as I follow. But I needn't worry. There is nobody about to notice. Gone is the time when neighbours linger at thresholds or lean on windowsills to pass the time of day. Winter is cruelly bitter this year. Firewood is as scarce as food. Energy is better preserved by staying indoors avoiding trouble, when neighbour is set against neighbour in this treacherous war.

The setting sun bleeds through coppiced beeches as the young woman hurries down the path. I keep to the animal track that runs parallel on slightly higher ground, and as I tread quietly over frosted leaves, I match her pace to conceal my footsteps. Where the trees thicken by boulders she stops abruptly, turning in my direction, and I drop flat against the ground, prostrating my body to be one with the earth as Lupo and the others taught me. Raising my head slightly, peering through dried bracken, I see her collecting pine cones and stuffing them into a cloth bag. When it is full, she continues on her way and I trail her through the forest until she comes to a huddle of old buildings set in a clearing. Next to a tobacco-drying tower stands a single storey stone house and from behind an old trough at the side of the door, she produces a key and lets herself in. After a while, the glow from a lamp glimmers through the glass and I watch as she draws the shutters, a single strip of light casting a beam through a broken slat.

When I understand that she is alone in this house, I slip away, the path lit by a pallid moon. The crackle of a twig in the woods beyond has me reaching for the German's revolver and I stop behind a beech trunk, blood draining from my veins as the sounds draw near. When a porcupine shuffles by along the path, near enough for me to hear the sound of its bristles knock against each other, my shoulders relax and I stifle nervous laughter.

I am tired now. The straw bed in the cattle shed where I have sheltered these last two nights awaits. Sausage and bread snatched from the plate of a drunk soldier will be my midnight feast.

Tomorrow I shall pay the girl a visit and engage her in talk. If my instincts prove me right, she is a likely candidate for us.

'Every man thinks meanly of himself for not having been a soldier.'
Samuel Johnson

CHAPTER ONE

England

1947

The thin envelope amongst the pile of post on the doormat bore an Italian stamp and, turning it over, Richard Moorhead saw that it had been sent from Corbello in Tuscany. His heart began to race. He slit open the letter with his forefinger. It took him a while to interpret the fancy Italian handwriting and some of the words were beyond him. He'd picked up a fair bit of the lingo working in the field hospital, but he was by no means fluent. Nevertheless, he caught the gist. His presence was requested for a ceremony on Sunday 4 May 1947 in the Town Hall of Corbello at eleven to thank all those who had worked so tirelessly for the town during the war. There would be lunch afterwards. Richard had never known Italians to celebrate anything without food. Even in the midst of war, there had always been a plate of minestrone to share, or a handful of polenta or beans.

The village school in Corbello in Tuscany was where he and his fellow orderlies had set up their field hospital, once the Germans had been flushed out and the allies had reached the defensive Gothic Line. The building was in a bad state when they'd taken it over, its walls pockmarked with bullets and obscene drawings scrawled by German soldiers. The medical team had operated in an old schoolroom on the ground floor, maps of the world stuck to the plaster walls, charts showing how to form the alphabet still displayed on the chalkboard. Someone had drawn horns and a moustache on a framed photo of Mussolini, its glass cracked. They'd had a variety of cases on that first day, ranging from a Tommy with half his belly missing, to a little boy who'd picked up a mine whilst herding goats. Neither of them survived. It had been a time of extremes: life and death in the balance each second of each day. Even when you slept, your dreams were full of death. Some nights there'd been no time to sleep. Some nights he couldn't. He'd close his eyes, but the day's events were still there. Men screaming for their mothers, mothers screaming for their children. Small wonder that it trickled back to haunt him even now.

The letter in his hand, he went to the French windows in the family home he had just sold, jingling pennies in his pocket, staring at the rain-sodden garden. Where the lawn used to be, a patch that Pa had dutifully dug for the war effort was choked with weeds between stalks of Brussel sprouts sticking up like knobbly fingers. At the bottom of the garden, the remains of an Anderson air raid shelter, its metal frame twisted and rusting, was a reminder of where his parents and younger brother had died. It was ironic that the house stood intact, its only scars a couple of cracked windowpanes in the scullery.

The bare floorboards creaked as he moved away to take a last look at the other rooms downstairs. There was still an acute housing shortage in England, anxious purchasers queuing all night for whatever trickled onto the market. Richard felt he had done his bit by easing the problem: this place was too big for a bachelor and it held too many memories. Next to the breakfast room door, he trailed his fingers down pencil marks where his mother had noted her sons' heights over the years. The kitchen was cold and the clock, which his father wound ritually at the end of each day, silent. He leant against the Rayburn cast iron range that had once belted out heat, making this room the hub of the house, and his mind wandered back to 1943 when it had all started. Memories, provoked by the letter from Corbello, reeled out like scenes from a film.

*

'Bring me up to speed with Cromwell,' he'd asked the fifth form. Richard had waited for a hand to go up but nobody offered. Instead, sixteen boys glared back. He had grown accustomed to scornful looks. He'd even stopped going to the local pub since the proprietor had begun to show reluctance to serve him. The beer was awful anyway, he'd told himself, watery and weak. Doubtless what they thought of him.

'Sir?' A pimply boy sitting at the back of the classroom had eventually stuck up his hand.

'Yes, Smythe?' He was captain of the Second XI, a mean bowler, a popular boy.

'Is there something wrong with you, sir? Like, a wooden leg or a fatal illness?' Smythe had asked.

Richard had hitched up both trouser legs to display his pasty calves. Sniggers from the boys. 'The last time I looked, there was nothing untoward about these limbs, Smythe.'

'Well, why are you not fighting, sir?'

Then others, with the usual bravery of numbers, had started to chip in. 'Sir. My brother is in the Air Force, sir, and he's younger than you,' a boy in the front row piped up.

'Is it because you're scared?' asked another.

'I'm a pacifist,' Richard explained. 'I don't believe in violence.'

The history of the Civil War was abandoned and Richard had guided the boys in a discussion about the rights and wrongs of war. They were more tolerant than some adults. A woman in town had spat at him recently. She'd told him, disgust on her face, as though she'd stepped in something nasty: 'My only son was killed at Dunkirk while people like you cower here. Shame on you!'

The grocer had gently scolded her. 'Now, now, Mrs Hawthorne, that don't do no good.' He'd pushed a couple of potatoes into her basket.

But what good were two extra potatoes when you wanted your son back? Richard hadn't responded to the woman; he could understand her commonplace reaction. Whenever he tried to explain his beliefs, it was always the same reaction: he was a coward, he was letting other people go to war while he led a cushy life as a schoolmaster in a boys' private school at the end of a leafy Surrey lane.

'There are plenty of older men who could do your job,' was another answer when he countered that teachers too were needed for the war effort. 'Be careful you're not getting others to wash your dirty underwear.'

The comments stung like wasps. Deep down he'd begun to wonder if they might hold a grain of truth.

At supper that night, his mother, reading his eyes, had said, 'More grief, son?'

'I've been asked to look for another job. The headmaster called me into his office and said my pacifism was proving awkward for some parents and that it was time to leave. If I'm honest, it's a blessing, Ma.'

His father had suggested he joined him as a warden. 'I had an old biddy sticking up for me the other day,' he'd said. 'A man in the shelter started up about me being a bloody conchie. "You leave him alone, he's a good man," she told him. If she'd had a rolling pin in her hand, as sure as eggs is eggs, she'd have used it. I was busy emptying waste buckets down a manhole and spreading bug powder while she tore into him. Not the most pleasant job in the world, but somebody's got to do it. It's useful work, lad.'

'I'll think about it. I heard they need teachers up in London. The children are going wild on the bomb sites with the schools closed.'

'Will you have to go through a tribunal again?' his father asked.

'I shouldn't think so.'

Richard thought back to the day when he'd had to present his viewpoint before a panel led by a County Court Judge. A stern woman sat on the board, her hair tightly crimped, her mouth pursed like a cat's bottom as she glared at him over her thick glasses. The judge had been a fair fellow, thank heavens. 'We are not so much concerned with your views, young man,' he'd intoned, 'so much as whether we think they are sound and reasonable.'

After presenting his case, the elderly judge nodding every now and again as Richard spoke, he had been granted conditional exemption. 'Continue as you were, young Moorhead. Your teaching skills are needed for our young people.'

'Quakers are looked on reasonably favourably. It's political activists they don't like,' Richard told his parents.

His father had nodded. 'Not like in the last war when we were dished out white feathers ten a penny.'

Richard watched as his father picked at dry skin around his thumbnail: a telltale sign that he was brooding.

'I want to prove I'm not a coward,' Richard continued.

His mother had served up supper. 'Eat up,' she said, lifting the lid from a casserole of mutton neck and dumplings. 'The butcher warned me there'll be no more where this came from for a while. It'll be vegetable pie tomorrow or whale meat, worse luck.'

While they'd eaten, they'd listened to the radio. Reception was poor and it squeaked and hissed through the broadcast of *Monday Night at Seven*.

'It's Barbara's birthday tomorrow, Ma, so I shan't be in for supper – nothing against your top-hole pies, of course, but I'm whisking her up town as a surprise, taking her dancing.'

His young brother had sniggered. 'You'd better get hold of some Jerry toecaps for her shoes. I wouldn't fancy your size tens treading on my plates of meat.'

Richard had smiled at Billy. He was better at tennis than dancing, which was how he'd met Barbara, over the other side of a net in the park. She wasn't that good at hitting the ball, but she had an infectious laugh and they'd soon abandoned their game and spent the rest of the afternoon chatting.

'We'll be back late, so don't wait up. We'll go on the bike, with the buses not running,' he said, getting up to help clear the table.

'You'd better warn her of your plans, son,' his mother said. 'You know what she's like with her fancy frocks. How will she manage on the back of a motorbike, all dolled up?'

'Perhaps you're right. Maybe we'll take in a film instead. They're showing *The Goose Steps Out*, with Will Hay. We could do with a good laugh.'

'Everyone could do with a laugh right now,' his mother had agreed.

'Can I come?' Billy had piped up.

'No room for three on the bike. Sorry. Maybe next time,' Richard had said, thinking he didn't need a fifteen-year-old gooseberry crowding in on his date with Barbara.

Halfway through the film, while Richard and Barbara had been canoodling in the back row of the Troxy, the air raid sirens started to wail. They'd been tempted to stay put, but the film clicked off abruptly and there'd been a rush for the exit. Usherettes guided the crowd, shining their torches down to show the way. Outside, the warnings continued and searchlights strobed the London skyline searching for planes. A middle-aged warden in a tin hat bearing the letter W called with quiet authority as they emerged from the cinema. 'This way, ladies and gents. This way.' He pointed to an Underground sign, an arrow underneath the words AIR RAID SHELTER.

Below stairs, it was already nearly full. People had staked their places before the latest raid, asleep on grubby blankets or on top of their possessions. A couple of men played cards on an upended suitcase; a woman knitted next to an infant asleep in a cardboard box. There were people huddled between the rails where trains had run in peacetime and others camped on the elevators. Richard and Barbara found a spot to lean against the wall next to a mother seated on an overcoat. A baby slept in her arms and a toddler snivelled beside her. Barbara crouched to wipe his nose and the mother whispered, 'Thank you, lady. It's the third night in a row we've had to turf ourselves from bed. Albie's tired and grizzly. I can't stand it when those sirens start up. Sets me nerves right on edge.' She pronounced the word like other cockneys, so that it came out as 'sireens'.

Richard and Barbara had chatted quietly, wondering how long the raid would last. 'Let's hope my bike is safe, otherwise it's a long walk back, Bar.'

She seemed more worried about her laddered stockings. 'Sylvia lent them to me. She'll be furious. She'll have my guts for garters.'

An old man had struck up Vera Lynn's latest song, his accordion echoing from the sooty tiled walls. A woman started to sing, her voice untrained but compelling. When she reached the line 'Keep smiling through…' others joined in. Those who couldn't sing tapped their fingers, nodding their heads in time.

Barbara snuggled into Richard. 'That's the spirit,' she said, dabbing her eyes. She wasn't the only one blowing into a hand-kerchief. Afterwards there was quiet in the cold damp place as people settled down for an uncomfortable night.

As Richard had begun to nod off, his arms round Barbara, there'd been an almighty explosion. The shelter rocked like a ship, the place filled with dust and rubble as part of the ceiling caved in and masses of people scrambled out of the way of falling concrete. For a moment or two there'd been eerie silence and then blind panic as mothers screamed for their children. And then, two men of Richard's age dressed in khaki uniforms appeared and calmly took control.

'Form an orderly queue,' the tall, bespectacled fellow said.

His companion added: 'No need to panic, folks, but we have to get everybody out of here. If anybody's hurt, Mr Dodds and I will tend to you as soon as possible, but in the meantime, leave your possessions and follow us.'

Richard had been impressed by the young men; he couldn't make out if they were from the Red Cross and their uniforms were not regular army.

'We could do with some strong fellows to help,' the one called Dodds had announced.

'Are you all right if I leave you, Bar?' Richard asked. 'I want to lend them a hand.'

'I'll stay with this lady.'

'Meet me later by the Shaftesbury Memorial.'

He'd squeezed her hand and pushed his way through the crowd to join the two young men. Only when he'd drawn nearer did he make out the letters QUAKER embroidered on their brassards. Dodds pointed to an elderly man slumped against the wall, his breathing laboured, his face grey. 'Take Mr Perkins here up the stairs,' he said quietly to Richard. 'And then we need to get across to Charing Cross, if possible.'

The frail old man was dazed and Richard had taken him gently in his arms, following Dodds, who was carrying a young woman. They emerged from the Underground steps to a scene from hell, their feet scrunching through glass, ankle deep. A fire crew battled to extinguish flickering, fiery tongues in gutted shopfronts, the sounds of glass cracking and falling bricks mixing with commands as they directed huge jets of water. A trolley bus had landed on its side, its rear end sticking up like an abandoned toy in a gaping hole. Somebody had covered the body of a child with a coat, and Richard stepped over a motionless girl, her pretty face untouched, the lower half of her body severed. He stopped, horrified, helpless, and Dodds had turned to call, 'Over here, mate. Keep following me. Somebody else will see to her.'

Rats scuttled from holes, finding paths through the blazing embers as flares floated and drifted down like petals from large yellow flowers scattered across the sky.

At Charing Cross, nurses had taken over and Richard followed his fellow Quakers back to the bombed Underground station to fetch more wounded and vulnerable. Lumps of soot blew everywhere, searchlights swirled in the acrid smoke and a bomb had pierced a water pipe, its powerful jet splashing onto the debris like a bizarre fountain. Richard helped a very pregnant woman back to the nurses.

'The baby's coming. Bleedin' 'ell,' she'd moaned. 'This un's picked a right time to say 'ello, an' all...'

Richard had been relieved to hand her over to the medical staff. Delivering babies was something he knew nothing about. At least, not then.

When the trio had finished evacuating the bombed shelter, they shared a brew of tea handed out by the Women's Voluntary Service.

'I was brought up a Quaker,' Richard said, pointing at the men's badges while they sipped hot sweet tea poured from a huge metal pot. 'But what uniforms are you wearing?'

'We're with the FAU,' Dodds had said, shaking Richard's hand. 'I'm Douglas Dodds, DD to my friends. Thanks for your help tonight.'

'I'm Richard Moorhead,' he said, introducing himself. 'FAU? What's that?'

'Friends Ambulance Unit. Resurrected from the last war. I'm surprised you've not heard of us if you're a Friend.'

'I didn't go to Quaker school.'

The other man had introduced himself at that point. 'I'm Percy Hythe. Neither did I, old chap. But I wanted to do something to help and I was lucky enough to find out about this outfit at my tribunal.'

'I need to find out more,' Richard said. 'Listen, I've got to find my girlfriend now, but how can I get in touch with you?'

'A few of us camp in an empty school in Whitechapel, but if you're interested in the FAU, you need to apply for a place at Manor Farm, up Edgbaston way. That's where we trained. Get yourself to London again and we'll fill you in.'

The two men he met that night changed Richard's life. The purpose of the FAU, they were to tell him, was to relieve suffering caused by war. This had resonated. Six months later he knew how to make a bed with envelope corners, roll up bandages, help a patient use a Nelson inhaler, carry out blood transfusions and stitch up wounds. He would go on to help save lives of countless men, women and children. One year later, he would sleep under canvas in Macedonia in the perfect camouflage of an olive grove, and eventually, he would work twenty-four hours non-stop in an operating theatre overlooking the Bay of Naples.

But it was where he landed up in Tuscany that would cause him to question his beliefs.

CHAPTER TWO

1947

Shaking away his memories in the cold, empty house, Richard picked up the keys and took them to the estate agent, before meeting up with Barbara in the pub. He was early and took his pint to a corner table where a mean fire glowed in the grate. He picked up the local *Observer*. There was a half-page advertisement for Plummers' department store and Barbara's pretty face smiled with flirty eyes from a photo announcing the 'latest in this season's hats'. The top of her face was fringed by a strip of net attached to a straw hat perched on her head. He couldn't see the point of this fashion; but he couldn't see the point of most things at the moment. Since he'd been demobbed from Italy, few things struck a chord. England didn't seem like a country that had experienced a huge victory: piles of rubble still clogged the roads and queues stretched outside shops, housewives waiting to buy even the most basic of goods. There was no sense that rationing would come to an end soon. During the war, he'd found a purpose for a while. After leaving his post at the school, he'd ended up with the Friends Ambulance Unit and, after training, was sent to join up with the 56th division, part of the Eighth Army. He'd been in the army, but not *of* the army and that had suited him fine. His duty was to save the wounded, according to the Geneva Convention, no matter what nationality, without having to go against his deeply held beliefs and fight.

'Hello, darling.' Barbara's hand on his shoulder brought him back to 1947 and The Fox and Crown. 'What a stink of a day it's been,' she said, collapsing into the chair opposite him. She undid the buttons on her bolero jacket and peeled off her leather gloves. 'I could murder a sidecar.'

'Come again?' he asked, not up to speed with Barbara's fads.

'You know,' she continued. 'Lemon, brandy, a dash of Cointreau. It's all the rage.'

He went to the bar to order and returned with a gin and tonic. 'No Cointreau, old thing.'

'Oh well,' she said, lifting the cocktail glass to her lips. 'Bottoms up, darling!'

She'd left a red lipstick imprint on the rim. The colour of blood. He shook his head to rid himself of the image of a dying soldier in Tuscany, but as she talked about her day, the face of a desperate Italian mother blurred into Barbara's and his hands began to shake, slopping beer down his shirt.

'Are you having one of your funny turns again, darling?' Barbara asked, a frown puckering her powdered forehead. She leant towards him, one manicured hand tapping his sleeve. 'Can I do anything?'

He shook his head, steadied his breathing. She was sweet but he was used to these panic attacks.

'It seems to be happening more and more, Dick.'

Soldiers had called him Dick. They had bandied schoolboy comments about him being the dick with more head, playing around with his surname. He'd taken the baiting; he was used to being picked on. More than once he'd been at the wrong end of a pair of fists. But Dick from Bar's lips sounded wrong. He'd asked her often enough to use his full name. He stood up, his voice raised. 'Call me Richard, for pity's sake…'

'Please, Richard. Calm down.' She reached for his hand and he attempted a smile, wiping sweat from his brow.

'Sorry, old thing,' he said, collapsing back into the chair.

'Talk to me. You're… so distant these days. I can't help you if you don't tell me what's going on in your head.'

She moved with a rustle of her wide skirts. The sound was like wind sifting through olive branches and he was back in Italy again. Barbara's face merged with the face of a terrified Italian woman and, once again, panic rose and his heart rate accelerated.

'I'm a mess. Not much fun,' he said, reaching for the remainder of his beer with hands that continued to tremble. 'You should find somebody else.'

Barbara frowned and bit her ruby red lips. 'That again. Look, Richard,' she said, huffing air in exasperation. 'I waited and waited for you to come back from the war. But… somebody different turned up. I don't know you anymore.'

He looked up, surprised at her spot-on statement. 'None of us can ever be the same after those years.'

She quickly glanced away, pulled out her compact case and examined herself in the mirror, turning her face this way and that, pushing back a stray strand of hair and – if he wasn't mistaken – blinking away a tear, checking it hadn't smudged her black mascara. Snapping it shut and returning it to her bag, she rose. 'Oh well, darling. This is pointless and I'm tired of it, quite frankly. We had a good run, and nobody can say I haven't tried.' She hooked her handbag over her arm before bending to peck him on the cheek, and in a voice that sounded braver than it was, she said, 'It's all a bit beyond me, I'm afraid. But…' She fiddled with her leather gloves, eyes glistening as she spoke. 'Please find a doctor who can help you.'

When Richard looked up, she was gone, the sudden draught from the door as it shut behind her, cold on his legs. He drained his beer and walked slowly from the pub along dimly lit streets to his digs, feeling like a heel, but knowing their parting was for the best. And he also felt relief. His feelings for Bar were not the same as before. They were two very different people. He'd written her a poem for her birthday last month and after she'd read it, she'd laughed. 'Well, I've never been described like that before. Write me a story instead,' she'd said. 'Or buy me a bottle of Dior. I never could stand poetry at school. Fancy describing me as a chaffinch.'

They'd been dragging along for too long. Two people who didn't fit. How could he explain to her what he felt inside? It was hard enough understanding it himself.

As he undressed for the night, the Italian airmail envelope rustled in his shirt pocket. Was there any reason why he couldn't accept an invitation to return to Tuscany in May? It would be approaching half term at the new school where he was presently teaching. A return trip to Corbello might be just the ticket; something to exorcise the ghosts that haunted his days and nights. He'd made plenty of friends amongst the locals and it would be good to look them up and share good food and wine with them. He lit his pipe and opened the window to the night air. Yes, it would be good to set foot on Italian soil again. This time, without the fear of death stalking him round every corner. Maybe it might sort out his head. Like lancing a boil to rid its poison. He didn't need a doctor or a shrink.

CHAPTER THREE

1947

The trip across Europe on the ex-military BSA M20 motorbike that Richard had purchased with part of his parents' inheritance was going to plan. The sidecar held a rucksack containing his few clothes, a couple of notebooks for his poems, his old manual typewriter, plus assorted camping gear. Snow lingered like thick slabs of cream along the winding road leading to the Gotthard Pass. That night, his thick featherdown sleeping bag kept him cosy inside the tent he'd picked up from an army surplus store. It was different sleeping under canvas this time: he knew he wouldn't be woken at some god-awful hour to report to the surgeon to assist with an amputation or to mop blood from shrapnel wounds. There'd been occasions when he had been hauled out of bed at 3 a.m. and worked through until 10.30 p.m. if things had been hairy, whilst gunfire, Flying Fortresses and Messerschmitts kept up their hullabaloo.

This night in the Swiss Alps was quiet, save for the occasional cry from a hunting animal. He sat in the dark for a while, gazing at the jagged outline of the peaks zigzagging along the Gotthard Massif. He thought he might have heard wolves howling in the distance, but he wasn't perturbed. They were far away and although he'd heard plenty during his stint in Tuscany, he'd never seen one approach a living man. There'd been sightings of packs near Monte Cassino feeding on putrefying bodies scattered all over the shop. The terrain had been rocky, the battle so fierce, that it had been impossible to bury every corpse.

It would be time to turn in soon. How many nights had he spent under canvas in the past years? Starting from the time of his training with the FAU, camped inside the leaking cowshed at Manor Farm in the countryside near Birmingham, where he had slept for six weeks at the end of busy days of exercises. There was a photo in the album he'd slung into the sidecar showing him at the farm back in late 1943 at twenty-three years of age – lean and fit. He was carrying two buckets of water into the kitchen, a broad smile lighting up his face; another snap had caught him shivering after wading across the stream, when he'd carried a stretcher with a volunteer bandaged up. He and his fellow stretcher-bearer had tipped their patient into the ice-cold water soon after the photo had been taken, but they'd got their come-uppance when it was their turn. The route marches over the countryside were all shown in the snaps, his shorts muddy and boots cloggy, his breath steaming in the crisp air.

There were other pictures of his move to London where he'd worked for a while in Bethnal Green and slept on a mattress on the floor of a church basement, watching ops by day and shifting screens for the nurses. The latter pages of his album showed the move abroad. There were fewer photos in this section; there'd been little time for recreation. Everything literally hotted up in Egypt where they'd slept in bivvies, as they called their tents, slung up behind the old Ford. When he had a chance, he'd scribbled lines of poetry in his notebook: words more vivid to him than photographs.

The flip and pull of sheets a-billow in a Sussex breeze.
Sail boats off Fairlight Cove.
Mirages
that wrench me from my dirty canvas tent,
snapping and heaving in this roaring desert storm.

*

On each of the mornings during his seven-day journey to Italy, Richard brewed a cuppa on his Primus stove and boiled a couple of eggs in the leftover water in the billycan. That generally kept hunger at bay until the evening when he pitched camp near a hostelry. The food he was served was good, much better than the toad-in-the-hole or Spam fritters with boiled cabbage served up at civic restaurants in London. It was a treat to drink wine again, but he limited himself to two glasses. He needed a clear head to navigate the roads that were still in a terrible state. Many had deep craters and he feared for his brakes after the many emergency stops that he'd executed to avoid steering his motorbike into holes.

His map for the journey was made of silk, a gift from an ex-soldier he'd shared pints with after the war. When he'd told his new friend, Fred, that he would probably return to Italy one day, the man pulled what looked like a handkerchief from his jacket. 'Take this, mate,' he'd said. 'I'll not be going back.' It was a map, issued by M19. An escape route that Fred told him, with a wink, had been smuggled to him in a parcel of games by the so-called Jigsaw Club. 'Take it, pal. It helped me find my way across the Swiss border when I escaped from my camp. Take it. I wouldn't go back to those mountains again, even if you paid me, so I shan't be needing it anymore.'

As the miles distanced him from England, Richard began to relax. It was strange, because once he crossed the border into Italy he was back in the place where he'd witnessed most misery.

Signs of war lingered everywhere: buildings half standing, their rooms open to the world, revealing intimate corners of bathrooms and bedrooms, bits of bedside tables, broken washing basins, mirrors that reflected the sky, curtains that fluttered to the outside, the better pieces of furniture long scavenged. As he drove through shabby towns that had seen action, he saw houses boarded up, shops closed, and an absence of people.

But there were signs of recovery too. Sheep grazed in the patchy fields and crops sprouted from the scarred landscape. Masons were busy building walls and carpenters perched up ladders were patching ruins, planks of new wood and roof tiles piled by the side of the road. On the outskirts of Milan, an army of diggers shovelled rubble with their giant crab claws and further down the main road, he passed flats under construction. They were ugly and square, with no gesture to the beautiful, centuries-old ornate *palazzi* buildings they had replaced.

On the fourth night, he ate in an *osteria*, the outside walls pitted with bullet holes and signs of battle. But inside a huge effort had been made and the dining room was freshly painted, and bright with colourful pottery and pictures. The owner limped over to his table and proudly presented Richard with a menu: fresh pasta, roast hare with vegetables from his own plot of land. Richard savoured it all, complimenting him in good Italian. When the owner realised that he was *inglese*, Richard was embraced warmly like a long-lost son, the women were summoned from the kitchen to shake his hand and he was offered a glass of *liquore* on the house. '*Evviva gli alleati*. Long live the allies,' they all cried. 'You saved us from further destruction.' They all chatted at once, exuding the warmth he remembered so well from his time in the little town of Corbello, where he had learned to speak Italian from his local friends.

Friendly hospitality continued all the way down past Milan, Bologna, Faenza and on the evening of the ninth day he turned off the war-scarred main Arezzo to Sansepolcro road, and steered his bike up the dusty winding track towards the little central piazza of Corbello. He was tired and dirty. For a moment he stood by a roadside shrine, a votive light flickering red on a shelf below an image of the Madonna. Next to her was pinned an unsophisticated note informing passers-by that this was the spot where three *partigiani* had been tortured and shot by the *tedeschi* on the night of 17 July 1944. These simple memorials littered Italy and he stood in sadness for a few moments, contemplating yet again the futility of war, gazing on the plain that stretched as far as the mountains in the distance. Below him, tobacco was planted in neat rows where he remembered trenches and immobilised tanks had dirtied the landscape. He could still detect where the trenches had been, from the paler grass and telltale poppies that grew in strips. Once upon a time, the landscape of this valley would have been a palette of tobacco plants, sunflowers, church towers and castles on the hills lined with cypress trees, like the backgrounds in a Renaissance painting.

Moving on, he entered the gates of the little town. The Italian flag fluttered once again outside the town hall, the *municipio* sign painted new, and tubs on each side of the steps freshly planted with geraniums. A gang of half a dozen boys had been kicking a football to each other between the lime trees when he'd pulled up, the roar of his 500cc motor sounding loud as it echoed round the stone buildings. The lad acting as goalie picked up the ball and wandered over, eyes agog at the arrival of the motorbike, the rest of the gang trailing behind. Richard's was the only vehicle in the square. A couple of mules were tethered outside the little bar and one by one a group of men who had doubtless been inside nursing tumblers of wine and playing cards emerged to investigate the source of the noise.

Then Richard felt himself being lifted from the ground in a clumsy bear hug. His old friend Pasquale, the village blacksmith, rushed over and kissed him soundly on each cheek. 'You came back, signor Ricky, you came back...' He used the nickname that he had invented from day one of their unlikely friendship.

And then, before Richard could count to ten, the square began to fill with other villagers as they straggled from their doors, shouting that one of the *inglesi* had come back, he'd really come back. Tables and chairs were dragged into the square, wine was fetched from cellars and the women began to organise a meal to welcome one of their heroes back. Richard began to relax in the warmth of their welcome.

CHAPTER FOUR

One hour later, before any food had arrived on the tables, Richard asked for a glass of water. The third tumbler of wine had taken effect and Pasquale teased him. 'Have you turned feeble in Inghilterra, *amico mio*? I remember how you could put away the *vino*.'

'Different times, Gorilla. Different times.'

The smile on the blacksmith's face dropped for a few moments and he sighed. 'You are right.' Shaking his head as if to shake off bad memories, Pasquale clapped Richard on the back. 'I will get your glass of poison, buddy,' he joked, 'but water won't put hair on your chest.' He had always joked with Richard about his pale hairless body when they washed the blood away at the end of a shift in the field hospital, stripping by the village fountain behind a temporary canvas screen. Pasquale was covered with thick hair and Richard had nicknamed him Gorilla; it was the same word in Italian. The Italian had been the first of the Corbello citizens to offer help to the medical unit, volunteering to carry stretchers, fetch barrels of water and do odd jobs in the ramshackle school the Medical Corps had requisitioned as their field hospital. Pasquale patched up holes, set traps for rats and forged parts for the trucks when needed. He spoke fairly good English with an American twang, picked up from watching American movies.

A little girl approached, hanging on to the skirts of a pretty woman carrying a carafe of water on her head and Pasquale lifted the little girl into his arms and threw her in the air. The child squealed with laughter. 'More, Babbo, more…'

He set her down next to Richard. 'Remember this little angel?' he asked.

'*Ciao*,' Richard said, a little puzzled as he couldn't recall this child. The slight pouches beneath the little girl's telltale almond-shaped eyes and her button nose told Richard of her condition. She smiled shyly, bringing her stubby fingers to her face. He noted too the wide gap between her front teeth and he knew that if he were to examine her palms, he would find a singular crease across their width.

'Is this my saviour?' the little girl asked of Pasquale and he nodded his head.

'Yes, this is your guardian angel. And he is our saviour too, Angelina, for he brought you to us.' Pasquale grasped the woman's hand and squeezed it, before she moved away with Angelina. He waited until they were at a distance before explaining.

'What happened to her is no secret here, but Rosa and I don't like to make too much of a fuss in front of Angelina. She's the child you rescued. Do you not remember? We have looked after her ever since. She's our daughter now.'

He pumped Richard's hand up and down, but with his gratitude, the memory that haunted Richard suddenly returned with a vengeance. He pushed his chair from the table. 'Excuse me. *Scusatemi*, I need the toilet.' He brushed past the blacksmith and hurried from the piazza. People turned to stare but nobody followed. They had known suffering; there was an understanding about grief in this place; the knowledge of when to step in and help and when not to talk was instinctive.

The town was not big but Richard soon found a quiet corner down an alleyway that smelled of cats and where half the houses were shells. A piece of torn curtain hung from the gaping window of an empty house, like a ghostly limb. He slumped down onto the step and watched a rat slide down an open drain. With trembling hands, he pulled his pipe from his pocket and struck a match, the flare lighting up his features, his stomach churning as he confronted memories of this place.

*

As crazy as it had seemed in the thick of war, Richard had gone for a walk on that summer afternoon in 1944. There was a dusty track, near to where the FAU had set up their station, leading to a hamlet in the part of the valley that was a kind of no man's land. The Germans still held the hilltop town of Corbello at that time. It was important strategically as it commanded the view of the main route between the two important cities of Arezzo, now liberated by the allies, and Sansepolcro, still occupied by the Germans.

Richard's destination on that muggy early afternoon had been a huddle of half a dozen houses where the men occasionally traded for eggs. The young woman who lived there with her tiny daughter and father was happy to swap a couple of slices of white bread in exchange and Richard had saved his dry breakfast slice for this purpose. Inside his shirt, he nursed a black and white kitten against his chest. Its mother had abandoned her litter at the back of the medical store, where she'd given birth. He and a couple of the men had adopted them, feeding them scraps of bully beef and slops of tea. Richard was taking one down for the toddler. The kitten might grow to be a good mouser and the child didn't seem to have any toys. But, apart from that, he'd wanted to get away from the hospital unit that day, unable to sleep after a particularly draining shift. There'd been harrowing cases to deal with: four more badly injured children brought in by anguished parents. The Senior Medical Officer had done his best, but it had been pointless. Then, just as they were cleaning up, a partisan had been brought into the blood room. He'd been shot and afterwards tied to a tree, petrol poured over him and set alight. A relative had carried him in, but he'd died in agony two hours later. Richard had needed to clear his head. It was the only way he could confront the next shift.

At four o'clock he'd set off alone down the track. In the distance, he could hear the dull thud of cannon fire and he wondered which poor town was being blasted to smithereens. Lines of a new poem he'd been plotting drifted into his thoughts:

> Bare bones of houses,
> Carcass walls, eye socket windows.
> An old woman, bent double,
> grubbing
> through rubble.
> Searching for a memory.
> Another shell explodes,
> A flash – the only colour
> In this grey Italian landscape…
> Tiles fall…

Wild blackberries hung heavy in a stretch of hedgerow and as he'd picked a handful, he tried to imagine himself back home, picking over fruit with his mother in the tiny scullery, helping her boil up jam, securing lids for her while the Kilner jars were still scalding hot. He looked forward to sitting in the yard of the Italian woman's simple farmhouse to sip ice-cold water from her well and to be apart from the company of the battle-weary for a while.

As he drew nearer the hamlet, he heard shouting and scream-ing and he squatted down behind an empty pigsty. From there he crawled on his stomach through the dry grass behind the farmhouse. The back door was open and he crept inside. An old man lay on the floor, an upturned cooking pot seeping carrots and potatoes into blood pumping from a wound in his stomach. Richard felt for his pulse, but there was nothing. He straightened up and moved with stealth to the small window that overlooked the farmyard.

A German soldier aimed his gun at the woman who sold eggs, her little daughter half-hidden behind her skirt. He was shouting at her in pidgin Italian, demanding she bring him a chicken. '*Portare pollo. Pollo…*' he shouted, and she, with hands clasped, was begging him to leave them alone, telling him there were no chickens, the *tedeschi* had taken them. 'There are no animals left,' she cried.

The soldier had his back to Richard and before he could think twice, Richard had lunged, bringing his left arm around the neck of the soldier, his right knee into the small of his back. A shot and a scream split the air simultaneously and, without hesitation, Richard pulled harder on the man's throat until he slumped forwards to the dirt. He ran to check on the woman lying yards away, her little girl screaming, 'Mamma, mamma' over and over. There was nothing he could do to help the woman. The top of her head was a mess from the bullet that had shattered her brain like a burst watermelon. Horrified that he had caused her death, he tried to take the child in his arms but her screaming intensified and she wriggled away, pointing frantically over Richard's shoulder. The German was on his feet again, grasping for his rifle. Richard got to the weapon first and used it without hesitation, even though the gun felt alien in his hands. In that moment, it was all surprisingly easy. Then, he had grabbed the child, fearing that the dead German might not be alone, and ran like the clappers back to the field hospital. Pasquale was lifting a box of medical supplies from a truck when Richard thrust the screaming child into the Italian's arms.

*

Pasquale found Richard in the shadows and sat down beside him, his bulk taking up most of the step. He had a bottle in his hand and he handed it to Richard. 'I couldn't find water,' he said.

Richard smiled. 'We'll share this,' he said, taking a swig of the red wine.

For a while they sat in silence, passing the alcohol between them. The voices of the townspeople and the chorus of cicadas were soon replaced by music from an accordion drifting from the square. Wine, food, music, companionship: the staples of Italian festivity.

'He was the only man I ever killed,' Richard said, slurring his words as the wine took effect. 'I'm not counting the poor bugger I dropped from the stretcher at Cassino, or the lad I gave too much morphine. They were goners, anyway.' He gulped down another huge slug of wine and spluttered as the vinegary taste hit the back of his throat. 'Maybe Angelina's mother would still be alive if I hadn't intervened that day... it haunts me, Gorilla.'

He turned towards his friend in the gloom. 'Nobody will ever be able to explain the point of war to me. What good ever came from killing? But I joined the ranks of killers myself.' He squinted at Pasquale, whose features blurred before his eyes. With all the wine he had consumed, Richard swayed even where he was sitting. 'I've heard they want to give me a medal, but I don't deserve any of this praise. I'm just another killer. I should never have come – I'll leave in the morning.'

'You rescued a child, Ricky. What else could you do?' Pasquale put his arm around the Englishman's shoulders and squeezed him. 'You gave Rosa and me our beautiful daughter. There was no one else left in her family to take care of her, so she became our family. Stay a while with us in Corbello so we can look after our hero.' He took the bottle from Richard's hands.

'Stay?' Richard asked. 'Why should I stay?'

'You came back here! That's a good enough reason to start with.' He pulled Richard to his feet. 'But come eat now. This guilt will pass, my friend, when you realise that there is more to life than dwelling on the past. We need to line our stomachs so that we can drink more *vino*. And then I'll find you a couple of *belle signorine* to dance with.'

'Dancing and killing don't go well together, my friend. I'm not fucking dancing.'

Pasquale shook his head and led Richard back to the piazza where he was swept into a whirl of merrymaking that he couldn't avoid. Whenever he tried to say that he wasn't a hero, he was given another glass to swallow by his friends and on that first evening back in Corbello, his clumsy feet clomped away the nightmares.

CHAPTER FIVE

It was just as well his head was fuzzy and he was suffering the hangover to beat all hangovers next morning because, on any normal day, he would have halted the ceremony before it began. Being back in this place had reinforced that he was no hero. He was a fraud. Pasquale had woken him with coffee as sludgy as mud, bitter as medicine, and suggested he got up and dressed in whatever smart clothes he could muster. Richard went straight to the trough outside Pasquale's smithy and plunged his head and shoulders into the cold water, gasping as he emerged, hoping to shake away the effects of last night's *festa*. Pasquale roared with laughter. 'Get this down you, loser,' he said, handing him a cup of something yellow, as Richard dried himself on a cloth.

'What are you poisoning me with now?' Richard asked.

'My own cure. Raw egg beaten up with sugar and a generous dose of *vino* Marsala.'

It was more pleasant than Richard expected. Nevertheless, his head still felt as though a dozen drummers were practising against his temples and, if he'd been able, he would have slunk off to sleep away the rest of the day.

In the centre of the small square which housed the twelfth century church of San Martino, the baker's, a little hostelry called Da Bruno and the town hall, a wooden stage had been erected and the place thronged with people from outlying villages come to attend the ceremony. Pasquale, bursting from a shiny dark suit that was short in the legs and arms, led Richard up the steps of the stage, where the mayor waited in his Sunday best, a wide sash of green, white and red draped from one shoulder and across his stout body. A small brass band began to squeak out the Italian anthem, almost in unison, and Richard winced as three trumpeters blasted out the first notes. Pasquale's mouth twitched and leant towards him to whisper, 'San Martino is the patron of drunkards, did you know? Better pray to him to cure your head.'

The mayor started a flowery speech. It was long and the crowd began to fidget, a small child wailed and nobody made an effort to quieten him. Richard caught some of the main points, although there were many long words he'd never heard before. It was fitting, the portly mayor started, 'That we stand together today in front of our little church dedicated to a saint who was also a soldier. More than a thousand years ago, he cut his cloak in half to give to a beggar. Our British friend today did not wear a cloak but he, along with others who could not attend today, gave a piece of himself, a slice of courage, to save the lives of our citizens, who are gathered on this stage to give thanks to him and the doctors and nurses who couldn't travel today from Inghilterra.'

He gestured to the other side of the stage where half a dozen men, women and little Angelina huddled, all beaming at Richard, who looked down at his feet in embarrassment. He had simply been doing his job; he'd done no more than others, probably less. They should be here instead and he was uncomfortable that he'd come all this way to bask in their praise, when inside he knew he was no hero. Logically he'd known that the ceremony would happen, but all throughout his journey he'd pushed thoughts of it to one side, telling himself that his return was about more than that.

Pasquale dug him in the ribs to remind him to stand to attention as the mayor advanced with a medal and, reaching up on the tips of his shiny shoes, placed it around Richard's neck. 'I hereby declare you an honorary citizen of Corbello,' he announced, stepping back as the townspeople cheered, a few of the men in the crowd whistling through their fingers to shouts of '*Evviva l'Italia.*' Richard watched as Pasquale lifted Angelina to pull on a cord, pulling open a small velvet curtain that covered a plaque on the side of the town hall. *Piazza degli Alleati*, he read. The town square had been renamed in honour of the allies. It was a great honour, and one he felt he personally didn't merit.

Later, as Richard and twenty or so dignitaries and officials sat down to another gargantuan feast of dishes of varied *bruschette*, home-made pasta, roasted quail and hare, Richard gazed at the company around him. The only person he actually remembered was Pasquale, sitting at the other end of the long table, chatting animatedly with his neighbours, knocking back Chianti like water. There were more interminable speeches to sit through that he didn't fully understand and Richard longed to escape. But he knew that this would be considered offensive behaviour. Italians enjoyed formal occasions.

He felt like an imposter. Why on earth had he come to the ceremony? He cursed himself for not thinking his return to this little town through: turning up on some kind of whim to bring himself closure for an act that stalked his dreams. Richard, drenched with sweat, ran his fingers around the collar of his shirt and wondered when he could make his escape. The Senior Medical Officer should be here in his place – or one of the doctors or nurses who had worked to achieve miracles under such dreadful field conditions. Or any of his mates in the FAU. The only thing that kept him glued to his chair was acceptance of this honour as a representative. Once he was back in England, he would look up the real heroes and put them in touch with the mayor of Corbello. It was they who deserved the attention he was being lavished and, in halting Italian, he said as much at the end of all the speeches.

After strong coffee and sweet liqueurs, and Richard's hand had been pumped up and down by countless important besuited men, he signalled to Pasquale and the two men wandered away from the square. They sat on the low wall that encircled the little town, and Richard got out his pipe, using his lighter first to help Pasquale with his cigarette, which smelled rank.

'You're not still smoking those filthy Alfa things, are you?' he asked, wafting the noxious smell away. 'They're made from wood shavings, Gorilla.'

'I am used to them. And they're cheap. Maybe I should get the hang of a pipe, like you.'

Richard chuckled and packed Erinmore mix into the bowl with his thumb. 'I need to stretch my legs after that affair. Thank the stars it's over. Where is it safe to walk without being blown up by mines?'

'Stick to the roads. If you see anywhere marked with signs, don't venture there. But a team of army engineers swept the area last month, so things are slowly improving. The bastards even put mines down by the riverbanks to trick fishermen and children playing in the shallows.' Pasquale patted his stomach. 'Tell you what, Richard, I'll join you. I need to digest this and it's easier to show you than explain where it's safe.'

The two men walked together down the dust road that circled the hilltop town like a necklace. Soon after reaching the plain, the path ran parallel with a narrow river that trickled through the valley. They stopped at a point where the water collected in a natural pool. 'When it's warmer, this is where the kids swim,' Pasquale said. 'During the war, the *tedeschi* commandeered it.' He smiled. 'I'm teased by my friends because they say I'm descended from the monster who used this as his bath.'

Richard smiled. There were myths galore in this fascinating country.

Pasquale continued, warming to his tale. 'The story goes that he was a big man, covered in hair, and known as Homo Selvatico or Agnollaccio. He preyed on shepherds, snatching their sheep, and this pool ran red with the blood from the beasts he devoured. One day, a young shepherd was told by a friar that the only way to finish off this beast was to use a golden bullet. He handed the shepherd a gold coin and blessed it, advising him to make it into a special bullet. The shepherd was successful and from that day, the Grand Duke of Tuscany granted him years of free hunting in the area.'

'Another story invented by the rich to grant themselves favours,' Richard said.

Pasquale pulled a face. 'That is the way of the world. It always has been.'

'All the fighting, all the wars over lands and riches. It doesn't change a thing. The killing is pointless.'

'But not if a people are being invaded and abused. It's natural to want to fight off the enemy when they threaten your loved ones.'

Richard shrugged his shoulders. 'Let's walk,' he said. He was tired of arguing his conscientious objector's corner, of explaining that he preferred to build a new world with a civilian service, rather than fighting to destroy the old.

They walked at a steady pace until they came to a couple of buildings surrounded by olive trees, some snapped at the trunk and bearing scorch marks from incendiaries. Pasquale wandered over, his feet crushing poppies and chamomile flowers in the coarse grass. He ran his hands over what remained of the trees. 'With careful pruning, these could pick up and there'd be a fine crop,' he said, turning to Richard, who was staring instead at the taller structure, a kind of tower soaring above a lower building attached at right angles, forming an L-shape, with a small court-yard between. He'd never walked out this way during the war.

'You're looking at the old tobacco-drying tower,' Pasquale said. 'It belongs to our Mayor Gobbi, but it hasn't been worked for years. He owns a lot of property round here. He has his fingers in many pies, that one.'

Richard pushed his way through a heavy door made from chestnut. Inside, two pigeons flapped their wings, the sound echoing loudly in the empty building like umbrellas shaken in the rain. The startled birds flew through a large gap in the roof, its rafters open to the blue sky. It was like nowhere else he had ever seen, so different from his parents' home in its avenue of identical, boxy houses. He'd imagined himself living in a small apartment in England but a strange thought popped into his head. 'This would make the most amazing place to live in,' he said.

Pasquale followed Richard into the ramshackle building. 'Are you crazy? Live in this dump? It's a long way from town; it's huge and likely infested with woodworm; there's no electricity. It will be freezing and draughty in winter. It stinks of smoke from years of drying tobacco. You cannot be serious.'

Richard gazed at the thick beams spanning the width of the tower, ideas flickering through his mind. 'A mezzanine floor up top, another floor between, huge windows to let in light,' he muttered to himself. 'It wouldn't need much furnishing. Once finished, the place would speak for itself.'

Picking his way over charred timbers and debris, he went outside and crossed the area between the tower and the squat building. He stopped at a well, its opening covered with a circular piece of wood, pushing the lid away and jumping back as a snake slithered from beneath. 'There's water, at least,' he said, noting with relief that the reptile was a grass snake and not a viper. During the war, one of the orderlies he'd worked with had taken to snake hunting in his free time. Richard hadn't joined in.

The walls of the squat building were slowly being reclaimed by moss and grass that grew in gaps that needed repointing and the door was padlocked. Richard tried to rub clean a patch in a small adjacent window and peer inside. But his view was blocked by a cobweb as thick as a curtain on the other side of the glass. 'Do you think your mayor will let me have the key to this place?' Richard asked. 'I'd like to take a better look.'

Pasquale banged his temple with his thick forefinger. 'Either you have drunk too much Chianti or you have sunstroke, but seeing as the sun isn't hot enough, I'll just go along with my original notion that you are crazy, Ricky.'

'I am serious.'

Pasquale shook his head. 'Well, buddy, if you are really serious about this, then let *me* make the first move to the *sindaco*. If you show that you're keen to our mayor, the price for this pile of shit will go up. You have to play it cool. He's a crafty devil. I don't trust him and I don't like him. I've never seen the guy laugh. How can you trust anybody who never laughs?'

'Is there no estate agent to deal with?' Richard asked, ignoring Pasquale's rant.

'Say again?'

'You know – an agent to act as intermediary. For a sale?'

'Our mayor is estate agent, bar owner, governor of the school, hospital, not to mention father to half the little bastards in town. It's Edoardo Gobbi we have to go to for most things, cap in hand. He's a slippery customer and I can't stand the man. I can only think that he bribed his way to getting voted as our *sindaco*.' Pasquale made an obscene gesture with his finger. 'He brings out the worst in me. But…' He paused. 'If you are really that keen on taking a look, who's to say that some passing tramp hadn't already broken into the place?' Pasquale picked up a metal reinforcement rod leaning against the well and used it to wrench the padlock from the door.

It was dark inside the smaller building and as daylight leaked in, an angry buzzing started up from behind the furthest window barricaded with lopsided shutters. '*Calabroni,*' Pasquale said, jumping back out of the door. 'I'm outta here. These can kill if they sting.'

For a big man, he was a real sissy, Richard thought. A hornet's nest wouldn't take much to sort. Still, he would leave well alone for now. Those insects had lived here before him and he'd find a way to persuade them to leave and nest elsewhere. He picked up a stub of candle in an enamel holder from a square table and lit it with his lighter, holding it up to see better. In the far corner a metal double bed had been partially screened by a grubby sheet hanging from a thick piece of rope tied to hooks in a beam. A thin mattress was rolled up at the bed end. A cooking stove with blackened pans, a pile of tinder stacked at its side, a chipped stone sink beneath the cobweb-curtained window nearest the door, a shelf with cracked plates and cups, a small mirror hanging on the wall and an old treadle sewing machine were the main contents. A ladder leant against a small storage platform above the kitchen area and everywhere were mouse droppings. He glanced at the newspaper on the table, a copy of *Il Popolo* dated 5 June 1945 and he remembered its significance: the date of the Berlin declaration, when Nazi Germany had been legally dissolved.

'Looks like nobody has lived here for a while,' he called to Pasquale outdoors.

'And do you blame them? Hurry up, crazy man. Rosa will be wondering where we've got to.'

Richard emerged blinking into the sunlight. 'This place will do up nicely. There's everything I'd need to camp in it while I renovate. I need a project.'

Pasquale shook his head. 'Now, you're really worrying me. If you like Corbello so much, why don't you consider one of the new houses they're building outside town? It would be safer in the event of earthquakes. You'd have running water, electricity, a bathroom with a toilet. Here you'd have to fertilise the fields.'

'Only for a while. Until I installed a modern bathroom.'

Richard loved Italians for their warm hearts and downright nosiness. But he needed his own space. There was no way he would sign up for an apartment in a communal block, ready-made or otherwise. This spot here, within sight and reach of the little town topping the plains, was perfect. Near enough but far enough away to heal his life.

'*Why?*' Pasquale asked the question that Richard probably should be asking of himself. 'Why do you want to leave your own country to come and live in a ruin like this? Why?'

How could Richard explain what he didn't really understand himself? He only knew that he craved a change and this was a good place to wipe the slate clean, give himself a new perspective. The short time he had spent in Corbello back at the tail end of the war had warmed him to this country. Strangely, a few hours earlier, he'd wondered why the dickens he had come back, but now he was seriously considering staying. Italy did that to him. It was a place of extremes – of passion; she had a way of drawing him out of himself, of damping down his usual Anglo-Saxon reserve. England, on the other hand, didn't seem like a country that had won a war. There was still rationing. Jobs were scarce. At the resettlement office, he'd been told to return to his teaching job. But there'd been no help offered with settling his mind. His parents were gone and he was a different man to the one Barbara had met before the war. Even if it had worked out with Barbara, the thought of marriage, a permanent job at a half-rate school as an English teacher of snotty-nosed kids, living in a semi-detached house and tending to a vegetable patch of a Sunday forever after, filled him with little joy. There was no challenge to it and the mere thought made his heart wither. There had to be more to life. During the war, with bombs falling around, dealing with horrific injuries, facing death any minute, he'd done a lot of dreaming; yearning for a peaceful world had helped him through those times. What was wrong with having a dream? Doing up an old tower in beautiful Tuscany was a good start.

CHAPTER SIX

Richard wore a tie and a clean shirt to the meeting in Mayor Edoardo Gobbi's office in the *comune*. He and Pasquale were ushered in by a pretty young woman wearing a tight skirt and white blouse, the buttons straining over her full bosom. Richard watched the mayor, whose eyes slid sideways to watch the woman's backside as she left his room. Then he rose from behind his desk to shake Richard's hand.

'Pasquale tells me you are wanting to view my tobacco factory outside Corbello. Sit down, signor Richard. Sit down. It's a pleasure to be in the company of a hero.' There was no chair for Pasquale, who remained standing by Richard's side.

Richard perched uncomfortably on the narrow wooden chair, embarrassed once again by the mayor's description and smiling inwardly at Gobbi's inflated description of the property, while the mayor re-seated himself on the comfortable leather swivel chair behind his desk. Richard was mesmerised by the sight of the ugly carved legs in the form of naked-breasted women supporting the desktop on their heads.

'Factory?' Richard said in English, as agreed previously with Pasquale. 'A factory to me conjures something larger. The buildings are in a very poor state.'

He listened as Pasquale translated something entirely different to what he had said. As far as he'd understood, it went something along the lines of Richard only thinking about the idea of buying somewhere at this preliminary stage. The mayor suggested that signor

Richard might instead prefer to view a couple of handsome villas for sale in nearby Anghiari. They were ready to move into. One had a swimming pool and the other, five hectares of flourishing vineyard.

'Pasquale, please tell the mayor that I'm not a rich *inglese* and that if he wants to get rid of his *ruin*, I *might* be up for it,' Richard said, looking straight into Pasquale's eyes, keeping his own face straight and noting the merest of twinkles in response.

Pasquale responded in his American twang, his voice equally as level. 'I'll tell him that if he doesn't sell it to you at a good price, we'll let his wife know he's been screwing his secretary, who, by the way, has the finest tits I've seen in a while.'

Richard tried not to let his amusement show, but he couldn't resist continuing in the same spirit for his friend's benefit, remembering what he'd said about Gobbi's corruption and hoping fervently that his words would not be translated literally. 'Perfect!' he said. 'And tell the mayor I'd like to take a proper view and *maybe* come back to negotiate. Tell him I don't want him to be there when I look it over, if at all possible, because his bad breath will make me keel over and it would put me off the sale.'

'Of course, signor Richard.' There was a slight pause before Pasquale continued in English. 'You're killing me with this, buddy. You owe me one fat drink for keeping my face straight. I'll pick an awkward time for viewing, like straight after lunch when he's probably in bed with his... assistant.'

A couple of days later in Da Bruno, Pasquale knocked on the door of the room where Richard was staying. 'I've had an interesting visitor,' he said as they walked to their usual seat on the town walls. 'The mayor's wife. She wants to talk to you and I've arranged to meet at the tobacco tower in one hour.'

Richard's eyes widened. 'Do you think she was eavesdropping on our conversation with her husband and heard all about his mistress's tits?'

'Once again, Ricky, you are being ridiculous. I thought the *inglesi* belonged to a sensible race. Shall we walk there or do I have to squeeze my arse into your machine again?'

'Let's walk,' Richard said, patting his friend's stomach. 'It will do you good. It's not that far.'

They made their way in silence out of the little town, Pasquale puffing a little as they strode along. The umbrella pines lining the road cast welcome shade. May was beginning to heat up, bees were feasting on pollen, and lizards scuttled across the path where the two men walked, their feet stirring up dust. An old man hoed around lettuce seedlings in a field near the river and he stopped to wave. Pasquale shouted over, asking if the old man had any chicken manure to spare and was told to come by later. 'I shall probably end up doing some little job for him in exchange,' Pasquale said as they continued their walk. 'A lock for his gate or repair of a tool, maybe.'

Richard liked this system of barter and wondered what he could offer, if the time arose. If he was to stay here, then he needed to come up with some way of making a living. A dream he'd nurtured over the past years was publication of his poems. During the war he'd scribbled lines whenever he could and compiled them in the form of a diary. Living in this place would offer a perfect opportunity to concentrate on pulling them into shape and he'd already imagined a study arranged on a mezzanine floor at the top of the old tobacco tower. Pasquale interrupted his daydream.

'Look! The signora is here already.'

A slim woman in her late thirties approached from where she had been leaning against a new grey Fiat Topolino, its roof rolled open. 'Good afternoon,' she said in heavily accented English, extending a manicured hand to Richard. 'Magdalena Camarlengo. I am Edoardo Gobbi's wife. How do you do?'

Richard noted the use of her maiden name, a practice commonly used in Italy. The tailored suit she wore was not the Corbello norm of cotton frock, pinafore and sturdy rubber work boots. She was deeply attractive, her dark hair curling to her shoulders and he reckoned he could span both hands round her waist, belted neatly with the narrowest strip of red leather.

'Delighted to meet you,' he responded. 'Compliments on your English.'

'I worked as personal assistant for a British captain helping the displaced at the end of the war. One picks it up very quickly when one converses with real people instead of studying from a book and Captain Graham was an Oxford lecturer before the war. He has invited me to visit your country, but… who knows?' She bit her lip and paused, causing Richard to wonder whether she had done more than interpret for her English captain. 'Anyway, to business,' she continued. 'I discovered from my husband that you are interested in my property.'

'*Your* property? I thought it belonged to your husband.'

'He likes to give that impression. But it was passed down to me by my grandparents.' She pulled a silver, monogrammed case from her crocodile-skin handbag and offered a cigarillo to Richard, who declined, but moved forward to light it for her. As he drew closer, he caught the scent of her perfume.

'A lot of his portfolio is in fact mine,' she said, tipping back her head and exhaling aromatic smoke into the Tuscan air. 'My parents were not interested in taking on the tobacco business but my grandfather hoped I might one day pick up the reins.' She turned to look at the property. 'I loved coming here when I was little. Nonno used to let me help stack the tobacco leaves to dry and stoke the fire with him. But the business was long gone even before war devastated our country.'

Pasquale intervened. 'Signora Gobbi, my friend would obviously like to take a good look inside before he decides anything and… in fact, he will probably want to look at other properties before he comes to any decision. Is that not so, Richard?' he asked, turning towards him with a barely perceptible lift of his thick eyebrows.

'Yes. Oh… yes. I definitely need to take a really good look and weigh up everything before deciding,' Richard said, to Pasquale's obvious relief.

Magdalena dipped into her handbag and produced a set of keys, closing the clasp again with a snap. 'Sensible man. Only fools rush in… There are three keys on this ring, gentlemen. Each labelled with the name of three different properties. All mine, *not* my husband's. Pasquale, I'm sure you know where the other two are. They are all uninhabited. If you need me, you know where I am.' She turned to walk to her car. The door slammed and she accelerated away in the opposite direction to Corbello.

'Wow!' Richard said. 'A husband would be a fool to get on the wrong side of that one. How in hell's name did they end up together? They seem an odd match.'

'An arranged marriage when she was very young,' Pasquale said. 'Her parents moved away from here to the city where she was born. They make them different there.'

'Too big, too small, too near other houses, no character, no project and too expensive.' Richard reeled off objections to the two properties they viewed later that week. One was an elaborate nineteenth-century villa in the centre of Anghiari, near the theatre. 'I wouldn't be able to fart or blow my nose in this place, without everybody knowing,' he said, standing on the balcony overlooking the busy square. 'Not for me.' The other property was a former bishop's house next to the church. 'Where the bells chiming on the quarter hour through the night would drive me bonkers,' Richard said as he bought another bottle of Moretti beer to share with Pasquale in the theatre bar. 'There's something about that tobacco property that speaks to me. I can't get it out of my mind.'

Next morning while Pasquale was busy in his workshop, sparks flying from his anvil as he worked to mend a cartwheel, Richard took himself off alone for another look at the tower without Pasquale, who would only try to dissuade him of the purchase. It was sunny again and he rolled up his shirtsleeves as he worked to detach the sidecar from his bike. He wanted to take a roundabout route to the property, to remind himself of the beauty of a landscape hinted at during the war: cypress-lined avenues meandering up to hilltop villages perched on ridiculously steep rises, churches and little chapels holding ancient treasures, simple shrines by the side of the road. It had been frustrating to be at war in a country that people had explored and revered over the centuries on Grand Tours, while he was trailing an army on the move.

Richard drove his motorbike along a track that led through tidy lines of vines, rose bushes planted at the end of each row, the vine grower's early warning system for aphids. He remembered how golden the shoots had looked at the end of the summer of '44, how vines drooped heavy with withering grapes, unharvested as battles waged and nobody could reach the fruit.

He passed a large farmhouse perched on the top of a hill, its commanding position no doubt chosen as a defensive point against marauders. Part of its *cotto*-tile roof was covered with sheets of corrugated iron and the bullet-scarred walls were shored up with metal poles. He asked himself if the day would ever come when he didn't think about war, and, deep in thought, he didn't notice a flock of scrawny chickens scratching in the track. A couple of birds scattered from his wheels, with squawks and flying feathers.

He pulled up to make sure he hadn't killed any and stretched his back, arms reaching for the cornflower-blue sky. The chickens had all, happily, escaped his wheels. In a cobbled courtyard in front of another abandoned house, he spied a fountain and went over to slake his thirst, his mouth full of dust from the road. He remembered passing a sinister notice during the war as he drove the ambulance along a similar powdery track: 'Drive slowly. Dust is Death!' it read. He'd slowed down and peered nervously towards the hills held by Jerry, in case dust had given away their presence.

The fountain was dry and he moved on. In a field beyond a lone farmhouse, a shepherd watched over a straggle of sheep and a large black dog barked a warning at Richard and charged the fence. Noting the gaps, Richard climbed quickly back onto his bike and roared away.

In the next hamlet, he stopped by a washing fountain where a couple of women scrubbed at clothes. They smiled shyly at him and giggled as he asked in halting Italian if he could drink from the tap. They shook their heads, '*Non potabile*,' said the braver of the two. Not for drinking. They pointed to a house opposite where a painted sign, BAR – OSTERIA, was propped against an old oil drum planted with roses. He thanked them and wheeled his bike over. The aroma of real coffee and something herby and delicious hit him as he approached, making his mouth water as he pushed through the curtain at the door. A plate of home-made ravioli filled with spinach and cheese and a couple of glasses of wine improved his Italian and he enjoyed a simple conversation with the owner and his toothless wife, smiles and handshakes exchanged when he promised to return again.

By now Richard was looking forward to his sneak view of the tower and its adjoining house. His heart sank when he saw a shining Lancia Aprilia parked outside. Mayor Gobbi appeared from behind the building, mopping his brow as he walked over. '*Chi è?*' he shouted, anger in his voice. 'Who is it?' He stopped short when he saw Richard and leant a spade against one of the olive trees. 'Ah, signor Richard. I was tidying up. This place…' he said, pulling a handkerchief from his pocket to wipe earth from his hands, 'it is in a terrible condition. It needs bulldozing.'

'No need for that, sir, surely.' Richard stopped himself in time from offering to take it immediately off his hands, remembering Pasquale's advice not to appear too eager.

'It is dangerous. The tower could fall at any time. I shall be asking the inspector of buildings to put a demolition order on the place.' Gobbi went to his car and produced a new chain and padlock and Richard watched in dismay as he secured the door that Pasquale had forced open. 'What are you doing here anyway, signore?' he asked.

Richard decided not to let on that he knew the property belonged to Gobbi's wife. There was no point in angering this pompous man. He wondered why the little mayor was so against him buying the place, and reflected on his comment about wanting to bulldoze the complex. It didn't make any sense that he'd been busy tidying up, as he'd put it, when Richard had turned up.

'I made a trip round the *strade bianche* on my bike this afternoon. When I was here in '44, I always wanted to explore these back roads.'

'You should take care. There are mines everywhere.' He turned to Richard, a frown on his face. 'Why don't you house hunt in Arezzo? Buy a fine *palazzo*? There is so much more to see in that city: the frescoes of Piero della Francesca, beautiful squares, excellent restaurants… there is nothing for *turisti* here.'

He stood, feet firmly planted in the scrubby grass in front of the tower, blocking Richard's path. Richard gave up on a sneak viewing and returned to his motorbike.

'I'll think about your suggestion, signore,' he said, swinging his leg over his bike and kick-starting the motor. If he had deliberately skidded so that a huge cloud of dust enveloped the mayor as he stood waiting for Richard to leave, who could have said?

CHAPTER SEVEN

Richard arranged to meet Magdalena Camarlengo outside her lawyer's office in the centre of Sansepolcro, in the square known as Piazza Torre di Berta. Where once a huge tower had soared to thirty-eight metres since the thirteenth century, there were now neat piles of bricks and massive stones arranged in rows for reconstruction.

'The Germans blew this up before they left the city at the end of July '44,' Magdalena explained, as they made their way through the avenue of rubble. 'There was no reason, other than disdain that Italy had swapped sides and joined the allies. The tower was of no strategic importance whatsoever and despite the anguished pleas of the bishop to spare it for posterity, its demolition was a purely destructive act. *Seventeen* bombs were laid in the tower; the rubble filled the whole of this square. When the tower exploded like a rocket into the summer sky and dust rained down afterwards, it was like July snow.'

'Your husband wants to demolish your tower too,' Richard said.

'Well, he will be disappointed, won't he?' she said as Richard opened the door for her to the lawyer's office.

It took no longer than half an hour to go through the formalities of signing purchase documents and sorting a bank account. On 1 June 1947, Richard became the proud new owner of a dilapidated Tuscan tobacco tower and adjoining dwelling.

'We must celebrate this event,' Magdalena said. 'I shall take you to one of my favourite places for lunch.' Her lawyer declined, protesting that he had another important appointment, and

Richard was pleased to have time on his own with this intriguing woman.

He followed Magdalena on his motorbike as she drove up the hill from the city centre along a dirt track. This time, he wore goggles and a kerchief around the bottom of his face against dust stirred up from the unsurfaced road by her Fiat Topolino, surprisingly nippy for a small car. She took the bends like a rally driver and he smiled as he kept up, enjoying the chase.

Her car pulled up outside a huddle of stone buildings and a church built into the hillside, a squat building with a simple metal cross crowning its terracotta roof tiles.

'Where have you brought me?' he asked.

'To where they serve the best food in the area. Follow me.' To the side of the church, they passed through an open gate and she pulled a bell hanging from an archway covered with red scented roses. The door was opened by a friar who smiled at her. '*Benvenuti*, welcome,' he said with a gentle smile. 'There are two places at the end of the table over by the window, signori.'

There followed an extraordinary meal served on wooden platters, with tumblers filled from jugs of strong red wine. A first course of home-made strips of thin *tagliolini* pasta, with a sauce made from slivers of truffles sourced from the woods, was followed by tripe, unlike any Richard had ever eaten: tender, succulent slices flavoured with tomatoes, olive oil and herbs, served with a vegetable that he had never come across before.

'It's only eaten at this time of year,' Magdalena explained. 'We call it friar's beard, or *lischeri*, but it has many other names. Delicious, no?'

It was very good, a cross between asparagus, spinach and samphire. Richard thought he might acquire some seeds and grow it in his garden. The idea of a new life, new experiences, new friendships, so far removed from his grey and panic-stricken existence back in England, was thrilling him like a renewal.

'I'd never have thought a monastery would have a restaurant,' he said.

She smiled. 'Friars have always welcomed travellers of all kinds, although there are plenty of people who prefer to eat in more luxurious places, but I like it here. Nobody asks questions of you. These friars were busy during the war... they hid many refugees in their crypt.'

'I've heard similar stories. I know that British POWs were helped by local priests but that not all the clergy supported the allies.'

'Since the war ended, we have been told to forget what went on, but... some things will never be forgotten.'

They were quiet for a while. Richard gazed at the view of the valley below, where mist threaded the city of Sansepolcro, her cathedral tower soaring like a needle from the haze.

'You're not from Corbello, are you?' Richard asked, after cups of espresso were brought to the table.

'Can you tell?'

'There is something more... worldly about you,' he replied, not wanting to say he'd heard about her life from Pasquale, but also meaning what he said. She was so different to everyone else he'd met in the village. She had a chiselled, classic beauty, her eyes dark and mysterious, and as she spoke, she kept sweeping her hair from her face, as if she was aware of the attention she aroused.

She laughed. 'I think it is because my father allowed me an education. I enjoyed studying languages at school and... I have always had a mind of my own.'

She looked up and Richard thought those eyes might be flirting with him just a little.

'The war was not so painful for me,' she continued 'We were occupied, but not all the *tedeschi* were bad.'

She paused and swallowed the rest of her black coffee. 'During the war I had an administrative role with a national body set up back in the 1920s known as the Fascio Femminile – we helped with single mothers and women struggling to bring up their children.' She paused. 'I was a good fascist in those days... like everybody else. We didn't see what was coming. Anyway... as time went on, I changed my allegiance although I remained at my job. When the allies rolled in and remained to sort out the mess with their relief agency, I was called in to interpret for refugees in our area and help them repatriate. I had studied English and they welcomed my help.' She stood up, her chair scraping against the stone slabs of the refectory. 'But now, I need a smoke, *andiamo*... let's go.'

'This meal is on me,' Richard said as he helped her into her jacket.

'Thank you, Richard,' she said, lingering close to him as she fastened her button. 'There's a box by the door to leave an offering. Guests are asked to leave what they can afford.'

He looked helplessly at her and, leaning over, she pulled a couple of notes from his wallet, a lock of her hair grazing his sleeve, her perfume strong. 'That will be sufficient,' she said. 'They will use the money to help others.'

They wandered behind the monastery, where a large vegetable garden with varieties of salads was planted behind formal hedges of lavender and box. Magdalena perched on the edge of a well in the centre and pulled a tin box of slim Wintermans cigarillos from her handbag, offering him one. He declined. 'I prefer my pipe, thank you.'

'Do you know, before the war, women were not allowed to smoke. If we wore lipstick, we were considered whores. We could be arrested for being bare-legged, and trousers on women were considered the devil's outfit.' She exhaled smoke fiercely. 'At least the war has resulted in more freedom for our sex. We even have the right to vote now.' She gave a sarcastic laugh before asking, 'I'm hoping that life for women in your country is better. Where do you live in England?'

'I was brought up in a suburb of London. In the county of Surrey.'

'Have you ever been to Oxford? William has invited me to come.'

'William?'

'Captain William Graham. The man I worked with after the war, helping the displaced. He's a lecturer at the university.'

'Oxford is a wonderful place. Most people have heard of our famous city.'

'He suggested I enrol in summer school there. I'm considering it.'

'What will your husband think about that?' He was surprised at himself for asking the question.

'I do not care what he thinks, Richard,' she said, turning to him, her eyes flashing. 'We have different needs now. He does not know it yet, but I shall leave him very soon.'

She looked at him, defiance and something else in her eyes that he couldn't fathom. She might have been coming on to him and she could equally have been warning him not to ask more questions. He wasn't sure. But when they parted not long afterwards with a handshake, her fingers held his longer than necessary and he was again confused. He waited for a few minutes after she left, her little car disappearing round the mountain bend, and this time he did not try to keep up.

During the first week of owning his property, Richard spent his days pootling around the buildings, drawing sketches of spaces he planned to renovate first. The panic attacks that he'd experienced in England had not returned and he felt more at peace with himself. He was sure that it was more than simply being distanced from Blighty. Tuscany, her intriguing people, the beauty of the landscape and her rich culture were calling for discovery. It was a fresh start for Richard and he was ready for it. He imagined how he would use the areas within the two buildings: where the light was best for a kitchen, where he would write, where he could install a stove for a living area. Would he sleep on the top floor of the tower or devote that to a study? One of the very first projects would have to be the installation of a modern bathroom in both buildings. He didn't fancy washing from a bucket of water fetched from the well in the thick of winter. Pasquale turned up a couple of times with food sent from Rosa, and over slabs of freshly baked rosemary focaccia, swilled down with a glass or two of Sangiovese, they talked through Richard's ideas. His friend recommended a local builder and carpenter.

'If you want me to help with any wrought iron work, then I'll give you a special price. How are you going to reach your mezzanine area, for example? Have you thought about a spiral staircase?'

They huddled over Richard's sketch pad, arguing amicably about the best designs.

Richard spent time doing nothing as well, soaking up the looks and sounds of his territory, nosing about it like an animal. A golden oriole sang to him from an umbrella pine. He took time to listen to its call, and he collected a basket of large pine cones for kindling. Pasquale had told him that the tree would fruit edible nuts for making pesto. 'I will bring Angelina and Rosa to collect them when they are ready and she will show you how to make the sauce.'

His favourite place as the sun set, was in the corner between the tower and the one-storey building, the L-shape felt protective, like a pair of arms. The day's sun was stored up in the stone walls and radiated warmth until late in the evening. Here was a place to relax at the end of a day's work and scribble lines of poetry, snatches of feelings, snapshots in words. He remembered what Magdalena had told him about the war bringing her and other women new freedom and the memory of a line of peasants walking in a sad line away from their bombed homes came to him. He had been travelling in the back of one of the field ambulances and they had overtaken a straggle of dejected refugees. He flicked back through his notebook and worked on the words he had jotted down, forming them into better lines:

They approach:
Bedraggled shadows,
Scarecrows.
A straggle of women,
Barefoot.
Trailing burdens of
Babies, and old folk with silver tears.
Brave women of Italy along a dusty track.
Lost women, crushed.

Richard struck through some phrases and leant back against the wall, recalling Magdalena's words at lunch. It seemed life in post-war Italy was changing for the women. Hopefully, women would no longer be lost and crushed in the world of men.

The bench where he scribbled his words was cobbled together from thick oak planks he'd found leaning against the tower and he'd balanced them on top of two concrete blocks in the shade of a straggling fig tree. Pasquale had warned him the fig tree would need removing – it was too near the house, but for the meantime it offered shelter and he looked forward to picking the fruit. That was it, he thought, sticking his pencil behind his ear, sitting back to breathe in his new life. He was looking forward, and the notion gave him energy and freedom, better than any medicine or tonic prescribed by a doctor.

Magdalena came to say goodbye three days after their lunch. 'I haven't even left Edoardo a note,' she said as they sat together in the courtyard, the sun glinting off a pile of empty twenty-litre demijohns that he'd come across at the back of the low building. He had an idea to place them as ornaments in a kitchen garden that he would design soon.

'He won't have a clue that I have gone to England,' she said. 'You are the only person I've told, so I trust you not to tell him. I can't stay here, Richard. If there were children involved, then I'd put up with him, but—'

'Life is short.'

'Indeed. The war has taught us both that, I think.'

He was disappointed that she was leaving. He hardly knew her, but she intrigued him. She was sassy, striking, but it was more than a sexual feeling he felt. She was feisty, determined and he had the feeling that there was more to her. Days spent with her might never be straightforward and he liked that idea.

'I wish you all the luck in the world,' he told her when she embraced him later before driving away.

'*Altrettanto*, the same to you. We are both starting off anew, Richard. *In bocca al lupo* to you. Good luck!'

Afterwards, he thought how bizarre it was: that she was leaving for where he had come from. He had forgotten to ask her for her forwarding address in England, but maybe it was for the best. Each of them was tearing themselves from their roots in order to escape, hoping that another culture might fill them afresh. Some might have said it was a form of running away, but he saw it as an adventure. After surviving a war, he felt he could survive anything. And he saw little risk in his Tuscan adventure.

*

At the end of the week, on a brilliantly sunny morning, Richard rolled up his shirtsleeves, and built up a sweat as he dug the perimeters of a temporary vegetable garden. Pasquale had given him surplus courgette, tomato and salad plants and he needed to plant and water before the early sun fried them.

After half an hour of digging over the hard soil, sweat pouring from him, he removed his shirt. He had already retrieved three mule shoes, the chains from an old yoke as well as a misshapen bottle from the soil. All these keepsakes would look interesting strung from the outside walls of the building as architectural salvage. He bent to pick up a piece of bone, thinking how unfortunate it was that he had selected the exact spot where all domestic refuse had been buried. So far, he had sifted through chicken bones, broken dishes, bent spoons, an old night pot, and other detritus of everyday life. As he pulled on the bone, he jumped back, his heart skipping a beat as his fingers touched what was obviously a human skull, a few hairs still attached to its leathery, withered flesh.

He continued to dig carefully, presuming that he had unearthed the remains of a soldier. It was happening all the time in this post-war period. The Imperial War Graves Commission was working overtime to identify victims and to contact relatives who continued to live in hope after receiving telegrams with the inconclusive words: presumed missing. Scraping away more earth, he revealed the shreds of what looked like a skirt and a faded scarf and reached the conclusion that the corpse was that of a woman. He stopped digging, knowing that he had to contact the local *carabinieri*. Whatever poor soul had ended up in the soil around his tower deserved to be recognised.

CHAPTER EIGHT

Richard was forbidden to pass the rope barrier that cordoned off his property. A stout *carabiniere*, wearing an ill-fitting uniform that looked as if it had been handed down by men of varying sizes, guarded the flimsy deterrent, warning him to keep away while investigations were carried out. The body had been carefully unearthed and removed to the mortuary in Arezzo.

'When can I have my property back?' Richard asked.

The *carabiniere* shrugged his shoulders. 'When the *maresciallo* has ascertained the corpse's identity and the reasons for it being there,' he said importantly. 'Such procedures take time.'

'There must be many bodies from the war found buried in unexpected places. Apart from soldiers, there were plenty of evacuees, people moving all the time to escape from bombings in the cities. Is there always such a fuss made when each of these poor souls is found?'

'Each of these cadavers once belonged to somebody, signore. We have to investigate further and gather up every clue and rule out foul play before you can come back to your property.'

It seemed to Richard that not much gathering-of-clues was taking place. The *carabiniere* spent most of his time leaning against the fig tree, picking his nails and teeth. And when Richard enquired at the *municipio* to ask if they could hurry up procedures, the mayor seemed to almost rub his hands with glee as he said, 'What a pity you didn't buy my beautiful villa in Anghiari. I'm afraid, signore, that the wheels of bureaucracy in our country are slow. Very slow indeed. You need to learn the art of patience if you are planning to live in Italy.' He looked up from his paperwork and glared at Richard. 'By the way, signore, I do not like that the tower was bought behind my back.'

Richard did not feel like retaliating that it was hardly his fault if Mayor Gobbi had not told him from the outset that the tobacco tower belonged to his wife. He kept quiet, preferring not to further delay permission to return to his property. The man seemed to wield a lot of power in Corbello. It was best to keep in his good books.

Richard took himself off to Florence for a week, treating himself to visits round the Uffizi Gallery. He learned how Botticelli's *Primavera* – a fifteenth-century masterpiece – had been smuggled from the gallery out to a nearby castle during the war, and had only been saved from a bonfire of artworks by a brave gardener who had got the Germans drunk on Chianti before they could set it alight. In the evenings he sipped Chianti himself at a little bar on the Ponte Vecchio, thinking about the spoils of war, mesmerised by the view of the reflection of the city lights rippling on the river Arno. It was the only bridge that hadn't been bombed during the July 1944 retreat by the Germans, who'd wanted to hinder the allies' advance.

There was progress on reconstructing the remaining bridges with scaffolding and signs of building all over the city, but it was a mammoth task. Wandering through the back alleys on several occasions he had to pick his way over piles of rubble still waiting to be cleared.

He couldn't wait to return to Corbello and the countryside. With its early summer green mantle, it was redolent of renewal and promise.

*

'It's definitely the body of a woman and, sadly, it is probably somebody I once knew well,' Pasquale told him on his return. 'You are only allowed to return to live in the place once the post-mortem has been completed.'

'Who is it?'

'They think she is Fosca Sentino. They identified the poor girl from the brooch found with the body. The former owner of the *osteria* came forward to inform the *questura* that his mother-in-law had given it to Fosca as a gift. She worked for him and used your property from time to time during the war.'

'What do you mean used?'

Pasquale pulled a face. 'People say that there were comings and goings while she lived there and Mayor Gobbi mentioned that she entertained men… *tedeschi* sometimes, but… from what I knew about her, it's unlikely. Gossip travels fast in a place like this and often takes the wrong turnings.'

Richard snorted. 'Nobody told me I'd bought a brothel. My God!'

'You know as well as I do how war turns lives upside down. She was the local schoolteacher; she had a young son to care for and no husband to help…' He shrugged his shoulders. 'If that was the only way to put food in her mouth… then who can judge?'

'So, somebody was out to get her, I suppose. A lynch mob, maybe, out to punish her for associating with the enemy. Poor woman.' Richard tutted. 'And what happened to her son?'

'Who knows what went on? They both disappeared at the end of the war, like so many of the dispersed.'

Another victim, Richard thought to himself as he rode his motorbike back to the tower, determined not to let the shadow of war cloud his new home. He'd penned his own despair at the futility more than once.

And I ask myself, 'why, oh why?'
If child is father to the man,
What happened to make him choose this madness?

The lines whirled around in his head as he tried to put them into shape. As he passed a fruit grove at the side of a house, he decided he would one day plant a tree in the spot where the poor woman's body had been found. It would serve as a sign of respect for another ruined life. A peach, or almond, maybe. Something sweet.

The local *carabinieri* had forbidden Richard to start renovations inside while they investigated the identity of the dead woman, so a few days later, under the hot June sun, he began work on his land at the back of the tower. He planned to clear stones from the overgrown patch of scrubby meadow earmarked for a future vegetable plot. Years of neglect meant that he needed somebody in the village to plough it for him but in the meantime, he was preparing the soil. The pile of stones was growing. He would use them for a perimeter wall. Pasquale had advised it might deter wild boar and porcupine from digging up the crops, particularly potatoes.

Pasquale had insisted that he stay with him and Rosa for the interim, and sleep in one of the bedrooms above the bar and restaurant that they had taken over at the end of the war, but it was by no means ideal and he couldn't wait to start work on restoring inside his property and move in. His frustration was lessened by working at the back of the house today. His view was of Corbello in the distance: a ring of ruined houses on its hill, dwellings propped up with scaffolding, sounds of hammering and cheerful song so different from the sounds of gunfire the first time he had been stationed with the FAU. Here and there in the meadows skirting the town, a sunflower nodded its heavy head in the warm breeze, like a signpost to better things.

He watched a shirtless man guide two oxen to plough, calling instructions to the two cumbersome, yoked animals as they dragged the blades behind them through reddish-brown soil. A young boy, a sack bag around his shoulders, walked behind, scattering seeds in the deep furrows. The child was healthy, compared to the children he had helped nurse, some horribly maimed from explosives left behind by the *tedeschi* and he hoped that the field had been properly swept. There were still warnings posted on the walls outside Rosa's bar and there were no-go areas in the hills, waiting for engineers to do their job of sweeping the land. Swathes of red poppies along the unploughed fields nearby marked the areas where trenches had been filled in with fresh earth. There were other patches of poppies elsewhere, marking places where victims of war had been hastily buried in this valley that had seen so much action. Representatives from the Imperial War Graves Commission had made preliminary investigations and marked off these graves for future work.

Richard straightened up to ease his aching back and decided to trespass into his own house to retrieve his camera from one of the boxes stored in there. The splashes of poppies were too beautiful to forget and he wanted to capture the scene. It might inspire him to write a line or two in the future. One day soon, he would fix up a corner in the tower and place his desk on a mezzanine area with bookshelves and an ideas noticeboard to pin his photos and notes.

As he turned into the courtyard, he was startled to see a young woman leaning over the well. A child of about four was playing under the apricot tree. He was tugging at its laden branches and laughing as the orange-yellow fruit fell to the grass.

'*Buongiorno!*' he said, feeding his arms into his shirt.

The woman jumped. 'Giampiero, *vieni qua*,' she said, calling the little boy to come, and the little boy ran over to her immediately and buried his face in her skirts, his bottom sticking out.

'I'm sorry,' she said. 'I didn't think there was anybody around.' She spoke clearly without dialect and he was pleased he understood her.

'*Prego*, be my guests.' He moved to the well and pulled on the rope to help her raise the bucket of cool water. 'I have some cups somewhere inside.'

'Don't trouble yourself, signore. We can use our hands.'

He watched as the boy drank first. The woman dried his mouth gently with her skirt and then she dipped in her own hands, cupping them and letting the water trickle in so that she could slake her thirst. Her hair was bound in a scarf and the end dipped in the bucket as she bent. She pulled it off to reveal two thick plaits of blue-black hair wound around her head. To Richard, she looked young to be a mother.

She wiped the water from her own mouth with the back of her hand, drops glistening on her olive-brown skin. 'Would you mind, signore, if we rested for a while in the shade? We've walked from Sansepolcro this morning and my little boy is tired.'

'Of course not.' He indicated his rudimentary bench between the two buildings. 'There is perfect shade there at this time of day.' Then he glanced at his watch. 'I've brought a picnic with me today but there's too much for me.'

'*Grazie*. You're very kind. It's a long time since breakfast and Giampiero has already eaten our panini.' She gazed down at the child. 'He is always hungry. I think he is making up for the time he lost during the war. I can't seem to fill him up.'

He smiled. '*Perfetto.* We can share.'

They followed him over to the bench and he fetched a basket from the tree where he had hung it to escape invasion from lines of ants that crawled along the edge of the building.

'You need to pour boiling water on them,' she said. 'They're a nuisance if they get into the house,' she said.

'That will have to be a job for the future. I'm not allowed to do anything to the interior of this place for the moment.' He didn't feel it appropriate to tell her the reason with her little son listening in. Children had gone through too many horrors in the last years. Now was the time to recapture innocence and trust.

'There are always rules and regulations to follow in our country,' she said, adding, 'Where are you from, signore?'

'Ah, you can tell I'm not Italian. And I thought I was beginning to speak your beautiful language quite well.'

She laughed. 'No offence. I mean, you speak it well, for a foreigner, but…' She looked at his dirty blond hair and blue eyes, his lanky frame and large feet. 'You don't look in the least bit Italian.'

He watched as a blush spread across her cheeks as she stammered an apology and he thought how refreshingly straightforward she seemed.

'Absolutely no offence taken,' he said, doing up the buttons on his shirt.

He arranged the spread that Rosa had packed for him that morning: portions of roasted rabbit left over from yesterday's supper, a salad of artichokes and wild leaves seasoned with olive oil and fresh herbs, half a rosemary-sprinkled focaccia baked in the *osteria* oven and a handful of flat peaches to finish off. The little boy grabbed at a piece of rabbit and the woman rebuked him sharply, reminding him of his manners, and he hung his head, biting back tears.

'It doesn't matter,' Richard said. He'd seen too many starving children during his time in the field hospitals. Scruffy ragamuffins with lice and rickets, orphans left to fend for themselves. They had to be stopped from overstuffing themselves with army ration biscuits handed out to them, their little bellies swollen from malnutrition.

'But it *does* matter, doesn't it, Giampiero?' she said, tipping the child's head up, her finger under his chin so that he had to look into her eyes. 'We know the correct way to behave, don't we?'

The child gazed up at her and when she nodded, he turned to apologise to Richard. '*Mi scusate*, signore.' Richard smiled and handed him the meat.

When there was nothing left of the meal, the little boy thanked both Richard and his mother and went to play beneath the apricot tree.

'I want my son to grow up civilised,' she said. 'We have gone through so much, but there is no need for him to turn into a savage.'

'I don't think there is any danger of that, signora…?' He trailed off, a question mark in his voice.

'My name is Fosca,' she said. 'During the war I lived here for a while.'

His mouth fell open. 'Are you Fosca Sentino? But… you are supposed to be dead.'

She looked at him, bemused. 'Yes, that is my name. But I can assure you, I am very much alive, signor…?'

'Richard,' he said, shaking her hand. 'But… I'm sorry to tell you, Fosca, but… everybody in Corbello believes that you are dead.'

'What do you mean?'

He lowered his voice and pointed to the area cordoned off with ropes, weeds beginning to grow again where the earth had been disturbed. 'They found a woman's body buried there. And the *carabinieri* worked out that it was the body of a Fosca Sentino. A young schoolteacher who had not been seen since the end of the war.'

She frowned. 'Well, they have made a mistake. *Eccomi.*' She pointed at herself. '*I* am Fosca Sentino. And I am alive and well.'

CHAPTER NINE

'Wait until I tell Pasquale,' Richard said, gazing in amazement at this woman resurrected from who knew where.

'You know Pasquale?' she asked.

'Yes. I'm living with him for the time being in his guest house.' He patted his stomach. 'And Rosa is feeding me up like one of their piglets. She is an excellent cook, but I can't wait to be back here living as a bachelor once again. This is incredible, signora Fosca. We should go and let everybody know.'

Despite the heat of midday, after folding up the picnic cloth into Rosa's basket, they started up the footpath to Corbello. Giampiero began to complain he was tired, and Richard scooped him up to carry him on his shoulders, the little boy placing his hands on each side of Richard's head to balance. While they walked, Fosca explained she had returned because she wanted to reclaim her teaching job and Richard told her he had worked in the school building at the end of July 1944 when the allies had used it for their field hospital.

'*Che combinazione*,' she said. 'What a coincidence. But I don't remember seeing you at all.'

'Me neither,' he replied, thinking that despite treating many civilians in those days, he would have remembered this young woman. Maybe back then her looks had been dulled by the war and its privations. She was not conventionally beautiful – her nose was a little long and her cheekbones prominent – but she had a pensive, sensitive air about her and looks to make a man turn twice in the street.

Fosca began to lag behind as the final stretch of the track led around the perimeter of Corbello. Richard stopped to wait for her, watching as she gazed up at the shells of houses that ringed the walls nibbled with bullet holes and shrapnel.

'Are you tired?' he asked.

'I am shocked. At the devastation,' she replied. 'It is far worse than I remember. This place was rebuilt after the earthquake of 1917, before I was born. It didn't deserve to be battered down again.'

'The Germans blew up many of the larger houses where they were billeted before they retreated. They were intent on destroying any intelligence before the allies arrived.'

'I do remember,' she murmured. 'But somehow my mind has pushed out the extent of it. I suppose I'd wanted Corbello to remain how it used to be.' She continued to walk. 'The mind is a mysterious place. It plays tricks on us.'

'Or we play tricks on the mind.'

She looked at him. 'Yes. I think you are right, signor Richard.'

He liked the way she pronounced his name: Reeshard. Her Italian vowels lingered to make his ordinary, English name sound exotic.

At the ruined gateway, where the green, white and red colours of the Italian flag flapped bright against old stones, she halted again.

'I am suddenly nervous.'

He set the little boy down. 'Don't be,' he told her. 'Why should you be? They will be pleased to see you again… risen from the dead.' He chuckled but she interrupted his laughter.

'We shall see. The last time I was here, it was difficult.'

He took her to Pasquale first, the sounds of blows on his anvil causing the little boy to approach with curiosity to see what the big man was doing. Little Angelina was playing with a rag doll in the shadows and when she saw Giampiero, she came over and took his hand. '*Ciao, bambino*. My name is Angelina. Who are you? Do you want to play?'

Fosca smiled. 'If only it was as easy for adults,' she said.

Pasquale wheeled round from his work and lifted the visor from his face. 'Fosca! Is it really you?' He strode over and grasped her hands, looking down at her with wonder. 'But we were convinced you were dead.'

'So I hear,' she said.

'Well, we must celebrate.' He lifted her in his arms and swung her round as if she were weightless. Giampiero circled round them, laughing and shouting, 'Me, me. Me too.' Then Angelina wanted a turn and Fosca began to laugh as the children lightened the atmosphere. The tension on her face began to ease. Looking at her smile, which lit up her eyes as dark as blackberries, Richard saw that she was more attractive than he had first thought.

Pasquale mopped his brow and dampened the fire in his brazier. 'Did you know that Rosa has taken over Bruno's *osteria*, Fosca? She does simple meals too. Come! We'll eat together and you can tell me what's been going on since we last saw you.'

He tucked Fosca's arm under his and Richard and the children followed up the alleyway into the small central square where shoots were beginning to sprout from severed plane trees. Children were playing tag and Angelina pulled Giampiero with her to join in.

'See who is come back to us,' Pasquale bellowed, his voice bouncing round the houses patched with wood and corrugated sheets. Shutters were flung open in the top storey of the school building, a couple of women at the fruit and vegetable stall turned in curiosity to stare and then averted their gazes, muttering to each other. The sound of a window being slammed was loud in the little piazza. And then an old man shuffled across and took Fosca by the arm, peering up into her face.

'Bruno,' she said, shocked at the appearance of the former innkeeper. 'Bruno...' She went to embrace him, but he held her at arm's length.

'I thought you were gone, like the others,' he said, tears moistening his rheumy eyes. And then he turned away to stumble to where he had come from.

Fosca stood still, her shoulders slumped, listening to the whispers of the women at the stall, whispers that stuck to her like burs. She turned to leave. 'I suspected it would be like this, but I hoped enough time had passed.'

Pasquale stopped her, barring her way, his arms clasped over his barrel chest. 'You are not going anywhere,' he said, his voice loud and clear. 'You are coming to the *osteria* and Rosa will prepare us a welcoming supper. And' – he raised his voice even louder – 'the drinks will be on the house tonight for anybody who wishes to come.'

Another shutter banging and the trickle of water from the village fountain were the only responses to Pasquale's invitation as the little group made its way to the bar.

Richard wondered what had happened to cause this unfriendly welcome. He understood that war did not stop automatically when peace treaties were signed. He'd been involved with enough civilian relief work with the FAU to know that grievances lived on. Apart from aggravating poverty and squalor, civil war in Italy had destroyed friendships and communities. At war's end, he had helped treat the most horrific injuries inflicted by lynch mobs on *nazifascisti*, on women who had slept with the enemy, or on black marketeers who had profited from people's misery, on informers and people suspected of being spies. There was a great deal of bloodletting, trial without courts, the desire to immediately avenge in case the *nazifascisti* went unpunished. For a while, before order was restored, people turned into wild animals. He remembered how he and the doctors had fought to save the life of a girl accused of sleeping with the *tedeschi*. She'd been found floating in the river Sovara with severe injuries to her head and abdomen, her hair completely shorn and her face badly mutilated. She had died and her attackers had hung around the hospital and cheered when they'd heard that she had passed away on the operating table. This inhumanity was yet further proof to Richard, if he had ever needed it, that war served no useful purpose.

Fosca was undoubtedly on the receiving end of some kind of grievance and he wondered what she had done. Pasquale had told him she had used the tobacco house to entertain men, he remembered now. She didn't seem that type of woman but he knew that war forced people to desperation.

None of the townspeople joined them for drinks in the *osteria* that evening. Fosca looked round the eating area and observed that nothing much had changed since she had worked there, when Aurelia and Bruno had run the place. The same black and white photos hung on the walls, showing scenes of haymaking, the first tractor to be bought in the town, schoolchildren performing gymnastics in the square, the procession for the feast of San Martino. Even the bar counter, where Pasquale was pouring wine into a jug, had the same glasses and decanters arranged on the shelves behind him.

Angelina helped her mother lay the table with a blue checked cloth, setting the cutlery down haphazardly, which Pasquale discreetly rearranged once she had returned to the kitchen to be with Rosa. Giampiero had found the piano in the bar and Pasquale fetched him a stool so that the little boy could reach the notes. It needed tuning but the discordant noise of the little boy experimenting on the keys was a useful cover to the awkward silence between Richard and Fosca as they sat waiting for their food.

Richard wanted to get to the bottom of the reasons for the poor welcome shown to this young woman, but he knew better than to barge in. He had only just met Fosca; they were strangers. But he felt sorry for her, watching as she nervously twisted her skirt. She and her son were yet more victims of a war that was supposed to have ended two years ago.

The door to the *osteria* opened with a clatter and the short, portly *carabiniere* who had guarded the site of the body, burst in. His uniform was buttoned tight and he was sweating.

'Signora Sentino Fosca?' he announced, removing his cap from an almost bald head. He stuck his cap under his arm, two slicks of oily black hair dislodging in the process, dangling over his eyebrows. He swept them back and came to stand opposite Fosca.

'*Sì, sono io.* Yes, that is me,' she said.

'You are under arrest.'

Fosca stood up, her face indignant. 'Why? What have I done?'

'We are investigating the murder of somebody with the same name and so far, you are our only lead.'

Richard and Pasquale interrupted the policeman.

'So, you are arresting her for murdering herself…' Pasquale said. 'Don't be ridiculous, *sergente*.'

'It's a joke,' Richard added.

The policeman replaced his cap and tried to stand taller than his one metre fifty-five centimetres. His surname, Gambacorta, was the bane of his life, for he had indeed been provided by nature with short legs. Despite ordering the town cobbler to add extra centimetres to all his shoes, it made little difference to his stature. 'If you will come with me, signora,' he said to Fosca.

The door opened as he spoke and the mayor entered.

'There will be no need for that, *sergente* Gambacorta. I can deal with this.'

'But, signor *sindaco* Gobbi, my orders are to detain this—'

'The orders have changed. I know this woman and I have spoken with your *maresciallo* in Arezzo. You can go now, *sergente*. Your superior officer will be in touch. I have made my telephone number available for his messages. I recommend you return to the *questura* to await further instructions from your superior officer.'

The little sergeant tried to exit with as much dignity as possible and when he had gone, Edoardo Gobbi sat down at Richard and Fosca's table. 'Welcome back to the living, signora Fosca. This is most unexpected.'

Fosca nodded and Richard observed how her eyes narrowed as the mayor addressed her and how she shrank back against the chair. There was obviously no love lost between these two.

'Your resurrection is most inconvenient,' he said with a half-smile. 'The *maresciallo* himself will arrive tomorrow. He will turn the place upside down once again and the case will have to be re-opened. Just when we thought the dust was settling.' The mayor sucked air through his teeth and looked Fosca up and down.

'But, why did everybody assume that I was the dead woman? I have been down the road in Sansepolcro all this time – if somebody had bothered to check.'

'We have been too busy trying to return to normal: there has been so much to sort with reconstruction of our town, caring for the sick, dealing with the displaced… the list is endless.' As Mayor Gobbi spoke, he waved his plump hairy hands in the air in little circles, his gold signet ring glinting.

Pasquale was called by Rosa to the kitchen and he reappeared with a dish of steaming ravioli and laid an extra setting for Gobbi.

'We concluded that the dead woman was you, Fosca, because of the brooch,' Pasquale said, leaning in to speak quietly, breaking the uneasy silence that had settled in the dining room.

'Brooch?' Fosca asked.

'*Sì*. There was a photo posted in the piazza showing items found next to the body and one was a brooch that Bruno recognised. He said that his mother-in-law gave it to you,' Pasquale said, serving out generous portions of Rosa's homemade ravioli. Giampiero ran to climb on his chair and Fosca distractedly tucked a serviette under her son's chin while she listened to Pasquale, concern etched on her face.

'When they found the brooch, there was no point in looking any further, as it seemed obvious that the…' Pasquale paused, as if searching for words and lowered his voice. 'It seemed to everybody that the… deceased person was you—' He broke off his explanation, indicating Giampiero with his chin, signifying that he did not want to talk about such matters in front of her son.

Fosca slumped back in her chair, a look of horror on her face.

'I need to see this brooch for myself,' she said.

Gobbi, his mouth full, waved his fork about. 'The *sergente* has it secured in the *questura* as evidence. I will arrange for you to see it as soon as possible, signora. Come to see me in my office. Pasquale, tell your wife that her ravioli are *squisiti*.'

Fosca toyed with her food, scraping most of it onto Giampiero's plate and Richard watched her, observing how pale and withdrawn she had grown. The incident with the policeman, and the knowledge of this brooch had obviously upset her.

Gobbi left without eating the main course. He excused himself, wiping his mouth clean of the rich red sauce and knocking back half a glass of Sangiovese wine, explaining he had work to do.

'I will see you in my office tomorrow morning, signora Fosca. Ten o'clock.'

'*Grazie*,' she mumbled.

When he had left and Pasquale was busy in the kitchen, Fosca turned to Richard. 'I need to check something in the tobacco house before tomorrow morning. Is that possible?'

'Legally, no. Inside is strictly out of bounds at the moment. But…' He paused. 'We are in Italia, where rules are made to be broken, are they not? We could go now and if we ask Rosa to look after your son, then we'd be quicker on our own.'

Fosca had no qualms about leaving Giampiero. Her little boy didn't even look up when she slipped away soon afterwards because he was engrossed in a game with Angelina. The little girl had bound him up with old rags as bandages and was using him as a patient. They were playing doctors and nurses.

The heat of the day was melting away as they took the path down towards the tobacco house. A group of youngsters was swimming in the river pool, their shrieks as they splashed in the water mingling with the loud chorus of crickets. At one stage, along a narrow section of the path, Fosca's foot skidded on dry gravel and Richard, walking behind her, caught her arm to stop her from falling. She turned to thank him with a smile that was both sweet and sad.

'What is it you need to check on?' he asked once they'd arrived. He fetched a large key from its hiding place under an old sink planted with rosemary and turned it in the rusting padlock. The door squeaked open and a couple of bats swerved out into the fading light. Fosca didn't flinch and he couldn't help comparing her reaction with the fuss that Barbara would have made. She hated spiders and creepy crawlies.

'*Pipistrelli*,' Fosca murmured. 'Many people believe that bats in the house bring bad luck or that they are evil spirits and foretell death.' She shivered. 'I've always hoped this isn't true.'

Even though it was dark inside, Fosca seemed to know exactly where she was going. Richard pushed open a shutter and tutted when the hinge snapped, leaving it hanging half on, half off. 'Another job to add to the list,' he muttered.

He watched as she pulled a stool to stand on and reached up to feel around a beam in the far corner of the kitchen area, the contours of her figure trim as she stretched.

'It's not there,' she said, collapsing down onto her heels.

'What were you looking for?' He held out a hand for her to jump from the stool but she managed without his help.

'I was hoping to find the brooch… hoping against hope…'

'You're not making any sense. Pasquale said that they found a brooch on the body of the woman they dug up. Are you talking about the same one?'

She let out a huge sigh. 'I was hoping that there'd been a mistake…' She hugged her arms to herself. 'I will find out more tomorrow when Gobbi shows me.' She started to shiver.

'Fosca, come outside and we'll talk there. It's gloomy in here.'

She followed him out of the door and waited while he bolted and locked it again.

'Let's sit on my bench,' he told her. 'Come… you look as if you need to talk.'

They sat in silence for a while and he waited for her to be ready.

'Thank you for the chance to unburden myself,' she said eventually. 'My story is like countless others of the war, I'm sure. Complicated. And difficult.'

'I hope you can trust me,' he replied. 'I know we hardly know each other but… go with your instincts, Fosca. Tell me only if you wish.'

He paused and looked sideways at her. She had a frown on her forehead that he wanted to smooth away. She reminded him of lines written by Auden, one of his favourite poets, about how life can leak away in headaches and worries. There was too much time wasted in worry, in his opinion. Now that the war was over, life should be seized, and every precious moment that remained, lived and savoured to the full.

As they sat in silence for a few minutes, he watched the twilight deepening, and it occurred to him that he hadn't thought to bring a torch to light the way back. He was just about to stand up to leave when Fosca started to speak, her voice so soft that he had to lean closer to hear.

'I fear that I know the identity of the dead woman,' she said. 'She was a good friend to me. I haven't seen her since the war. I thought she might have returned to her home city of Torino.'

'I'm a good listener,' he replied. He understood the therapy of unburdening oneself. In the field hospital he had sat up late many a night, holding the hands of men, young and old, reassuring them that they were not alone, even as they took their last breaths. 'Talk to me. It might help.'

It seemed to Richard that talking in darkness made it easier for Fosca and even from her first words, it was as if she was telling the story to herself. He sat back and let her pour it out.

CHAPTER TEN

Fosca's Story

Late winter 1943 and early January 1944

The summer of 1943 was to be our last together. On the final night with my beloved Silvio, our son was tucked up in his washing basket by the side of our bed. Our final hours together raced like eagles chasing and swooping on their prey. How glad I am that we didn't sleep one wink that night. Maybe Silvio had a premonition we would never see each other again. We talked softly about the first time we'd met by the village fountain, how he'd winked at me as I filled my bucket and how I'd blushed and splashed him for being cheeky. As we lay together in our tangle of sheets, we whispered of our future and how we would live one day in a free Italy. We had no plans for a formal marriage; we'd said our vows to each other up in the mountains six months after we'd first met. The bread and wine of a religious ceremony could not have sealed our bond any tighter than the bread and cheese we'd taken with us to the meadows and the promises we'd made to each other.

Now that Silvio is gone, that time plays over and over in my head: the summer hours we spent making love, the windows open to the still hot air to catch an occasional breath of breeze to cool our glistening bodies. From the ceiling above our bed, I'd hung bunches of grapes on hooks to dry for winter and Silvio had remarked that it was like sleeping beneath frescoes on a painted ceiling. Twice in that final night, I'd lifted our little son from his basket to feed and Silvio arranged a pillow behind us. He stroked our baby's downy head, never taking his eyes from his son as he suckled. 'You and he keep me going, Fosca,' he'd whispered. 'You two restore my soul.' We didn't speak of where he was going with his partisan fighters on the following day. But I knew it was down towards the coast where the *tedeschi* were busy constructing barriers to stop the allies battling up from the south. Silvio and I had an unwritten agreement that there was no talk of war in bed.

From where I sat, propped against the pillows, I'd watched as Giampiero screamed with colic, his little legs bunching up against Silvio's chest, as he paced the wooden floor, rubbing the child's back, humming lullabies until he slept, each drawing comfort from each other. And long after our baby slept, his tiny fist curled around his *babbo*'s thumb, I stored the image in my heart. Afterwards, we made love and I tried not to cry. We couldn't get enough of each other that night. Thank God we didn't make another child. Thank God for that at least – there was little else to give thanks for in that brutal time. How could I have cared for another child on my own in this hellish world? It was hard enough to look after Giampiero on my own.

In the midst of winter 1943, when I'd been without my Silvio for weeks, the village school closed and I lost my job as *maestra*. The girl I had employed to look after Giampiero left town with her family and for a while I continued my work, teaching some young pupils at home, Giampiero on my knee, but that was eventually taken from me. 'The *tedeschi* have requisitioned the school building for their men,' the leader of Corbello *comune* told me one morning. 'I am sorry, signora Fosca, but you have to find somewhere else to live. You have one week before the German soldiers move in.'

I had no relatives. As a child, my home had been with the nuns in a foundling hospital after I was abandoned on their convent steps. It has been a dark, gloomy night, apparently, and so the name Fosca, with the same meaning, had been chosen for me. The only connection with the past that I possessed was a scrap of material patterned with tiny acorns, pinned to the shawl that the nuns found me wrapped in.

With no family to turn to, and knowing nobody in the village would have room for us in their tiny homes, I began to grow desperate, but then a woman told me about Edoardo Gobbi, who owned a deserted tobacco house two kilometres from the village. I went straight away to his office in the town hall where he worked at that time as the *comune*'s registrar.

He looked up from a list of names he was scrutinising in a ledger. 'You will have to take it as you find it, signorina.'

'Signora,' I corrected him, moving Giampiero to a more comfortable position on my hip.

'It hasn't been lived in for more than a year. The caretaker lived there with his wife and family but they moved back to Sicily. I can't do any renovations for you.' He shrugged his shoulders. 'In these difficult times, where would I find materials?'

He was not a bad looking man, although inclined on the stout side, his hair slicked back with oil. His clothes were well cut and his shoes looked expensive. For some reason I couldn't warm to him. Maybe it was the way he looked me up and down, his gaze slow and lazy, lingering too long on my breasts. He made me feel naked and I hoped he wouldn't be the kind of landlord to turn up unannounced. The rent he asked was low and I had found nowhere else, so we shook hands. I released my hand from his sticky soft palm and wiped it surreptitiously on my skirt.

Giampiero chose that moment to tell me he needed his next feed, opening his mouth to complain in a lusty cry. Gobbi looked up from his paperwork. 'If you need help with your baby, my wife is the chief administrator for the Fascio Femminile in this area. If you need clothes for your child or to trace where your

husband is, signora Gobbi will help.' He narrowed his eyes. 'Is
he a prisoner somewhere?'

'I do not know,' I replied. That was all the information he
would get from me. I didn't want any help from the *fascisti* and I
mumbled, '*No, grazie,*' and turned to leave. I'd heard about these
women. Once you were on their books, your life was no longer
your own. I would manage without them.

Two days later, one of the parents helped me move my belongings
from the school apartment in his donkey cart: a box of clothes, my
precious sewing machine, a couple of pots, books, and blankets for
Giampiero. I managed on the little savings I had, eking these out
with an occasional private lesson. My payment was in kind: every
now and again I would find outside my door half a dozen eggs,
a handful of potatoes, darned clothing for my baby, or, if I was
lucky, a plucked pigeon or a rabbit. Food was scarce for everybody,
although people living in the cities were far worse off. I valued
these offerings, more precious than if they'd been gifts of money.
As I sowed seeds for tomatoes, salad and courgettes in a sheltered
spot near the tobacco house I prayed that Silvio would return.

I spent my days in a terrible fug of denial and hope. One of
Silvio's friends had visited me, bringing the red cravat that Silvio
always wore, torn and spattered with blood. I fell to the ground
as the partisan told his story. The last his band of men had seen
of Silvio was after a mission to pour sugar into the petrol tanks of
the *tedeschi* trucks parked outside Pesaro Station. They had wasted
no time in retaliation, shooting partisans and civilians, stringing
them up from lamp posts and, after they were dead, shooting at
their bodies for target practice. After two days their corpses were
unrecognisable. After my initial shock, I refused to believe that
Silvio was gone and I prayed there'd been a mistake – that he had

dropped the scarf as he ran away, as a kind of message to me. All I could do was hope, even though my hope grew thinner every day.

When winter deepened its bite, bringing frost and icy winds, I couldn't keep Giampiero warm in the semi-ruined house and my milk dried up. We were hungry and when hunger gnawed, all I could think about was food. My baby was covered in welts from fleas and bed bugs and he cried at night. I knew what I had to do. There was no help to be had from anyone in the village – people could barely feed their own families. And apart from Silvio and Giampiero, I had no family.

One day wrapped up in all the clothes I owned, we left the tobacco house and I took the longer route to the city of Sansepolcro. I told myself it was in order to avoid roadblocks, but I knew it was to prolong the moment when I would hand my baby over to the same nuns who had cared for me.

The convent of Santa Maria della Misericordia was in the centre of town. I was stopped at the entrance to the city walls at the Porta Fiorentina by two *tedeschi* soldiers. '*Documenti*,' they barked, in their strange accents, but when they saw me struggling to search for my papers, with Giampiero's weight and the bag in my arms, they waved me on impatiently. I hurried along Via della Misericordia. The street was bleak. Several of the houses were boarded up. I saw the letter 'J' scratched in chalk on two doors and I knew what that meant. The Jewish community had been persecuted throughout Mussolini's rule and I shivered at the thought of families dragged from their homes. There was a poster on the wall:

JEWS WANTED
PAYMENT FOR EACH INDIVIDUAL:
MAN: LIRE 5,000
WOMAN OR CHILD: LIRE 2 TO 3,000
RABBI: LIRE 10,000

There was no pity left in this world and I hugged Giampiero tight to my breast. If it hadn't been for him, I would have pulled down the poster and torn it to pieces, but who knew who might be watching through the shutters in the buildings as I passed? At the convent, I made my way immediately to the back of the imposing building. Sheets fluttered on a line strung across the courtyard and I smiled at the toneless drone of the nun who had always cared for me, her singing drifting to me from an open window.

'You still can't sing, Madre Caterina,' I said, grinning as I pushed open the double doors of the kitchen. 'Which makes the two of us. I am sure it's your fault that I can't hold a note. It must have been the example you set me.' My delight at seeing her again made words spill from my mouth and I was ready to burst into tears.

The nun turned around from the sink where she was washing cabbage leaves and, wiping her hands on her spotless apron, she opened her arms. Then, seeing the bundle in my arms, she hurried over.

'What have we here, Fosca?' she asked, one hand on my shoulder and the other parting the shawl to better see my son.

She took Giampiero and gestured me to sit down. 'What a cherub,' she said, planting a tender kiss on his face. 'He's like you, Fosca.' She looked up. 'Have you eaten, child? You look all in. Fetch bread and cheese from the cupboard, left over from lunch.'

I could have found my way around the kitchen blindfolded. It was the place I'd retreated to whenever everything became too much to bear. When I was bullied by the boys or scolded by strict Madre Rita for my scuffed shoes, untidy plaits or mistakes in arithmetic – whatever small misdemeanour she could pick on – Madre Caterina was always my safe haven. She let me hide under the table or knead bread with her on the scrubbed *madia*, the wooden storage chest where flour was kept and bread left to rise. 'I come from a big family,' she'd told me often enough. 'Each year my parents just had to look at each other and there was another baby on the way. A world without children is an empty world. You can come to my kitchen whenever you want, Fosca.'

Madre Caterina had lost her plump figure, her cheeks hollow and pasty white. 'Are you all right?' I asked her. It was a stupid question. There was a war raging. Nobody was all right. Her response was predictable.

'Are any of us, Fosca? Everything is scarce, especially goodness and love.' She paused and looked at me. 'And you?'

I shrugged. 'The same as everybody. It's not easy, is it? My husband is missing, Madre.' I didn't feel like telling her I was unmarried. In my eyes I felt married. But in hers, without a religious ceremony, I would be considered a single mother, a *ragazza madre*. There were plenty of us about since the outbreak of war.

There was silence for a few easy moments and I watched her rock my child, her body moving gently with the maternal instincts denied her by religious vows of chastity.

'Will you look after him for me? Until the war is over?' I blurted.

'It's not so safe here, Fosca. You've seen for yourself that the *tedeschi* are everywhere in the city. Up until now they've left us alone, but we've heard dreadful things. Your little one would be far better off staying by your side.'

'I can't feed him any longer. He'd starve to death with me. I need to find work and then I can pay our way. But I can't find work if I have to be with Giampiero all the time.'

She sighed in pity. 'I suppose one more mouth won't make too much difference. We already have nine little scraps at the moment, Lord bless them. Mother Superior has talked about moving us up to the mountains to avoid the bombs. Leave it with me. I shall talk to her.' The nun looked up at me, regret in her eyes. 'I'm afraid we can't offer you shelter at the moment, Fosca. I'm so sorry. I hope you understand.'

She placed my little boy gently in a basket containing kitchen towels. 'When did you last eat a proper meal?' she asked.

'Yesterday.' There was no point in telling her that all my food had been finished days ago and that I'd been surviving on watery gruel made from wild salads, the roots of bishop's lace, *funghi*, thyme infusions and anything else I could glean from the countryside. I was very hungry. I'd saved my last heel of bread for Giampiero and a rind of Parmesan for him to chew on. He was teething and it helped soothe his sore gums. But he needed milk too and the woman who usually sold it to me had lost her last cow to looting *tedeschi*.

Giampiero chose that moment to wake up and opened his mouth wide in an angry, hungry howl. Madre Caterina heated a small pan of milk and pulled a feeding bottle from the shelf. 'Here, feed him and I'll make you both *pan cristiano*.'

My eyes watered. She'd remembered my favourite snack. While Giampiero guzzled his milk, I watched Madre Caterina cut four slices of *toscano* bread and dip them in whipped egg, milk and cheese. Then, fetching a heavy frying pan, she poured in a splash of oil and fried the eggy bread until it was crisp.

I mopped up the last of the crumbs with my fingers and she held my son on her lap while he chewed on a crust of bread clutched in his dimpled fist, and without looking me in the face, she told me what I knew already. 'It's best you disappear now without making a fuss, Fosca *cara*. It will be easier for both of you. And I'll explain everything to Mother Superior when you're gone. Come up to the mountain retreat in a month to see him. Give the poppet time to settle.'

I knew it was the right thing to do but my heart ached already. I couldn't look after my little boy properly and work at the same time. He would be safer with the nuns. I stayed put for a few moments longer and then I gave her the little puppet I had made from part of his daddy's red cravat. 'This is his favourite toy, Madre. Don't let him lose it.'

'Go now, while his tummy's full. Don't worry about him, Fosca. I'll look after him – like I did you.' She handed me my son for a final cuddle and busied herself packing half a dozen eggs, cheese, sausage and bread and wrapping it all in a piece of cloth, before stuffing it into my bag and taking him from me again.

Tears blinding me, I left. I could hear him cry as I hurried away, and I wept for the whole journey back to Corbello. When I arrived at the tobacco house, I curled myself into a ball on the bed and wondered what to do next.

CHAPTER ELEVEN

Fosca

On a crisp Saturday morning in December, I began my trail round Corbello to search for work. The grocer didn't need me. 'I'm sorry, signorina,' he said, 'there's nothing much on my shelves anyway. I'm shutting shop next week.' He shook his head. 'Try the *osteria*. The *tedeschi* like their food and wine. Bruno is open all hours.'

The little eating house known as Da Bruno was buzzing with soldiers, where a stove threw warmth from its corner. One of the men whistled as I entered and I pulled my headscarf further over my face. A young *tedesco*, his khaki shirt open at the neck, was playing a jazzy tune on an upright piano, a cigarette dangling from his mouth. As I passed, he stopped playing, stood up and gave an exaggerated bow, blocking my path. There were laughter and comments exchanged which I didn't understand. If I hadn't known better, I might have described the atmosphere as convivial. Some of these blond young men sitting at tables looked no older than children themselves, but I knew their kind was responsible for killing children, women and the elderly in cold blood. Just as I was turning to leave, thinking that I couldn't possibly bring myself to breathe in the same air as these murderers, Bruno Gavelli came from behind the bar carrying a tray of full wine glasses. I knew both his sons; the youngest had attended my lessons at the primary school. The oldest boy, Gennaro Gavelli, was only seventeen but he had been deported to work in a factory in Germany. Bruno smiled a harassed welcome. 'Signora Sentino, go into the back kitchen. My wife will be happy to see you.'

Aurelia, Bruno's wife, was bent over the stove turning *crescie sfogliate*. My mouth watered at the homely aroma of flat breads made from flour, lard, milk and water, a popular winter snack. 'Signora Fosca, welcome.' She pushed back strands of hair that had worked loose from her scarf and her hands left streaks of flour on her face. 'As fast as I make these *crescie*, they disappear. I can't keep up.' She gestured to the sack of flour next to the stove. 'I dread to think from where they looted this, but… we have to keep in with these monsters,' she said, lowering her voice, 'to try and get Gennaro back in one piece.' A tear trickled down her cheek and fizzed off the hot plate.

Fourteen-year-old Ennio smiled shyly at me and I went to sit beside him. 'How are you?' I asked. 'Have you been continuing with your school work?'

He was busy peeling a mound of potatoes and he shook his head. 'There is no time and anyway, I have other things to do.'

'The child does nothing but talk about running off to fight with the *partigiani*, but I keep telling him he is only fourteen, signora.'

'If I am old enough to be killed, then I am old enough to fight so that others won't be killed,' Ennio said.

The boy had logic, and there was nothing I could say to deny this statement. The *tedeschi* had killed children far younger than Ennio. 'You must keep safe,' I said. 'Your parents need you with them now that Gennaro is in Germany.'

I watched as he peeled a potato, stabbing at it with his sharp knife as he sliced it into chips. I thought how difficult it must be to endure the presence of the enemy in his own home.

'How is your mother?' I asked Aurelia.

'Much the same, signora. She has good days and bad days. She's upstairs on her own at the moment. I have too much to do down here to keep her company.'

'Let me sit with her for a while,' I offered.

I climbed the narrow stairs to where Nonna Zina was in bed. She stirred when I entered the room above the bar. Piano music and men's laughter drifted up through the wide oak floorboards. I helped her into a more comfortable position against her pillows as she grumbled about what a nuisance she was.

'I wish they would play songs I know,' she said. 'When my husband was alive, we entertained our customers every Friday and Saturday night. I played the piano and he sang. He had a beautiful tenor voice, signora. People travelled from villages all around to listen.' She warbled an aria from Puccini's *Tosca*, 'E lucevan le stelle', her voice thin and quavery, but still tuneful.

I clapped my hands when she finished and she laughed.

'They used to tease me in the convent and call me Tosca, instead of Fosca,' I told her. 'Because I *can't* sing.'

'Everybody can sing, my dear.'

'Some better than others. I promise, my voice is truly terrible.'

'Tell me how you've been,' she said, patting the bed. 'It's lonely up here. Fill me in on all the news.'

I sat down near her and told her how I'd taken my little boy to the nuns, how it had broken my heart but I hadn't known what else to do. I told her how I was looking for work now that the school was shut. It was a relief to open up. I'd been on my own in the tobacco house for days. I even shed a tear while I was talking to the old lady, but I don't think she noticed because the room was dark and her eyesight poor. We chatted for a while until her eyes drooped with fatigue and I tiptoed from the room.

Ennio was gone when I came down to the kitchen and I stayed to help his mother, rolling up my sleeves and washing dishes at the sink. She was worried about her son in Germany, and asked me if I knew any Italian who spoke German and could find out where Gennaro was. 'He is too young to be all those miles away.

And Ennio is so angry that he's been taken from us. I'm afraid he will do something foolish.'

I promised her I would see what I could do to help.

'*Grazie*, signora.'

'Please call me Fosca.'

She smiled shyly. 'You are very welcome here, Fosca. Please come again.' She placed half a dozen warm *crescie* in a paper bag as well as a quarter of a salame and thrust them in my hands. 'We can't give you money, Fosca, but you are always welcome to share what little we have to eat and if you can spare an hour every now and again to sit with my mother, it would help me.'

I preferred to leave by the back door rather than push through the throng of soldiers in the stale air of the bar. As the afternoon wore on, they had become rowdier as the drink flowed. On my way back to my empty house, I wondered how I was going to earn money to pay for Giampiero's keep at the convent. I could keep my hunger at bay with handouts from my friends, but it wasn't enough. I needed to bring in some lire.

On the Saturday before Christmas, I trudged up the frosty path to Corbello. The trees stood still against the iron-grey sky like ghostly limbs, and I shivered. My shoes were wearing thin and I'd packed them with straw to stop the holes, but that didn't prevent cold from nibbling at my toes. It was nearly Christmas Eve and I didn't want to be alone. I'd packed a couple of thrillers with gaudy covers – *gialli* – for Ennio that Silvio used to devour, reasoning that if the boy couldn't continue his schooling, at least he could keep up his reading. I'd run up a couple of scarves on my sewing machine for Nonna Zina and Aurelia from scraps of material, selecting the least threadbare remnants and edging them with a line of lace unpicked from an old nightdress. They were simple gifts but I didn't want to arrive empty-handed and trespass on their kindness.

The windows of the *osteria* were steamed up and, pushing open the door, I saw that once again there was a full house. In the bar area, a pretty girl with a tangle of curls was singing, accompanied by the same *tedesco* soldier, ash from the cigarette in his mouth threatening to spill onto the keys. She held a red scarf in one hand, waving it with little flourishes as she sang a popular folk song of a girl asking her boyfriend to hand over his handkerchief so she could wash it in the fountain. It was a simple tune that the German was managing to follow, improvising chords.

She caught my eye as I entered and I stood listening to her beautiful voice and the words I knew so well. When she reached the final verse, where she should have sung about hanging the handkerchief on a thorny rose bush to dry, she changed the words. Holding my gaze in hers, without her expression flinching, she sang in dialect of how she would strangle all the men in here with the cloth and spit on their corpses afterwards. The room was full of *tedeschi*, there were no local men in the bar at that time of night to hear what she sang and I prayed that none of the soldiers understood our dialect. It was a foolish, dangerous act. But as I turned to push open the door to the back kitchen, I grinned at her audacity.

'Who is that girl?' I asked Aurelia, busy as ever, cutting strips of *pappardelle* pasta to dry on a clean cloth spread on the table. 'She has some cheek.'

'That's Simonetta. She comes and goes. I think she was studying in Turin for a while but she has relations here. The place livens up when she comes in, but she hangs around those soldiers too much for my liking.'

'It's not because she likes them,' I said, recounting her performance.

'They all like *her*. She needs to watch out.'

'It looks to me as if she can take care of herself.' I went over to Aurelia and gave her a peck on the cheek and handed her my gifts. 'I'll pop up and see Zina.'

'She'll love that. She's been off colour for a couple of days.'

Zina was dozing but she sat up when she heard me come in and smiled. 'Have you come to keep me company again, Fosca?' she asked.

'*Sì*, Zina,' I said, pulling a shawl round her shoulders. 'And I've brought you a little something for Christmas.' I handed her the scarf and she held it up close to her eyes. '*Che bello!* I haven't had a gift for years. *Grazie!* You are a kind girl.'

She talked to me of past Christmases, how she had loved the snow when she was a young girl and had learned to skate one year when the pond at the back of the *osteria* had frozen over. 'I remember we had a party and my mother roasted chestnuts and served them in twists of paper. I still adore the smell. We collected them from the forest each year. I met my husband on Christmas Eve too.'

I encouraged her to tell me more. 'It was at the well,' she said, a smile on her lips as she recalled. 'The water was frozen and he took me to another source of water – a stream that gushed further up the hill and he filled my bucket. In those days, we were never allowed to meet a boy on our own. But nobody suspected that fetching water from the well would lead to romance. From that day on I hurried to meet him every day. At the well, we had our first kiss. He was very handsome.' The old lady patted her hair as she finished. 'And, though I shouldn't say so, I was pretty back then too. And I never told him I'd known about the spring up the hill until much later, after we were married. *Of course* I knew about it all the time. Fetching water was one of my daily jobs for my family.'

I laughed and told her about Silvio, and what a coincidence it was that we had both met our husbands by wells, and she held on to my hand while we were lost in our memories.

'Fetch me that box from the top shelf,' she said eventually. 'I have a Christmas gift for you too.' I lifted down a little square box made from chestnut. 'My husband carved this,' she said, tracing her arthritic fingers along the details of a pair of inlaid lovebirds carved from bone. 'This is for you, Fosca,' she said, pulling out a brooch. 'There's no point in keeping it hidden away in my box.'

'No, Zina,' I said. 'You must give it to your daughter.'

'I have already given Aurelia what I wanted to give her, *cara*. No, this is for you.' She pressed it into my hand and closed my fingers over it. 'Wear it and think of me.'

The oval case was silver, designed to wear as a brooch or on a chain. Within the glass, two locks of hair were woven into E and Z. 'My hair and my darling Enzo's,' she said. 'And if you press and slide the back,' she said, fumbling to show me, 'it opens up.'

I had no jewellery of my own, growing up as I had with the nuns. 'I will treasure this, Zina. *Grazie dal cuore*. Thank you from the heart.' I pinned it to my blouse and bent to kiss the old lady. She smelled of lavender and talcum powder and she held me close for a while. I stayed by her bed until she nodded off.

When I arrived downstairs, Aurelia looked up from her pasta making. 'You shouldn't have bothered with this,' she said, fingering the scarf that she'd already tied around her head.

'It's my pleasure.'

She smiled. 'Well, you're a clever seamstress. And very kind.'

I showed her the brooch; I didn't want her to think I had stolen it or taken advantage of an old lady and she smiled.

'I'm pleased. But keep it somewhere safe, Fosca. In these times, you never know. We have all hidden our special things.' She lowered her voice. 'We all know the *tedeschi* are more than light-fingered. I would hide your sewing machine too, if I were you.' Then she handed me a knife. 'If Mamma's asleep, keep me company for a while and peel these while we talk, there's a love,' she said. 'Those brutes love to eat potatoes with everything – even with a bowl of pasta, would you believe?'

It was warm and cosy in the kitchen with the fire crackling in the vast fireplace where a cauldron of minestrone, hanging from a blackened chain, simmered in the heat.

'When are you going to see your little one?' she asked after we'd worked in silence for a few moments.

'I want to try to see him over Christmas, but it will depend on the weather,' I said. 'The sky looks heavy with snow.'

'Stay here with us tonight, Fosca, and set off tomorrow. That will shorten your journey and we'll see if there's anybody to give you a lift to the city.'

'Would you mind? It's so cold and lonely in that old building.'

'If you don't mind sleeping in the kitchen?'

'Of course not. Now, give me another job, Aurelia.'

'See if Bruno wants help in the bar.'

Her husband was grateful for an extra pair of hands and I was relieved when he told me he would serve the men where they sat if I stayed behind the bar to decant wine into jugs and wash glasses. I had no desire to squeeze between the narrow tables and be touched by drunken soldiers. The bar was full to bursting since I had arrived. More customers had come in and I recognised one or two of the Italians from the town hall, including my landlord, sitting at a corner table playing cards, as well as the local doctor who had delivered Giampiero. The pretty girl was still there, talking to the pianist. I caught one or two words of English as she laughed at something.

I worked on late until the last of the drinkers had left and Aurelia and Bruno had climbed the stairs to their beds. Then I wrapped myself in a blanket by the stove, and lay on the mat, watching the dying embers, touching Zina's brooch on my blouse from time to time and planning where I would hide it in the tobacco house. I knew I had done the correct thing in leaving Giampiero in the care of the nuns. It would have been impossible to look after him properly with this job. But that thought didn't stop my heart yearning for him. It didn't take long for me to fall asleep that night. It was good not to be alone.

CHAPTER TWELVE

The snow that had threatened in the days before, failed to fall. The sky that Christmas Eve was a blaze of blue against which rags of clouds drifted like sheep. But it was still freezing cold. Aurelia and Bruno had found a way for me to get to Sansepolcro to see Giampiero. The girl called Simonetta who had sung in the bar was in need of a lift herself, apparently. She'd found one as far as Anghiari with the doctor and she could loan me a bicycle to ride to the city for the remaining eight kilometres. I didn't like to own up that I'd never ridden a bicycle in my life and I would walk the remaining distance. I would deal with that problem when it arose.

Dottor Negri was impatient to leave. He thrust a couple of white pinafores at us and told us to tie back our hair. 'If we are stopped, you are my nurses on your way to the hospital,' he told us. 'I'm not allowed to give lifts as a rule – I'm only supposed to drive on medical business – but as it's Christmas, I'll see what we can get away with. I'm hoping the guards will be more relaxed.'

Simonetta shook hands with me and sat in the passenger seat, after gesturing to me to climb in the back. I'd never ridden in such a smart car and as the doctor drove fast down the winding road, I had to hang on to the door handle to stop myself sliding on the leather seat. At the first roadblock, a lone German soldier waved us on – but we had to stop at the second and third. Each time, I noticed that Simonetta scribbled something down afterwards in a small notebook and stuffed it down her front. The doctor spoke to her softly as he drove, but I couldn't catch what they said to each other above the noise of the motor. As we passed through the hamlet of Le Ville, I was dismayed at the heaps of rubble lining the road where houses had once stood. A gaggle of children stretched their hands out as the car passed and I couldn't help thinking how easily my own son might become one of these begging urchins one day if I didn't care for him properly. I needed to find a more permanent way of earning money for his keep.

At the hospital in Anghiari, where a sheet bearing the red cross was slung across the *cotto* roof tiles, we returned our pinafores to the doctor and I listened as he and Simonetta made arrangements for their return journey. I thanked him and told him I would find my own way back as I wasn't sure how long I would remain with the nuns.

'I'll take you to where my bike is kept,' Simonetta said, dragging me with her. 'It's not far.'

To this day, I cannot explain why I allowed myself to be persuaded to accompany this girl I hardly knew. I did not even know how to ride a bike. Why go with her? But there was something about her. Maybe it was because I felt so alone and craved company of my own age, or maybe it was simply because Simonetta was so vivacious and compelling.

I followed in her wake and we crossed the road and slipped down an alleyway that led to the main square. I remembered how, before the war, the nuns would bring us orphans in crocodile file to see the living crib outside the convent church of Santa Croce. Townspeople dressed up as Mary and Joseph, there were real sheep, and shepherds playing on bagpipes. Three kings knelt in fancy costumes and a real donkey and cow stood over a wriggling baby in a manger. The nuns told us Saint Francis might have watched the same scenes we were enjoying. How innocent and trusting we all were, nursing our twists of newspaper filled with hot roasted chestnuts, our wisps of breath spiralling like smoke into the December air, believing implicitly in the stories the nuns wove us.

Now, outside the church, instead of a Christmas pageant, there was a pile of sandbags, and barbed wire coiled round a huge crater in the middle of the square where a bomb had fallen. Where once banners of the different historical districts adorned windowsills on the ramparts, red and black flags hung stiff in the December air. At the far end of the square, a soldier guarded a passageway and Simonetta swore softly. '*Porca miseria*, the swine are everywhere.' She tugged my sleeve and pulled me through a door. 'Follow me,' she said. 'I know a shortcut.'

I kept up with her as she ran to the top floor and knocked on a door. It was opened by a striking woman wearing a man's beret. The two kissed and embraced closely, the older woman whispering something that made Simonetta giggle. When they separated she stared me up and down.

'And who do we have here?' she asked, her voice deep, educated, her accent, like Simonetta's, from the north.

'She's a friend, Maria,' Simonetta told her. 'I need to get to number six.'

The woman stood back to let us in and we followed her to windows that gave on to a small balcony. To my surprise, Simonetta climbed over the railing and slid down the roof. 'Follow me – the tiles are sound. You won't hurt yourself, Fosca. Come!'

I moved gingerly and followed her as she trod over more tiles to another space. 'The next part is the hardest. Don't look down,' she told me. The roofs of the little hilltop town stretched away like ploughed fields of tiles.

We were between two buildings now, separated by a gap of almost half a metre. One slip and I would hurtle to the alley, twenty metres below. What was I doing following this mad girl across perilous rooftops? I stopped, my legs wobbly, my heart pounding.

'I *promise* you'll be fine,' she said, coming back to join me. 'One stride and you're there. Watch me!' She repeated the crossing to show me how and held out her hand from the other side as I stepped over the abyss.

'*Brava*,' she said, moving stealthily across a flat roof where ragged clothes, crisp and motionless in the freezing sunshine were strung across a washing line. My fingers brushed against them and I banished thoughts of slippery, ice-covered tiles, hoping that we didn't have to return the same way. Simonetta opened a door and we descended a narrow staircase to the ground floor. She inched open an older door leading to a dusty courtyard. At the far end a covered area housed old boxes and a cart half eaten by woodworm. Simonetta squeezed herself behind the piles of rubbish and I heard her yelp before she reappeared pushing a man's bike, its wheel frames packed with straw where inner tubes had been removed.

'I hate mice,' she said. 'There's a nest behind there.' She shook her head and shuddered.

I laughed, thinking how absurd it was that this girl could jump fearlessly across rooftops but was scared of tiny mammals.

'Here's your transport to Sansepolcro,' she said.

'Wasn't there an easier way to get to the bike?' I asked, unimpressed with our rooftop antics.

'Well, thank you so much, Simonetta. You're so *very* kind,' she replied with sarcasm. 'There was a guard posted in that square, in case you hadn't noticed, and we wouldn't have got to this end of town the normal way.'

'And how will we get the bike back over the rooftops?'

She pulled a face. 'You're disappointing me, Fosca. I thought you had more sense. There is more than one route in and out of this town.' She pointed to her eyes and head.

She was blunt, so I would be too. 'There's no need to be sarcastic. I need to get to Sansepolcro, so if you point me in the direction of this other wonderful route, I'll set off right now. And I don't need the bike.'

'So, you prefer to walk in those, do you?' she said, pointing at my old shoes, my toes gaping through holes I'd tried to plug with hay.

'Yes, I do. Because I've never ridden a bike before,' I confessed, my voice sounding like a petulant child's. I'd never had the opportunity. None of the nuns owned bikes. Silvio and I had walked, hitched rides or used the bus when we wanted to move about.

'Well, now's your chance to learn,' she said. 'Either that, or you can walk the eight kilometres in the freezing cold. And that will mean you'll have less time to spend with your son. Have you considered that?'

'How did you know about my son?' I snapped.

'Bruno told me. It's not hard to discover information, you know. Especially in a small town like Corbello.'

She held the bike upright, standing to one side, gripping the handlebars. 'Climb aboard,' she ordered. 'Now's your chance to learn. It will make life easier for you and we've plenty of room to practise.'

I watched as she removed one of the handlebar grips and stuffed a roll of papers inside the hollow tube, before replacing it. It would be at least two hours' walk to Sansepolcro, and who knows what would happen to my poor feet along the way. I had no idea how long it might take to learn how to ride a bike – a minute? A day? But trying now seemed like the best option.

She supported the bike as I perched on the saddle. She told me to place my feet on both the pedals, while she held on. 'Balance first,' she said. 'Look ahead and push down on the pedals, first with one foot, then with the other.'

I wobbled at first as I took my feet off the ground, but then before I realised what was happening the bike was moving and she had let go. 'Steer! Steer to the left,' she shouted, as I careered directly towards the old cart. When I wrenched the bars too suddenly, the next minute I fell, cushioned by a pile of rotting rubbish heaped next to the cart.

'Don't you disturb those mice,' Simonetta said. She was doubled over laughing as I lay there, my bottom in the air, and then I was laughing too and our hilarity echoed round the courtyard, causing a couple of pigeons to flap away over the roofs.

'Come on,' she said, wiping tears from her eyes. 'We'll have that guard investigating this noise before long. We need to scarper. Hop on behind me and I'll take you myself. Let me do the steering for today.'

I am surprised that we weren't stopped on that crazy wobbly day as Simonetta cycled down the back roads from Anghiari, with me clinging on to her for dear life on the pillion, the world racing by in a blur. It was exhilarating, terrifying and dangerous rolled into one. A couple of *tedeschi* soldiers waved us on with grins on their faces as we hurtled, shrieking, towards a roadblock near the city entrance. The doctor's hunch had been right and the fact it was Christmas Eve helped. The soldiers were less vigilant than usual and, afterwards, I was to realise that Simonetta had been banking on that too. I didn't realise it at the time, but the lending of the bike to me was part of her plan to use me to smuggle information within the resistance.

Our cheeks were flushed and Simonetta's hair was a mad tangle when she skidded to a halt next to a ruined farmhouse not far from the city walls of Sansepolcro. 'Come in and share a glass of wine before you push off,' she said. 'We've both earned it.'

She pushed the bike round to the back of the building to a barn, its roof barely intact. 'Welcome to one of my humble abodes. Take this while I open the door,' she told me and I held the bike as she pulled a key from her jacket and undid a huge padlock securing the rickety entrance.

'That's my double bed,' she said when we were inside, and she pointed to a ladder leading to a hay-strewn platform. 'And come and see my kitchen.'

I followed her to the far end of the barn where sticks of firewood and ash on the cobbled floor showed recent activity. 'Take a seat,' she said, indicating a circle of half a dozen sawn-off tree trunks, 'while I find us something to eat.' She pulled a lump of dried sausage and a couple of apples from a small metal meat safe hanging from a beam. 'It's the only mouse- and rat-proof spot in the building,' she said with a grimace.

I was hungry and the spot of mould on the sausage meat was easily ignored when we washed it down with a generous beaker of wine. It loosened my tongue as well.

'You seem to be here, there and everywhere, Simonetta,' I commented as she cut slices of apple to share.

'That's just about it. I move about a lot in the hope I'll become a figment of the imagination,' she said, a grin on her face.

'Who are you, really?' I asked.

She pulled a face. 'Good question. How much time do you have, Fosca Sentino?'

'I'm anxious to see my little boy, but...' I liked this girl with a sparkle in her eyes. I'd never met anybody like her.

'You live in that old house next to the tobacco tower, don't you?' she asked.

I gasped. 'How do you know?'

She tapped the side of her nose. 'There's not much I don't know, *amica mia*.' She went to fill my glass again and I covered it with my hand. '*No, grazie*. I'm going to the convent from here. I don't want the nuns thinking I've turned into an unsuitable, alcoholic mother.'

She smiled. 'Listen. I will come and find you in your little house one day and we'll talk. And in the meantime, I need a favour from you.'

'If I can, I'll be pleased to help you in return for the lift and my supper.'

She smiled. 'I want you to deliver the bike to a bar in the centre of town. In the corner of the main square. All you have to do is to leave it outside, pick a sprig of rosemary from the bush growing outside and enter. Place the rosemary on the counter and tell the woman serving that you are sorry, that you broke a piece off. She will answer, "No problem, take it." That's all you have to do, Fosca. Then, leave the bar and go and find your son.'

'Won't the bike be stolen from outside?'

'No. Don't worry.'

It seemed very mysterious to me, but nothing taxing or harmful was involved and it seemed the least I could do.

'*Va bene*, Simonetta. Fine. Thank you for the lift and… I'll see you soon, hopefully.'

'How will you get back to Corbello?'

'I'll find a way.'

She nodded. '*Brava*. I like a woman with initiative. Where there's a will, there's a way.' She stood up to embrace me, standing on tiptoes to plant a kiss on each of my cheeks. She was at least a head shorter than me and her frizzy hair tickled my chin. She led me to the door of the barn and I hurried away, turning to wave at her before rounding the ruined farmhouse. I couldn't wait to hold Giampiero in my arms again.

I pushed the bike along the flat, empty streets, void of Christmas revellers, and, my simple task accomplished, I hurried back to the Convent of Santa Maria, picturing the moment when I would hug my little boy and gaze on his beautiful little face, wondering how much he had changed during our time apart.

CHAPTER THIRTEEN

Nobody answered when I pulled on the convent bell, so I made my way to the kitchen at the back. The shutters were closed on all the windows and as I hammered on the door, a cat ran over to me from the laundry building. It rubbed itself against my legs, mewing plaintively. I bent to scratch it behind the ears, cursing inwardly at my stupidity for not checking before making the trip. Madre Caterina had told me that they would be moving to the retreat in the mountains, but I hadn't counted on it being so soon.

'Have they left you all alone, *micia*? Poor pussy! There's nothing for it but to catch mice.'

I wanted to weep. I had no idea how to reach this mountain retreat. In all my years at the convent, I had never been there. There was nothing for it but to make my way back to Simonetta's barn, in the hope that she was still there and I could beg a lift back to Corbello.

Snow began to fall in soggy flakes, finding its way through all the gaps in my thin clothing and shoes. It was almost dark when I was stopped by a guard at the main gate of the city. He was huddled against the stone walls, trying to shelter from the driving snow. My documents were in the pocket of my skirt and I fumbled for them with frozen bare fingers.

'*Freddo, freddo,*' he muttered impatiently in guttural Italian, stamping his feet against the cold, urging me to hurry up. '*Sbrigare.*'

In my haste, I dropped my papers on the wet ground and he waved his bayonet, indicating I should pick them up. As I bent,

I felt his fingers fumble up my skirt and I screamed and leaped away. A second guard appeared from a doorway where he'd been sheltering with a cigarette. He was older, his face kinder, and he shouted at the young soldier, who muttered a sulky '*Buon Natale*,' and all but pushed me through the gates. I could hear the voice of the older man berating his fellow soldier as I quickened my pace. Old women and young girls had been raped by *tedeschi* soldiers and I trembled at my near escape.

Snow continued to fall in drifts and my skirt was soaked by the time I arrived at the barn a quarter of an hour later. Light filtered through a gap in the wooden walls and I pushed the door open. As I turned to close it against the weather, I was seized from behind for the second time that evening. Before I could shout, my mouth was covered by a hand. I bit down as hard as I could and a man swore, grabbing at my hair and yanking me to the ground.

'Leave her be, Lupo. I know her.' I was relieved to hear Simonetta's voice, shouting, and she bent over where I lay on the barn floor.

'She shouldn't come creeping in on us like that,' the man called Lupo grumbled, sucking the blood from his palm where I had sunk my teeth. 'The bitch is lucky I didn't draw my knife.' He was wiry with sharp features and his eyes flashed in anger.

Simonetta helped me to my feet and I rubbed the back of my head.

'Are you alright?' she asked. 'Sorry about my friend. He's hot-headed.'

'My hot head has rescued us from more than one tricky situation,' he retaliated.

'Come and sit by the fire,' Simonetta said, her arm around me as I looked warily at Lupo. 'You're soaked through. What happened?'

I filled her in about the deserted convent, as well as the incident with the guard and she shook her head. '*Bastardi*. It's best not to wander alone in the dark.' She poured hot liquid from a pan into a chipped cup and handed it to me. 'Get this down you and I'll rustle up some dry clothes. I know the way to the nuns' mountain retreat. There may be a way yet of you managing to see your son for Christmas. All is not lost.'

The drink was bitter and scalding hot and I began to thaw, my heart lighter at the possibility of seeing Giampiero. Simonetta reappeared with a bundle of clothes and, ordering Lupo to turn his back, I changed into a pair of men's trousers and a thick cotton shirt. She threaded a length of string through the belt loops, pulling it tight around my waist and handed me a felt beret. 'Once you've pushed your hair off your face and into this, we'll soon have you looking the part,' she said, laughing.

I was glad there was no mirror because I was sure I looked ridiculous, but I was happy to be dry.

Simonetta dished out three portions of thick vegetable soup and we dined by the fire that Christmas Eve, the flames playing shadows on our faces.

'I'll see you at dawn with the others,' Lupo said, standing up to leave. He wrapped a thick, woollen scarf around his neck and nodded at me. 'Sorry about earlier, signorina,' he said.

'It's signora,' I corrected him. 'No harm done. By the way, you can call me Fosca.'

He nodded. His smile transformed his face and I saw he was a fine-looking man, no longer the thug he'd first presented.

Simonetta accompanied him to the door and they talked in low voices for a while before she returned to the fire. 'Best we put this out, cosy as it is. There's not much firewood left. You can sleep with me tonight,' she said, pointing to the platform above. 'We have an early start. Thank God the snow has stopped.'

We didn't remove our clothes. The straw smelled sweet and Simonetta pulled a moth-eaten horse blanket over us and we settled for the night.

'I think I can trust you,' Simonetta said, breaking the silence.

I'd been staring through a gap in the roof to the left of where we lay, remembering how I'd tried to keep myself awake on the nights before Christmas when I was little, willing a sledge to appear in the sky. I wondered if Giampiero was asleep and if the nuns were able to conjure some magic for the children.

'What do you mean you trust me?' I said.

'You must be wondering what I am up to, but you haven't asked.'

'The war has taught me not to ask questions. But I have my mind and my eyes and I don't miss much,' I replied. 'You are a *partigiana*, I think. My husband was a resistance fighter too.'

'I know. I met him. Silvio was very brave.'

I sat up then, adrenalin suddenly coursing through my veins. 'You know Silvio?' But then excitement was replaced by cold dread as I thought again about her words. 'You said "was". It's never been proved to me, Simonetta,' I said, grasping her hand. 'But I've always felt that he wouldn't come back. Deep in my heart, I knew... but I have been denying all this time that he's gone.' I touched my chest and she nodded her head.

'I'm so sorry, Fosca.'

I broke down and she took me in her arms, rocking me back and forth like a mother would rock a child, until my crying stopped. Even though I had felt Silvio was dead, her confirmation was painful.

'He was courageous. One of the best, Fosca. If it's any consolation, he died immediately.'

She settled me down, pulling the blanket over my shoulders and kept hold of my hand as she talked.

'What I am going to tell you will be hard to hear. But you need to know about it, Fosca.'

Simonetta paused and I wondered if it was because she was searching for the right words.

She sighed deeply before continuing. 'Nobody was saved, and the *tedeschi* were like savages. Bent on revenge because two of their men had been shot the previous week. Ten *partigiani* were rounded up in retaliation and stood in front of a firing squad. Afterwards they were strung from lamp posts to be used for target practice. Their corpses were unrecognisable when they were taken down.'

I looked up. 'I need to know exactly where they were laid to rest,' I said, my tears falling again. 'I need to know for sure that Silvio was one of those boys.' I pulled my hand away from hers, still clinging to a hope that Silvio was not amongst them. She'd said their corpses were unrecognisable. If Silvio had not been identified, there was still a chance he was alive.

'When the time comes, we shall find out where they are buried and pay our respects. I promise you.' She tried to take me in her arms again, but I shook my head and squared my shoulders. If Silvio had been brave, then so must I.

There was aggression and resolution in Simonetta's voice when she continued to speak. 'I have vowed to do everything in my power, until my last breath is spent, to avenge these deaths and get back our freedom, Fosca. One day, when we have time, I will tell you more of why I am in Tuscany. But for now, we should catch some sleep. Tomorrow is a big day for us. We are banking on a Christmas gift for the *resistenza*. The *tedeschi* are in for a shock.'

Her voice grew steelier as she continued. 'I belong to a group that works to sabotage the *tedeschi*. You will meet them soon.'

*

It was still dark and I was in a fitful sleep when Simonetta shook me in the first hours of dawn.

'We need to move quickly. Put these on again. They're dry.'

I pulled on my skirt and blouse and when I climbed down the ladder, I hardly recognised Simonetta. She looked like a child with her long curls tamed in two plaits. 'Are you willing to be one of us today, Fosca?' she asked. I thought of Silvio, and I nodded.

'*Brava!* Then, you need to be a good actress and remember what it was like to be pregnant.' She lifted my skirt and fastened two bullet belts around my middle, packing them out with strips of cloth. This was followed by what she told me were fuses and wires which she wound round and round my waist. 'Wear this too,' she said, handing me a grubby apron to tie on top of my bulky skirt. She stood back and nodded. '*Bene*,' she declared. 'Fine – you look about seven months gone… Your baby is ammunition for our fighters in the hills. Are you sure you want to do this?'

I nodded, the image of Silvio in the forefront of my brain.

'I am doing this for my son,' I replied. 'And for his freedom.'

'Good girl. *Brava!* Chances are we won't be stopped by anybody, but you never know. If we are, I shall explain I'm taking you to hospital and that's when your acting skills will be put to the test. It will be the second time you go through labour pains.'

The belts were heavy, causing me to stoop, which Simonetta told me added to the look of a woman in late pregnancy. She helped my feet into thick socks and gave me a pair of men's work boots, which were too large for me but better than my flimsy, worn shoes. At the last minute, she handed me a pistol, demonstrating quickly how to use it if necessary. It felt cold and deadly against my stomach as I concealed it and I hoped I wouldn't have to fire it.

The early morning air stung my face as I stepped into the dark outside to follow my friend over compacted snow. The promise of being reunited with my son later that Christmas Day spurred me on as I tried to keep up.

We saw nobody as we made our way across the frozen vineyards, the runners stretched along wires like the arms of Christ crucified. Our feet crunched over the snow under the faint moonlight and a dog barked in the distance, breaking the silence of early morning.

I almost fainted when two *tedeschi* loomed from the gloom, torchlight blinding us temporarily. Simonetta muttered under her breath and hissed at me to start moaning.

'*Documenti! Dove andare?*' one of them shouted, waving his rifle, demanding our papers and asking us in broken Italian where we were going.

Simonetta pointed at my stomach. '*Ospedale,*' she said and I doubled over, making a sound that I hoped would pass for a labour pain.

The second soldier laughed. '*Der Jesuskind italienisch,*' he jeered, and his comrade laughed too, waving us on with their bayonets. Once again, the feast of Christmas had come to our aid. Simonetta put her arm around my shoulders to support me, and when they were out of sight, she exhaled a huge sigh of relief. '*Porca boia!* Damn them to hell. There were no sentries posted there the last time I checked. You did well, Fosca.'

I was shaking now. If I'd been searched by them, that would certainly have deprived Giampiero of a mother. As I stumbled on, I started to question myself. Why was I putting myself in such danger? But once more I remembered Silvio – his sacrifice and the sacrifices of others. What was the point of Giampiero growing up in a world dominated by *nazifascisti* tyrants? It was plain to me that I should join in with the fight against oppression and hope that the struggle would bring a better future. For too many years we had suffered tyranny. It had started with Mussolini and even though he was no longer our ruler, he continued to issue orders from his Republic in Salò by Lake Garda through his militia. He had attracted thugs of all kinds to his group of blackshirts and the *tedeschi* were adding now to the reign of terror.

We climbed steadily, the path narrowing until we reached a crossroads. Three mules were tethered to a rusting metal cross. Lupo and another man appeared from behind a tree and greeted Simonetta. Both men were dressed in white, a camouflage against the snowy night, and each of them carried a gun slung on their backs.

'Fosca, you ride with me,' Simonetta said, 'until we reach the convent.'

'We need to move fast,' Lupo said. 'We only have two hours left until daylight.'

He helped me climb up with my unwieldy load to sit behind Simonetta, who had leapt without any difficulty onto the largest mule. Lupo slapped the animal's rump and I clung to Simonetta as the animal moved up the path, its hooves slipping on the icy stones. I must have looked like Mary on her way to her stable, the bulge on my stomach hard and cumbersome.

Just before the summit, Simonetta stopped and pointed to a track leading to the right. 'This is where we leave you, Fosca. Go down there for about one kilometre and you'll come to an old hermitage. That's where your son is.' We slithered off the mule's back and she lifted my skirts, helping me remove my burdens and packing everything into saddlebags. '*Grazie*, Fosca. Wish us well.'

'Where are you going?' I asked. The weapons I'd carried were surely the 'Christmas gift for the *resistenza*' Simonetta had mentioned. Who would they be taken to? And how would they be used?

'Best not to know. We will have more favours to ask of you, Fosca.'

I waited until the mules and their riders trotted away into the early morning mist that sifted through the branches and when I could no longer see or hear them, I turned down the path. The noise of my boots tramping over the snow seemed to magnify in the still air and I willed myself not to imagine what might be hiding within the thick forest lining the path. There were no stars and only a faint moon to guide me, but the strip of frosty white path drew me on until it eventually opened into a clearing. At the far end, I made out a dull flicker of light and as I crept nearer, I realised it was a candle set behind a small window. I had arrived at the retreat.

Madre Caterina, up early to pray, opened the door to my tap and took me in her arms. '*Buon Natale*, Fosca,' she said. 'I had a feeling you would come. You will be Giampiero's best Christmas present. He will love it, *cara mia*.'

For twenty-four hours within the cloistered world of the sisters, we tried to forget about the war. They had baked chestnut cakes and made *guanti di San Giuseppe*: deep fried, sweet pasta shapes known as the gloves of Saint Joseph. Each child they had taken in received a pair of warm hand-knitted socks as well as simple gifts – crocheted hand puppets for the girls made from odd bits of wool and wooden animals for the boys carved by an *inglese* whom the nuns were harbouring. They told me they'd thought he was dead when they'd come across him when out looking for firewood. He was a pilot who had bailed out over the mountains before his plane crashed. 'He has a head injury,' Madre Caterina had said. 'He is like another of our children. He can't remember his name, but he had an identity tag on him. His name is Frank Williams, so we call him Franco.'

I watched as he played with the children, giving them piggybacks, shaping aeroplanes for them from newspaper. Wherever he had come from, he had a way with children. Maybe he was a father. He was a good-looking man if you ignored the right-hand side of his face, horribly burned and mutilated.

'I wonder if he has family waiting for him,' I said.

'Who knows, Fosca? In the meantime, he is safe with us. He can't speak, so at least he can't give away his identity through words, and we dye his blond hair each week. He seems to like it when we massage his head. It comforts him.'

He was yet another displaced victim chewed up and spat out by this awful war. I felt fleeting sadness until I lifted Giampiero for another cuddle and he squeezed his little body close to mine. That night, I held him close on the narrow bed in one of the cells, gazing on his perfect face and dimpled wrists, relieved to know that he was in safe hands with the nuns.

At around midnight, I woke to the sound of a huge explosion. Giampiero slept on but I crept to peer out of the tiny window. In the valley below, huge flames licked the sky in a brilliant red glow and I wondered if Simonetta and her friends might be responsible for this display.

Simonetta came for me late the following afternoon while Giampiero was having a nap. She asked the nuns if she could borrow two habits for us to wear, promising that we would return them as soon as possible.

'They'll be even more careful at the control posts today after what happened last night,' she told me when we were changing from our ordinary clothes. 'I'm depending on you again for your acting skills,' she said.

The nuns seemed to take to Simonetta and we were each handed a basket of little apples and pears. '*Buon Natale*,' Madre Caterina said, embracing us both. 'Christmas blessings. This is all we can spare. Take care, my dears,' she whispered. And when I told her I would send money up as soon as I could, she told me not to worry and that she would remember us both in her prayers.

On our way down the track, Simonetta stopped and pulled two revolvers from under her habit. She hid one at the bottom of each of our baskets and asked me if I still had my pistol. 'Just in case,' she said. 'But I am hoping our weapon today will be these.' She swung the wooden crucifix and beads around her head like a lasso and grinned and I smiled at her childlike fun.

Simonetta knew shortcuts through the forest but we walked the last fifteen kilometres along the main Arezzo road. I could hardly believe my eyes when she waved down a *tedesco* truck. When it stopped, she asked the driver for a lift, bowing her head meekly when they agreed. They were only going as far as Anghiari, they said, but told us to climb up behind. Two fresh-faced soldiers, looking no older than seventeen, sat with us looking cold, sleepy and morose. I clung on to my basket as we jolted over the bumps. If I'd dropped it and the revolver was revealed, it would have been difficult to explain why a nun had a weapon. The soldiers even helped us down when we stopped, one of them clicking his heels together and snapping a salute. It was only when the truck had bumped away out of view that my heart calmed down.

'You have to take risks in this business,' Simonetta said as we continued our journey along the straight road into Sansepolcro. 'It's the only way.' We were stopped twice more. Once by a soldier who waved us on and the second time by a fresh-faced, overzealous Italian militia youth who peered at us and questioned us about the photos in our documents and why we hadn't been photographed in our habits. 'We are novices,' Simonetta explained. 'We haven't yet taken our solemn vows. But we can still pray for you, can't we, Annunziata?' she said, turning to me. I bowed my head and nodded. My knees were trembling so much – I was grateful for my long habit so he didn't see them shaking. 'Of course, sister,' I replied. 'We shall say three decades of the rosary for you and your family.'

He waved us on and ten minutes later we were back safe in the barn at the edge of Sansepolcro. It had been a long trek and we both flopped onto the straw, exhausted.

'You have passed the test, Fosca,' Simonetta said, leaning on her elbow to look down at me. 'You did really well today. *Brava!*'

I was too tired to reply. Once again, I'd been swept up by Simonetta into something I'd never have dreamt of doing in the past. She said I had passed a test but I did not realise that night how far I would venture with Simonetta and the *partigiani* in the coming months. In the end, none of us really know what will happen to us from one day to the next.

CHAPTER FOURTEEN

1947

Fosca stopped talking. There was a chill in the air and a sprinkling of fireflies flitted between dark shapes of bushes. She shivered and Richard was about to ask her if he could fetch a jacket to put around her shoulders when she blurted out, 'I fear that the girl who was buried here could well be Simonetta.' She stood up, rubbing her arms against the cold. 'That is all for now, signor Richard. I'm sorry I've talked so long. Perhaps I will tell you more about her another day.' Her voice was flat, as if she had expended too much energy in narrating her story.

Richard stood too, not sure what to say. The war still casts its web, he thought. Everybody had a story. He was humbled that this young woman was telling him hers. He hadn't understood every word because at times she'd spoken fast and he'd had to concentrate to catch the bones. Through his medical training and own experience of the last years, he knew the psychological benefit of talking through worries and fears. He didn't always practise himself what he'd learned. It was easier to keep everything in.

'I'll walk you up the hill. Let me fetch a torch from inside, wait there,' he said.

'There is no need. If you knew how often I have taken that path back and forth to town, I could almost do it with my eyes closed.'

'Nevertheless, I am coming with you. I would never forgive myself if anything happened.'

'The war is over, signor Richard. What could possibly happen to me?'

She was right, he thought, but nothing was impossible – especially given the reception she'd received from most of the Corbello inhabitants. He insisted that Fosca and Giampiero stay with Pasquale and Rosa that night.

'Where else will you sleep?' he asked her, when she refused.

'We shall come back here, and shelter against the walls. It wouldn't be the first time we've slept rough.'

'And if it rains? We are due a storm.'

'Then we shall get wet. Water never harmed anyone.'

'Well, if you stay here, then so shall I. I wouldn't be able to sleep easy if I knew you were down in this place on your own. And it seems senseless to return to Corbello in the dark to fetch Giampiero and then come down again to this place.'

She turned angry then. 'I know how to look after myself, signor Richard. What do you think I've been doing all this time? I don't need a man to think for me.'

'I don't doubt it. But I work on the premise that a little bit of help is worth a lot of pity. And…' He played a mean card. 'I am thinking about your young son and how much cosier he will be in the dry. And a breakfast of warm milk and Rosa's fresh bread and home-made jam to wake up to.'

Rosa and Pasquale moved Angelina into their room with them that night, letting Fosca and Giampiero snuggle together in the bed that Nonna Zina had once occupied. Fosca lay awake for a while, the window ajar to the night air. When rain began to patter on the leaves, as predicted by Richard, she was glad he had persisted in his argument. He seemed a good man and she wondered why he had decided to come and live in the middle of the Tuscan countryside so far from his own country. It seemed the war had stirred up everybody, spun them around to fling them wherever they landed.

As she drifted into sleep, her son's body warm and soft against hers, her last thoughts were of Simonetta with her mischievous smile, her tangle of curls. She had only just begun telling her story to Richard, and she wondered if she would ever tell him the rest. Certain things could be too dangerous for him to know, and too dangerous for her to even speak of.

Simonetta appeared later to her in a dream, jumping from roof to roof like a butterfly, a full moon silvering her wings. If the body signor Richard had come upon was Simonetta, Fosca knew she must find out how she had ended up there. Something was not right.

Next morning, Fosca left Giampiero to play with Angelina, who was more than happy to have a playmate, while Fosca went to her appointment with the mayor to look at the brooch found with the body. Once she saw it, she would know if the poor girl found in the garden was Simonetta, or some other unfortunate. And if it *was* Simonetta, there were other things she needed to discuss with Gobbi.

'Some of the children in the town taunt Angelina because she is different,' Rosa had confided while Fosca helped her wash up the breakfast dishes. 'And I think that she will always be happier with younger children who haven't picked up the prejudices of their parents.'

'Back when I was the teacher here, I tried to instil kindness into my pupils,' Fosca said as she hung the big coffee cups back on their hooks. 'Words and numbers are not the only subjects they must learn at school.'

'She doesn't like the teacher now. And I am not sure he enjoys teaching either.' Rosa untied her apron. 'He's a war invalid and I feel he would rather be anywhere else than in the classroom.

The women at the fountain think he will offer his resignation soon, *grazie a Dio*.'

Fosca was encouraged by this piece of information and stored it for later use.

'I shouldn't be too long this morning, Rosa, and then I'll be out of your hair.'

'Please don't worry, Fosca. It's good to have another woman here. And Angelina loves your little boy.'

'Yesterday I was all set to turn tail and return to the nuns, but a good night's sleep has restored me. Thank you for welcoming us. But... I only wish that everybody in the village felt like you and Pasquale. *Grazie*. As soon as I can find work, I will find a place of our own.'

'Good luck with that. Most of the houses in Corbello are shells and families are crowded together with relatives in whatever shelter they can find until they can raise the means to mend their own.' She sighed as she measured out handfuls of flour onto the kitchen table and fetched eggs to mix fresh pasta for the midday meal. 'It will take a long time to return to how life used to be.' She paused. 'If it ever does.'

'*Coraggio*, Rosa,' Fosca said, reaching over to squeeze her friend's floury hand. 'Slowly and surely it must happen.'

Mayor Gobbi was shouting into his phone when Fosca knocked on his office door. She couldn't help but overhear his heated words. He was talking about a woman. That much was obvious by his blasphemous language. When she heard the way he kept referring to this woman as nothing but a prostitute, Fosca was terrified for a moment he meant her. '*Porca boia. Quella donna è nient'altro che puttana*.'

He slammed the phone down and ushered Fosca in, shutting the door firmly behind them. 'You will find out sooner than later when people start their tittle-tattle,' he said as he collapsed into his swivel chair. 'My wife has left me and nobody knows where she has disappeared to.' He pulled a handkerchief from his pocket and wiped sweat from his brow. 'And now you have turned up out of the blue, scattering pigeons when they were beginning to settle in their lofts, bringing the wretched *carabinieri* in your wake.'

'Are you expecting me to apologise for being alive?' Fosca said, her voice cold.

'Your resurrection, *cara* signorina Fosca, will mean that we shall now have to determine the identity of this dead woman in order to stop the *carabinieri* from snooping and poking into our affairs. You haven't been here to witness the goings-on in town since the end of the war: the rifts between families, recriminations, witch-hunts... we were beginning to resume our lives and now this...' He dragged his hands through his hair. Fosca noticed that the roots were greyer than the rest and deduced he was due for a fresh application of black dye.

The man was in a stew. She chose to ignore that he had called her signorina instead of signora. Only she knew that she wasn't legally married, and she'd always told people that she was and corrected them when she was addressed as signorina. But she knew from past dealings that it was important to tread carefully with this man. She cleared her throat. 'I've come about the brooch found on the body. I need to see it with my own eyes.'

He stood up and pulled open the top drawer of a wooden filing cabinet, lifting out a folder and a brown package sealed with official labels and stamps.

'I visited *sergente* Gambacorta and he loaned this for the morning. It will save you from visiting the *questura*. The cells there are not very comfortable. I hope you appreciate the favours I am doing you.'

He threw the package onto his desk and Fosca watched, biting her lip as he broke a seal and extracted a smaller parcel from within. Her hand went to her mouth as she peered closer. She picked it up. There were zigzag scratches on the back that hadn't been there before, but there was absolutely no doubt it was the same silver brooch that Nonna Zina had given her. There was the delicate carving of two lovebirds, and opening up the case she saw the 'E' and 'Z' inside, woven from hair.

Her eyes travelled to the piece of red cotton cloth protruding from the brown package: Simonetta's distinctive red spotted kerchief that she had always worn. Many had been arrested for this alone – red being a symbol of resistance. As the realisation hit that her friend was dead, Fosca gave a quiet cry and collapsed against the wall.

Gobbi watched her while she recovered. Although there was a carafe of water on his desk, he didn't offer it and she didn't ask.

'This brooch was given to me by Bruno's mother-in-law,' she confirmed. She rubbed at her eyes, determined the tears that threatened should not spill. 'And I think I can tell you the identity of the dead woman too, because I loaned her this brooch. I knew her as Simonetta Ferro.'

The mayor sighed in exasperation as she continued. When she'd left to meet Gobbi this morning she knew she would need to bring this up. She felt a quiver of fear but did her best to gaze at him calmly. 'And you knew her too. She was involved in the assault on the train and what happened afterwards. Just as you too were involved.'

Gobbi's head jerked up at these words. He was silent for a long moment before saying coldly, 'You seem to forget, signorina, that we had an agreement never to talk about that.'

'That agreement no longer stands as far as I am concerned. The war is over. You told me lies and led me on. I can never forgive you for that. Be very careful, Edoardo,' she said, deliberately dropping his title. 'I know more about you than anybody else in Corbello.'

He hissed at her to keep quiet. 'This is not the right place to talk about such matters. *Porca boia.* Why did you have to turn up? All this belongs in the past. What is the point of raking it up again?'

'I'm not raking anything up. I'm reminding you of facts. But I do wonder what the citizens of Corbello will think when they find out about the past dealings of their mayor. Incidentally, who did you bribe to win the position?'

His look was menacing now and she hoped that he wouldn't notice how her legs were shaking. Despite her visceral fear of this man, she braced herself to continue. 'If the woman in the mortuary is Simonetta, I want to know how she died.'

He threw up his hands at this. 'Like thousands of other war victims: during an air raid, from a gunshot wound, by stepping on a booby trap, from starvation… the people from the War Graves are busy all the time with these corpses that turn up under farmers' ploughs, in mass graves, caves. War is death. Death happens in war.' He pulled out a linen handkerchief from his jacket pocket and mopped his brow.

'And do they examine the why and how of these corpses?' she asked.

'Well, *we* shall find that out now, won't we?' He glared at her, his eyes menacing, full of threat. 'The *carabinieri* will want to carry out further investigations. Do not be surprised if the *maresciallo* calls you in for further questions.'

'If he does, then I shall have a lot to tell him, won't I?'

Fosca turned to leave, unsurprised that this man had not offered a single word of condolence for the loss of her friend.

She needed to breathe fresh air and return to the innocence of her child. Before she opened the door, her hand lingering on the knob, she turned to him. 'Two things, *sindaco* Gobbi,' she said, stressing the word. 'I want my brooch returned to me as soon as possible and…' She paused. 'I hear that there might be a vacancy for a teacher soon in Corbello and I shall apply for my old post.'

She accepted his mumbled, 'I shall see what I can do,' as a resigned affirmative. If the job did not come her way, she would certainly start to spread gossip in the town about the mayor and his involvement with the partisans during the war. She could not prove it but she had the strongest of feelings that Edoardo Gobbi was somehow involved in Simonetta's demise and she was determined to get to the bottom of it. She didn't have much money to spare and couldn't afford to stay at the *osteria* for too long. But once she got her job back – and she was quietly confident that Gobbi would make sure that happened to preserve his reputation – then she and Giampiero would be able to move into the little apartment beside the school. As she descended the steps of the town hall, she felt faint and had to grasp hold of the railings. She had thrown down her gauntlet. To some, her threats to this man would sound like blackmail, but he was a nasty piece of work – she had experienced his devious ways herself – and there was only one way to deal with a villain, even if it went against the grain: like for like.

Richard was drinking coffee in Pasquale and Rosa's bar when Fosca returned to fetch Giampiero. He held up his cappuccino, a broad smile on his face. 'Join me, Fosca. I'm celebrating. I've been informed that it won't be too long before I can move back into my tower and start renovations. What will you have? A glass of Prosecco, maybe?'

She shook her head. 'Too early for me. A coffee would be wonderful. *Grazie.*' She sank into a chair and Giampiero ran over to sit on her lap. She kissed the top of his curls, breathing in his child's smell of milk, the outdoors, of innocence She wanted to protect him from all the evils of the world but he wriggled loose of her embrace.

'Mamma, you're squeezing me too tight,' he said, looking up at her.

'*Scusami, tesoro.*'

Looking over Giampiero's head to Rosa as she set coffee on the table, she said, 'I'm afraid I was right about the brooch, and I recognised other possessions of Simonetta's.' Her shoulders slumped, her face showing her dejection.

'I'm very sorry,' Richard said, leaning over to touch her arm. Fosca looked down in surprise at his hand resting on her and moved to pick up her cup. Rosa bustled over and added a measure of *anice* liqueur to Fosca's coffee. 'This will help settle you,' she said. 'What a shock.'

When Rosa had returned to the kitchen, Richard surprised himself by issuing an invitation to this woman and child whom he hardly knew.

'I have plenty of room in my property if you need somewhere to stay for a while. There's the house down there not being used,' he said, wondering even as the words came out of his mouth what he was doing, cluttering up his life. Did he really want the peace that he had craved shattered so soon? But he felt sorry for her and it was true that he had the space. He could take up temporary residence in the tobacco tower and let her use the house. Maybe she could teach him more Italian and cook and clean for him in lieu of rent. He understood all about courage in its various forms. And from the little he knew about Fosca, it seemed she was bravely struggling.

'It's just about habitable but you'd have to draw water from the well and there's no electricity. The place is dry and clean enough.'

'You are very kind,' she replied. 'I might take you up. But only until I get back my teaching job.'

The deal was sealed with another round of coffees and this time Richard took his strong and black and tried a slug of *anice*. He felt almost like a local and the aniseed taste was more than pleasant.

Fosca, Giampiero and Angelina wandered down towards the tobacco house a couple of days later, Fosca feeling the need to escape from the poisonous atmosphere of Corbello beyond the walls of Rosa's *osteria*. She was also aware that the children were getting under Rosa's feet in the kitchen where she was making *biscotti* and preparing for a wedding party. Rosa was grateful when Fosca offered to keep them occupied until supper time. 'If there are wild asparagus or flowers of malva in the woods, Fosca, gather some for me for the wedding salads, please.'

The trio stopped to dip their feet in the little stream that trickled its way to the big pool where older children played. Fosca tilted her face towards the sun, relishing the warmth, thinking how lucky she was and how sad that Simonetta had been denied a future at such a young age. She had barely turned twenty-one when they'd last talked. What had happened to her since then? How long ago had she died? How did she die?

The children's laughter pulled her from her thoughts and she told herself to concentrate on the present. Moving over to the water's edge, she showed Giampiero and Angelina how to use mud at the edge of the water and shape it into little bowls to dry in the sun. Angelina needed more help than Giampiero, her fingers clumsy on the clay. She would always need extra guidance, Fosca thought, but Rosa and Pasquale were good parents and she was a lucky girl. Sometimes parents were ashamed of children born like Angelina and misguidedly kept them locked up, believing that they had done something wrong in producing a child who, in their eyes, was not perfect. Angelina was bonny, her smile and laughter always present, and she was very gentle with Giampiero.

'Can we go and see signor Richard now?' Giampiero asked when the children had eaten their afternoon snack: a *merenda* of bread and goat's cheese. 'I like him. He's fun and he lets us explore.'

The idea of sharing her concerns about Simonetta appealed to Fosca. Maybe bouncing ideas off Richard would help.

'We'll only stay a little while. He's very busy.'

Richard looked anything but busy. A straw hat covering his face, he lay in a hammock manufactured from an old army blanket tied with thick rope and secured between two stout olive trees.

The children ran over and began to rock him, so that the hammock tipped him out. 'No peace for the wicked,' he said, lifting each of the children up and dumping them in the middle of the blanket, tickling them until they begged him to stop.

'I'm so sorry for disturbing you,' Fosca said, a smile on her face as he approached, brushing dust from his knees.

'Don't be. I was being lazy and needed to be disturbed. I have so many jobs, you wouldn't believe, since the *comune* gave me permission to continue with work on this place.'

'And the *carabinieri*?'

'They finished their measuring and removal of samples this morning. But, to be honest, any clues will have long disappeared.' He lowered his voice as he told her that Simonetta's body was to be examined again later in the week.

She bit her lip, not wanting to picture her friend's lithe body in any other way than the last time they had been together.

'I am not sure how to start, but I am determined to find out what happened to her,' Fosca said eventually, looking over to the children, who were squealing at the fun of swinging in the hammock.

He followed her gaze. 'Don't worry. It's perfectly secure. If it takes my weight, they'll be fine.'

The thought that he would make a good father flashed into her mind but she squashed it down. Giampiero had a perfectly good mother.

'That loathsome Gobbi tried to palm my concerns off by telling me that Simonetta was just another victim of war. But if a local person had found her body, they would surely have taken her to the cemetery rather than bury her all alone down here. From what I can gather, she couldn't have been blown up by a mine. I saw her scarf… it was intact. And the brooch too, save for a few scratches on the back. You worked in a hospital on bomb victims, Richard, didn't you? Am I wrong to think like this?'

'I understand your reasoning. If she'd been shot by soldiers passing through, they wouldn't have had time to bury her. Burial parties usually looked after their own, sometimes with a hastily dug grave, or a pile of stones placed over the body.'

He paused. 'But I was the one who found her and she was buried quite deep and her body and most of her clothing was intact.'

'There is something not right.'

'Let's see what the investigation comes up with, Fosca. Try to put it out of your mind until then.'

'It's hard. She… she was my friend.' She hadn't told him the rest of her story yet, and so he could not appreciate the concerns she felt. Simonetta had always thrown herself into everything without weighing up the danger. She'd got away with it on so many occasions, but her luck had obviously run out. What had she been up to? And who with? The questions stormed her brain and she longed for answers.

'Right!' Richard's chirpy tone surprised her, jolting her away from memories of Simonetta.

'Fosca, I came here because I realised that sometimes the best way to deal with our past pain is to distract ourselves. So while the children are occupied, you can help me start on a project. The well. The bucket keeps catching as I draw it and tips out water. I need to repair the brickwork, but it's a job I'm loath to do on my own in case I go hurtling down and am never seen again. Would you mind keeping an eye on me when I descend?'

'*Certo!* And I can keep an eye on the children at the same time. A mother develops eyes in the back of her head quite early on,' she said with a smile.

Richard fetched another length of rope from a coil hanging from a rusty nail on the house and secured one end to the trunk of the fig tree and the other round his waist.

'That fig will have to come down,' she advised. 'If it grows any bigger, the roots will disturb the house. It might even be the cause of damage to the well.' She pointed to the olive trees. 'And they need to be pruned to produce better harvests.'

'I'm impressed. A horticulturalist as well as a teacher.'

'I enjoy gardening. Madre Caterina – the nun who practically brought me up – she taught me a lot. I loved helping her in the kitchen garden.' She shaded her eyes and gazed across the couple of hectares of land. 'There's an awful lot you could plant here, you know: peach trees, almonds, apples, pears, quinces and kumquats and, behind the house, there's a perfect sunny slope for vines. You could become self-sufficient. Buy some hens and a goat or two.'

'Well, I might come knocking on your door for advice.'

'It would be wonderful to *have* a door,' she said, puckering up her mouth ruefully. 'If I am successful in applying for the teaching job, there's an apartment too. But who knows if that will happen? It depends on that man…'

'You don't like Mayor Gobbi, do you?' Richard started his descent of the well, his voice echoing in the confined space.

'You could say that.'

'That makes two of us then. Or, three even.'

'What do you mean?'

'I met his wife before she did a runner. She was not enamoured either.'

'Magdalena is a strong woman. Too strong for Gobbi. It was never a good idea to get on the wrong side of her.'

'Good luck to her for leaving him, I say. In fact, she was the true owner of this place. I bought it from her.'

Fosca suspected that Magdalena had seen Richard coming. It would not have been past the woman to pounce gleefully on a foreigner prepared to buy a run-down wreck simply because he had a romantic notion. In her opinion, it would be cheaper and easier to build a new house from scratch. But she said nothing.

'There are a couple of bricks that have worked loose down here on a ledge,' he called up. 'I'll need to tidy them up and set them back in. Stand back while I throw them up.'

The old bricks landed at her feet. Fosca leant over the mouth of the well and saw that Richard's legs were extending across the width and his head had disappeared into an opening in the side of the well wall. Many older wells were built with these openings on each side, about a metre from the top. They were used for storing food and to keep meats cool during the summer months. Plenty of country people had tried to hide possessions in such places when they'd been forced to flee their houses when villages were cleared by the *tedeschi*, but it was such an obvious hiding place that often these goods had been stolen by the time the home-owners returned.

When he emerged from the well, his hair caught up with cobwebs, dust smeared on his nose and forehead, Fosca's eyes widened at what he held up: a piece of metal about the size of a brick.

'Look what I found, Fosca. I do believe this might be a bar of gold. It's certainly heavy enough.' He whistled. 'What is the law about finders keepers in Italy? This could pay for restoration of the tobacco tower and more besides.'

The grin on his face reminded her of a little boy who had been presented with a new bicycle. His excitement changed to concern as Fosca put her hand to her mouth and collapsed onto the side of the well.

'What's up, Fosca? Are you ill?'

Fosca knew exactly what Richard had found. She took the brick from Richard's hand and ran her fingers over it, shaking her head.

'I'm not unwell, Richard. No. But, I can't believe what you found.'

'What, Fosca? Tell me.'

'You finding this here. It makes me even more suspicious that Mayor Gobbi had something to do with Simonetta's death.' She looked up at him and saw he was shaking his head, confusion written all over his face.

'I don't understand.'

'This is indeed a gold bar and it's part of a haul that Gobbi snatched with the help of the *partigiani*.'

He shook his head again. 'Are you going to fill me in? I'm not sure I follow.'

'It's easier if I start by telling you more about Simonetta, my friend,' she told him as he climbed from the well. 'She was braver than any woman I've ever met. We spent a lot of time together in this place and she is linked to what you have just found. I am certain of it. And so is Gobbi, I'm sure.' She paused, her gaze directed to where the children were playing. 'I hate the idea her story will be forgotten. She deserved better than to end up in a hastily dug grave.'

She moved to sit on Richard's bench, placing the gold bar at her feet as she began to talk.

'Simonetta wasn't her real name. It was Natalia. But that was before I met her…'

CHAPTER FIFTEEN

Simonetta's story, summer 1943

Turin

For twenty-year-old Natalia, creeping out at night from the hiding place had become a compulsion. She would wait until Papà's snores broke the silence of her prison. Her little sister Francesca didn't sleep much – she was in bed all day now. Natalia hated to see her thin hair and scrawny arms. She was like a ghost, her once beautiful eyes dull. Where they were constrained, high up in the eaves, the air was cloggy and clammy, a perfect breeding place for mosquitoes that had turned her skin red and scabby.

'Be careful,' Francesca whispered, and Natalia put her finger to her mouth before bending to kiss her younger sister on her hot cheek. She had another fever.

In her other hand Natalia held her shoes. She'd chosen dark clothes again for the night: a pair of slacks and a dark blue shirt, so that she would merge with the shadows. Tiptoeing across the bare floorboards like a cat burglar, she was careful to miss those that creaked. During the day, she watched routines of people in the piazza below the soap factory from the tiny attic space where the family were hiding. There was a small, vented window where a torn curtain offered a gap to spy through. At night, the street beyond was empty because of curfew and so far, she'd never noticed soldiers patrol in this corner of Turin.

Natalia had oiled the hinge on the door to the attic with a can she'd found in a cupboard. Her *papà* and mamma hadn't noticed the pieces of rag that she'd placed beneath the legs of the table that blocked the door. She eased away the table where she studied and slowly opened the door, holding her breath in case it squeaked. Then, she unpinned the length of material that concealed the exit through the large wardrobe placed on the other side against the attic door to where they were hiding.

Two months of being caged like a bird had started to feel like two years, and yet it was worse than being caged birds. They couldn't sing or laugh, they had to whisper to each other or use hand signals and when her sister suffered one of her coughing fits, she tried to muffle the sounds with her pillow. The previous week their mamma had found blood on the pillowcase. Francesca needed medicine and Natalia knew how to get it.

Down the ladder she climbed from the storage area, each rung taking her a step nearer to a couple of hours of freedom. The machinery in the room below stood silent – during the day it was a cover of sorts to the family's presence upstairs. The scent of soap powder and chemicals cloyed in her nostrils, and her bare feet stuck to the salts and powders spilling from bins as she tiptoed across the floor.

The owner of the soap factory was a true friend. A few years before the outbreak of war, their *papà* had moved them away from their home town of Anghiari in Tuscany, where there was little work, and taken them to Turin to set up this soap factory together with his old friend, signor Zanelli.

Once Mussolini's anti-Semitic laws had come into force in the late thirties, their situation turned from difficult to worse. It was so unjust that they were no longer considered true Italians. She and all her other Jewish friends were banned from attending university where she had begun her studies in pharmacy. Then, after a few months, Papà was unable to work any longer at the factory and he lost co-ownership. Somebody had reported that he was Jewish and he was forced to do hard labour with other Jews – breaking stones for road building.

For a while, once a week, the girls were able to attend a type of college where Natalia tried to keep up with her pharmacy studies. It was near the synagogue in Via Sant'Anselmo, but that was no longer possible since the *fascisti* had thrown petrol at the walls to burn it down. Since the Germans marched into Italy in 1943, like a khaki-green snake, Jews had begun to be hunted everywhere and their *papà*'s work colleague, signor Zanelli, had been more than courageous to offer them a safe haven. The overzealous *repubblichini* and Italian SS would certainly have thrown him into prison or shot him if the family was discovered hiding in the makeshift cubbyhole above his factory.

Once in the open, Natalia breathed in the night. Nero, the factory cat, emerged from his hunting spot on the wall and flopped down at her feet, turning onto his back on the cobbles. She bent to tickle his tummy, wishing she were a cat, free to wander where she wanted.

She kept to the walls as she moved through the outskirts towards the city centre. A dog barked and she froze, but the sound was coming from a few blocks away and she wasn't the reason for its alarm. Natalia heard the cry of a baby and the soothing voice of its mother through shutters open to the heat and she moved on until she reached the house of her friend, Maria. The door was unlocked and, checking there was nobody about to see her, she slipped inside and climbed the stone staircase to Maria's apartment.

Maria, also dressed in dark clothes, handed her a package. 'That's all I could get,' she said, hugging her close. 'You will have to make it last. I'm sorry.' Maria worked at the chemist in Via Roma.

'I took it while the manager was out for his coffee,' she told Natalia. 'But if he checks, I'm in deep trouble.' She drew her fingers across her throat and Natalia squeezed her arm. '*Grazie*, Maria. You're one in a million.'

So many of Natalia's so-called friends had stopped talking to her, abandoning friendship in the fear of being branded as acquaintances of Jews. In one sense, she didn't blame them – they had been fed so many lies. When newspapers like *Il Lambello* told their readers to hate Jews and suggested Jews should all wear brightly coloured bracelets to warn against infection, when they printed lies about how Jews were profiting from the war and described them as rabid dogs, then it was hard for the credulous to distinguish the truth from lies.

But Maria was so much more than a friend. The two girls had fallen in love and it was torture for Natalia to be apart from her beautiful girlfriend who understood her like nobody else. Maria had once described their being together like the brief flowering of a delicate poppy as it unfurled fragile, papery petals. Separation was the moment the petals shrivelled and died.

The clock struck two on the cathedral bell-tower as they emerged onto the dark street below Maria's home. Her parents stayed in their country house each weekend, but she worked on Saturdays, so the family apartment had become a Saturday meeting place. They made their way to the boulevards, ready to hide behind the columns if anybody appeared. Next to frayed notices exhorting citizens to eat less sugar and salt (which few had tasted recently anyway), and next to the propaganda images of American soldiers killing little children, there were posters advertising sums of lire for the capture of Jews. There was money to be earned for handing them over to the authorities so that they could be deported, imprisoned or worse. Natalia ripped down a cartoon of a Jewish man, his tongue being cut off with a pair of scissors. As she tore it into shreds and scattered the pieces, she frightened herself with the vehemence of her anger, for she felt like cutting off the tongue of the designer of this vile propaganda. Pulling stumps of chalk from their pockets, the two girls wrote in bold letters on the brick walls. **EVVIVA LA CLN** – Long live the committee of national liberation – **EVVIVA LA RESISTENZA**. And, like shadows, their simple but fraught mission completed, they kissed before blending into the darkness of the alleyways and dispersing to where they had come from.

After creeping back up through the soap factory and inching the door open to her prison, she yelped as Papà's strong hands grabbed her and pulled her inside. 'Where have you been, foolish girl?' he said in a hoarse whisper. Her sweet, kind father shook her in fury and fear. 'You are placing us in danger. What if somebody followed you back here?' he said, shaking her again.

Her mother stood behind her in the gloom, wringing her hands. 'You don't know who is spying on us, Natalia,' she said. 'There are plenty of people happy to report us and take the reward.'

Natalia knew they were right, but she also knew there was little point in her family existing like rats, hiding away in the dark, nerves shattered, their health ebbing away. That kind of life might last forever and she didn't want to live this way any longer than she had to.

'I've been out to find medicine for Francesca,' she said, handing her father the package by way of a peace offering. He shook his head as he took it and ordered her back to bed. Francesca was awake, holding out her arms and Natalia climbed in beside her. She could feel her ribs; she was as fragile as the thin shell of a bird's egg and she wanted to weep. Nobody realised that they were sisters when they first met them. Francesca's hair was fair and her features were delicate, her eyes a deep, deep blue. Natalia was dark, with an athletic build although not very tall, and her eyes were almost black. As they lay close, she whispered to Francesca in the darkness and told her that soon the war would be over and they could leave this place. But she didn't believe her own words.

There were several bombing raids in the next few days, the sky lit up in vivid flames of orange and yellow as plane after plane shed its load. They felt vulnerable and powerless in their top floor eyrie – like birds in the highest nest on a tree about to be felled. The two sisters clung to each other, shaking as each bomb fell, the ground shuddering, the whole building swaying and threatening to collapse with each load spewed from the sky.

After the worst night of bombing, before first light, signor Zanelli crept up to their hiding place to talk to their *papà*. After he had gone, they had a family powwow. Their parents and Zanelli had decided they should escape to the mountains above Turin where they would be safer. Several Jews had already escaped to the Val d'Aosta and they could join them there. Signor Zanelli had told them they would be hidden for the journey in large crates holding consignments of soaps. He had organised false documents and destroyed their genuine papers. From now on, Natalia would be known as Simonetta Ferro and Francesca as Maria Cristina Ferro. Natalia liked the new surname – it meant iron. It made her feel strong. The photo of her was grainy, but whoever it used to be, she resembled her a little, save for the fact that her hair hung in two long plaits. Natalia wondered who she was, if she was still alive or living far away in another city.

That evening the two girls giggled as Francesca braided Natalia's thick curls to get her into her new role. Their *papà* said that persecution of Jews was worse in big cities like Turin and Milan and they would be safer in the countryside, but to Natalia's mind, they would never be totally safe anywhere as long as this war continued.

'If we are to survive,' their father said, 'we have to present new faces to the world. We are no longer the Lombroso family – we are now *famiglia* Ferro.' He paused and rubbed his face before continuing, his voice quiet. 'But we shall always be the same people inside.'

Natalia watched as her mother slipped her hand into her husband's, a rare demonstration of affection.

'Never forget,' he said, 'how proud we are that the first Jewish prime minister in Europe was Italian. Luigi Luzzatti's name should never be forgotten. And remember all the famous Italian Jews who contributed to the importance of this nation: those who introduced printing to Italy and all our famous Jewish authors, poets, scientists and inventors. Each and every day we should strive to be the best people we can be, and remain proud of our heritage.'

Their mother blew her nose softly when he had finished whispering these words to them. Natalia wondered if this tyranny would ever end, and how long it would be before she started to feel restless and miss Maria once they were marooned in the mountains. But she also wanted her sister to get better and for her family to feel safe, so she tried to banish these thoughts.

On the night before they were due to leave, she had to say goodbye to Maria. When she was absolutely certain that everybody was asleep, Francesca's eyes shut fast and her parents' snores proof enough, she crept once more from the hiding place and let herself out into the city. The streets were a mass of rubble that she had to clamber over to find her way to Maria's place. The familiar landmarks, like the wonderful avenue of plane trees, were now stumps in the ground and she watched as somebody hacked at the fallen branches for precious fuel. She passed a family asleep on the street under a sheet stretched above their heads, a small fire glowing next to them, where an old lady sat, her hands extended to the hot ashes. The old lady watched Natalia with blank eyes as she passed by. The night wasn't cold, but she supposed the old woman was looking for comfort from the flames.

The bombings had been directed at the bigger factories like Fiat, Westinghouse and the Dalmine steelworks, but not all had hit their mark. Blocks of apartments where ordinary civilians lived had also been razed to the ground. She crossed the river Po where a prostitute stood waiting at the end of the bridge, slinking back into the shadows as Natalia hurried by. The Corso Vittorio Emanuele was blocked with stones and fallen timbers. There was no way forward and she feared for Maria's home in nearby Via Pio Quinto. Everywhere in Turin was a war zone, the city reduced to deep craters, fallen cables and hungry displaced citizens.

Without warning, the habitual sirens started up, quickly followed by the unmistakable drone of approaching planes. The sky trembled like a violent thunderstorm and then everything lit up in a blaze with gunfire coming from all directions, adding to the sickening sounds of the crashing of buildings, people screaming and the whine of falling bombs. Natalia covered her head with her hands and dived for cover behind a pile of rubble, grazing her knees as she landed. When there was a lull, she dashed like a cat from shadow to shadow. When she reached the main piazza Vittorio, she found herself in plain view of a German anti-aircraft battery and she dropped down to crawl on all fours. Suddenly, a German soldier appeared from a doorway. For a minute they stared at each other in total silence. Then, a man shouted an order and the soldier looked at her, shaking his head before turning away. Once she was out of his sight, she tore away back across the bridge as if she was being pursued by a pack of lions, knowing that she had had a lucky escape.

But the nightmare only worsened. When she returned to where Zanelli's soap factory should have stood, there was nothing but fire, black smoke and water spurting from somewhere where machinery should have been.

'Mamma, Papà, Francesca,' she screamed. A man who had been searching through the rubble tried to drag her away and she lashed out, cursing at him to let her go, rushing forward to tear at the mound of smouldering debris with her bare hands before everything went black.

CHAPTER SIXTEEN

Simonetta

They told her that she regained consciousness thirty-six hours later. Natalia woke to the concerned, kindly faces of signor and signora Zanelli peering over her. She lifted her hands. They were swaddled in thick bandages and when she tried to raise her head from the pillows, everything swam.

'You have to rest,' signora Zanelli said, pulling the sheet up that she'd tried to kick away. 'Your injuries are nasty. Are you hungry, my child? Could you manage a bowl of broth?'

'Where is my family?' she asked and signor and signora Zanelli looked at each other. Without them telling her in words, the expressions on their faces told her everything and she started to weep. Her whole body hurt but the ache in her heart was the worst pain she had ever experienced. She closed her eyes and wished that she could die too.

'I'm so, so sorry, Natalia,' signor Zanelli said.

'My name is Simonetta,' was all she could say and then she started to sob, as she remembered how she had practised saying the new names with her sister, who had looked forward to a better life in the mountains.

'I'll sit with you for a while,' signora Zanelli said when her husband left the room and Simonetta shook her head.

'Please, I want to be alone.' She turned her head to the wall.

Later, she recalled that they did their best. They had found her in the hospital and persuaded the doctor in charge of the overcrowded ward that they could look after her at home. She knew that she was ungrateful for their kindness, but she couldn't see any point in living. A doctor came to dress her burns and stitch the wound on her head where a tile had landed from one of the buildings during the raid. He told her that she was lucky to be alive. The scars on her hands would heal but she knew her heart never would. After ten days or so, signor Zanelli came into the little box room in their home where they were nursing her and sat on the chair beside the bed.

'Natalia—' he started to say and she interrupted him, her voice cold.

'My name is Simonetta.' She persisted with this new name, wanting to cling on to the last happy hours she had spent with her family, when they had been thrown a lifeline. It made them feel closer and so, Simonetta she wanted to remain.

'Simonetta,' he said, trying again. 'I have found you somewhere else to go. It's not safe here. The *nazifascisti* are searching houses in this area and if they find you here—'

'They will arrest you too,' she said, looking up into his kindly eyes. 'I'm so sorry. You've been kind and I am selfish.'

'You are not selfish, *mia cara*. You are sick.'

He paused, fiddling with the ring on his hand. 'You have been through too much for a girl of your age.' He swallowed, searching for words and Simonetta felt sorry for him. He had been courageous in harbouring her family.

She reached out to touch him with her bandaged hand. '*Mi scusate*, signor Zanelli.'

'Your friend, Maria,' he continued. 'She came to find you. She's in the next room. Would you like to see her?'

Simonetta gasped. 'Please.'

He showed Maria in and left them alone. Maria lay down on the bed and held her until she was ready to talk, smoothing her tangled hair that peeped from under the bandages. 'Oh, Maria.

I've lost everything,' Simonetta said, tears trickling down her face. 'And I thought you were dead too. Why couldn't I die with my family? It's only because I went to find you, to tell you that we were leaving that I'm still alive, but I want to die too.'

'Shh! Shh!' Maria said, dropping soft kisses on Simonetta's cheeks. 'Don't talk like that. I'm here now. I'm here to help you for as long as you need me, *anima mia*.' Then she talked about the new plan that signor Zanelli had come up with. How he had tracked down a cousin of Simonetta's father in Anghiari in Tuscany, where they once lived. It would be safer for her there. Safer for her mind too. 'You can make a new start and get away from the misery of Turin. It will be easier all around. And I will come with you. I could never leave you, Natalia. You are the other half of my soul.'

Simonetta shook her head. 'You must call me Simonetta from now on.'

Maria shrugged. '*Va bene*. That is fine. A different name will never change you from the girl I love. We can travel together; you are still weak.' She paused before adding, 'He is a good man, your signor Zanelli. He has sorted all the travel arrangements and documents and he told me of your new identity. It is for the best.'

'My name is Simonetta,' she said again, as if repeating it would convince them both. She sighed and shook her head. 'Oh, Maria, what else is there for me to do, but accept? *Grazie*.'

If Maria hadn't been with Simonetta during those early weeks in Tuscany, Simonetta would have given up. Slowly, her sorrow turned to deep anger at the war, towards the stupid politicians who had succeeded in reducing Italy to such a mess. Very quickly, she realised that she and Maria were nothing but a nuisance to her cousin. He had seven children and their arrival meant extra mouths to feed. To tell the truth, she didn't much care for him either, because of his politics. He'd rejected his Judaism. And he admired Mussolini, believing that their deposed leader would come back one day from the Republic of Salò to rule the country again.

The girls soon found jobs at the Misericordia Hospital in Sansepolcro, cleaning wards, and were able to move out. It was hard work but they felt useful. They were provided with beds in a dormitory on the top floor of the hospital and simple, starchy meals of pasta once a day. Simonetta couldn't stop thinking of her family who she would never see again, and felt that she was existing from day to day by a thread, despite Maria's loving presence.

One late afternoon near the end of a long shift, as she was scrubbing the floor near the main entrance, a scruffy young man with a beard beckoned to her to approach. When she drew close, he grabbed her and thrust something hard into her side. 'Don't scream,' he said calmly and quietly. 'If you make a fuss, I'll shoot. And I'm not bluffing.' It was a gun he held against Simonetta's side and he pushed it harder into her ribs. 'Listen carefully: I need you to find a stretcher and I need a doctor.'

'There is no need to threaten me,' she answered, trying to push him away.

'Be quiet,' he said, gripping her arm. 'No discussions. You're too young and pretty to die. Do – what – I say.'

She called Maria over. 'Fetch a stretcher.'

Maria saw immediately what was happening. Together, they followed the young man outside to a figure slumped under a tree. It was a young woman in a bad way: unconscious, her face grey, the front of her dress caked in blood.

They carried her into the *sala operatoria*. *Dottoressa* Bianca was in there alone, scrubbing her hands clean when they entered. She was a popular woman: a hard worker with a generous heart. Someone had told the girls that her *fidanzato* had been killed in

Libya early in the war, and that she had dedicated her life since to mending people's bodies and minds now that her plans of marriage and children were ruined.

'I will help you,' she told the scruffy young man firmly, taking in the situation. 'But you have to leave my theatre.' She stared him in the eye. 'And you can put that weapon away. This is a hospital not a battlefield.'

The young man pushed his gun inside his jacket. 'I'll be waiting outside. *Grazie, dottoressa.*' He bent to kiss the woman on the stretcher with a tenderness totally in contrast with the rough way he had handled Simonetta. Then he shuffled away, leaving the smell of sweat and cordite behind.

'You had better hide him in the cellar. There are *tedeschi* and militiamen everywhere.' *Dottoressa* Bianca pointed to Maria and told her to accompany the young man and she told Simonetta to close the door. 'You will help me,' she said. 'And do exactly what I say.'

Simonetta wasn't squeamish. She had started her pharmacy studies at university before Mussolini had forbidden young Jews to continue with their education. She knew something about human biology and had attended a few anatomy lessons, including performing an amputation on a dead body. She copied *dottoressa* Bianca as she finished scrubbing up and tied a mask around her face. 'You will hand me each instrument when I ask,' the doctor said, her voice calm and authoritative. 'What is your name?'

'Simonetta, *dottoressa.*'

Dottoressa Bianca cut the bloodstained dress to reveal a gaping wound in the girl's stomach. 'If this girl lives, it will be a small miracle,' she said as she started on her work.

At the end, she sewed the girl's wound up with neat stitches and Simonetta couldn't help thinking of the hours her mother had spent, sewing embroidered cloths and sheets for her trousseau.

Simonetta had never seen the point of all that. Her mother had filled a chest with linen for her daughters, but Simonetta had never any desire to marry, unlike her sister. Francesca had spoken often about the type of wedding she wanted when the day came: of the long lace dress she would wear and the matching veil, the roses she would arrange in her bouquet. Simonetta choked back a sob at the memory and the doctor glanced at her. 'You have done really well, Simonetta. Is it too much for you, this blood?'

She shook her head. 'No, *dottoressa*. I was thinking of the family I lost, that is all.' She willed herself not to cry, annoyed that sorrow struck in unexpected moments.

The doctor's eyes were full of compassion. 'People who have not lost a loved one cannot understand the pain,' she said. 'Let us hope that we do not lose this young girl too. But she will need nursing through the night.'

Simonetta offered to sit by her, promising to call one of the nursing sisters if necessary. *Dottoressa* Bianca allowed the young man to sit with the patient for a while, after making sure he cleaned himself up, and she found him fresh clothes from a patient who had passed away, as well as a pair of sturdy boots with odd laces.

He talked to Simonetta quietly as they sat together that night, the expression on his face tender as he spoke. The young girl was his sister. Simonetta watched him as he checked on the window, explaining that it would be his escape route, if necessary, testing that the window would open easily and how far it was to the ground if he needed to jump. There was something animalistic about him, Simonetta thought, with his hunted, wary look. His fists clenched and, biting back his tears, he told her how he had returned to his burning village. 'My sister was raped, stabbed and left for dead after a troop of *tedeschi* ordered the place to be cleared in retaliation for the death of one of their men. She wasn't the only one to suffer.' He looked up at the ceiling as if trying to contain the tears that welled in his eyes. 'The monsters went on to violate two pregnant women and…' He stopped talking, his fists clenched together, his head bowed. '… gouged out their unborn babies…'

Simonetta was horrified. She couldn't comprehend such brutality, but she realised it must be true, for how could anybody invent such stories? He was a *partigiano*. She knew that already. It had been obvious from the start and the *dottoressa* had known this too. Simonetta had heard rumours that the doctor was a good woman, that she had hidden refugees in one of the wards where patients with contagious diseases were held.

The partisan told Simonetta that his name was Lupo, but that it was not his real name. She immediately felt an affinity with him. Both of them were people with two identities. Most of the *partigiani* had different names; it was better that way, he told her. She learned there were several bands in the area hiding in the mountains and their numbers were steadily increasing. They were made up of young soldiers who had absconded from the Italian army as well as escaped POWs and German deserters.

Simonetta told him her own story and he listened intently.

'We need more women, Simonetta. To work as *staffette* to deliver messages and spy on enemy movements. In many ways it is easier for you women to blend in. We have girls who have smuggled guns to us in the bottom of a pram and old women who hide medicine and food in deep pockets within their clothes.'

'I am desperate to play a part. I lost my whole family.' Simonetta clenched her fists, her voice raised in anger.

He touched her arm and told her to hush. 'You would need to stay calm. There is no place for emotion in our fight.'

She raised her eyebrows. 'You say that, but how can you not feel emotion after witnessing what these barbarians are doing to us?'

'You misunderstand me. I meant that we need to have our wits about us. To remain calm, think on our feet when danger is all around. And each of us has a part to play that others do not need to know about. It is best not to share too much.'

She was quiet for a few moments. She watched as the man called Lupo bent over his sister and then buried his face in his hands. Simonetta closed the dead girl's eyes and drew the sheet gently over her head.

'I have listened carefully to your words,' she said, her hand on Lupo's shoulder. 'And I want to help.'

She was drawn to the *partigiani* initially through her grief, but as time passed and she was to witness acts of brutality and hear of massacres of innocent people, the *resistenza* became her reason for existence. She didn't care where she lived. As long as she had somewhere to sleep, food to line her belly and Maria by her side, that was enough.

CHAPTER SEVENTEEN

1947

Richard was ripped from the past when Pasquale turned up, carrying little Angelina and Giampiero on each shoulder.

'Faster, faster, *asino*. You're a very slow donkey,' they squealed.

'And you're very heavy sacks of flour,' he said, setting them down next to Fosca and Richard.

'I found these two scallywags making their way up the path. Did you not realise they had escaped?' Pasquale said.

'*Dio mio*. What an awful mother I am,' Fosca said. 'I am so, so sorry.' She pulled her son to her. 'You should never run off like that,' she said, half-scolding, but with relief in her voice as she pulled leaves from her son's curls.

'But you and signor Richard were ignoring us,' Giampiero said, pulling away, 'so we set off on an adventure. We didn't find any tigers though, did we, Angelina?'

The little girl took her thumb from her mouth. 'No tigers. Just Babbo.'

'No harm done. It was just as well I was walking down to see what you were up to,' Pasquale said. 'Rosa sent me to tell you she has lasagne in the oven.'

'Mamma, *ho fame*,' Giampiero said. 'And Angelina is hungry too, aren't you? That's why we ran away.'

The little girl nodded and patted her tummy. 'I'm as hungry as a wolf.'

'Oh goodness,' Fosca said, jumping up from the bench. 'What time is it? I'm so sorry, Pasquale.'

Richard checked his watch. 'Nearly six thirty. I could run you up to the *osteria* on the motorbike. It won't take long to hitch up the sidecar. But there's not going to be room for you, Pasquale.'

'No matter,' he replied. 'The walk will do me good. Rosa is always saying her husband is twice the man he used to be.' He winked at Richard.

Fosca bit her lip. 'Rosa serves the evening meal at seven and there's no way we can get there in time if we walk. I'd promised I'd give her a hand with waitressing. Do you really not mind?'

'It will be my pleasure.'

The children loved the bumpy ride up the hill in the sidecar, urging Pasquale on with squeals as he attempted to race them for the first few metres. But they quickly left the big man behind. Fosca sat gingerly on the pillion, gripping the bar behind to support herself. Once or twice she gave a little shriek as the bike jolted and Richard turned his head to tell her to hold on to him so that she didn't fall. But she wouldn't. And he didn't insist. She was glad when they pulled up outside the *osteria*. Thanking him quickly, she hurried into the building with the children.

Richard ordered a couple of beers and sat outside waiting for Pasquale to arrive up the hill, thinking over Fosca's account of her war, and of Simonetta's. It was easy to overlook the experiences of ordinary people. Ten minutes later, Pasquale turned up, the big man plonking himself down, huffing and sweating. He downed his beer in one go. Richard bought a couple more to take back to the tower and put his head round the kitchen door to wave a goodbye in the direction of Fosca, who was turning meat on the griddle. He wanted to remind her of his offer of accommodation, but she looked far too busy. The invitation was there if she wanted to take it up.

As he made his way down to the tower, he looked forward to spending the night on his own instead of returning to his bed at Rosa's. A sandwich and beer would do him fine. Later on, he lay in his hammock staring up at the stars, his mind filled with Fosca's story. Yes, he'd seen the war and had helped patch up countless wounds. But trying to survive as a civilian in an occupied country he knew very little about.

Swinging gently to and fro he thought of what Fosca had related about Simonetta, the girl in the grave. A body was one thing but a story that fleshed out her bones was another. He was curious to know more, and what linked it all to the gold he had found in the well. He looked over to the shapes of the tobacco tower and the little house shrouded in the night and he shivered before hauling himself out of the hammock and making his way to his makeshift bed.

Three days later, Rosa lent Fosca an old pram to transport her few possessions to the tobacco house. She packed in bags of flour, rice and a basket of early flat peaches, as well as a couple of jars of passata. 'Please don't cut yourself off down there, Fosca,' she said as they embraced. 'And when you feel the need of a woman's company, remember I am here.'

Fosca arrived in a flurry of laughter, Giampiero, perched on top of the contents in the pram, urging her to make the pram go faster like a chariot. Richard looked up from his notebook where he had been scribbling ideas.

'I am taking you up on your kind offer, Richard, but only until the teaching job comes my way,' Fosca said as he came over to help guide the pram over the uneven ground.

'Please don't worry, you're not disturbing me.' He pointed to the little house attached to the drying tower. 'You and Giampiero can sleep in there. It will be good to try out living in my tower. We'll have separate entrances and our own space. Please don't keep apologising.'

Thereafter, if she began to apologise, he would start singing a tune, or block his ears and she would smile contritely and shrug her shoulders.

Fosca was a hard worker. Within a week, the house was transformed with a coat of whitewash splashed over the internal walls. The flagstones in the kitchen area were scrubbed clean, bringing out tan, gold and brown hues. Richard stood, hands on hips, marvelling at the change, and wondering if it was her need to distract herself from war memories that made Fosca throw herself into the tasks. She hadn't mentioned Simonetta for a few days, but he saw her face darken whenever she looked over at the spot where the body had been found.

'You've done well, Fosca. I was thinking of replacing these slabs, but they look fantastic. *Grazie.*'

'*Prego!*'

She also seemed to take delight in feeding him, teaching him about local dishes and flavours. He'd never eaten anything so good as when she carried over to the tower a dish of home-made pasta with a sauce of pesto made from herbs growing wild in the meadows or, on another evening, *pappa al pomodoro* – a soup with the main ingredient of *toscano* bread, flavoured with tomatoes and basil. And she introduced him to fresh broad beans eaten raw with thin slices of pecorino cheese drizzled with honey from Rosa's bees. All these dishes were typical *cucina povera*, homely country cooking from recipes passed down through the generations.

'I love the way you cook your vegetables,' he said, when she'd stuck a tray of tomatoes sprinkled with breadcrumbs, garlic and chopped parsley into the outside oven after baking a batch of loaves. 'In England, our vegetables are boiled to death.'

She'd cleaned the bread oven at the back of the house of years of spiders' nests and was pleased that it still drew properly. Home-made pizza on a Sunday evening became a ritual and after three weeks, he suggested they ate together in the evenings, the three of them. 'It doesn't make any sense for you to carry over the food for me to eat on my own in the tower.'

Giampiero had asked him more than once if he was a prince living in a tower, like in the stories his mamma told him at night and the little boy had drawn him a picture of a man wearing a crown, leaning from a turret.

'The women in Corbello will have something more to gossip about at the fountain. They will say I am living in sin with you,' she said one evening as they drank coffee after supper.

'Do you mind?' Richard asked, wishing he could take a photograph of her sitting opposite him in the candlelight. She looked like a woman in a Renaissance painting, her hair falling over her shoulders. Dreamy, a far-off look in her eyes.

She shrugged. 'Let them think what they want. They do not know who I really am. Their lives are very narrow.'

Richard hadn't made much progress in starting work on the tower, preferring to try out different places for sleeping and writing, still testing the light and feel of the place. At the moment it reeked of smoke layered onto the stones from years of drying tobacco leaves from the fires stoked below. There were vents in the walls, which let in some light but he planned to widen them and install picture windows to capture the valley views. He'd made a few other decisions: he wanted to insert a middle storey and he would definitely sleep on a mezzanine floor built on the top level. He fancied the idea of a roof terrace or a large balcony where he would sleep on hot summer nights. Through a missing tile in the roof, looking south, he could see across the valley and the fields to Corbello, the dusty road coiling round the hill like the patterns on the shell of a giant snail. He pictured how the town might look, once repairs were completed. Would Corbello ever feature on tourists' postcards?

Apart from causing many thousands of dead, the twentieth century's two major wars had undone hundreds of years of heritage across Europe, razing monuments to the ground and displacing works of art from their rightful places. His experience of war had only shored up his Quaker belief that it was fundamentally barbaric; nothing could persuade him otherwise. But it was time to forget about war, look to the future and concentrate on the simple things in life. He looked across the yard to where Fosca was draping washing on the bushes to dry and decided he would construct her a washing line. She was singing in her truly dreadful voice, and it made him smile.

The windows sparkled and she made plain linen curtains to pull closed at night. Some of the panes were cracked and the frames needed patching, but with cobwebs removed, daylight spilled into the room. Richard pictured the space with a couple of rugs, easy chairs and pictures on the walls. 'I need to go hunting for furniture and bits and pieces. Will you help me with your female eye?'

One market day they headed to Arezzo. In the main piazza – largely undamaged, compared to its surrounding streets – there was a holiday atmosphere. Crowds thronged round the stalls selling everything from cheeses, cured meats, fruit and vegetables to clothes, bric-a-brac and furniture. Richard lifted Giampiero onto his shoulders as they wound their way around the square towards the furniture section.

He stood for a while gazing at an untidy arrangement of war souvenirs for sale, wondering how anybody could find interest in these maudlin leftovers of battle: British and German helmets, brass bomb casings converted into ashtrays and pen holders, a tattered USA flag and a pile of servicemen's blankets, which a group of women were fingering, exclaiming at the quality of the

American cloth. Fosca told him they were prized for dyeing and converting into warm winter coats. But all Richard could think of were the men who used to own these possessions and wonder if they were amongst the dead.

Fosca was an expert haggler, managing to get the price of aubergines, sweet red and yellow peppers and a punnet of cherries down to far less than priced. 'What is your signora doing to me?' the elderly fruit vendor exclaimed to Richard, who, liking the supposition of Fosca as his wife, watched in awe as she bargained. 'I bet she drives a hard bargain with you on a Saturday night, eh?' the old man said, the cigarette in the corner of his mouth waggling as he chuckled and swung the brown paper bags around to twist the corners shut.

After an hour of meandering, they sat at a table outside a bar, Fosca opting for an espresso, Richard a Peroni, and Giampiero frantically licking at a chocolate gelato that dripped down his wrists in the hot sun. All around them was noise, colour and cheerful friendliness.

'Thank you for bringing us, Richard,' Fosca said, wiping sticky cream from Giampiero's mouth and fingers. 'I'm glad we came.'

'You're very welcome.' She looked pretty today, he thought, in her full-skirted, tight-waisted black and white polka-dot dress. It made a change from the drab skirt and blouse she wore most days. When they passed by a stall selling straw hats, he encouraged her to try on a couple and he bought her one with a wide brim, decorated with silk flowers.

'*Bella, bella,*' the young stallholder said as Fosca viewed herself in the mirror. And, yes, she did look beautiful, Richard thought. He had not been oblivious to the admiring looks she'd attracted as they dawdled at the stalls.

At the far corner of the Vasari loggia, they came upon another stall selling second-hand goods. Richard examined a gramophone player, a stack of classical discs of Chopin's nocturnes tied with string catching his eye. There were partial sets of dinner services, a tarnished candelabra, a top hat that he tried on, much to Giampiero's amusement. When Richard plonked it on the boy's head, it covered his face completely and rested on his shoulders. A tall wardrobe painted in colourful Tuscan style was pitted with shrapnel damage. Fosca opened the doors to reveal sliding shelves down one side and a clothes rail in the other half.

'Do you like it?' she asked.

He wrinkled his nose. 'Too fancy for me.'

'It would look good in your kitchen for storing pots and pans, don't you think?' she said.

'Something plainer, maybe?'

She picked up a couple of books and waved them triumphantly. '*Ecco!* You asked me to help you with my language, so we can start your Italian literature lessons with these, Richard. These, at least, I know about.' She flicked through the pages. 'Ungaretti, Montale… they are recent poets and I think you will like what they say.'

It was fun to wander round and survey what was on offer. At midday, the bells in the elaborate *campanile* of Santa Maria della Pieve, the tower of the hundred holes, rang out the angelus. A flock of pigeons and white doves flew up and over the square like fluttering handkerchiefs and the vendors began to pack up their stalls. Richard watched Fosca go up to a woman who was lifting a dressmaker's dummy up to a cart and after a short discussion, she passed it to Fosca, who, with a huge smile on her face, held it up triumphantly to Richard. 'This will help me, because until I return to teaching, I plan to set up a little sewing business.'

'Wonderful!' he said, although not understanding anything about sewing. He had no idea what purpose the item served. Barbara had been interested in fashion and her hats and flamboyant dresses made from materials that made her look like an exotic butterfly had intrigued him. Not having any sisters, and his mother always wearing plain clothes, this passion for fashion was a delightful puzzle to him. 'It's going to be interesting travelling in the sidecar with that thing to hang on to,' he added.

She clapped her hand to her mouth, 'Oh, *scusami*… I didn't think.' She called over to the woman, who was harnessing an old horse to her laden cart, that she had changed her mind, but Richard pulled on her arm. 'No! It will be fine. I'll go slowly and you can sit behind me with Giampiero in the sidecar together with your new purchase. But next time we come shopping I think I will borrow Pasquale's truck.'

'If you will allow a next time.'

She chuckled and he wanted to pin her smile to her face and dispel the sadness so often there.

Fosca settled Giampiero into the sidecar and wedged the dummy in behind him. Then she mounted the bike, tucking her dress beneath her. He turned to her, looking like a frog in his goggles. 'Make sure to hold tight to me once we get going,' he said, with a cheeky smile.

To Fosca, as they bumped over the partially repaired road back towards Corbello, it felt strange to cling on to a man after so long, but eventually she relaxed, moulding her body against Richard's spine as he negotiated the winding road to the pass of Foce dello Scopetone.

Richard stopped the bike at the summit to let the motor cool down while they ate a picnic in the shade of pines and poplars. From a stall in the park at the top of Arezzo, they'd bought half a litre of wine and thick slices of pizza wrapped in greaseproof paper. For Giampiero there was a bottle of juice with his slice of margherita, and they completed their lunch with a bag of cherries, Richard betting the little boy on how far they could spit the stones.

Fosca laughed. 'You're teaching him bad manners,' she said. Giampiero's mouth was stained pink from the fruit and his face was red from the exertion of spitting as far as his little lungs would allow.

'In years to come, when he returns to this spot with his girlfriends, he can boast he planted all the cherry trees around,' Richard said as he placed his helmet two metres away from where they were sitting. 'There'll be another ice cream for you, young Giampiero, if you can spit all your stones into this.'

Fosca lay back in the grass, squinting at the light that splintered through pine needles on the trees above. The crickets were loud at this time of day and, together with the laughter of her child and the fizzy-buzzy hum of a bee on the daisies poking through the coarse grass, they were perfect, relaxing sounds. She had a momentary pang about Simonetta. It was all too easy to block her from her mind, the pain of war memories too heavy to constantly bear. Just as she felt her eyelids grow heavy, a hot squirming little body flung itself on top of her. 'I've won another gelato, Mamma. For spitting so well. *Andiamo*, let's go. Hurry! Richard said we could stop at the first place that sells ice creams.'

Fosca held on to her son, tickling his podgy tummy and blowing raspberries on the skin beneath his shirt. She buried her face in his milky soapy smell and didn't want the moment to stop. It was these little things of peacetime that were precious, she thought. During the past years, a picnic in the mountains had been out of the question; you never knew if soldiers were around the next bend or a sniper was aiming at you from the rocks, or when the dark shadow of a Messerschmitt might appear over the horizon. People had moved about quietly, merging into the background, attempting to avoid danger and death. In her heart she knew that she was wrong to keep avoiding the issue of Simonetta's death. Sooner or later she had to confront it. With the help of this kind Englishman, who had no axe to grind, maybe she would find a way.

Richard helped pull Fosca to her feet and she brushed blades of dry grass from her creased frock. 'The only place to find *gelati* will be Anghiari,' she said. 'Nobody up here will possess a refrigerator.'

'I know the perfect place – if it's still open,' Richard said. 'I went there with the hospital unit at the end of the war. We can enjoy a sundowner while his lordship eats his second ice cream of the day.'

'And from then on, *gelati* will be rationed,' she said as she made sure that boy and dressmaking dummy were safely wedged into the sidecar. 'He'll be sick.'

Climbing back behind Richard, it felt normal this time to place her arms around his waist. The air was beginning to freshen and she moved closer to his warmth and stayed there until he pulled the motorbike up in the old market square, beside the monument to Garibaldi. His stone fingers were extended in a pose towards the hills from where they had just travelled. Here too there was plenty of war-damage: several buildings propped up with stout timbers, the pale pinks and yellows of the façades pocked with holes and bullet marks. But the *pizzeria/ristorante* halfway up the square was doing a roaring trade: locals and a few tourists sipping their cocktails that a smartly dressed waiter carried to them, balancing his tray on the tips of his fingers as he wove through the tables.

'What does he do when he needs to get undressed?' Giampiero asked.

'What do you mean?' Richard asked.

And when the little boy replied, 'If the tray is glued to his hands, how can he take off his shirt and put on his pyjamas?' Richard chuckled.

'It's not glued, my cherub, he's clever at balancing the tray,' Fosca explained, ruffling her son's curls.

From then on, while the adults enjoyed their tall glasses of iced Campari, Giampiero walked solemnly around trying to balance a drink mat on the edge of his chubby fingers, happy when another child joined in with his game.

Fosca envied the uncomplicatedness of children, and she raised her glass to her lips while she watched her son, the setting sun's rays dancing for a moment in the bright red bubbles of her drink.

'We'll have to do this again,' Richard said, leaning back in his chair, looking content and relaxed. 'Once I get the place ready for furnishing, would you accompany me to the market again as my interior design advisor?'

'I'd love to,' she replied, smiling. He had already asked her to come along today for her 'female eyes', as he'd put it. But she would be more than happy to join him again, for another golden day like today.

Back at the place she was starting to refer to as 'home', Fosca tucked Giampiero up in bed, and afterwards, prepared a dish of baked aubergines and mozzarella. Richard carried out the kitchen table from the tobacco house and produced a bottle of Sangiovese wine that Pasquale had given him. When the last drops were finished, Fosca sat back in her chair. She couldn't let any more time go by without dealing with Simonetta's death, despite trying to push it away. There and then, she resolved to share her thoughts with Richard about what might have happened to her friend.

'If I told you more about Simonetta and what we did together, then I hope you might be able to help me fit together the missing pieces of the puzzle. I've tried to switch off about it and continue with a normal life for the sake of Giampiero, but my mind won't rest until I find out what happened to her. The feelings go too deep.' She paused, watching for his reaction. He nodded encouragement and she continued. 'Her story will be new to you; you will be more objective and have clearer ideas than my muddled head. But the story is long.'

'I am not going anywhere, Fosca,' he said softly. 'I am all ears, as we say in *inglese*.'

She was grateful for his understanding, and as she looked at him with both sadness and relief, she had the strangest feeling that he would do anything to help her.

CHAPTER EIGHTEEN

Fosca and Simonetta

January 1944

My heart was aching to be with my little son, but I knew Madre Caterina would take great care of Giampiero. Simonetta was a good distraction to me in those first lonely days without him. I never knew what she would come up with next. What Simonetta had related to me about her life in Turin, the way her family had been persecuted for being Jewish, her great loss at their death, had made her into the fighter she was. My life was tame in comparison but it was about to change.

'I've told you about my past,' Simonetta told me as she threw another stick on the fire in the barn, 'because I want to involve you in our fight for freedom. We need more people to join us. I think you will be of great use.'

I looked at this girl with her hair tied in two thick plaits, her clothes filthy and torn. She was small in stature, younger than me but she possessed the courage of a lioness. I noticed the faint scars on her hairline for the first time and the discolouration on her hands from burns she'd suffered in the bomb raid that had killed her family.

'I have a young son to think of,' I reminded her. 'He comes first. Always.' As soon as I'd said those words, I felt cowardly, as if I was inventing an excuse, but I had to be honest with her.

'And what kind of world do you want your son to inherit?'

'A world with a mother in it. He has already lost his father and he has no grandparents. The only other person in the world who cares for him is Madre Caterina: a nun with no family to take over when she is gone. If anything happens to me, Giampiero will be quite alone.'

'We are both orphans, then. We have that in common,' Simonetta said. 'You and I – all of us – need a world that is better than the one we live in now. And we have to fight to achieve a different kind of Italy and to rid our country of the *tedeschi* and our own Republican *fascisti* who have brought us to ruin over the last twenty years. I have to tell you that there are thousands of women up and down the country who are allying themselves to the resistance.'

I was quiet, reflecting on what Simonetta was saying. I knew in my heart that was right. She didn't need to tell me about suffering, but I had grown used to staying in the background, keeping my nose clean. I didn't know if I would ever possess her courage. At that point, I said nothing, but it was as if Simonetta could read my thoughts.

'What about if we asked small things of you?' she said. 'The tobacco house where you live, for example. It could be another safe house for us.'

'It doesn't belong to me. My landlord could turn up at any time of day or night.'

'We would only use it from time to time. I move about a lot. It's best for my type of work not to stay in one place for too long.'

I thought about that for a few moments: how Simonetta knew her way about the area even though she was from a city much further north and how people seemed to trust her. Maybe it would not be so bad to have her company occasionally. I'd taken to dropping in at the *osteria* a lot, I realised, because I felt lonely. But I still wasn't sure about involving myself in dangerous missions. First and foremost, I had Giampiero to consider.

'It would be good to see you from time to time,' I heard myself saying. 'So, come to me, if it helps.'

She smiled. '*Grazie*, Fosca. Now let's see what we can rummage up to eat.'

Two days later and I was back in Corbello, alone at the tobacco house. The place was damp, with the fire unlit in my absence over Christmas. Mice had nibbled the blanket on my bed and I swept droppings from the table in the kitchen area. The wind howled that night, rain lashed at the windows and found its way through gaps between loose roof tiles. I slept badly and when I woke, I needed company. So, I made my way up the muddy truck to Corbello – thankful for the watertight, oversized boots that Simonetta had given me – to see if I could help with Nonna Zina. The thought of living with her family and abandoning the lonely tobacco house crossed my mind as I trudged beneath the dripping trees, but they had little food and space to spare for themselves. It was not in my nature to intrude on their kindness.

The door to the *osteria* was closed and a sign on the door told me they were shut due to family bereavement: *CHIUSO PER LUTTO*. I went to the back and knocked. Aurelia opened the door. She was dressed in black and when she saw me, she held out her arms. 'Nonna died last night, Fosca. She went peacefully in her sleep.'

I was sad, for I'd grown fond of the old lady. I sat with the family for a while after I'd paid my respects to Zina's body laid out upstairs. There were no flowers at that time of year, but the family had cut branches of myrtle and rosemary to place beside her and a single red votive candle flickered on a shelf in the soft light. I reflected on the passing of life and Simonetta's words rang in my ears, making me feel ashamed that I had been reticent in our talk the other day to become involved with the *partigiani*.

Sitting beside the old lady whose life was spent, I resolved to do what I could to make the world a better place for those of us left. I touched her cold waxen hands arranged on her chest, a set of wooden rosary beads entwined around her fingers and, after bidding farewell to her family and relatives in the kitchen, I hurried back to the tobacco house. I needed to find a hiding place for Nonna Zina's brooch that she'd given me the last time I'd visited. I had said I would treasure it forever, but if the time ever came for me to have to sell it, then I would. I looked around the room and eventually I found the perfect place. In one of the beams straddling the washing area where I kept a bowl and jug on a stand, there was a small hole, an imperfection in the wood. I wrapped the brooch in a strip of dark rag and, dragging over a stool, I balanced on it to probe my fingers within the empty knot. The gap was bigger than appeared to the eye and I managed to push the brooch over to the left. Stepping to the floor, and checking upwards, the brooch was impossible to see from any angle.

I knew that Simonetta would come to find me again sooner or later. In the meantime, I used my sewing machine to patch and mend the few clothes I owned. I cut up an old thick skirt to make a pair of warm trousers and shirt for Giampiero. During the day I hunted for firewood for the stove and for anything edible I could forage. One day I pounced upon a treat: a clump of winter mushrooms growing through the frost on a tree stump, and I collected them to add to a handful of polenta for my supper. I found chestnuts stashed in a hole at the base of a vast beech tree, most likely hidden by squirrels or dormice, and I stole the hoard to roast as a treat. As a substitute for coffee, I picked acorns from the ground to grind. As a child, I'd spent hours working with Madre Caterina in her vegetable garden or gleaning plants from the wild in the meadows that bordered Sansepolcro. It had been a chore back then, but now I thanked her for everything she'd taught me. From the woods I gathered cleavers, the leaves of purple deadnettle, chickweed and garlic mustard for winter salads and soups, and rosehips for infusions. Occasionally I would hear the rattle of gunfire in the distance and the rumble of heavy vehicles on the main road, but I saw nobody until late one night.

I woke to a rattle of stones on the window. I thought at first it might be hail, but creeping from bed to peer out, I saw Simonetta looking back at me in the moonlight. 'Let me in,' she mouthed.

'It's perishing out there,' she said when I opened the door. She hugged me quickly, her clothes damp from the night air and she handed me a sack. 'Potatoes, flour, coffee, cheese, salami, rye bread and oranges,' she said as she finally produced a bottle of wine from her haul of goodies. 'And don't ask me where I got them from.' She winked and I drew her inside. We huddled near the stove, which I stoked with handfuls of pine cones and bark.

'We'll save the wine for tomorrow,' she said. 'I'm frozen, it will only make me feel colder.'

It didn't take long to prepare her a drink from dried lemon balm and rosehips. She pulled a face. 'Remind me to source sugar or honey for next time I come. How do you drink this stuff?'

I liked the bitter, aromatic flavour. Maybe I was more used to a simple diet than this well-travelled girl. We shared hunks of bread and cheese and as it was well after midnight, we climbed into my bed and huddled together for warmth for the remainder of the night. My sleep had been interrupted and it eluded me now, but Simonetta dropped off almost immediately. I lay there, the moonlight shining through the tiny window onto her. She looked impossibly young. Her face was streaked with dirt and there were dark shadows beneath her eyes. As she slept, she murmured and her hands twitched. I pulled the cover around her, feeling very protective.

In the morning we had a feast of a breakfast. I stored away the rest of the food she had brought me in my cupboard, and we sat and talked.

'Fosca, I need you to hang around the *osteria* more. Fighting is stalled at the moment with this bitter weather. The allies are dug in and the *tedeschi* are playing a waiting game. In the meantime, we need you to find out anything you can. The *osteria* is always full of *tedeschi* and militia.'

'But I don't speak German. What use could I possibly be?'

'We know there is somebody spying on us. We don't know who but we've been thwarted recently on some of our missions. Our leader, Lupo, and others of our group were arrested a week ago after we tried to cut electricity lines to the headquarters of the *tedeschi* and we believe that information is being passed on by somebody. We need to find out where the men have been taken. Anything – I repeat *anything* at all – could be of use.'

'But wouldn't it be easier for you? You were in the *osteria* when I first saw you. That pianist, he seemed to be coming on to you – and I heard you talk in English.'

'They were words from a song I know. I speak very little English and anyway I am too well known in there. Besides, they suspect that I stole his gun. If I go in, then I'll be arrested straight away.'

'How did you do that?' I gasped.

She smiled. 'Simple. The stupid fools take off their holsters and hang them over the chairs. It's as easy as stealing food from babies when they have drunk too much. I slip my jacket over the back of the chair and then pick up the gun and holster with it when I leave.' She winked. 'I can teach you many tricks of the trade. And when I have to flirt, I *flirt*,' she added. 'Men are so foolish.'

I shook my head, thinking how fearless she seemed, how close to the wire she lived.

'So, what do you say? Can you do this for us?'

I hesitated, but then remembered my resolve as I'd sat by poor Nonna Zina's bedside. 'Of course, Simonetta. I'll try. So, how will I get the information to you?'

'Don't worry. I will come to you. And as it works out, then we shall devise systems for leaving messages. Thank you, Fosca.' She hugged me. 'Remember – anything at all is of interest to us. The times the men come in. Who they are. On which nights. The vehicles that pass. Who the big drinkers are who might give away information. And flirt if you have to.' She stood up to go, collecting her rucksack and jacket from where they had been drying by the stove.

'Before you go,' I said, reaching for the stool, 'this is where you can leave messages when I'm not here.' I stood on the stool to show her my hiding place and pulled out the brooch. 'This was a gift. It's silver. Maybe it has some value.' I pressed the back to show the secret opening as Nonna Zina had shown me, and handed it down to Simonetta.

'I have a friend who could value this for you,' she said as she closed and opened the back of the brooch again. 'Do you want to me to ask if it's worth selling?'

'Yes. Money for my son is more useful to me than jewellery.'

'Leave it with me,' she said. She pulled a chain from inside her shirt and threaded the brooch through the loop before slipping it within her clothing. 'Don't worry, I'll take good care of it. And, before I forget, I got you this.' She pulled a parcel from her rucksack and tossed it over to me. I caught it, looking at her questioningly.

'If you need to earn money for your son's keep, use this. It's a silk parachute. I noticed your sewing machine. Perhaps you could make clothes from the material: petticoats, shirts, nightdresses.' She smiled.

After Simonetta had gone, I opened the package. There were metres and metres of silk. I imagined sewing a beautiful nightdress – how it would feel to the touch; how it could make a woman more desirable in bed. I'd never worn one with my Silvio. I didn't need to. He kept me warm in other ways in the few short months we'd had together. But I could sew one for another woman. I wondered who was getting married next in Corbello. There had been many hastily arranged weddings during this war because of the fear of no tomorrows. Maybe Bruno would let me put up a notice in the *osteria* to repair and make garments. I decided to visit him later that afternoon. That night, before I settled down on my bed, I pulled the photograph of Silvio nearer to me. His smile gazed back at me; it was in his beautiful brown eyes. Silvio had always been ready to laugh and cheer me up. I wanted him there next to me. I held the frame to my breast as tears trickled down my face. I feared it would never happen again, but I wanted to believe otherwise.

CHAPTER NINETEEN

There were more soldiers in the restaurant trying to keep warm than the last time I had been. That winter of 1944 was the hardest for years, and war made it harsher. Snow that had fallen at the beginning of January still lay on the ground, dirty and stained, and it wasn't difficult to understand why fighting had stalled in the mountains. This time I entered the *osteria* via the main entrance and, with Simonetta's words ringing in my ears, I made a mental note of the number of men. There was a woman tonight, seated at the table with a group of *tedeschi* soldiers and Italian militia-men. She wore a fox fur around her neck, and bright red lipstick smeared her mouth. I didn't have to think too hard how she had managed to get hold of cosmetics. We country girls had our own more innocent methods to make ourselves prettier: we bit our lips to make them redden or made lipstick from dried rose petals crushed into petroleum jelly. Silvio had liked the look and taste of my lips when I'd eaten raspberries.

I banished those memories and concentrated on the present. I thought I might have recognised the woman as the mother of one of my pupils, but I couldn't be sure. Simonetta had given me a small notebook but warned me not to keep it on me, and to hide it in the tobacco house where the brooch used to be. I tried to memorise the scene in the *osteria* by inventing rhymes: *The girl in red will end up in bed. The man at her table was willing and able.*

The latter part of my rhyme referred to a well-dressed Italian in his late thirties: my landlord, signor Gobbi, and husband of the fascist woman, Magdalena, in charge of the group of fascist women in town. When I had taught at the school, she was always dropping by with leaflets and bundles of second-hand clothes for the children in greatest need. To my mind, she was more interested in checking on allegiance, rather than dishing out charity. Signor and signora Gobbi wore shoes of soft leather and better quality clothes than ordinary people could acquire. No doubt they were in thick with black marketeers. Gobbi was in conversation with the German pianist with whom Simonetta had sung the night I'd first seen her, before Christmas. I doubted if the *tedesco* could have played a tune well that evening, the way he was slurring and slumping in his chair from too much grappa. The girl with the lipstick moved over to sit on his lap, picking up his cap from the back of the chair where he had hung it and pulling it down on her own head, giving him the flirty eye from beneath the peak. I made a note of the skull insignia and shuddered at the ugly image. It meant he was an SS officer. All this information I stored in my brain to transfer later to my hidden notebook.

Aurelia was busy in the kitchen rolling out a sheet of pasta dough. A pile of greasy dishes sat by the sink and I fetched a pan of water standing in the ashes and set to work, happy to immerse my arms in warm water and dry out my damp clothes in the fuggy kitchen. 'It's lonely down in the valley,' I said as Aurelia turned to stare. 'Let me help you.'

'I've only a portion of pasta to give you in return,' she said, sprinkling a handful of flour over the dough to stop it from sticking to her rolling board.

'*Perfetto.* That is more than enough for me.'

'With this freezing weather, more and more soldiers come into the *osteria* to eat. They tell me they prefer this to their army rations. But it's getting harder to find the ingredients.'

'Bruno should ask them to provide them. They've taken so much from our people and it's no doubt ended up in their canteen.'

'But can you imagine what would happen if we used produce stolen from our own neighbours? The war is bad enough without adding more enemies to the list.'

Aurelia worked her anger out on the pasta, pressing too hard on the rolling pin, holding it up roughly to see how thin it was. If she didn't curb her anger, there would soon be holes in it.

'Let me, Aurelia,' I said, taking the long *mattarello* from her. 'You wash the dishes and I'll make the pasta.'

It was soothing work, and it took me back to my childhood and the afternoons when I'd helped and hindered Madre Caterina in the convent kitchen. She'd taught me that pasta should be rolled out so thinly that if you placed a love letter beneath, you should be able to read the words through it. I'd giggled and told her that nobody would ever write me such letters. And I'd been right. Silvio and I had so little time together; there were never any letters exchanged. Plenty of kisses, yes. Memories of our brief time together, my beautiful son and a photo were all I had. And if I wasn't careful, I would be wearing a hole in the image of Silvio's face, because I touched it so often before I went to sleep each night.

Within the hour, we were ready to serve up and Aurelia asked me to put on a clean apron hanging on the back of the door and to wait on the tables. And that is how another small contribution to the resistance started: gleaning snippets of information from careless comments in Bruno's *osteria*, and noting routines. It was like picking over what was left in a potato field after harvest. Small offerings to feed an empty stomach. It was hard work and my feet ached at the end of that first long day. I kicked off my shoes and rested my toes on the stone flags beneath the kitchen table as I sat later with Bruno and Aurelia to share leftovers of pasta. The sauce, made from bottled zucchini and peppers, was delicious, but Aurelia warned her store of jars would soon come to an end.

'Thank you for your help tonight, Fosca. Whoever would have imagined a schoolteacher at work in my humble kitchen?' Bruno said as he mopped sauce from his plate with a hunk of black rye bread. It had been a long time since any of us had seen white bread.

'Whoever would have imagined that our country would be in the midst of a civil war?' I replied and he grunted. 'Besides, I would rather be down here working, being useful to my friends, than doing nothing up in the tobacco tower all night.' And I was being useful to more friends than them, I thought to myself.

'I cannot imagine a time when it will be over,' Aurelia said. 'I don't know how we can continue to feed people when we have no food to put on their plates.'

'You should speak to your German customers,' I said. 'Like I suggested. If they want to continue to eat here instead of in their canteen, then that is the only way. Let them provide you with ingredients.'

'Easier said than done,' Bruno said.

'Speak to the Italians who come in here too,' I said. 'They know which Germans to approach. Signor Gobbi, for example. He's in thick with them.'

'It feels to me like I am collaborating if I do that,' Bruno said, lowering his voice.

'Then, close the *osteria*,' I said, leaning back in my chair to see his reaction.

'But it's my life. The only one I know. My grandfather started this business. It would kill me to close this place.'

I had to be careful how I presented my advice. From various disparaging comments that Bruno and Aurelia made about the

National Guard and the men who fraternised with the *tedeschi*, I could tell which way this couple leaned, but it was hard to be absolutely sure of anybody's politics during this time. I chose my words carefully. 'This place is important to Corbello,' I said, leaning forwards, resting my hands on the table. 'You need to keep it going for the sake of your friends and family who have always lived here. One day this war will come to an end and Da Bruno must still be here, at the heart of the community. Your *osteria* needs to be a place that has always been and always will be.'

I didn't know whether he understood what I was trying to convey. I couldn't tell him that his little eating house was the ideal location to integrate with the enemy: a place to observe and pick up information that might help in the fight to bring them down. I couldn't spell all this out bluntly and I couldn't involve them directly. It was too dangerous. I hoped, at the same time, that the people of Corbello would not accuse him afterwards of getting into bed with the *tedeschi* and that when they came to understand what Simonetta and I had been doing, Aurelia and Bruno would not hate us for having used them.

'Would you mind if I continued to help you occasionally?' I asked. 'I have time on my hands.'

There was a pause while they looked at each other. It was Aurelia who spoke first. 'It's no secret that there is a lot of work to keep the *osteria* running. With Gennaro missing…' She paused and bit her lip.

Bruno placed his hand on top of hers and continued. 'And now we have sent Ennio away to stay with my brother in the mountains. We were worried that he would be deported too.'

'So extra help would be really welcome,' Aurelia said. 'Maybe once or twice in the week?'

'We can't pay you much, I'm sorry. But you can share supper and keep any tips that come your way,' Bruno said.

'Then, that's settled,' I said, pushing back my chair and fetching my coat from its hook on the door.

'Wait!' Aurelia said. She felt my coat and tutted. 'That can't keep you warm in this weather. I've been sorting through Mamma's things. Come upstairs and choose a couple of her garments. They're old-fashioned, but you're a clever seamstress, you can alter them. Come!'

Upstairs, at the end of the old lady's bed, now made up with a clean white counterpane, a crucifix laid on the pillow next to a single wilting red rose, she opened a wooden trunk. The scent of dried lavender wafted into the bedroom. She pulled out an old-fashioned two-piece costume in heavy burgundy wool, a long skirt with plenty of material, patched and worn in places, but good quality. The jacket was a bolero, with leg of mutton sleeves edged with black braid.

'This was her Sunday best,' Aurelia said, holding it up. 'Moths attacked it but she darned the holes so neatly. Look!'

I peered at the tiny, almost invisible stitches.

'You should keep it for yourself. I could adapt it to fit you,' I said.

Aurelia fingered the material. 'No, Fosca. You are young and you'll get more use out of this.' She laid the outfit on the bed and folded it carefully, pulling a shawl from the trunk to wrap around it. 'And take this too. There are many more. She loved to knit and crochet in the evenings by the fire. Take it to keep you warm.'

'Thank you.' I asked her then if she could spread the word for me about alterations and mending. 'And I have silk to make underwear,' I added. Aurelia found a piece of paper and told me to write a simple advert, promising to hang it up next to the price list in the bar. Then, she hugged me before letting me out of the kitchen door.

After the warmth of the kitchen, I felt the chill of the night air keenly and pulled Nonna Zina's shawl round my shoulders. As I reached the end of the short alley leading from the piazza, I saw two men ahead, the glow of their cigarette ends pricking the dark. I thought about turning back to take the longer route down from the town, but then the idea came to me to linger in the alley and listen to what they were saying. Simonetta had asked me to be alert. Here was an ideal opportunity. One of the men was my landlord, signor Gobbi, and the other, the German pianist. Why were they out here in the cold? The *tedesco* slurred his words but his Italian was good and I moved closer, pulling the shawl over my face and stepping quietly to slip into the shadows.

'What were they like, those wretched *ebrei* who lived in my lodgings?' the German was asking. 'The grand piano is wonderful. If I could find a way to get it back to Germany, I would. I may well take it up to the camp to while away my boredom. Was the musician who lived there beautiful, Gobbi? Some Semites are exquisite… I remember a pretty girl in Venice called Devora – wonderful breasts and legs. She was like a gypsy – so free and easy, her skin like velvet.'

The men laughed.

The pianist was talking about the family who owned the Villa Felice, a beautiful house on the edge of town, where some *tedeschi* officers were billeted. They'd fled their home long before their arrival. I'd taught their son, Abramo, a bright boy. His mother was a concert pianist. I hoped they were safe.

'If my Führer could hear me talking about fraternising with the inferior race, I would be in deep trouble.'

I didn't catch Gobbi's reply. There was the sound of a lighter snapping shut and the scent of tobacco wafted towards me before the German continued their discussion.

'You are sure you have identified the best spot?' the German asked. 'The bridge spanning the valley? I will make sure the goods are stored in the back wagon and that I'm on it with a few of my less enthusiastic soldiers.'

'I already told you I will talk to my contacts, Manfred. Leave it with me.'

I shuffled forwards to hear better and my foot sent a loose stone skittering down the cobbles. I fully expected the men to come for me but the sound was covered by the *tedesco*'s coughing, loud in the frosty air.

'What is in these *scheiss* cigars? Good God, man.' The German coughed again before continuing. 'If you need more materials, let me know in good time. And the *banditi* must change the signals so that the train stops in the right place.'

'Of course. You can rely on me to convey all this,' I heard Gobbi say.

'It's freezing out here. Now, buy me another glass of grappa to seal our agreement,' the German said, 'although I have to say our German schnapps is infinitely superior. I missed it when I was studying music in Venezia.' His voice grew louder as the two men approached and, thinking quickly, I stepped along the alleyway and called to them. 'Signori. Bruno sent me to collect up empty glasses and to ask if you need another drink in the warm?'

The German pianist swayed. Gobbi caught hold of him. '*Attento*, Manfred. Watch yourself on the snow. You don't need another grappa.' And looking at me intently he said, 'Signorina, you should be careful about wandering alone at this time of night.'

I mumbled a thank you and hurried away as best I could over the snow, slipping now and then on the icy descent. It took longer than usual to reach the tobacco house and my imagination played tricks on me. Each bush was a man huddled in the black of night, waiting to spring; each movement in the undergrowth was a wolf ready to attack and tear me to pieces. When a wild cat darted across the snow, I stifled a scream, my legs reduced to a quiver. I kept checking over my shoulder at the slightest rustle, expecting to see the two men following me and I decided, halfway back to the tobacco house, that I would ask Aurelia and Bruno if I could sleep in Nonna's bed on the late nights I worked in the *osteria*.

Before I climbed into my lonely bed, I jotted down everything I had observed that evening and pushed my notebook back into the hiding place in the beam. I was sure Simonetta would be interested in what I had heard between Gobbi and the *tedesco* called Manfred, and wondered when she would contact me again. Although I was weary from helping at Bruno's, I couldn't sleep and I padded over the cold stone flags and pushed the kitchen table against the door, hoping that it would alert me if anybody tried to break in.

CHAPTER TWENTY

Light was draining from the cold kitchen as I sat a few nights later at my treadle machine. My fingers were cold and it was time to set a match to the fire to prepare an infusion of rosehips and see what there was to eat. As I nursed kindling to catch fire, there was a thunderous knocking at the door and I jumped. 'Let me in, signorina Fosca. I know you're in there.'

I remained still, frozen by the hearth. Whoever was there knocked again. 'I've come to ask you about altering garments.' Then I recognised the voice. It was my landlord, signor Gobbi.

I crept to peer through the window. He stood there alone and I unbolted the door.

'I saw the notice in Da Bruno and they tell me you are an excellent seamstress, signorina, as well as a good schoolteacher,' he said, pushing his way past me.

I wondered why he had come to the tower at so late an hour and not spoken to me at the *osteria*. I pulled my shawl across my breasts, and moved to the chimney where the poker lay. If he laid a finger on me, then that would be my weapon. Instead, he surprised me with a blunt question.

'You have a child, do you not, signorina Fosca? Should you not have thought about his safety before joining in with your...' He paused before coming out with, '... so-called *partigiani*?'

I took a step back, aware that the first flicker of shock on my face had given me away. 'I d-don't know what you are talking about, signore.'

'Oh, but I think you do. I've watched the way you hover when you serve the *tedeschi*. I'm not stupid, signorina Fosca. And the way you suddenly appeared in the alleyway the other night. If *I* can detect that you're acting like a little spy, don't think that others are not suspicious. You're very amateur. You should stick to being a schoolteacher.'

He moved closer to me and tilted my face up with one finger and I brushed his hand away.

'I won't molest you, signorina, don't worry. That's not why I have come. I'm a married man, as you well know. Magdalena is more than enough for me to handle.'

He laughed at his own quip and went to sit at the table. In the uneasy silence, I watched him as he peered about the room. 'You have made this place look almost homely. The caretaker's wife before you was a slut; the place was always filthy. All it needs now is the laughter of a child. You must miss your little son.'

My stomach turned over but I tried not to change my expression. 'What do you want?' I asked.

'Contacts, signorina. I need to speak with your friends. It's very important. For the sake of your child, it would be wise to do as I ask.'

I looked at him, trying to gauge the degree of his threat. Was he was telling the truth or tricking me?

'Tell whoever you are working with to meet with me,' he continued, thumping a jacket onto the table. 'And see what you can do with this hole in the right elbow.'

'I don't know what you mean by contacts, signor Gobbi,' I told him. 'What are you talking about?'

He drew so close to me that I smelled garlic sausage and wine on his breath. 'Do what I ask you and I will tell you where your husband is.'

The poker fell from my hands at his words and I thought my legs would give way. '*Gesù Maria*. What are you talking about? Silvio is dead.'

'What if I know otherwise, signorina?'

I grasped hold of the lapels on his jacket. 'How? Where is he? Tell me.'

'He has been sent to the workers' camp.' He removed my hands and my eyes bored into his, trying to read his expression. Was he telling the truth?

'Do what I ask of you with your contacts and I will use *my* contacts to set him free.'

'How do I know you're not spinning me a lie?'

'You don't, signorina. You will have to decide that for yourself. But if you want to see your husband alive again…'

'W-where shall I tell them to meet? What time?' I was angry my terror was showing in my voice and, to hide the fear and doubt in my eyes, I picked up the jacket from the table to examine the tear.

He smiled then. 'Amateur, signorina, very amateur. I thought at least you might spin your yarn of innocence a little longer. Tell your leader to come by himself – that I will be alone – and to meet at the old hunting lodge on the Scheggia Pass. Three o'clock, in three days' time. *Buona notte!* Gobbi paused at the door. 'And do not tell anybody about your husband. If you want to see him again, we keep that information between ourselves.'

He strode away, leaving the door open and I hurried to pull the bolt across and fetch the pistol that Simonetta had showed me how to fire, my whole body shaking from the shock of hearing about Silvio. I remained in the shadows in the far corner of the kitchen, a blanket over my legs like an old woman, questioning whether Gobbi was telling me the truth; grasping at the possibility of seeing my beloved Silvio again. Simonetta had told me he was dead, but she'd also told me the bodies of the partisans were so mutilated that it was impossible to identify them. Yes, I'd been given his red scarf but many partisans wore these around their necks. The militia arrested people for wearing red garments, interpreting these as signs of rebellion. Even carrying an umbrella, like the *inglesi*, was a reason for being arrested on suspicion of subversion.

My reasoning was like a tangled ball of wool as I sat there wondering what to do for the best. In the end, I decided I would convey the message for the meeting to Simonetta, but I would not tell her about Silvio. I couldn't take that risk. If Silvio was still alive, I had to do everything in my power to get him back.

Each time the house creaked, I jumped. Outside the trees waved their branches across the sky as if to taunt me and I strained my ears for the sounds of a truck arriving up the track or the marching of soldiers' boots as they came to arrest me for being a spy. When something scratched against the windowpane in the gusting wind, I shrank back against the wall, but it was only thorns on the climbing rose and my shoulders relaxed a little. At one stage in the night, I considered escaping to the convent to be with my son, but I was worried I might be followed. Paralysed with fear and uncertainty, I sat in silence. I let the fire go out. The crackle of burning twigs would have impeded my listening. Slowly my eyes grew accustomed to the gloom. The sky was pricked with stars that night and moon shadows cast grey light on the dirt floor of the kitchen.

My head started to droop with fatigue where I sat, when more tapping against the kitchen window jolted me from the edges of sleep and I heard Simonetta call, 'Let us in.' I sped to pull open the bolt and fell into her arms, weeping with dismay. 'I failed before I even began,' I said over and over. 'I failed. I'm no good at spying for you.'

'Quick, give me the grappa!' Simonetta said, gesturing to a woman behind her.

'This is Maria,' she said as the beautiful young woman I had first seen in Anghiari handed her a goatskin pouch. 'Drink!' Simonetta said, bringing it to my mouth. I spluttered as the spirit hit the back of my throat.

She crouched down by me and I watched as Maria moved to the window, a rifle poised against her shoulder.

'What did the bastard do to you?' Simonetta asked.

'He didn't hurt me. He came to tell me that he wants to meet the *partigiani* at the hunting lodge on the Scheggia Pass three days from now.'

Simonetta exhaled and moved over to Maria. 'Do we trust him?'

'We should at least find out what he wants. He's an active member of the *repubblichini*. He might be useful to us.'

'He mixes with the *tedeschi*,' I said. 'Especially the pianist. The one called Manfred.'

'Major Manfred Hansen,' Simonetta said. 'He's half drunk most of the time.'

'I overheard them as they planned together outside Bruno's,' I continued 'Something about a train and a viaduct or a bridge, I think – and about changing the signal. They need your help.'

'I say we meet him. We have little alternative and I'm sure that is what Lupo would do,' Maria said. 'But we'll make sure to have back-up—'

Simonetta interrupted. 'But what if he does the same? If he brings soldiers? What if it's a trap?'

Maria swung around from the window. 'But Fosca says she overheard them talking… they are definitely up to something.'

'They didn't know I was listening, I'm sure of that,' Fosca interrupted.

'It's not like you to have cold feet, Simonetta,' Maria said. 'We *have* to meet him. We can't ignore him. Perhaps if we open this line of communication it will be a first step to getting Lupo and the others back. And to finding out who is passing on information on us to the *tedeschi*. It could be this Gobbi fellow himself. If he tries anything, then we shoot our way out. But let's see what he wants.'

The two of them left soon afterwards. Simonetta had told me to try to stay calm, and reassured me I had done well, but I was full of uncertainty. Gobbi had picked up that I was spying in the *osteria*. My already shaky world was starting to disintegrate. Once again, I considered running away to be with my son, but I knew this was the coward's way out and so far, I believed that only I and my *partigiani* friends knew where Giampiero was. I shivered at the thought of his hiding place being discovered. Climbing on top of the covers, fully clothed, I listened to the sounds of the night, hoping that what Gobbi had told me was true and that soon I would have Silvio beside me again. But I fretted about what I had helped set in motion. Like it or not, I was now involved.

CHAPTER TWENTY-ONE

1947

Fosca rubbed her hands across her eyes and stopped talking.

'It's late,' Richard said, watching her with concern. 'We've had a busy day and… your story is upsetting you.'

She looked up. 'Yes, I am tired. There is much more to tell you. This is only the beginning, but… I need to find out how Simonetta died, Richard. Could it be to do with finding the gold bar in this place? In my bones I feel that Gobbi knows something.'

He pulled her to her feet. 'There is plenty of time, Fosca. You need to sleep now. And don't worry about the bar of gold we found in the well. It's safely hidden in a niche in the fireplace.'

'Good,' she said. 'I am tired, Richard. I will go to my bed now.' She yawned and arched her back. 'Giampiero is an early riser.'

She talked to him as if in a daze, her mind in another place and Richard understood this only too well.

Before they parted for the night, she thanked him. 'It helps talking to you. I've kept many things deep within me for a good while.'

'I know exactly what you mean. We say, a problem shared is a problem halved.'

She smiled. 'I like that expression. We say it too. But, until now I haven't been able to share,' she said. She glanced at him, a shy realisation on her face. '*Grazie*, Richard. *Buona notte*.'

*

Richard woke to Giampiero calling him and the smell of coffee drifting through the window openings. 'Signor Richard. Mamma says breakfast is ready.'

It was half past nine. He couldn't remember when he'd last slept in so long. Pulling on a shirt, he opened the door of the tobacco tower to a blaze of sunshine. Beneath the shade of the fig tree, Fosca had laid the kitchen table with a gingham cloth and was pouring coffee into large pottery cups.

'Wow! You are spoiling me again. Thank you, Fosca,' he said, rubbing his hands together. He sat down next to Giampiero, whose cheeks bulged like a little hamster.

'I told you my son wakes early. He helped me make a cake this morning, didn't you, *figliolo*?'

'I broke the eggs for Mamma but one of the shells fell in the mix and we took ages fishing out the bits.' Giampiero held out his plate as Fosca sliced a sponge ring.

'It's a good thing I like crunchy shell cake then, isn't it?' he told the little boy.

'That's not what it's called. It's a *ciambella*. And we boiled the other eggs too and if you want jam on your cake, there is some from Rosa. Strawberry. My favourite.'

'Don't talk with your mouth full, Giampiero,' his mother said.

'You taught me an expression last night, so here is one for you, Richard,' Fosca said as she poured hot milk onto his *caffelatte*. '*Il buongiorno si vede dal mattino.* It means that we should start the day as we mean to go on.'

'And we say exactly the same thing. We have more in common than you think, Fosca.'

She nodded her head. 'So as it is such a sunny day, I will make a start on tidying your courtyard and clear it of thistles and dandelions. I found some pots that I can fill with wild flowers. Giampiero will help me collect the seeds, won't you, *tesoro mio*?'

'As long as I can get muddy and you don't tell me off, Mamma,' he answered, his face smeared with jam.

She smiled and once again Richard was struck by the transformation. She was more relaxed this morning. She looked beautiful, her hair bound up with a bright cotton scarf tied close to her head. Her hair swept back from her face emphasised her perfect bone structure.

'It all sounds *perfetto*. I shall be busy stripping tar off the beams in the tower.'

They broke for a simple lunch of *spaghetti alla carbonara*, followed by a bowl of fresh apricots. Richard drank a glass of wine but Fosca stuck to water. 'Otherwise the jobs won't get done,' she explained.

'Do you always push yourself like this?'

She shrugged. 'It's the way I was brought up. By the nuns. They didn't approve of idle hands.'

Giampiero climbed onto her knee and she wiped clean his sticky face and kissed the top of his curls. 'Are you tired, little one?' She rubbed his back and Richard watched as the little boy's eyes closed and she carried him gently over to the hammock.

'Coffee?' she asked on her return.

'Let me make it for you.'

'In Italy men don't do these things.'

'Can't they be trusted?'

She gave him a long look. 'Trust is something I am having to learn again.'

'I'm only offering to make you a coffee!'

She gave him a wry grin and sat down. '*Va bene*. If you can make it and it is drinkable, then I accept.'

Later, when they sipped at their espressos, she asked, 'What was your childhood like?'

'Loving. Ordinary. I had a younger brother.'

'Had?'

'He and my parents were killed in an air raid.'

She leant across the table and patted his hand. 'I am sorry, Richard.'

'It seems we are both orphans, you and I. Something else in common.'

'But the difference is I never knew my parents. I can't imagine what it must be like losing a family when you have known them through your childhood. If I were to lose Giampiero, my heart would be wrenched from me.'

'Do you know anything about your parents?' Richard asked. 'Did the nuns in the convent have no record?'

She shook her head. 'The only thing I have is a tiny square of material.' She started to collect dishes from the table and he helped her.

'There is no need, Richard.'

'I insist. If I am lucky enough to have meals cooked for me, then it's the least I can do.'

'Do all *inglesi* help around the house?'

'No, not all. But many do. My father always polished our shoes. He carved the joint on a Sunday, wound the kitchen clock at night, helped my mother bring coal into the house for the stove.'

She widened her eyes in astonishment. '*Mamma mia.* I like it. Men in Italia are used to being waited on.'

After the plates were washed and she had stacked them to dry, she fetched the photograph of Silvio and pointed out the square swatch of faded green material, patterned with tiny acorns inside the frame. 'Madre Caterina, who looked after me most of the time, told me that this was pinned to my shawl when they found me on the steps of the convent. This is the only link I have with my past.'

He watched as she ran her finger over the image of the young man in the photo frame. He had a strong face, a thin moustache on his upper lip and a twinkle in his dark eyes.

'And this is my Silvio,' she said. 'The man I lost twice.'

'Twice?'

'The second time was far harder.' She set the photo down on the table between them. 'But enough of that. Let me pour us a *digestivo* and you can tell me about the world. You told me about your travels in the war. I have never been further than Sansepolcro. I've spun the globe to my pupils in the classroom many times and always wanted to visit new places.'

'I hadn't been abroad until I joined an ambulance unit,' he said, sipping the strong, bitter *amaro* from a tiny glass.

'Are you a doctor?'

'No. I'm a medical orderly. I knew nothing about medicine before I joined the Friends Ambulance Unit and trained with them. But I learned more than they taught me through the work I did during the war. We travelled through many countries.' He drew in his breath to prepare himself for yet another explanation of his beliefs.

'I'm a pacifist, Fosca.' He waited for a look of scorn but her expression didn't waver and he continued without interruption.

'My parents were Quakers. A Christian community who believe in peace. I was brought up a pacifist.' He used the English word for it, not knowing the Italian.

'*Pacifista*,' she said back to him slowly. 'The word comes from the Latin for peace, does it not? *Pace*, in Italian.' She looked at him. 'If you had children, would you do the same?' she asked. 'Bring them up not to fight for their country?'

'I would talk to them about my belief but they would be free to make up their own minds. But, Fosca…' He paused, searching for words. 'I believe I *did* fight – in a different way. To help with the effects of war. To help damaged people.' He broke off, forcing back the image of the gun that he had used, feeling like a hypocrite. He wasn't sure if he could talk to her yet about that episode.

She looked over to where her son was asleep. 'When they are yours, it is hard to let them make their own way. I think one of the most difficult things I ever did was to separate from my baby during the war.' The faraway look returned to her face. 'But I did it for the best. I did it to protect him.'

'That is all we can do, Fosca. Our best.'

She poured another measure of *amaro* into his glass. 'So, tell me about the world you saw, Richard.'

'I wouldn't describe it as a holiday. We were constantly on the move. Our unit would always try to be twenty miles or so from the fighting.'

He rose from the table. 'I'll fetch my album to show you some photos.'

'Please.'

The album was in a box at the back of the tower and before returning to the table, he glanced through the door to where she sat, wondering what she thought of his pacifist beliefs. He knew now that she had been involved with the partisans, that her husband had been killed in the fight for freedom. She had given nothing away in her reaction to his stance. Did she think less of him now? It mattered to him. The realisation was like a punch in the stomach.

He pulled his chair closer to hers and turned the pages of the album. He'd taken several photos in Tobruk of abandoned desert stations: overturned guns, empty ammunition boxes, tangled telephone wires, mangled and rusting tanks, makeshift direction posts and petrol cans – contrasted by photos of desert flowers and a plateau overlooking a blue, blue sea. There were fewer photos of Cassino. There, in that hellhole, where bodies lay unrecovered for days and the stench turned his stomach, they'd operated on more than one occasion for twenty-four hours without stopping, but he didn't talk to Fosca about that. He only told her that he never wanted to witness anything like the results of that battle again. The barrage of guns had not ceased throughout the night while the wounded from both sides were brought in.

There was a single photo of Richard in a rare lull, showering under a large can of water swinging perilously from an olive tree and she laughed and told him he would have to erect a shower like that outside the tower. There were a few more from the end of war when he was involved in relief work: his friends in the FAU, shirts off in the baking sun, leaning from their truck windows to reach out to a gaggle of children with grubby outstretched hands, hoping for sweets and bubble gum, like the Yanks were known to dish out.

'As you can see, there was no time for sightseeing,' he said, a note of sarcasm in his voice. 'But it gave me a glimpse of a wider world. Those years I spent with the unit were certainly different from my years as a schoolmaster.'

'You never said that you were also a teacher,' Fosca said, shutting the album.

'I told you: we have many things in common.'

'I'm afraid that if I told you the rest of my story, you wouldn't agree. I think we are quite different, Richard.'

'Mamma. *Ho sete.* I'm thirsty,' cried Giampiero from his hammock.

Fosca rose and Richard laughed. 'Are you fetching the little Italian man a glass of water?' he asked.

She glared at him. 'I am being a mother to a little Italian child.'

*

They returned to their tasks for the rest of the afternoon. After Giampiero was settled for the night, Fosca served out their supper of rabbit portions roasted with fennel and tiny potatoes. This time she accepted a glass of wine and it seemed to loosen her tongue.

'You keep insisting we have a lot in common,' she said, finishing her second glass. 'But when you hear what I have to tell you about where the gold came from, you might change your mind.'

CHAPTER TWENTY-TWO

1944

Fosca

A couple of mornings after Gobbi had come to find me in the tobacco house, I awoke to something tickling my nose and I shrieked, sitting bolt upright in bed.

'*Dormigliona!*' Simonetta said, a piece of straw in her hand and an impish look on her face. 'Sleepyhead. You will have to learn not to slumber so deeply. What if I had been a *tedesco* waking you up to have his evil way with you?'

I pulled a face and sat up, trying to make light of what she'd said. 'If he looked like a film star and had the physique of a god, then I would take advantage of him. It's been a long time.'

She grinned. 'I do not believe that for one minute.'

'For heaven's sake, Simonetta. Do you always turn up like this without warning? You nearly gave me a heart attack. What time is it anyway?' I asked, sitting up and rubbing my eyes.

'Half past five. I've been back to Anghiari with Maria and the others while you've been sleeping your life away. We've been putting together our plan to meet with Gobbi.'

Simonetta sat on the edge of the bed while Fosca pulled on her clothes.

'Maria can't stay in Anghiari any longer. The place is overrun with *tedeschi*. We think that your place would make a better base for a while. And we can keep an eye on this Gobbi chap who's been pestering you.'

'I don't agree that this is safe, Simonetta. Gobbi is aware you come here. He could spring an attack anytime. Even I have the jitters about staying here. Anyway, who are these people, besides Maria? Do I know them?'

'They'll be here soon. We stagger our journeys. It's best not to move around together. They're a great bunch. We need to discuss what we are going to do about getting our leader Lupo back. Now, are you going to make me some coffee to go with these cakes?'

I widened my eyes at the currant buns that Simonetta pulled from her bag, wondering how and where she had found them.

'I only have coffee made from roasted grape pips to offer you in exchange.'

'*Fantastico!* Now stir your stumps and get dressed while I light the stove. They'll be here soon. I wouldn't trust some of the boys near a scantily clad woman.'

While she waited, Simonetta reminded me of how she had met her missing leader Lupo at the hospital in Sansepolcro with Maria, when he'd brought in his wounded sister for treatment. 'She died. He's so angry all the time, Fosca. Lupo is not his real name… of course few in the group use our real names. They endanger the lives of their loved ones by being in the *resistenza*. Lupo is a good name for him. He's fierce and wild like a wolf… and very brave. We need him back.'

Maria and a couple of young men slipped in at about seven o'clock. She asked me how I was, and after shaking my hand, she moved about the building, peering through the windows, looking in the fireplace and opening cupboards.

'She's checking for places to hide and for escape routes,' Simonetta whispered.

The two women greeted each other with a long embrace. Maria wore the same black beret as on the first occasion we'd briefly met before my flight over the rooftops. She had a delicate beauty, her oval face like a plaster statue of a Madonna, her skin unblemished. Her almond-shaped eyes were hazel and dreamy but I was to learn that this gentle expression belied ferocity. If Lupo could be likened to a wolf, then Maria was the tigress. She was no Santa Maria, as I would find out in the coming days.

'*Bene, bene*,' she said finally on completion of her tour. 'This will do fine for the time being.' She pointed to the men. 'You two will take it in turns to be on guard in the tower at all times. There's an air vent next to one of the wide beams large enough to sit on and watch the road.'

'I'm not sure that this place is safe or that Gobbi can be trusted. How do you know he is not springing a trap on us with this request for a meeting?' I said.

'Don't worry,' Maria said. 'We have been keeping an eye on him. He's being trailed as we speak and we have decided to risk using your place for the time being. We know what we are doing, Fosca *cara*.'

I hoped she was right. I jumped as, suddenly, a rope dangled from the roof and two diminutive figures slid down to the floor, landing in a somersault and jumping back up to bow low before me. 'Primo,' said the first introducing himself, followed by the second man, who doffed his cap. 'Secondo is my name. Second to none.' The others laughed at the look on my face.

'Meet our private circus acts,' Simonetta said. 'They like to make spectacular entrances.'

The two men were short and lithe and they bowed again before shaking my hand. Before I realised what was happening, Primo had whisked the shawl from around my shoulders and done it up as a turban on his head, while Secondo swayed up from the ground like a snake. I smiled. Maria told them to settle and to save their performances for later. There were other members of the band that I would meet later, Simonetta assured me. When

I thought that all the surprises were over, the youngest member turned up. As soon as fourteen-year-old Ennio from the *osteria* arrived, he gave me a warning look. I gasped, my mouth wide open, lost for words at the thought that this child should be involved with a band of *partigiani*. Bruno and Aurelia would be horrified to see the one son left with them putting himself in such danger. When Simonetta had first suggested that the tobacco house could be used as another safe house for the *partigiani*, I'd never expected that I might have to lie to my friends.

'Signorina Fosca, do NOT on any account tell my parents that I am here.'

'But—' I stammered.

Simonetta interrupted me. 'Ennio has important news for us, Fosca. He's found out where Lupo and his own brother ended up after their arrests, and we need to get them back.'

'Near my *zio*'s farm in the mountains,' Ennio began, 'I noticed a lot of activity. Maybe fifty of our *italiani* working and *tedeschi* guards watching over them. They have heavy machinery and a couple of dozen mules and the men work all hours digging trenches and moving rocks.'

Maria took up the thread. 'We know that they're constructing defensive barriers. Eventually they will cross the terrain from the east to west coast. Hitler wants to stop the *alleati* from pushing north to Austria. We heard from Radio Londra that the allies are south of Rome at the moment, held up at Monte Cassino.'

'I watch the men most days from the woods near my uncle's house,' Ennio continued, standing up, his eyes ablaze. 'And I couldn't believe my eyes when I spotted Gennaro, signorina Fosca. And the other day, more prisoners arrived at the camp. They were tied together with barbed wire around their ankles, their feet torn and yellow from bruises. One of them – a tall thin man with a beard – said something to the guards. He was the only one who talked. I didn't catch what he said, but he was beaten there and then until he fell to the ground. And I really did see my brother, I promise you. Gennaro hasn't been sent to Germany as we all feared. He's working up there.'

'And the new prisoner can only be Lupo,' Simonetta said. 'He matches Ennio's description.' She put her arm round the boy's shoulder. 'Ennio is to be applauded. He used his wits and remained hidden all the time even though you can imagine how much he wanted to make contact with his brother.'

'The men sleep in huts but there are guards on duty day and night,' Ennio said.

'We should do reconnaissance of our own,' Simonetta said. 'To make absolutely sure. Maybe it will be possible to storm the camp and rescue them.'

Maria held up her hand. 'No! That will only result in reprisals. It will achieve little and we will lose sympathy with our local friends if we are not careful. They've already lost their livelihoods, their food and stock, not to forget sons and husbands.'

'We need to plan this carefully,' Simonetta said, turning to me. 'Fosca, we need you more than ever to keep your ears open in the *osteria* for more information. In the meantime, Maria, you're right. We must spy on the prisoners. Record the shifts the guards work and their numbers.'

Although my insides had turned to water, I forced myself to participate. 'How can I help you in this?' I asked, desperate to be involved after what Gobbi had revealed to me about Silvio. Maybe he was in this camp? 'Can I help too with observing the prisoners? If anybody were to stop me, I could say I was looking for firewood on the mountain as there is none in the valley. If somebody lent me a mule, it would help with my disguise.'

Ennio made a noise through his teeth. 'Pshht! There are no mules to lend, signorina Fosca. The *tedeschi* have stolen them all to carry materials for the defences. They steal everything from us.'

'We can find you other tasks, Fosca,' Simonetta said. 'As you have your son to think about, we will not put you in unnecessary danger.'

The two young men in the shadows whispered to each other. I wondered how happy they were for women to be commanding the discussion. In her fireside talks with me, Simonetta had talked of the revolution that was quietly brewing in Italy. Women had always been expected to keep quiet, to behave meekly, to keep the fires going in the home and provide food for the table. Mussolini considered the Italian woman as 'the angel of the hearth', *l'angelo del focolare*, and we were considered inferior to men. Our Duce had expected women to marry and produce as many children as possible, preferably boys for the *patria*, fatherland. Young boys, indoctrinated by fascist propaganda that had started back in the 1920s, were taught from very young that war was to the male as childbearing was to the female. Everyone was encouraged to provide sons for Italy and tax exemption was granted for any family with more than six children, whilst bachelors were taxed heavily.

I listened while Maria and Simonetta talked through the plans. More men would be needed to stake the camp and if an attack was eventually mounted, another partisan band would be called in to make up the numbers. 'If we can liberate others along with his brother, then so much the better,' Maria said. 'But before we rush to finalise details, we need to meet with Gobbi and see what he has to say for himself.'

I was torn then between the possibility of Silvio being among these men, and asking my new friends to liberate him too, and, on the other hand, trying to put this attack off in case it jeopardised Gobbi's promise to deliver my husband back to me. I kept quiet.

I know now that I was wrong to do this, that I was acting almost like a traitor through not being open with my friends, but I was desperate to see Silvio again.

'Ennio,' Simonetta said. 'You are a brave young man. But you have to return to your uncle tonight and—'

'I want to help too,' the young boy interrupted. 'If I hadn't told you about the camp, you wouldn't know where your leader is.'

'Everything has to run as normal,' Simonetta insisted. 'I know you are dying to tell your parents about Gennaro, but they will know soon enough. Keep it as a wonderful surprise for them, eh?' She chucked the lad under his chin.

'Simonetta is right, Ennio,' Maria agreed. 'If we act, it has to be by surprise. Reveal nothing to your parents. We must not make ripples in the water before we build the bridges. And in the meantime, we will agree to meet with Gobbi tomorrow. He sounds the type of man who would not listen to a woman, but he has no choice. Let him know, Fosca, that we are prepared to meet. And remember to always keep your eyes and ears open.'

As I prepared for my next shift at Bruno's *osteria*, mindful that somehow information was being leaked to the *tedeschi*, I took more care with my appearance as I dressed and chose a low-cut blouse to wear that I'd run up from Simonetta's silk. Each time I bent to place heaped plates of Aurelia's home-made gnocchi on the tables in the *osteria*, I offered a tantalising glimpse of my cleavage. The *tedesco* called Manfred was at his usual place at the piano, playing Lili Marlene, a couple of men singing along to the tune that was popular even with Italians. Simonetta had confirmed that he was an officer, a major – an assault leader of the *Jäger*, the infantry division. She'd identified this from the insignia on his uniform.

I hovered over the tables as much as I could, feeling a little ridiculous at the displays I was putting on, but hopeful it would distract anyone from wondering why I was so attentive. A couple of Italian women were seated at a table with four soldiers, leaning close to them, revealing more cleavage than I ever could. I wondered for a minute if they might be the traitors. But I'd never seen them in Bruno's before. They looked more like women from the coast, brought up to the mountains for the night. They would know nothing about local goings-on and so I dismissed them as suspects.

Gobbi was standing at the bar nursing an after-dinner *digestivo*, watching me with hawk eyes. I had to find the right time to convey him the message that the *partigiani* had agreed to meet and, in my nervousness, I dropped a couple of plates and cracked a glass as I returned them to the kitchen and Bruno asked me if I felt sick.

'Sorry, Bruno. My mind was on my son,' I said. It wasn't a complete falsehood. I'd been pushing away worries that I would be denying him a mother by participating with the *partigiani*. I lingered longer to wipe clean the tables and smiled back at the men who stared at me, dragging out flirtatious behaviour from somewhere, hoping that Silvio would forgive me and understand. My landlord had now moved to a corner table where he was playing cards with three other *repubblichini*. I could sense he was watching me between rounds. He called over as his partner shuffled the next hand. 'Can I offer you a drink, signorina Fosca? You're looking very *carina* tonight.'

'I don't drink, signore,' I told him. 'But I'll fetch you another glass of grappa.' When I returned with Gobbi's drink he told me to keep the change. I pocketed the lire, thinking of the women from the coast resorting to selling their bodies to survive and earn money to provide for their children. Life would have to be truly rock bottom for me to ever follow that route.

'And how are you finding living in my house?' he asked. 'Is it warm enough?'

'Is anywhere warm enough this winter?' I said, hoping he would not drop by again to find out for himself.

'And did you finish altering my jacket?' he asked, grabbing my wrist as I turned to move away. 'My wife doesn't know one end of a needle from the other. This girl is very good, by all accounts,' he announced to the men sitting at his table. The way he said it sounded lewd, as if he was describing me in bed. The men smirked as Gobbi pulled at the waistband of his trousers. 'With all these privations, I have lost weight. When can you adjust these for me too?'

'Now?' I suggested.

'I could bring them to you later so that you can measure me, and fetch my jacket at the same time.'

'No need for that,' I said. 'Signora Aurelia has allowed me to set up a space in the *osteria* for taking measurements. I'll pin them this evening.' There was no way I wanted him to arrive unannounced at the tobacco house, in case Simonetta and the others were there.

'Now will do fine,' he said, standing up, excusing himself from the other players. 'No cheating while I'm gone.'

He followed me into the storeroom and I made sure to keep the door ajar. I didn't trust him to keep his hands off me as I started to pin the waistband, my hands trembling. As I'd suspected, there was no need at all to alter his trousers.

'Well?' he said, pushing my hands away. 'The answer?'

'They are willing to meet you. Three o'clock tomorrow at the Pass. But what about my husband? When will I see him again?'

He sighed. 'Be patient and you will see him again.'

It wasn't the answer I wanted. He returned to his card game. His friends departed soon afterwards and when I came out of the kitchen later with a cloth to wipe down the tables, Gobbi and the major were alone, sharing a bottle of brandy, their heads bent close over a piece of paper. As I worked, I glimpsed a sketch of a line crossed at regular intervals with tiny dashes, like a railway line on a map, and I stored the image in my head before the officer turned the paper face down. Gobbi's eyes narrowed as he caught me looking and immediately sent me off by ordering a plate of bread and ham.

I told Aurelia I wouldn't sleep in Nonna's bed that night after my shift like usual, and made my way back to the tobacco tower, turning around every now and then to check that I was not being followed. I didn't trust Gobbi and if I had been the leader of the group, I wouldn't have had any truck with him. And yet, he had promised me that Silvio was alive. Once again self-doubt flooded in as I thought of Simonetta's courage. She was so capable and inventive. In comparison, I felt like a *donnetta*, a little woman, insignificant and passive, despite her telling me that I was playing an important part.

The tobacco house was shrouded in darkness, silent as a tomb, the tower like a giant looming at its side, and I sighed at the prospect of another sleepless night filled with fear. But the house wasn't empty after all. As I lit a candle and stirred ashes in the grate to coax flames, Simonetta hissed to me from the other side of the room, 'We're here, Fosca. Close the shutters.'

'I delivered the message,' I said, my shoulders relaxing at the relief of not being alone. When I'd barricaded the kitchen against the night, Simonetta, Maria and I sat by the fire drinking wine from metal beakers. They told me that the others were already up in the mountains, staking the place where Ennio had seen the prisoners. I wished I were with them to see if Silvio was there too.

'I delivered the message to Gobbi.'

'You've been wonderful.' Simonetta squeezed my hand. 'You have done more than your share, *cara*. We couldn't have managed this without you.'

'I wish I could believe that.'

'We all do our bit towards the cause in different ways,' Maria said. 'Courage comes in many forms. Do not be hard on yourself, Fosca.'

'Like the shapes in a puzzle, we are all different but we come together to form a whole,' Simonetta added. 'But I've told you before, *cara*, that it's best not to know too much. It is not wise to know everything of what each person does.'

She'd talked to me of her torture. I was sure this was what she was alluding to. 'There was a hotel in Turin,' she'd told me one evening, 'where the *tedeschi* interrogated women whom they suspected to be *partigiane*. It was called the Nazionale. An ironic name, stuffed as it was with the enemy and no Italian allowed to be a guest there.' She'd paused and stared into the flames before her words came out like bullets from a pistol. 'I told the *bastardi* nothing, so they raped me. Men can be worse than pigs.'

She'd never mentioned the incident again or gone into further detail, and I never asked her to. But it had explained the scars I'd noticed when she bathed: the paler pigmentation of new skin around her nipples and little circles on the backs of her hands doubtless scarred by burning cigarette ends. She'd escaped, she told me, by feigning stomach cramps because of her monthlies and asked to go to the toilet. Left alone, she'd forced her slight frame through a tiny window and fled for her life. Simonetta had remained quiet for a long while after her revelation. Usually, she was the centre of discussion but I was growing to understand that her constant gaiety was a front, her bravado masking her fears.

We were tired but it was comforting to sit together near the warmth of the hearth. As we drank, we became merry and I laughed that night when the two of them performed imitations of rich fascist women they had come across.

Simonetta screwed her hair up and tied it with a length of string. 'Pretend for a while, that the string is velvet ribbon and these are real,' she said, stuffing a sack up her front to make a large bosom. 'And that I am Il Duce's bitch, Claretta Petacci.' Then she smeared charcoal around her eyes and jam around her mouth and minced across the room, waggling her bottom from side to side, pouting and making eyes at Maria.

Maria pretended to be Mussolini and shouted at her to produce more babies for the nation. She marched about, kicking her legs like I had seen the *tedeschi* do when they stormed into Sansepolcro. It was a good thing the tobacco house was a long way from Corbello and nobody heard us shrieking with laughter that night.

It was late when I turned in. I left the curtain round my bed open to watch the girls as they sat close, catching the last warmth from the fire. From the corner of my eye, I saw Maria grasp Simonetta's hand and gently kiss her scars. Simonetta smoothed back her friend's hair from her eyes. Not long afterwards, they wished me *buona notte* and they disappeared to the far corner where they shared an old mattress stuffed with corn leaves. I listened to the rustling of their movements and their stifled giggles. Many of us girls had cuddled together at night in the convent dormitory to find a closeness that we had never experienced from a mother. It was something I understood, but once I had met Silvio, I'd known I preferred to lie with a man.

I wondered how tomorrow would end. Maria had insinuated that I might be needed too. It took me a long time to get to sleep that night. What had I let myself in for?

CHAPTER TWENTY-THREE

I was invited with them to the Pass and, with trepidation, I accepted. 'Now that you are one of us,' Simonetta said. 'You can come along and see how we operate. We'll disguise you well. Don't worry.'

'But you said it was best not to know too much?'

'Maria and I think you're ready. But we don't want Gobbi to recognise you, so make sure you keep behind the others. Take it as another trial.'

Once again, uncertainty filled me and I thought of my little boy. But I needed to understand how Gobbi worked. Was he telling the truth about Silvio or stringing me along to his advantage?

By the time Maria and Simonetta had worked their magic, I swear that even Madre Caterina, who'd known me since a baby, wouldn't have recognised me. I was a young man. My face daubed with charcoal, the first shadows of stubble sprouting on my upper lip and chin. With my hair scraped in a bun under a moth-eaten woollen cap, a scarf pulled up my face, dressed in baggy, evil-smelling trousers and a shapeless darned sweater, the only thing that could give away my sex was my voice. My pistol was in the pocket of my trousers. I was threatened with raw turnips for a week if I opened my mouth. The hardest thing was not to break into laughter at my own ridiculous appearance as I filed up the Scheggia Pass with Simonetta, Maria and the others. I was last but one, a young man with a rifle taking up the rear. We followed an animal track and arrived early.

At the whine of an approaching motorbike, Maria ordered us to hide. Gobbi parked at the side of the white road and as he walked towards the ruined hunting lodge, the young man who had been behind me on the ascent crept towards him and brought his arm around his neck. I stayed where I was, watching Maria and Simonetta move nearer, their revolvers pointed. Gobbi struggled and the young partisan growled at him, 'Move again and you're dead.'

Maria ordered him to turn around. I saw the look of distaste on Gobbi's face when he observed her. 'You asked us here to talk,' she said. 'If I think for one minute you have brought anybody else up here, then my comrades will not hesitate to kill you.'

Gobbi winced as the grip on his neck was increased.

'*Vi giuro.* I swear on my life. I am on your side, comrades. Relax. I can't talk to you like this.'

'Walk into the woods,' Maria ordered, and she pressed her revolver hard between Gobbi's shoulder blades.

They stopped in a clearing of pines and Gobbi turned around slowly, his hands in the air.

Maria had covered the lower part of her face. Her eyes glinted steely cold as she spoke. 'You say you are on our side.'

'Yes.'

'Prove it. But keep your hands up.'

'I have a proposal for you, comrades,' he said.

Maria jutted out her chin. 'Go on. We're listening.'

'One of the *tedeschi*—'

'The major who you are so pally with.' It was a statement, not a question.

'Correct. I suppose your little spy told you. She's not exactly Mata Hari.'

When I heard his words I was shocked, but I remained behind the others, as Maria and Simonetta had instructed.

'Get on with it,' Maria said, brandishing her gun.

Gobbi began to lower his hands, but Maria stepped forward and after emitting a whistle, other *partigiani* emerged from the trees. I stood close behind the tallest man. Gobbi was frisked and a knife and gun that he had concealed under his trousers were found.

'What about the agreement to meet alone? This charade is ridiculous… I know who you are anyway.' Gobbi spoke menacingly, focusing on Maria and Simonetta, disgust on his face. 'This is a dangerous game for women.'

'Get to the point,' Maria said. 'Why did you call us here?'

'The German major who plays the piano in Bruno's *osteria* needs help. In return there will be guns and ammunition.'

'What kind of help?'

'An attack on a train that the Wehrmacht is sending north from Arezzo, full of stolen goods and, more to the point, weapons. Sub-machine guns. Mausers.'

Maria blew through her teeth. 'You're wasting our time. What do you take us for? Why would a *tedesco* want *partigiani* to blow up one of his own trains and give us gifts in return? It makes no sense. It's a trap.'

'It makes sense if you know what is travelling on that train.'

'Indulge me.'

'A vast quantity of gold. Secretly withdrawn – or liberated, shall we say – from the Banca d'Italia. On its way to line Hitler's coffers.'

There was a pause while the *partigiani* exchanged looks of disbelief.

Maria lowered her gun and ordered Gobbi to sit on the ground. 'So you and this *tedesco* make off with the gold, and blame it on us. And we are expected to be a party to this heist? What's in it for you?'

Gobbi glared up at her. 'Why should we let gold that belongs rightfully to our nation, disappear before our eyes? But, more to the point – apart from your group acquiring more weapons – you could bargain for more.'

'Meaning?' Maria asked.

'In return for helping, there is a way that the major can arrange the return of your leader. The young man who was arrested after your little stunt with the electricity lines.'

'How do you know who our leader is?'

Gobbi shrugged his shoulders. 'Please put your guns away, I am on your side. Don't you think I know what goes on with my own *paesani* in my own home town?' He narrowed his eyes as he stared into the eyes of Maria, his glance sweeping over the rest of us. 'Do you believe that I really like the *tedeschi*, my friends? The way they have invaded our country, sweeping in like a crazy hurricane? The way they kill and rape our fellow countrymen, steal our treasures, loot and lord themselves above us? I hate them just as you hate them.'

'To the onlooker it doesn't seem that way. You seem to like cosying up to them in the bar.' This from Simonetta, her fists clenched at her sides.

'Because I am *furbo*. I am clever, cunning, call it what you will. Do you really believe that I am a true *fascista*? I am a survivor and the *tedeschi* are stupid. While I talk to them in the bar and pass the time of day, they don't suspect my true feelings, because I am artful. Unlike poor Fosca, who you have set right in the firing line. Forgive me, but if your group is to flourish, you need to select your members better.'

When he spoke those words, I shrank further back into the trees but he wasn't looking at me.

'And the major? Why are you working with him? Do you count him as one of the stupid?' Simonetta said.

Gobbi paused for a few seconds, a quizzical look on his face. 'The major is a survivor. One of life's chancers. And he lacks the usual fervour for Hitler's cause. He speaks disparagingly of his leader and when he is drunk, I fear for his outspokenness. In short, signori, he is more interested in the gold on this train and his own rosy future than who wins the war, willing to betray his own countrymen for the sake of this treasure. I admit I'll take some of the gold myself – and why shouldn't I? But you and I, together, we have a chance to strike against the bastard *tedeschi* and win some weapons in the process.'

There was silence.

'We need more details before we can decide to proceed,' Maria said.

'You need to come to a speedy decision,' Gobbi said. 'The train is scheduled for next Friday.'

Maria looked at the others and they nodded. 'You come with us, signor Gobbi. I still don't know if I can trust you.'

'I understand. I would be the same. How can I reassure you that I want to help you in the good fight? I can be very useful to you with my German contacts, you know. I have an idea. Another way for you to get your leader back. With an exchange of prisoners. Think about it. Why don't we adjourn to my tobacco house to discuss this further? I believe that is a regular place for your meetings, is it not?'

There were further looks exchanged between the young resistance fighters. This man knew too much.

'I left my motorbike over there,' Gobbi said, pointing to where his Benelli was propped against a pine.

'You're coming with us,' Maria said as one of the partisans pushed the motorcycle further into the woods. 'You can return to collect it later. If it is still there,' she said, prodding him onwards.

*

One of the men stood guard at the window of the tobacco house, the other at the back door while Maria, Simonetta and Gobbi talked through the plans. I positioned myself the furthest I could from Gobbi and kept my face covered, my head in my hands, especially when I heard Gobbi ask where I was.

'She is working tonight and staying at the *osteria*,' Maria told him.

I listened as she explained how it would be necessary to join forces with another group of partisans on the other side of the valley. Ten able-bodied men at least would be needed to carry the gold and weapons, two strong men to uncouple train carriages and a further two to commandeer a signal box further down the railway line. Gobbi left towards midnight and after he had gone, the group hastened to gather their few possessions together.

'Even if he is trustworthy – and we don't know for sure yet – we definitely have to relocate,' Simonetta said. 'This place is no longer safe. All of you: find somewhere else to sleep, tonight. Fosca, if you can, keep an eye on Gobbi in the next few days. Tail him, but be careful. We don't want to lose you too. Do you think you can do that?'

My head told me not to do this. It spelled danger. Gobbi knew exactly who I was, and knew I was involved with the partisans. There was Giampiero to think of. But my heart was full of Silvio, and my heart won.

'Of course I can,' I replied, hoping I sounded more confident than I felt.

'There is another person we should include,' Primo told the group. 'He's a priest and an expert in explosives. He was a military chaplain in the Balkans. They call him Don Bomba, but his real name is Don Giovanni.'

Secondo smiled. 'He's a good man. You'd never tell that he's a priest if you didn't know already. He rarely wears his soutane. We knew him when we were in the *balilla*.'

Primo nodded his head. 'Yes. He'd tell the *repubblichini* that he was taking us boys for a hike in the mountains to strengthen our legs, but when we stopped for our midday *panini*, he would sit us down and tell us how we should all be rising up against the Duce to fight for freedom. He's one of the best.'

'In fact, he suggested we try out for the circus in Arezzo. Our parents were only too pleased to get rid of us. Two mouths fewer to feed,' Secondo added.

'And better than being sent off to the seminary,' his brother concluded.

Maria nodded approval. 'Yes, I've heard of this man too. Get him involved.'

They departed one by one into the night, like players exiting from a stage. Maria and Simonetta told me they'd be sleeping in a stable they had used before, on the road to Anghiari. It was warm and dry, except when the cow they were sharing the hay with had evacuated her bowels and it splashed onto Simonetta's clothes. 'If that happens again, we will really look and smell the part of *contadine* peasant women,' Maria had said as she held her nose. The pair dissolved into giggles as they headed out of the door. I smiled at their light-hearted antics, wondering if there would be much laughter in the days to come.

CHAPTER TWENTY-FOUR

I'd never met a clergyman like Don Giovanni, otherwise known as Don Bomba. He was tall, lean, with a face like a Roman Emperor. Primo and Secondo had told us he had scraped together stashes of explosives and whatever he could pick up by scouring abandoned military bases. This unusual priest had hidden them in crypts and cellars of various convents, monasteries and stables around the valley of Corbello.

By now, Gobbi had acquired the extra gelignite that was needed from the German major, who had also agreed to arrange the release of Lupo and young Gennaro once the gold was secured. I tried to talk to him on my nights at Bruno's to remind him of his promise to release Silvio but there'd been no opportunity. He was intent on ignoring me. The *partigiani* had come one final time to the tobacco house and there'd been heated debate amongst them about Gobbi. All the while, I kept the secret about Silvio to myself. How I wish now that I hadn't.

'We need absolute assurance about the return of Lupo and Gennaro before we agree to proceed.' Simonetta was adamant as she spoke. 'Gobbi has it all his own way at the moment. We are taking a huge risk and we could walk away with nothing in the end, simply to line the pockets of two greedy men.'

'Perhaps we should also make sure to get a cut of the gold,' Maria suggested. 'Think how it would help our cause, the weapons we could get hold of from its sale: the vehicles, the bribes we could offer.'

'Forget about the gold,' Simonetta said. 'If we get our side of the bargain and Lupo is once again in our midst, then that is enough. The gold would be difficult to get rid of.'

'I suppose you're right. As long as we do get those promised weapons. Sub-machine guns and anti-tank weapons will be useful,' Maria said. 'You're right, Simonetta.'

'Yes, the gold would only be a nuisance and hard to get rid of without trace,' Don Giovanni said. 'Although I would dearly love money for when this war is over: funds for rebuilding our schools and hospitals. Money to help shattered lives.'

'We have to hope that Gobbi does what he says,' Simonetta said. 'He keeps saying he is one of us. Let's hope he puts his money where his mouth is.'

'Or his gold,' was Maria's wry retort. 'He will have made sure there is a large cut for him, no doubt about it.'

And all the while I listened my hopes were pinned on Silvio being released with Lupo and Gennaro. I wasn't as intent on the cause of freedom. I wanted the father of my child back with us again.

On the afternoon before the planned night attack, Simonetta, Maria and I accompanied Don Bomba in disguise. At the gateway to Corbello, he asked two German sentries how long it had been since they'd last said their prayers.

'If you like, I can give you a blessing,' he said. 'I understand how difficult it is for you to attend Mass at this time. But I'm sure your mothers back home in Germania would want me to be looking after your souls – just as I am looking after the empty stomachs of my congregation.' He gestured to the baskets, topped with vegetables, tied to the sides of the mule he was leading.

The youngest soldier, probably no more than eighteen years of age, stepped forward and inclined his head for Don Bomba to make the sign of the cross. After reciting the Latin words of benediction, he handed the soldiers holy pictures of the Virgin Mary and we were all waved through, pulling a laden mule behind us. Beneath his cassock, around his waist, Bomba had earlier wound detonation wire and under the loaves and turnips on top of the pannier baskets, if the soldiers had searched, they would have found a couple of light machine guns and ammunition. We three plump nuns at Don Bomba's side had Red Devil grenades stuffed down our bosoms, gelignite in the fingers of our gloves and pistols beneath our habits. We were waved through with the priest. 'Bless you,' Don Bomba said. 'And try to come to Mass one of these days. Every Sunday morning at nine o'clock in my church of San Antonio.'

Once our band of four and our mule had left the main track leaving Corbello, we took a path that skirted fields set aside for tobacco. Where green shoots would appear in a couple of months, the earth was now hard with frost.

I was picking up valuable information from my new companions, each step bringing me nearer to reuniting with my Silvio. They talked of winter as a transparent season, when the fascist militia tended to mount attacks. It was an ideal time for capturing resistance fighters, easier to catch them when undergrowth died back and most trees were bare of leaves.

Don Bomba knew every inch of his parish and his route led us eventually through dense pine forest. As we trekked along the path, the sounds of our footsteps muffled by fallen pine needles, we were joined at stages by other fighters. They also had mules and by the time darkness began to fall, we numbered twenty, including Edoardo Gobbi, the lynchpin to the whole mission. By now he knew for certain that I was one of them but he paid little attention to me. We were armed with whatever weapons Don Bomba could muster, and the men had been selected for their strength. The contribution of Primo and Secondo was crucial to our mission.

There was no need for torchlight that night. A crisp, sunny day had given way to a star-filled sky, the moon providing enough light to show the silhouettes of the mountains. We women pulled off our nuns' habits and carefully removed our loads. Those who had been instructed to do so took up position along a ridge in a chestnut grove overlooking a single railway line that curved before a viaduct. This was our target and the timing had to be perfect.

The plan involved the signal box at the sleepy station of Molin Nuovo, seven kilometres further up the line, being taken over one hour earlier. The signalman, trussed up by two masked men, would be forced to demonstrate how to change the signals before the viaduct. As we *partigiani* in the forest took up positions, Simonetta turned to me, sighing with relief when the signal cranked down to its stop position.

In the meantime, two of the burliest *partigiani* crept to the part of the ditch adjacent to where Don Bomba had calculated the final two carriages would stop. Primo and Secondo, dressed from head to toe in black, slipped down the steep riverbanks beneath the soaring spans of the viaduct. Carrying all the equipment they needed – wire, a slim metal detonator wrapped in sheep's wool, and the almond-smelling gelignite – the sounds of the two men's descent were muffled by the roar of the river coursing through this point in the narrow valley. They were sure on their feet, stealthy and agile from their circus performances. They would use all their clever climbing skills to attach a bomb underneath the train line, high on the viaduct itself. My heart thumped in my chest as I watched them disappear into the darkness.

Above the noise of crashing water, words from two *tedeschi* sentries drifted down from the bridge as they passed each other at regular intervals. It took roughly twenty minutes between each time they crossed. We waited to see Primo and Secondo reappear, and every time I heard the sentries approach, my heart rate accelerated like the sounds of galloping horses' hooves in my ears. I was terrified that the two *partigiani* acrobats would be detected.

But they had planned their tasks carefully and allowed time for Primo to skilfully scale the middle block of the viaduct. Secondo threw him a rope with a small bag of sand attached to weigh it down. Primo waited for the right moment before lobbing it through the bridge railings.

With the clock ticking and the rope secured, I watched, my heart in my mouth, as Primo shimmied up to the head of the column and hung there like a spider from a ceiling under the iron trusses of the railway lines until the two sentries crossed paths again. Once the sentries moved off he continued his work.

'He's packing gelignite into the cracks now,' Simonetta told me, her whispers drowned by the waterfall, 'and then he'll insert the detonators.' She held up her hand, her fingers crossed, and I did the same.

After moments that ticked past like hours, we saw him slide down the rope and Simonetta squeezed my hand. 'We're on,' she said and Maria gave a thumbs up and let out a sigh of relief.

As quietly as they had approached the bridge, the two circus performers slipped away. During their climb back up the ridge, a couple of loose stones skittered down the bank causing a mini landslide of grit.

'Oh, *Gesù*,' I hissed, grabbing hold of Maria's arm. They would surely be seen now. The men froze against the ground as one of the sentries shouted and trained a searchlight towards the spot where they lay prone. It was a gift sent from God, we all said afterwards, that a couple of roe deer chose that moment to bound away metres from where they lay. The sentries took pot shots at the animals and then continued their patrolling of the bridge, their laughter floating across to us.

A distant whistle sounded as the rumble from the approaching train announced the countdown. There was a screech of metal on metal as the train pulled to a halt before the stop signal and shouts from its passengers. A handful of soldiers jumped from the front carriages and walked towards the guards on the viaduct. A discussion ensued, the men walked towards the signal and our hearts skipped beats as we prayed the ruse would work.

At the back end of the train, Hansen's role in the plan was to order his men to stay aboard. Thus, the successful uncoupling of the two last carriages by the couple of dark clothed *partigiani* went unobserved. Ten minutes passed before the signal cranked back to go, the soldiers mounted the train again and with a hiss of steam, it huffed towards the viaduct.

'Now the fun begins,' Maria said as she pointed to a spark beneath the metal wheels.

The spark fizzed along the short length to the detonator, unnoticed by all those on the train as it continued to travel down the line, before a gigantic boom shook the countryside.

I jumped. It was like nothing I had ever witnessed. It sucked the breath from my body and I put my hands to my ears as the viaduct shuddered, flew up into the air, and tumbled like Giampiero's building blocks. All of the carriages bar the final two toppled like toys into the ravine. The night sky lit up like a blood orange in a seething, flaming ball of smoke and explosions and I trembled all over.

As planned, we immediately scrambled down to the railway line, the mules slithering with us towards the two remaining carriages. A dozen or so *tedeschi* spilled from the doors of the remaining carriages, the crack-crack of their gunfire starbursts in the dark. I watched Maria run towards the train firing her machine gun and to my horror, her body took the full impact of a hand grenade, parts of her body cartwheeling and somersaulting to the forest floor. Simonetta pulled two grenades from her underwear – screaming like a demon as she aimed at the train. I froze, my hands to my mouth as Gobbi tackled her to the ground. 'Save it,' he shouted. 'You'll kill the major. Save them for later.'

I ran to Simonetta, pulling her back up the hill, desperate to drag her away but she pushed me off. Her face was white. I had never seen such a look of hatred. The next minutes passed in a blur of flames and cries from the wounded and dying.

Apart from Maria that night, there were no other fatalities amongst the *partigiani.*

Two figures emerged from behind the train, their hands raised; one had a wound to the chest and he was supported by the piano player, his major's uniform pristine, the skull insignia on his cap glinting in the firelight. 'Hold your fire! *Non sparare*! I have ordered my men to put down their weapons,' he shouted as he edged forwards.

Gobbi, flanked by *partigiani*, moved over to the two men. They searched them for weapons and then tied their hands behind their backs. Simonetta had run over to where Maria had fallen, but there was nothing she could do and Don Giovanni knelt over her, his head bowed in prayer. While he was busy, I watched as Gobbi raised his revolver to the temple of the *tedesco* standing next to Hansen and dispatch him with one bullet. The priest turned, a look of disgust on his face as he shouted, 'But he had surrendered.'

'He pulled a gun on me,' Gobbi lied. 'It was me or him, *padre.*'

The priest shook his head as he observed the rope around the dead man's hands.

It was clearer than ever Gobbi was not to be trusted. More and more I loathed him but more and more I longed for Silvio, so I kept silent about the murder I had witnessed.

'This is no time for philosophy and confession,' I heard Gobbi say. 'There is work to do. The explosion will have alerted all the *tedeschi* in Tuscany.'

I joined in with the file of *partigiani*, passing boxes from the carriages to pack on the mules.

The animals loaded, the combined group of resistance fighters parted ways and I saw Gobbi lead a mule and its load of gold back in the direction of Corbello.

When our group arrived at Don Giovanni's church, I caught up with Simonetta as she sat smoking, her body trembling. She watched in a daze as the men unloaded the boxes from the mules and carried them to the crypt.

Half a dozen tombs had been opened to conceal the haul, their heavy stone lids pushed back into place as each one was filled.

The ties around the *tedesco*'s hands were removed and, so far, the major seemed to be going along with Gobbi's plan for the exchange of prisoners, set up with Maria and the others. I'd even seen him help carry and unload some of the boxes and he'd sworn in ripe Italian at the weight.

The task completed, Don Bomba ordered everyone to disperse and to await instructions. 'If I need you, look out for the white sheet hanging from my window and as soon as you can, meet at the crossroads to Corbello.'

He turned to the German. 'I will shelter you in the presbytery and, as will be arranged, we will let you go as soon as our leader and the boy have been released. For the next few days, you are to remain upstairs in bed. You will be my housekeeper suffering from typhus. If the house is searched, we are banking on them not disturbing you.'

'I hope the bed is comfortable and you have an attractive nightdress for me to wear as well as some detective stories to read,' the major joked. But no one was in the mood for his humour.

Simonetta had disappeared. We had taken part in a scene from hell. And still I was no nearer to being with Silvio. My task now was to pin Gobbi down and remind him of his promise. The birds were beginning their chorus and light dusted the sky pale pink as I hurried back to Corbello. I knocked and knocked at the door to his big house in the piazza, but there was no reply. And no sign of the mule that he had led away from the train, bearing his gold.

CHAPTER TWENTY-FIVE

.

Back in the tobacco house, I couldn't sleep. The scenes I had witnessed that night crowded my head: screams of the injured, the dead, the blood. Maria. I couldn't get warm. As I went to fetch an armful of kindling from outside, I heard shouts in the far distance and in the half-light of early morning, I jumped when I saw a figure slumped against the fig tree. It was Simonetta.

'Can I come in?' She gazed up at me, her face streaked with dirt and tears.

'Where have you been?' I asked. 'I waited for you at the church, but you disappeared.'

She fell into my arms and her shoulders heaved.

'Maria… Maria.'

'I know, *povera* Simonetta, I know, you poor girl.' I held her as she wept.

When she was still, she wiped her tears with her sleeves. 'I can't stay here long. It's too dangerous. And it's not safe for you either, Fosca. Don't stay here any longer than you have to. Move… Gobbi is too much in the know and I don't trust the bastard or that shifty *tedesco* toad.' She looked up at me, her eyes red and puffy. 'Maria didn't die in vain, did she? We did what we set out to do, didn't we, Fosca?'

I nodded and when I tried to take hold of her hands, she pulled away. And then it came pouring out: how she'd returned to the woods above the viaduct to bury Maria.

'But there was nothing left of her.' She sobbed. 'I hate them, Fosca. I have so much hate for them.' She held up her hands, dried blood and dirt on her fingers, and her words were awful to hear.

'A wounded *tedesco* jumped from behind a rock and lunged. I fell and he was on top of me, Fosca.' She held up her hands, turning them this way and that, staring at them. 'With these, I gripped his throat. I throttled him. Hatred welled in my heart and I heard my dead parents, my sister, Maria – all spurring me on. I gritted my teeth and squeezed with a strength I never knew I had… My fingers dug into his throat, his muscles engorged and my nails ripped his skin. And then he flopped on me and even after his death rattle, I clung on with these fingers as his blood continued to seep between them. Warm, sticky.'

I tried to take her in my arms again but she wouldn't let me. She sat as still as stone, staring, her face like marble as she whispered. 'I ran until I came to a stream and I plunged my arms deep in the freezing water, rubbing and rubbing as the *tedesco*'s blood stained the water red. But I can't get them clean.'

I looked at her hands, dried blood and flesh stuck deep in her fingernails.

'All I can see in my head is my beautiful Maria. Like a doll smashed to the ground. She was all I had left in the world, Fosca. Because of two greedy *bastardi*, lusting after pieces of gold, she is gone. Forever.'

She looked at me, her eyes almost savage. 'I swear on all that is sacred that I will have my revenge, Fosca. Mark my words.'

She collapsed to the ground, her shoulders heaving as she sobbed and I lay down beside her on the cold earth, rubbing her back, speaking to her like I used to with my own baby. Slowly, her crying ebbed, her body went limp and I coaxed her inside as she shivered like a frightened animal. I filled a bowl with warm water from the pot by the hearth and gently bathed her hands, my fingers massaging hers. The plucky Simonetta I knew was somewhere I couldn't reach, her shoulders curved, head bowed. When I patted her skin dry, she murmured a thank you. 'I have to go now, Fosca. I can't stay here. The *tedeschi* are ransacking Corbello in their search for us. And you too – you must find somewhere else to stay.'

She pulled a piece of paper from her pocket. 'I was meant to deliver this, but I can't now. Do it for me, please, Fosca. Deliver it to the militia in the town hall as soon as possible. Remember everything that Maria and I taught you and make sure it isn't traced back to you. Be careful.'

She strangled a sob and kissed me on both cheeks. '*Arrivederci*, Fosca. Good luck.'

'I'm worried, Simonetta. Stay awhile. I'm afraid for you.'

'Fear is an indulgence. Don't worry about me.'

She was through the door before I could ask her more.

The message was written on the back of a flimsy propaganda leaflet issued by the Republican Guard. The image on the front portrayed the graphic slaughtering of innocents by allied bombs.

On the back, scrawled in capital letters, I read:

WE, THE 5TH DIVISION OF ARETINE FREEDOM FIGHTERS, HAVE CAPTURED MAJOR MANFRED HANSEN. WE WILL DELIVER HIM TO YOU IN EXCHANGE FOR THE IMMEDIATE RETURN OF GAVELLI GENNARO, AS WELL AS THE MAN KNOWN AS 'LUPO'. THEY MUST BE ACCOMPA-NIED BY GOBBI EDOARDO, ALONE.

AWAIT FURTHER DETAILS.

Of course there was no mention of the exchange of my Silvio on the note. How could there be? Gobbi had warned me not to mention to anybody about our agreement. But I should have mentioned it to Simonetta and the others. If they had asked for two men in the exchange, surely they could have asked for a third? I had missed my opportunity and now I was deeply involved in this hornets' nest.

While I filled my arms with firewood, I could hear Simonetta's bitter words of revenge in my ears and I wondered where she would hide now. She had told me not to fear for her. But I did. She was frail. Losing Maria would make her more reckless for the cause. She had nobody left, and I vowed that from now on I would show her how much I loved her. Giampiero, Silvio and I would be her family and give her a reason to live.

Just before sunrise, using the speckled mirror by the washstand to guide my hands, I combed my hair into two large pompadour curls and rolled the ransom note into one of them. Before that, I practised slipping the ransom note in and out of a fold I had tacked into the inside of my blouse sleeve and then I set off for Corbello, carrying a basket of laundry and Gobbi's mended jacket.

At the archway leading to the piazza I was stopped by militia guards, who took time to frisk my body through my clothes. I wondered if they could detect the somersaulting of my heart. What I was doing was risky. But I knew nothing had been achieved in the war without taking risks; my new friends had repeated those words so often during their discussions. The men pulled the linen from my basket and threw it on the muddy ground, but they didn't think of searching my hair. I showed my papers when prompted and made my way on shaking legs to the town fountain, where half a dozen women were pummelling sheets and clothing.

'My well is frozen over this morning,' I explained and they moved over to make room for me.

'You're lucky you don't live at the school anymore, signora,' the middle-aged woman next to me muttered, looking over to where a couple of German soldiers stood, their rifles at the ready. 'I didn't get a wink of sleep last night. Those *bastardi* turned our homes over searching for one of their men. Did they not come to knock on your door?'

'I heard nothing,' I said. This at least was the truth on this day of lies that I was weaving.

'*Beata voi.* You are fortunate. But if I were you, I'd leave this area while you can, signora. God knows what will happen next.' She lowered her voice as she told me that word was spreading that the *partigiani* had blown up a train and taken one of the officers as prisoner. 'There will be trouble, mark my words.' She scrubbed her sheet with ash paste. 'Those heathen *tedeschi* pulled my best linen from our bed and trampled all over it with their hobnailed boots. And they bayoneted the pillows. There are feathers everywhere.'

'I can't believe you didn't hear the rumpus,' the woman who used to clean the schoolrooms said to me. 'They barged in and stole my sewing machine and all of Giuseppina's trousseau: the set of towels I'd embroidered for her, the lace, her nightdresses... As soon as I can, I shall find a place to hide what we've got left.'

'Don't be so sure they won't find that too.' An older woman at the far end of the fountain chipped in. 'Anyway, there is far worse to worry about than your linen. Stop fretting about the things you might lose, *donne*. It's the lives of our families we should fear. You mark my words, women, there will be reprisals for what happened last night. The *partigiani* are a nuisance. They never think about the effects of their shenanigans.'

'Hush, Annunziata! Don't spread fear,' I found myself saying.

'It's not fear I'm spreading, signora Fosca, it's the truth. You're too young to understand.'

It was neither the time nor the place to give a speech about why the *partigiani* needed to resist the occupiers, or to explain to these women that everything that resistance fighters were doing was for the benefit of all people who craved to live in freedom.

Simonetta had talked to me at length on our evenings together about the women she had mixed with in Turin, before her family were killed. How a handful of them had managed to mobilise thousands to take part in uprisings. It had started as a movement to help disbanded soldiers, the sons, fathers and husbands of women like these at the fountain. Women had turned away from their brooms and sewing needles, transforming themselves from insignificant members of the household to wily and bold *partigiani*, learning new skills to back up the men in the resistance and become vital members themselves, stirring up strikes and demonstrations in the factories. I knew Turin to be a big city; I am more of a country girl and in the countryside, change is slow to happen. Nevertheless, change was needed. I could see that. But I said nothing. I bowed my head meekly and dipped my soiled laundry beneath the cold water, keeping one eye on the soldiers guarding the piazza. When I'd finished squeezing water from the linen, I piled it back into my basket and walked purposefully towards them.

'I need to take this to the *comune*,' I said slowly to the German soldiers in simple Italian, holding up a package that contained Gobbi's mended jacket. I pointed to the tall building where foreign black, white and red flags hung limp in the damp, still air. 'I need to go in there to deliver this to signor Gobbi.'

They looked inside the package and peered into the basket of wet laundry, then waved me on. I recognised the republican guard at the entrance to the town hall. Aldo, who also worked as the town street sweeper, raised his hand as I approached. 'My son is missing his schooling, signora Fosca,' he said. 'We try to persuade him to read his books, but we're not teachers. He won't listen to us.'

'Maybe I can drop by to see how he is doing,' I told him. 'He is not the only child in the same situation.'

Aldo nodded his approval. 'You are welcome any time, signora.'

'Aldo, I need to deliver this jacket to signor Gobbi. Is he in his office?'

'Up the stairs and second room on the left, signora,' he said.

I was perfectly aware of this. Before he became mayor after the war, Gobbi was the town's registrar and I had registered Giampiero's birth with him. I also knew the whereabouts of the pigeonholes where post was left for all civil servants and members of the Military Guard.

'May I first use the toilet in the *comune*, signor Aldo?'

He fetched the key from a hook inside the main entrance and handed it over. 'We have to stop any old body from using it,' he explained.

I knew this too. Only a few houses in the town as well as government offices had a toilet.

'I must have eaten something to upset my stomach,' I said. 'Thank you so much. I'll give the key straight back.'

The door locked, I peered at the mirror on the wall and pulled the hairpins from my curl to draw out the ransom note. Then I stuffed it into the slender fold stitched in my sleeve. My hands all fingers and thumbs, it took longer to pin my hair back to how it had been. When I'd finished, I pulled the chain to flush the toilet and returned the key to the guard, mumbling, '*Grazie* and *a presto*. See your son soon.' I sincerely hoped I would one day be able to teach again in the school where I had been so happy.

The hardest part was next: to deposit the ransom note in the correct pigeonhole without being seen.

Gobbi was not at his desk, so I left the jacket in his office and scribbled a note with the amount he owed. The door to his wife's office was ajar. She was typing and looked up as I walked towards the pigeonholes.

'Signora Fosca, I haven't seen you in a while,' she said, rising from her desk, coming into the corridor to greet me. 'Tell me, did you manage to arrange accommodation for your little boy?'

Magdalena looked as impeccable as always in her tailored suit. Her hair was swept on top of her head in a fashionable bow, her eyebrows tweezered to look like two minnows. Together with her husband, Gobbi, they stood out from the rest of us in our threadbare garments.

Conscious of the treacherous, whispery rustle of paper up my sleeve, I smiled at her as we shook hands. 'He's quite safe, signora Magdalena,' I said. 'I sent him away.'

'I'm sorry you didn't think we could be of assistance. Please don't forget that the offices of *il* Fascio Femminile are here to help you. All you have to do is show us your party documents. You do still have them, signora?'

Her eyes bored into mine like a cat intent on its prey and I shivered. 'Perhaps you are cold?' she asked. She returned to her office and handed me half a dozen skeins of wool from a box on the floor. 'Take these. Knit something for yourself and your child. And, don't forget, we are here for you. The office is open every Monday and Wednesday morning.'

'I need to speak to your husband, signora,' I said. 'Will you tell him?'

'Of course. But can I help?'

'No, no,' I replied, plucking an excuse from the sky. 'It's about a broken window in the tobacco house. It needs repairing.'

I took the wool but I had little desire to engage in more conversation than necessary. Of course I still had my fascist party documents. All citizens were obliged to carry them at all times, although most were no longer faithful to Il Duce. Steeling myself to walk away slowly and calmly, I thought how much more complicated subterfuge was than I had imagined. Simonetta had advised me to act naturally, but it wasn't easy. The ransom note was still up my sleeve, like a splinter that needed to be removed. With signora Gobbi watching, I couldn't leave it in the militia pigeonhole and now I had no idea how to deliver it.

I checked the piazza. Aldo wasn't at his post. It was ten o'clock, the hour that Bruno served up coffee in the *osteria*, and the little square was empty. Even the guards had disappeared. My heart pumping crazily, I double-checked to see that nobody else was in the piazza and pulled the note from the pocket inside my sleeve. Then I crouched down to leave it in the middle of the town hall steps, securing it with a stone so that it wouldn't blow away. There was a sudden gust of breeze and the note flapped under the stone like a fish on dry land.

CHAPTER TWENTY-SIX

1947

Fosca stopped talking, her hands clenched in her lap. 'I never saw Simonetta again. I should have kept her here with me that night. Maybe she would still be alive now.' She looked over to the tobacco house.

'There was so much going on in my head, Richard. It was full of what Gobbi had promised about my husband,' Fosca said, with a deep sigh. 'And I felt that I had messed up the only independent task that Simonetta had asked me to do. On top of everything else, I was fearful how my little boy would manage without a mother. But I should have stopped Simonetta from leaving the tobacco house. She was in a dreadful state, desperately bent on revenge.'

'Should have are two words that never help,' Richard said. 'I have had to tell myself that over and over.'

'What do you mean?'

'I've told myself since the end of the war that war and death are synonymous. They cause a scar on our souls that will never heal if we don't let it. There is really no point in dwelling on something that should have or should not have happened.'

'So you're saying I should forget?' Her voice was raised in anger. 'Because I can never do that. I need to know where the rest of the gold ended up and why Simonetta died and I shall never give up. I feel there is a link and I owe it to my friend to solve the questions in my mind.'

'And I understand that. I'm talking about coming to terms with events. Moving on.' He was quiet for a moment.

'I'm not explaining myself well,' Richard continued, running his hand through his thick blond hair. 'I told you I'm a pacifist, Fosca.' He paused. 'But despite that, I killed a German soldier while I was here. In doing so, I also caused the death of a young mother. And that is something I have had to come to terms with, otherwise I'd go crazy.'

She looked up at him. 'Did you kill in self-defence?'

'I suppose so. But chiefly because there were other lives in danger.' He stopped, as if hunting for words. 'But that went against everything I believed. I'd been taught from before I was in short trousers that war is totally wrong under any circumstances.'

'To me, what you did was self-defence. What else could you have done?' She paused, her head down. 'You are not the first to react this way in war… and you will not be the last.' She sighed and turned to him, her voice animated. 'And surely, despite what you believe – peace *needs* to be defended, does it not?'

'I grant you that. And that is why I joined the ambulance unit. To do my bit for peace. We looked after the injured on all sides, no matter what nationality. Medical men have no enemies. At war's end, when the Germans surrendered, we set up a joint dressing hospital to treat all the wounded. I shook hands with German doctors and worked side by side with their orderlies. I carried in stretchers with them, shared food and drinks.'

'Was the woman you say you killed the mother of Angelina?'

He looked up sharply. 'How did you know that?'

'Oh, Richard. It's common knowledge in Corbello. You don't need to hide it. And you are considered a hero for trying to save her.'

'I am definitely not a hero.'

'None of us sees ourselves as others do.'

He laughed then. 'Listen to the pair of us. Dishing out wisdom but not taking it on board ourselves.'

'It's what you told me the other day. A problem shared…'

'… is a problem halved,' he joined in, and they laughed.

'How about a coffee?' she asked. 'Any more wine and I'll be talking more rubbish than I already am.'

'It's not rubbish, Fosca. None of it is rubbish.'

He followed her into the tobacco house and watched as she sniffed the coffee grains and spooned them into a Moka pot, compacting it with the back of a spoon.

'How we missed real coffee during the war,' she said.

When they returned outside, Richard continued their conversation. 'You talked about messing up with the ransom note. What happened?'

'The exchange went ahead, despite my clumsy efforts.'

She poured two coffees into small cups, adding sugar to Richard's and a measure of aniseed liqueur. 'The handover happened on a freezing cold day at dusk, in an open area on the Scheggia Pass near the castle of Montauto. Lupo told me all about it, much later. He described the whole event like a game of poker, the transaction enacted without a word spoken, each party suspicious and taut, expecting a surprise card to be played in the showdown and the pot to be won by nobody. Those were his words.'

Fosca asked Richard if he wanted more coffee and he held out his cup.

'My Silvio was nowhere to be seen, but Gennaro and Lupo were exchanged for the major. And Simonetta drove them off in a laundry van. I remember Lupo saying he was scared witless by her crazy driving.'

'So, it wasn't a failure. The ransom note worked.'

'Yes.' She bit her lip. 'Oh goodness, this is like confession time for me, talking like this. It brings back those days of sweaty palms when I was a little girl in the convent. When we had to confess our sins every Saturday, so that we could take communion the next day.' Fosca shook her head. 'Honestly, when I think of what I considered to be a sin: eating two ham rolls instead of one or pulling the plaits of the little girl who sat in front of me in the classroom. Ridiculous!'

'For the Roman Catholic soldiers whom I looked after on the wards, confession was important. They told me it eased the conscience after they'd spoken to the padre.'

'You told me I am courageous, Richard. But I am really not. I wasn't honest with my fellow *partigiani*. When Gobbi promised to bring Silvio to me and told me not to reveal to anybody that he knew where Silvio was, I was naïve. I wanted Silvio to be returned together with Lupo and Gennaro. So I kept quiet about Gobbi. Maybe if I had told the others, Simonetta would still be here.'

'I don't follow.'

'I helped the *partigiani* because I was trying to help myself. What I did wasn't for the good of the cause.'

'In the end we do what we have to do.'

'I listen to what you are saying, but I am still ashamed.'

'You're far too harsh on yourself, Fosca. What you did, what you've had to put up with… you are amazing. Why would not revealing about Gobbi's promise make any difference?'

'It might have warned the *partigiani* off if they knew how devious Gobbi was. That man should not be the mayor of Corbello. He is not to be trusted.'

There was silence between them, each wrapped in their own thoughts.

'I ran away after a while,' Fosca said. 'It was too hard to stay in Corbello. There was too much sadness. Being with the nuns in the mountains was an escape and that time with Giampiero was precious. I had to get to know my little boy all over again.'

She fiddled with a curl, rolling it round and round her finger. 'But Simonetta was always on my mind. She still is.'

'It's certainly strange that there was only one piece of gold in the well. And Simonetta was found nearby.'

'Exactly. Why, why, why? That word is like the beating of a drum in my head. It won't stop until I solve these puzzles.'

'Tell me what happened afterwards, Fosca. Let's try to unravel this tangle in your mind.'

CHAPTER TWENTY-SEVEN

1944

On the morning after the exchange of prisoners, I was helping Aurelia roll out pasta dough when the church bells started to ring. I had taken to sleeping on the kitchen floor of the *osteria* since Simonetta had warned me against staying in the tobacco house. Outside we heard shouting, dogs barking, gunfire. I rushed to the window in the eating area and saw the parish priest slumped on the ground, blood soaking his white surplice. His pet truffle dog guarded his body, snarling at a *tedesco* who lifted his rifle to aim at the animal. Another shot rang out and the Lagotto Romagnolo whimpered before sinking lifeless across his master's body. A truck screeched to a halt in the piazza and *tedeschi* soldiers jumped from the back and started to hammer and kick on doors.

'Quick, we must hide, Aurelia. In the cellar,' I said, pulling her away from her work.

'My boys,' she cried. 'They went out this morning. Where are they?' She had just got Gennaro back from the prison, and he and Ennio had gone out for the day, gathering firewood for the kitchen stove.

'I'm sure they'll be safe,' I told her, bundling her down the stairs. 'They'll hide in the woods.' We squeezed behind barrels of wine and waited. There were more shots outside, the sounds of china smashing upstairs and heavy footsteps on the floorboards as voices of the soldiers yelled, '*Raus, raus.*' I don't know for how long the confusion lasted but eventually we heard a vehicle roar off. Silence followed. Aurelia and I crouched in our hiding place, clutching on to each other, waiting.

'I think they've gone,' I whispered, after minutes that stretched like hours. 'I'll go and look.'

Aurelia pulled me back. 'Stay here. It's not safe.'

'I'm sure they've gone. Listen to the quiet. I'll be careful. I won't be long.'

Outside, fires were burning. The square was strewn with pots, a sheet hung from a window. I bent to check on the priest but he was dead, his eyes staring at the sky. Then I heard the sound of running footsteps and I darted into a doorway, cursing myself for having ventured out too soon.

Aurelia's boys passed by me where I was pressed against the door. They were about three metres away from the *osteria*, and I was about to call to them when two shots split the air. It was all I could do to stop myself shrieking a warning, when the boys crumpled to the ground. Ennio crawled across the cobbles to where I was cowering, his hand outstretched. 'Mamma, Mamma,' he whimpered, blood trickling from his mouth, and I covered my mouth with my hand to stifle a sob.

Minutes later the German piano player marched past, flanked by two soldiers, their heavy boots a menacing sound on the cobbles. They mounted the steps to the town hall and, speaking in heavy Italian, the major ordered the townspeople of Corbello to come out of their houses and listen to what he had to say. 'I give you all my word,' he called out, his words piercing the silence, 'that you will not be shot. But if you do not assemble now, then more lives will be lost.'

Nobody moved at first, save for a cat that jumped from a windowsill to lap at a jug of spilled milk and then I saw Gobbi exit from the *comune* building followed by his wife, Magdalena. They stood on the steps close to where the tall, blond major towered over them. From the far end of the piazza, an elderly couple and a young boy struggled from their home, the old man's stick tap-tapping on the stones as he advanced. I went to help them and together we made our way to the centre of the square and stood by the fountain. Others began to emerge from their homes, fear etched on their faces. They joined us and we huddled together until there were about fifty Corbello citizens standing before the German major.

'Today, my senior officer, *Oberstleutnant* Wagner, ordered your priest to be shot as an example to the rest of the town because he was trying to warn of our approach.' The major's words carried to us. 'If we are to live together without further bloodshed, all citizens of Corbello need to understand that they cannot kidnap officers of the German Reich. I leave it to you to spread the word to those of your friends who escaped when your priest sounded the alarm. You have my word that, as long as your… *banditi*…' He paused before using the word. 'As long as your *banditi* continue to act irresponsibly, then more lives will be taken in reprisal. Warn your *partigiani* that we will hunt them down and bring them to trial. Anyone who shelters them will be punished. And by punishment, I mean shot. There is a reward for anyone who reveals their whereabouts.'

The major paused and I watched as looks and muttered comments were exchanged in the square. My insides turned to jelly. There were plenty of starving people ready to claim that money.

'You should understand that we have been lenient this time, but we shall not be in the future. It has taken all my powers of persuasion to prevent further bloodshed, but I cannot guarantee this again.'

The three Germans saluted each other and their words '*Heil Hitler*,' echoed round the piazza.

Everyone turned towards Aurelia as she shrieked, 'Ennio, Gennaro, *figli miei*.' She had found her sons. She knelt over them, screaming for help, her hands clasped, and I hurried over, calling for Bruno.

Gennaro died immediately, Ennio shortly afterwards. The *tedeschi* refused them burial at first, but a straggle of villagers returned to their homes from where they'd hidden in the countryside and, one by one, we joined in defiance against our occupiers. Despite the guns trained on us, Gennaro and Ennio were lifted from the piazza and carried into the *osteria*. The women helped Aurelia prepare and wash their bodies. Bruno strode into the church, his head held high, and removed the crucifix from the altar and held it aloft when we all processed later to the little walled cemetery. We followed behind, the bodies of the boys arranged on the back of a cart lined with clean tablecloths from the *osteria* and branches of sweet-smelling pine. There were no roses to gather to lay on the mounds of earth but we had our voices and sang hymns we'd learned as children, the words ringing proudly in the winter air.

After we had buried the boys, I stayed on at the *osteria* but I thought my heart would break like Aurelia's and Bruno's with the unbearable sadness that permeated the place. Downstairs I cleaned and scrubbed, helpless to know what else to do for them, my angry tears dropping onto the wet flagstones as I rubbed them clean. Aurelia stayed upstairs, sitting beside her sons' empty beds. Silence was a shroud, pierced by Aurelia's wails of grief. Bruno sat at a table drinking glass after glass of red wine, the plates of food I prepared untouched.

'There's no more work for you here, Fosca,' he said after two days, looking up at me through bleary eyes.

'Let me stay to help you.'

'Your *partigiani* have destroyed us.'

I could have been false and told him I didn't understand what he was talking about, that they weren't my *partigiani*. But I wasn't good at bluffing, like Simonetta. He would have read the lie in my eyes. I had played my part with them in a mission that had been a step too far. And my involvement had been spurred on by Gobbi's promise of returning Silvio to me. Fearing for my own sanity, and longing for my son, I decided to leave. But first I needed to check if Silvio was up at the camp. I couldn't rest until I did this.

Ennio's boots were sturdier than mine and I took them from under the bed Aurelia insisted on leaving untouched, the bedclothes rumpled from the last time the boys had slept there. Gennaro's thick trousers and sweater hung on the back of their door and I took those too, knowing that Aurelia would be upset, but the boys were gone now and my need was great. I'd listened to Ennio's descriptions of the camp he had observed. I knew the climb up to one thousand metres was steep. I couldn't keep to the road, used regularly by troops, and so my way was through the woods with rocks, gullies and thick brambles to push through. Without saying goodbye, I slipped away from the *osteria* to sleep for a few hours down at the tobacco house. At dawn, I pulled on the cap that Simonetta had given me and set off into the gloom.

I saw nobody on the first part of the journey and used the road for the first hour. But when the birds began to sing, I pushed into the forest, the branches dripping as I climbed. Twice I came across grazing deer and they scampered away as soon as they caught my scent. The climb grew steeper and I picked up two sticks to help me. As the sun rose in the sky and the morning haze lifted, I made out hamlets studding the hillside and in the far distance the city of Sansepolcro sprawled in the plain. I was hungry and my breakfast that morning was water from a stream and a lump of bread and cheese that I had stuffed into the pockets of Gennaro's trousers.

Voices drifted to me through the trees. I hid behind a boulder. Peeping through ferns, I watched as a line of men, escorted by a dozen German guards, marched down the road below. Most of them were my countrymen: dark haired, shorter than their guards for the most part. My heart beating, I strained my eyes to see if Silvio was amongst them but he wasn't there. Perhaps he was back in the camp. As the men walked away down the hill, I knew that the only way to be sure was to make my way towards the camp and watch.

After a further half an hour, the final stretch brought me to a rise. Below me lay the camp: about twenty wooden huts arranged in lines penned in by a high fence and at each end, two guarded watchtowers. I craned forward to see better. And that was when a hand went over my mouth and something cold dug into the back of my neck.

I was pulled to my feet and frogmarched down to the camp; I slipped a couple of times and the guard pulled me roughly to my feet and prodded me again with his rifle. A couple of prisoners looked up from where they were digging a trench, pitying looks in their eyes. I shouted out in Italian, '*Cerco* Silvio. Silvio Sentino. I'm looking for Silvio.' And I was rewarded with a kick to the back of my legs and I buckled to the ground. To still my terror, I pictured Silvio. He was relying on me to find him and that gave me strength to conquer my fear.

The forest grew darker still as a shadow loomed over me and I looked up. It was Gobbi's friend, Major Hansen, who had organised the attack on the train as well as the exchange of prisoners. My rough descent must have caused my hair to escape and he pulled my cap from my head. 'Well, well, well,' he said in Italian. 'What have we here but the little waitress from Bruno's? You are a long way from Corbello, signorina.'

'I was searching for firewood, signore. It has all been cut near the town. I…'

He interrupted my excuse with a laugh. '*Quatsch!* I don't believe that rubbish for one moment.' He pulled me to my feet and handed me my cap. 'The hat does you no favours either, signorina.' Then he took my arm firmly, his fingers digging in through Ennio's jumper, barking something to the guard, who clicked his heels together and gave that ugly salute. The major pushed me into his hut and I prepared myself for the worst. But what was to happen was bizarre.

Inside, it was warm and furnished with an assortment of quality furniture including an armchair upholstered in a rich velvet, a brass bed draped with fur coverings and a patterned rug. To my further surprise, in the far corner stood a grand piano and my mouth fell open. He watched me as I surveyed the space.

'I cannot live without my music, signorina.' He lifted the lid and proceeded to play a piece of classical music, an aria from *La bohème* by Puccini, a tune all us Italians recognise from a young age. He stopped after a few bars. 'Sentimental nonsense, don't you think? But it tugs at the heartstrings, nevertheless.' He sang the words to the bars he had just played. '*Che gelida manina* – what a frozen little hand. Are your hands cold after your trek up the mountain, signorina?' He walked over, squeezed my hand hard and looked down at me, his voice brusque. 'Now, tell me what you are really doing up here. Who are you spying for?'

I stuttered my answer. This man was charming one minute, the next threatening. Had this madman shot Ennio and Gennaro in the piazza after killing our priest? Was it my turn next?

'I'm searching for my husband.'

His eyebrows shot up. 'And who is this lucky man?'

'Silvio Sentino. I was told that he was in this camp.'

'And who told you this?'

I hesitated. If I told him that it was Gobbi, who had warned me not to tell anybody, and if Silvio wasn't in this camp after all, would it jeopardise my chances of seeing my husband again if he was elsewhere? 'One of the women at the fountain said somebody had said they'd seen him on a working party up here. I don't know who it was,' I babbled.

'Very convenient.'

He sat at the piano again and played a few arpeggios, his fingers flying over the keys. And then he turned to me. 'I think I believe you, signorina. Your reasoning is like the plot of an operetta.' He smiled. 'So convoluted that it is probably true.'

He lifted a crystal decanter from a side table and poured himself a measure of clear liquid. '*Prost! Salute!*' he said, raising his glass to me. 'I won't offer you my schnapps, signorina, or should I say signora, now that I know you are a married woman? I know Italian women quite well and you do not tend to drink much alcohol.'

Then he seated himself in the armchair and crossed his legs. 'I tell you what I shall do, signora. I like Italians. Our smiling commander, Albert Kesselring, doesn't. He doesn't like the southern temperament. He thinks you are all degenerate. But I studied music in Venice. I learned your beautiful language there and I grew fond of your race and one day I want to return to that beautiful city. I was treated hospitably and now it is my turn for repayment.'

He leant over to the side table and poured himself more schnapps. I willed my legs to stop trembling, distracting myself by gazing on the items dotted around this bizarre space. A silver candelabra on an ornate side table, two oil paintings of a sea scene. I wondered from where they had been stolen. My anger mounted and helped steel my resolve. How dare these brutes march in and wreak havoc on our beautiful nation. I clenched my fists as the major continued to talk in his stilted Italian.

'It is most regrettable what happened in Corbello. Two young boys and a priest killed unnecessarily because of the *partigiani*. Maybe they were innocent, maybe not. Your *partigiani* scrape up all kinds of strays to do their work.' He knocked back his drink and set the glass down. From his desk drawer, he produced a file and, opening it, he ran his long finger down a list. My heart quickened as I waited for him to pronounce Silvio's name. After interminable seconds he looked up and shook his head.

'I am very sorry, signora. You have been misinformed. There is nobody here of that name on this list – dead or alive.'

I let out my breath and staggered back, holding on to a chair to stop myself from falling.

'You are grown very pale, signora.'

I couldn't speak. My mind filled with a mixture of despair and hatred. I had let Gobbi dupe me and I was angry at letting myself believe in a ridiculous dream. But I refused to cry. I would not cry in front of this man and, although my heart was breaking, I pulled myself upright and waited for whatever punishment was to come next. But there was no punishment.

'I am leaving for Corbello in five minutes, signora. And I will give you a lift. But perhaps tonight you will do me the pleasure of dining at my table in the *osteria*. Tell your boss that you are having the evening free to eat with me instead of serving.'

I couldn't believe my ears. I was so flabbergasted that I said nothing, just stared at this conundrum of a man.

'Unless of course you wish to enjoy the fresh mountain air and walk back the route you came?' he said.

I accepted his offer, hoping I would be safer travelling in his car and stammered a *grazie*. But as for dining with him, there was no way that would ever happen. I dreaded to think what Bruno and Aurelia would make of me dining with the enemy.

*

He dropped me off in the centre of the piazza, ordering his driver to open the door of his shining black car, the German flag fluttering in the air. The women at the fountain looked up as I climbed out and they turned to each other, whispering behind their hands. It would be all round Corbello within the hour that I had been seen consorting with a German officer, but there was no time to explain what had really happened. I had to get away from Corbello as quickly as I could. I'd had a lucky escape but I was not going to chance another.

CHAPTER TWENTY-EIGHT

I flew down the track to what had become my home over the last few weeks to fetch my few possessions: the clothes I'd made for Giampiero, my precious framed photo of Silvio, and together with some scraps of food, I tied everything up in Nonna Zina's shawl to carry on my back. At the last minute, I lifted my skirt and concealed the pistol that Simonetta had given me. Its barrel cold against my stomach, I sat for a moment in the semi-gloom of the kitchen by the cold hearth, thinking of all that had happened within these walls. My induction into the *partigiani* had been brief, tragic and, in my eyes, pointless. I was a failure. It was hard to lie, to pretend, to adopt a false persona. Simonetta was a natural, made for resistance. It may have been because she had suffered more than I had; maybe the nuns had brought me up to be too honest. And I always had the safety of my little boy in the forefront of my mind and that was why I couldn't commit, like my friend.

Pulling the door to the tobacco house to, I hurried down the path towards the main Sansepolcro road. When a truck loaded with *tedeschi* soldiers passed me and screeched to a halt a little way ahead, I felt oddly unafraid as I hurried towards it, even though the soldiers were heavily armed. The instinct to survive was strong in me that day. I felt there was nothing much else that could harm me now.

'Lift, signorina?' the driver asked. 'We go to Sansepolcro.'

'Halfway will be fine. *Grazie*,' I said, remembering the occasions when Simonetta and I had dressed as nuns and been offered a lift. I followed her advice: to be daring, take risks, be a little cheeky. I managed a smile and a flutter of my eyelashes as a soldier in the back reached out his arm to help me up and took my bundle. He shunted up the wooden seat to make room and smiled. '*Buona sera, signorina.*'

I shivered as I responded to his greeting and as the truck pulled away, he pulled a scarf from around his neck, thinking I was cold. '*Sehr kalt. Freddo,*' he said, handing it over and I accepted with a brief smile. As the truck increased in speed, the scarf flew up in the current like an arm waving goodbye and I wondered when I would next see Simonetta. I began to feel a little proud of myself as I sat surrounded by the enemy.

From where the soldiers dropped me, it was another hour's walk up to the mountain retreat. The clouds were full of rain and a keen wind began to stir. I'd handed the scarf back to the soldier and I was cold but once I started to walk, the blood pumped around my body as I paced up the stony mule track. Rain deluged down as I rounded the final bend, the candle in the chapel window still flickering its welcome to any passing pilgrim. I couldn't wait to cuddle my son.

When I knocked at the door, I must have looked like a vagrant – my wet hair clung to my face, my clothes were muddy and the nuns didn't recognise me at first. Then they called for Madre Caterina, who came running, her arms open wide to welcome me. 'He's eating his supper,' she said, even before I asked. She looked me up and down, at my grubby clothes, at the exhaustion I must have shown in my face. 'But before you meet him again, let's make you presentable for the little man.'

It was like coming home. The nuns had brought me up; their way of life was ingrained in me. Madre Caterina boiled water for me to bathe, adding a bundle of rosemary to lend fragrance, and went to find fresh clothes. 'It is all we have for the moment,

Fosca,' she said, as she held up a novice's habit of cream serge. 'The material is good, and will keep you warm.' She spoke to me softly as she sponged my back and helped me wash my hair with lavender lotion, combing my tangles for me afterwards as I sat by the stove in the kitchen.

'The priest in Corbello was shot by the *tedeschi*,' I told her. 'I thought Silvio was in the camp nearby, Madre.' My tears soaked into the thick material of the habit. 'But I was deceived.' I turned to look into the kindly face of the nun, the nearest I had to family apart from Giampiero. I hoped she wouldn't ask further questions. All the fight had gone out of me and I was desperate to switch off from the events of the past days. 'I had to get away from Corbello. May I stay here for a while?'

'Rest for a couple of days, Fosca. Get to know your little boy again and then we shall find you something to do. We have more children sheltering with us and they are in need of a teacher. The Good Lord has chosen to send you to us at the perfect time.'

I was so relieved she didn't want to question me further on what had gone on since we'd last talked. She understood me. She had known me all my life.

Giampiero was shy at first and, just as Madre Caterina hadn't crowded me, I waited patiently for my little son to come back to me slowly. Of course I wanted to smother him with cuddles and kisses but I controlled myself, sitting in the nursery room that the nuns had converted in the sacristy area to the side of the chapel altar. I observed him as he tottered around, landing every now and then on his bottom, padded with a towelling napkin. The sacristy was warmed by a small stove and where priests' vestments and sacred vessels had once been kept, the nuns had arranged a couple of baskets to use as little beds and someone had carved small chairs from tree trunks and made a simple table from planks.

'There is no priest here at the moment to officiate at Holy Mass, so for the time being this space is perfect for our little ones,' Madre Caterina explained. She led me into the priest's bedroom. 'We thought you could use this as your classroom, Fosca.'

It was easy to settle back into a way of life that I had always known, the day structured between worship and work. Although I was grateful to have a safe place away from Corbello where the people of the town would judge me for imagined dealings with the *tedeschi*, I was silent during the time of prayer, and kept my scepticism to myself of the notion of the Good Shepherd, instilled in me from an early age. Where had He been when Silvio was taken from me? Where was He now when our country was occupied by a brutal army, our people punished for something they never asked for? Where were the five thousand loaves and fishes that we so desperately needed?

In my saddened, weary mood, I picked what I needed from my days spent in the retreat to build myself up again and tried to put behind me everything I had done for the *partigiani*. I stilled the little voice that whispered to me that I hadn't done anything for them – I had done everything for myself. The love for my son, the tenderness shown me by these good women, a clean bed to sleep in and simple food was all I needed. And in time, my slow, brown thoughts were turned to colour as I spent time away from the scenes I had witnessed and I forgot about Simonetta for a while.

Franco, the big *inglese* who I remembered from my last visit as a pilot whose plane had crashed in the mountains, turned out to be the carpenter who had crafted the little chairs and tables. The right side of his face was still a puckered mess and he struggled to speak, so he developed a mime language. The children adored him, particularly a little boy not much older than my Giampiero. Franco was particularly gentle with him.

Madre Caterina told me they had named the child Tommaso Paradiso. 'He was left at the convent on a freezing December night in a basket on the feast day of Saint Thomas. He is blind, Fosca. But Franco acts as his eyes.'

I'd noticed how Franco kept a careful watch on him and sat next to him at mealtimes, helping guide the spoon to his mouth, cutting potatoes into tiny chunks to feed him. The two had formed a special bond and the younger children too climbed on Franco when he dropped to all fours and pretended to be a horse or wobbly donkey. The most prized toy in the nursery was a set of wooden animals and an ark he had carved and the younger children played with them for hours. For Tommaso, he had devised a series of rings in increasing sizes to thread over a wooden cylinder and he'd made a recorder from a reed, and the little boy blew tunes he made up.

'Could you make me a blackboard?' I asked, miming the shape with my hands. Whenever Franco saw me, he pulled off the black woollen cap that the nuns had knitted to keep him warm and nodded his head like a gentleman. Madre Caterina told me that they had stopped colouring his hair dark and, instead, he shaved his scalp each morning to stop his blond hairs showing. His manners were those of an educated man and I wondered what he had done before the war and how he had ended up in Tuscany. To whom did he belong? Was there a family missing him? Whenever he looked puzzled at what we said, I drew for him on a scrap of paper and he smiled his crooked smile and nodded with enthusiasm when he understood.

Before long, my classroom was equipped with slates for the children to write on and lumps of chalky stones, all sourced by Franco from the forest. If I wanted a box made or geometrical shapes for the little ones to learn with, Franco would produce something within hours.

Winter turned to a warm spring and we were able to move outside to the small cloistered area during the day for our lessons. War seemed far away but now and again I worried about Simonetta. How was she managing without Maria? I missed her.

Occasionally a vapour trail from an aeroplane would drift across the sky, reminding me that war continued, impossible to tell whether from enemy or ally, flown by men whose lives might be over at any second. If I had been able to pray, my prayers would have been for no more wars and no more young lives to be lost. What was the point of raising sons and daughters for them to be slaughtered in their prime? As I watched my son play in the grass, picking at daisies with his stubby little fingers, I wanted time to stop still. Up here we were cocooned by nature. The bees were busy on the yellow celandines and primroses, the lazy sound of their hard work mingling with the song of the warblers that led the chorus of birds in the woods. In the little vegetable garden behind the church, the nuns had tilled the soil, ready for sowing seeds.

The brightest of the children in my little schoolroom were the twins: Roberto and Ria. They would soon celebrate their tenth birthdays and the nuns asked me to arrange something special for them.

'Those children are more innocents who have lost family, Fosca,' Madre Caterina told me one day when I was helping her hang out the washing, passing her the pegs as we talked. 'After they were left with us, they refused to talk because they were so traumatised. They've developed a secret language that only they can understand. Franco has helped them mime when they need something. The only relative they have is an uncle who comes to visit from time to time.'

What a motley band of lost souls we were, flotsam washed up by the sea of war and salvaged by the nuns.

Franco and I planned a party for the twins. 'What would you like to do on your birthday next week?' I asked them at the end of a difficult lesson. I'd set the older children a writing exercise: 'A special day'. Not a single word had been produced by Roberto. Instead he held up a picture of a cat that he'd sketched with his pencil. It was good: a more than lifelike tortoiseshell cleaning itself, one leg lifted in the air like a ballerina. Then he flipped the page to the other side and I looked in horror at the image of the same cat, decapitated. Ria had written a simple three-line poem.

My Special Day

It was the day before.
After that they were no more.
And now I hate, I hate the war.

It twisted my heart to guess at what was going on inside their little minds. From then on, I started the school day with a half hour of art, letting them express their feelings in any way they could.

Roberto had drawn a cartoon story of a little boy who didn't want any more birthdays. To be ten meant that his age was going to have two numbers, like old people. He didn't want to grow older. He wanted to go back to when he was eight years old, to be with his parents and the rest of his family.

Without these children to care for, I'd have slipped easily into spoiling my only child but I had suddenly become a mother to more than one and I felt useful again. This little group began to restore my confidence and gave me a new purpose, besides caring for Giampiero. But some nights, fear stalked me, my mind filled with questions. Where was Silvio? How was Simonetta? And my friends, Aurelia and Bruno... what did they think of me now? And then I would gaze on my sleeping child, his eyelashes fanning on his plump cheeks and remind myself he was all that mattered.

CHAPTER TWENTY-NINE

We did our best to make the twins' birthday unforgettable. Franco introduced a game where the children were blindfolded – all except little Tommaso Paradiso, who couldn't see anyway – and turned them round and round three times, handing them a length of unthreaded rope that was supposed to represent a mule's tail. On the side of the convent wall he had scratched two outlines in chalk – one of a nun bending to weed and the other, the hindquarters of a mule. The children had to pin the tail where they thought best. Laughter echoed round the cloister when all the tails seemed to land on the fat behind on the nun's sketch.

As part of the games, we practised dabbing dye extracted from red sorrel onto the faces of the children. If we gave a signal by clapping our hands, then they knew they had to scuttle into bed. The last one to do so was out of the game and if anybody made the slightest sound, then they were out too. It was an excellent opportunity to practise a plan we had devised in case of a raid. We were to pretend that we had an isolation room in the convent, full of contagious patients covered in rashes.

We ate the twins' birthday meal in the shelter of the cloister. Although the days had a promise of summer-to-come in the air, there was still a chill wind for May. At the very moment that Madre Caterina carried the chestnut and apple cakes, decorated with flower petals and blue and pink ribbons, from the kitchen, three men slipped into the cloisters. Without thinking twice, I stood and clapped my hands. There were shrieks as the children scattered to run and hide in their beds. I cursed myself for having left my pistol under my pillow. War had seemed not to touch us any longer and I had relaxed my guard. From the corner of my eye, I saw Franco pick up a heavy spade and conceal himself behind a column.

'Fosca, *come stai?*' the tall, thin man standing between his two slight companions asked and then I recognised him and my gaze fell to his boots and the mismatching laces.

'Lupo!' I said, starting towards him, my arms outstretched.

He put a finger to his mouth and I stopped midway. Franco looked on in puzzlement.

Roberto and Ria had halted in their party game when they saw him and they ran over. He crouched down to embrace them, toppling backwards to the grass as they jumped on him, shouting, '*Zio* Piero, *zio* Piero.'

My mouth fell open. 'You're their uncle?'

He removed the cap from his stringy lank hair and extended his hand, winking as he introduced himself to me with his real name. '*Piacere*, signorina. Let me introduce myself properly. I am Piero Bonaventura. Here to visit my special niece and nephew on their special birthday.' Then he gestured to Primo and Secondo, who proceeded to cartwheel and somersault across the cloister, juggling coloured balls and producing sweets and silken scarves from behind the children's ears.

After the excitement had died down and the children were playing with the balls, I sat with Lupo for a while. Madre Caterina discreetly placed a bottle of altar wine with four glasses on the ground next to Lupo, asking us not to tell Mother Superior. When she left us alone, I asked after the others.

'The group has broken up. We're all scattered,' he said and told me that since the last mission, it had been too dangerous to stay together. 'I haven't heard from Simonetta in a while. I think she's returned to Turin. She was very active up there before she came to Tuscany, organising riots amongst the factory workers. Knowing Simonetta, she'll have thrown herself into that again.'

Simonetta would never be the same after losing Maria, I reflected. Not having Silvio by my side had changed me, but my son had kept me going. Simonetta only had the cause of resistance left to her and I couldn't imagine her taking a back seat. I worried about her future.

Lupo sipped his wine and grimaced. 'A little sweet for my liking, but beggars can't be choosers. *Salute!*' he said and we drank to good health.

'You left Corbello so suddenly but I'm glad you're back with your son, Fosca. You seem calmer.'

'As calm as anybody can be in these times. Why didn't you tell me before that your niece and nephew were up here? And that you knew the nuns?' I ignored his comment about my departure.

He shrugged his shoulders. 'As you well know, it's prudent to share as little information as possible about ourselves.'

Giampiero tottered over, hand in hand with little Tommaso. He walked slowly, almost guiding his little blind companion and I marvelled at the sympathy and intelligence of even the youngest of children.

'We heard on Radio Londra that the *tedeschi* are about to withdraw from Arezzo, Fosca. There'll be more fighting as the allies work their way towards us. And Mussolini has ordered his *repubblichini* to hunt out conscripted soldiers on the run. You and the nuns should be on your guard. There are worse times ahead.'

That was the end of our brief conversation because the twins came over to climb on Lupo's knees. It was a joy to hear their little voices as they chattered with him. But I couldn't get used to hearing his real name. To me, he would always be Lupo.

'I'll miss you, Lupo,' I told him when he bid us goodbye after dark.

'Will you, Fosca?' he asked, pinching my cheek affectionately.
'A little,' I replied, smiling.

On the following day, we moved the children's beds into the
church to make it resemble a hospital ward, fearful of the arrival of
the militia guards that Lupo had warned us of. The children were
delighted that they didn't have to bathe each day and from then
on, their red spots were topped up with dye each morning. We
told them the party game might have to be played again one day
very soon. We didn't want to scare them with the real reasons and
we bribed them with the promise of cake for the best performers.

Lupo's warnings proved true a few days later, when in the
middle of an arithmetic lesson, gunfire sounded in the woods. I
clapped my hands and shouted at the children to run to their beds.
The game was on. When they were safely tucked up, a small group
of Italian militia guardsmen appeared up the track. They were
young, rowdy; a couple of them had rolled up their shirtsleeves
and another was taking potshots at squirrels in the trees.

Madre Caterina pushed me back from the door into the
convent as they drew nearer and with her arms folded across her
bosom and her feet planted firmly on the worn steps, she asked
the young men in her sternest voice, 'Can I help you, *giovanotti*?'

'I shouldn't imagine so,' one who seemed to be the leader of
the unruly gang replied and the others sniggered. Even from
where I stood behind the door, I could smell alcohol.

'We are here to look for any man who has failed to report for
conscription to the Republic of Salò,' he said, buttoning up his
camouflage jacket.

Madre Caterina laughed but I could hear nervousness in her
voice. '*Bravi! Coraggiosi!* Coming all this way to search for men
in a convent full of sick nuns and children.'

Her sarcasm only served to annoy the Italian, and he pointed to his black runic collar tabs, almost spitting as he ordered the nun to show him more respect. 'We are legionnaires conscripted with the Waffen-SS and we have orders to search this place for *partigiani* and draft dodgers.'

He pushed past and when he saw me in the hallway, he looked me up and down, his gaze lingering on my breasts as he fingered his beard, his eyes narrowing as he spoke. '*Ragazzi*, lads, what have we here? Is this beautiful girl a nun or a child, do you think? What was the name of the missing woman that Gobbi added to our list?' He barked a question at Madre Caterina. 'Who else do you have living with you?' His gaze did not waver from me.

My heart stopped. I hoped he couldn't read the terror in my eyes when I'd heard the name Gobbi.

'This young novice is a trainee doctor.' I was grateful that Madre Caterina intervened at that moment. I was too shocked to think of a reply. 'We have an epidemic of smallpox and she is treating the sick,' she said.

'A doctor, you say?' he said, leering at me. 'Then, maybe you can help my friend Giacomo.' He swung round to indicate one of the guards. 'He has a bad attack of the pox, but a pox of a different kind.' The others sniggered when their leader said, 'Unbutton your trousers, Giacomo, show the lady doctor your rash.'

Madre Caterina stepped forward. 'This is a place dedicated to God. Kindly reflect on what you say, remove your caps and show some decency.'

The men's caps remained firmly on their heads, the skulls on the peaks proving their allegiance to the Italian division of the German SS. Although they were *fascisti*, these boys had been raised to respect God and nuns. I was quaking inside, but took courage from Madre Caterina.

'You must be aware that smallpox is highly contagious, *signori*,' I said. 'I suggest you mask your faces. In the last week we have lost three sisters and two children. We buried them yesterday.' I hoped this would be enough warning and they wouldn't ask to see evidence of graves.

'So, you think I will believe that old chestnut?' the bearded legionnaire asked. 'Don't you think that trick has been played on us before?' He put his arm round my shoulder, the gun in his hand pointing under my chin and I tried to shrug him off, but his grip was firm. 'Signorina, lead us to your make-believe hospital. We will help you do the rounds and inspect your so-called patients.'

Madre Caterina stepped between us and he pushed her roughly against the wall, her head bouncing back from the hard stone from where she slumped to the floor. 'You stay here, old woman. I had more than my fill of pious crones when I was growing up.'

'Leave her alone,' I shouted, crouching down to see how she was.

'I'm fine, Fosca. Only winded,' Madre Caterina gasped.

I was yanked up by the veil I wore during the day and I lashed out at the bully, but he caught my arm and forced it behind my back so that I screeched with pain.

'Mm! I do like a pretty woman with spirit,' he said, pinching my cheek hard between his fingers. '*Bellina, tu sei.*'

'Take your hands off me. And... use *voi siete* when you address me,' I corrected him pointedly, trying to keep my voice firm as I reprimanded him for using the familiar form of 'you'.

But he laughed again. 'Hear that, lads?' He put his arms round his companions. 'Listen to that! A grammar teacher as well as a doctor. What other talents does she have, I wonder?'

'If you follow me, I will find you masks,' I interrupted, trying to inject a steeliness into my voice that I didn't possess.

This comment seemed to disturb his friends. There were mutterings about whether this was such a good idea; what if they caught smallpox? 'Come on, Emilio. *Andiamo*. It's not worth it.'

I opened the laundry cupboard and found four small linen towels and handed three of them out and tied one around the bottom half of my face to cover my nose and mouth. As they fumbled to tie their knots, I wished I wasn't alone. Lupo would have snatched their guns in their unguarded, drunken state. My own pistol had been permanently concealed beneath my long skirt since the day of the birthday party when I had carelessly left it under my pillow, but it was no use against three armed men.

Taking the long way round to the chapel, I worried how convincing the children would be. They were so young, and there were bound to be giggles from under the bedclothes.

As I walked through the cloisters, the leader grabbed me again and forced me up against the wall. He pushed himself against me, kissing me, groping my breasts. I struggled and when his tongue pushed into my mouth, I bit hard and he slapped me. '*Puttana*,' he hissed. 'Hold her, boys, while I finish off what I started.' My arms were seized by the two men and I screamed as loudly as I could. There was the sound of grunting and Franco loomed from behind a pillar, bringing the full force of a pickaxe on the head of their leader.

In the confusion that followed, I pulled my pistol from beneath my long skirts and aimed it at the second man's head. '*Non gioco più*,' I screamed at the top of my voice. *This is no longer a game*, all the pent-up anger at what had happened driving me to kill. The man turned to grab me, an expression of incredulity on his face that I shall never forget, before I pulled the trigger and he fell head first to the floor, joining his leader with a sickening crunch as skull made impact with stone and blood trickled over the floor.

'*Non sparare, non sparare*,' the remaining injured man begged, clutching his arm. I gave him no mercy and pulled the trigger again to finish him off.

We had killed three Italian soldiers, their blood staining the flagstones of the convent cloisters, which for centuries had been trudged in silence and prayer. One by one the nuns slipped into the cloister. When she saw what had happened, Mother Superior pulled out her rosary and kissed the cross at the end of the beads. Then she quietly ordered the bodies to be removed and buried in the woods, the flagstones to be scrubbed and preparations to be made to immediately vacate the place.

Reaction to what I had done hit me moments later. By my own hands, I had killed two men. I couldn't stop shaking. Madre Caterina hustled me to the kitchen where she sat me down and prepared a calming tisane of valerian. 'Fosca, you did what you had to. Those devils violated you and might have gone on to harm the children.'

She urged me to drink up and moved around the kitchen, pulling items from the cupboards and putting them in baskets. 'We have to leave this place. And quickly. Other soldiers will come to look for those men. You must pull yourself together and pack the minimum for yourself and Giampiero.'

She left to warn the others and prepare a bag of clothes for the children and before nightfall we were on the move again, like nomads. There was a cave nearby called La Buca delle Fate, and as shadows fell and the moon appeared like a watery star, we set off in a straggly disparate group of women, children and one war-damaged man. The cave name – the fairy hole – sounded enchanting, and I invented stories for the children to encourage them up the mountain as we climbed the stony path.

On the outside, I might have appeared calm, but from what they had let drop, Gobbi had sent those Italian militiamen to find me. I hoped with all my being that he would not cast his web again and find us in this place.

CHAPTER THIRTY

Ten days later

The cave was dry and well hidden. A stream gushed into a rock pool nearby, so we had fresh water to drink and cook with. Outside it was warm but the sun never reached the inside where we sheltered and it was always damp and chilly. It was hard to keep the children quiet and together with the nuns we were a group of sixteen in all, with various annoying habits that required us to be extra-patient with one another. One of the nuns sniffed constantly, the twins took ages to settle and another child thrashed about with nightmares. We had to sleep on sticks and moss, huddled against each other and only lit a fire at night so that the smoke would not be detected. There was little to eat. We lived on water, apples, bacon fat and dry black bread that Madre Caterina had hastily gathered on the day we left the retreat. We began to lose weight and the children, starved of sunlight, looked like pasty wraiths. I was worried about Madre Caterina. She had no appetite and had developed a cough. More than once I noticed her pass her food to the children and I chastised her for not looking after herself. We slept while the sun baked the countryside. It was safer to live under cover of darkness and turn our days into nights.

When our food ran out, I decided to venture from the cave to see what I could find in the nearby town of Anghiari. Franco wanted to accompany me but it was easier to go alone. 'You look too English, Franco. They will shoot you.'

He cleaned my pistol and gave me his binoculars and after kissing Giampiero goodbye and entrusting him to the care of

Madre Caterina, I crept from the cave. At the entrance, I turned to watch for a few seconds. My son was curled up on the nun's lap and they were playing a game with her hands. I held the image in my heart.

In the thick forest, I followed the stream down the hill in the direction of the town, stopping now and again to use Franco's binoculars. In the distance, plumes of smoke rose from the main road in the direction of Arezzo. The muffled sounds of cannons firing backed up what Lupo had informed me about the approach of the allies. A sliver of hope brightened my mood and I continued to descend. When I heard voices, I dropped to the undergrowth, gritting my teeth when I realised that I was lying on an ants' nest. I didn't dare move, despite bites to my thighs. Two *tedeschi* were calling to each other not far from where I hid and, without warning, a loud explosion rent the air. A pheasant perched on a shrub nearby squawked, its wings beating the foliage like a caged bird and I dropped the binoculars in fright. Laughter followed and I peeped through the leaves. One of the soldiers held up a large trout that he must have dynamited from the stream. My heart rate slowed down as I watched the men walk off, laughing and chatting to each other as they disappeared, but I stayed where I was for at least ten minutes. When I felt sure their fishing expedition was over, I shook my skirt free of the ants and pulled it up to my waist. The tops of my legs were covered in red welts and I soaked myself in the refreshing stream water to relieve the stings. For a fleeting moment, gazing up at the canopy of trees arching over me like the vast roof of a cathedral, I thought how wonderful it would be to stay here forever, to turn into a water baby or a fish with no responsibilities. But it was a foolish thought, and I continued my descent towards the back end of town.

The front walls, with the long terrace that once used to house pots of oleanders and where in peacetime townspeople walked up and down for their Sunday *passeggiate*, was where the *tedeschi* had concentrated their anti-tank weapons. My destination was the apartment where I'd met Maria for the first time, when Simonetta had taken me on our crazy rooftop flight.

The door to the entrance was ajar. I waited for a few moments to make sure nobody was about and then slipped in. My feet scrunched over broken glass as I moved about. The mattress had been half pulled off the bed, great slashes revealing its woollen stuffing spewing out like entrails. A painting on the wall had been used for firing practice. Holes pierced the eyes on the faces in the portrait and I shivered at the destruction. The purpose of my visit here – my hope of finding food in the larder – was probably pointless. But I was in luck: a jar of tomato passata remained on the back of a shelf next to a cloth bag containing dried borlotti beans and I took them, dropping them into my bag together with a colourful darned shawl hanging from a hook behind the door. I remembered Maria wearing it. She had told me a gypsy sold it to her and I smiled at the memory of our outrageous fashion shows in the evenings at the tobacco house. I turned to leave, and then I was pulled backwards, kicking as I was dragged from the room. 'Don't say a fucking word,' a man's voice hissed and I recognised it immediately. It was Lupo.

I turned and he held up his finger to silence me and pulled me behind a curtained alcove, pressing me back with him behind a rail of fusty-smelling clothes. The fur from a coat collar tickled my nose and I willed myself not to brush it away in case the movement revealed our presence. Footsteps approached.

'I swear to you I saw somebody come in,' a woman's voice said. 'It wouldn't be the first time they hid in this place.'

'There's nothing left in here,' a man replied. 'The looters have taken everything. It was probably a cat. Leave it.'

'But there are rewards for deserters—'

'Blood money. Leave it. Let's go.'

The woman continued to grumble as they departed, their feet kicking against broken crockery as they retreated down the stairs. Lupo let go of me, his revolver in his hand and beckoned me to follow. We climbed the stair to the roof and, just as I'd done with Simonetta, crouching low as we moved, he guided me across the rooftops to the door of a storage room. Inside, we talked in whispers.

'I came to find you and the children again,' he said. 'Where did you disappear to? How are my twins?'

I filled him in and told him about the cave where we were sheltering, explaining that we were desperate for food, and medicine for Madre Caterina, who was ill with a fever.

'There's a reward up for information on those missing guards. You need to be extra careful. Fosca, tomorrow night, all being well, I will bring you food and medicine. But be careful when you leave here. Wait until dusk. Arezzo is on the verge of being liberated by the *alleati* and any day now, they will be here, *grazie a Dio*. The *tedeschi* and *fascisti* know it and they are jumpier than ever. They shoot before they ask questions. Be extra careful.'

On that warm, fuggy day, five days later, we should have been sleeping. The cicadas started up their chorus, bees droned on the wild raspberry flowers that flourished near the cave and then the lazy summer sounds were drowned out by the relentless boom of cannon fire and the *takka-takka-tak* of machine guns somewhere really close. The children clung to the nearest adult and some of the nuns started to pray on their knees. The air turned misty and an acidic smell drifted into the cave and I urged everyone to cover their mouths with whatever we could. 'It's phosphorous,' I told them, 'from smoke bombs. Move the children to the back of the cave.' The twins started to cough and, covering my own face, I went out to the stream and tore my petticoat into strips and dipped the pieces in the water. I had no idea if it would help but we made the children wear them tied over their mouths and noses. 'Pretend we're cowboys,' I told the little ones, trying to turn it into another game, despite the terror in my heart.

The barrage of battle continued for hours until later that day when the volleys of gunfire decreased. Occasionally there was an explosion and then the earth trembled again, soil sifting from the roof of the cave onto our heads Thankfully the children had dozed off and we discussed in low voices what to do for the best. We had no idea which way the fight was going so we stayed put. Then, soon after nightfall, chanting voices drifted to us through the shadows, in a language I didn't recognise.

'To me, it sounds like a call to prayer,' Mother Superior told us. 'For the Sikhs or Gurkhas, I am not sure. I know that they fight with the allies.' She was a wise, educated woman and we took comfort from what she told us. The thought that the allies were so close could only be a good sign.

In the morning, the gunfire had ceased completely and Franco mimed that he wanted to go and see what had happened. When we told him it was too dangerous, he shook his head, a frown on his face. He would be quiet, he told us, lifting his big feet up and down as daintily as a dancer. Thirty minutes, he told us, holding up his fingers to communicate to us.

While he was gone, we fed the children with the last of the food that Lupo had brought us a few nights ago and the children helped sweep the cave with brooms we had made from twigs collected from the forest.

Franco's face was one huge crooked grin when he returned, his eyes smiling with excitement where his scarred face could not.

He scratched in the dust of the cave floor, *INGLESI*, and held up both thumbs, gesturing us to follow him.

'We should be careful,' Mother Superior said. 'Only one person should accompany Franco. The rest must stay here.'

'Let me go,' Madre Caterina said.

'You can't,' I said, 'your cough would give you away if we need to hide and you're not strong enough. I'll go.'

After I kissed Giampiero, Franco and I crept warily down the forest path towards the sounds of vehicles and tramping feet. From the shelter of rocks, we watched a line of tanks and trucks camouflaged with netting and branches, and a long file of troops dressed in brown khaki progress along the road. Some of the men were bare chested, some bronzed from the scorching sun, while others were burned red on their pale skin. I noticed other soldiers with dark skin, some with long whiskers and wearing turbans on their heads, marching erectly, their rifles across their shoulders. 'Are those the Gurkhas and Sikh soldiers?' I asked Franco and he nodded, raising his thumb.

Franco rose to his feet, gesticulating at the men below and a shot whistled over our heads. I pulled him down and then he produced a grubby white handkerchief from his pocket to tie to the stick he'd used to climb down the hill and waved it above us from where we crouched. We scrambled down the path with difficulty, our hands raised above our heads in surrender.

We were confronted by a tall soldier with ginger hair and freckles sprinkled like paint splashes across his face. He was flanked by two other men, their rifles trained on us all the time. Franco held up his identity tag for them to see and the tall soldier peered at it, his eyes widened and then he pumped Franco's hand up and down, a broad smile on his face. Franco held up his hands to signify that there were more of us in the hills, pointing back to where we had come from.

I wanted to cry and shout and dance about with joy. Surely it meant that the war was over. When Silvio returned from whatever camp he was confined in, then we could be a family again. Maybe I was foolish, but I was still clinging to this notion. Hope is always the last thread to snap.

CHAPTER THIRTY-ONE

Events unfolded like one of those dreams from which you don't want to wake. The children were made a fuss of as they were lifted into the back of an army truck and their mouths were soon smeared with melting chocolate dished out by the smiling soldiers. Packets of cigarettes were given to the adults, whether we smoked or not. Franco was busy scribbling words on a notepad for one of the men sitting with us, his face animated, his lopsided grin making his face appear even wonkier than usual. We were driven to a spot near the river Sovara where a field hospital had been set up. I was very impressed. The *inglesi* had not been in our area for long, but they had already erected a large tent and I saw camp beds lined up neatly inside with several wounded men receiving attention. I couldn't help thinking that, with their help, I might be able to track down Silvio as these people seemed so efficient. And maybe Simonetta would turn up. I had to hold tight to Giampiero; he had scampered over with the other children to the soldier with the chocolate, and they all held out their little hands for more. I pulled him back and told him not to be greedy, but who could blame them? They had endured months of privation.

While we waited to be seen, I watched as Franco, now being called Frank by these soldiers, was treated with cheery kindness. A good-looking soldier who spoke Italian handed him a hot drink and Franco showed it to us: dark brown, like muddy soup. His face lit up and he held it as if it were a glass of precious wine.

The soldier introduced himself as Maurice and told us his mother was Italian. He said something to Franco and then translated for us: '*Il primo tè inglese da molto tempo.*' His first cuppa in a long time.

Maurice went off, reappearing with an armful of uniform and before long Franco looked like all the other *inglesi* in his khaki shorts and shirt. But he still wore his rubber boots. I think it was difficult to track down army leather boots large enough. More soldiers gathered around, thumping his back, exchanging jokes as they looked over to us. Our Franco was turning to Frank before our eyes and he looked like he belonged amongst these men.

A truck with a red cross painted on its wheel shields drew up and two stretchers were carefully lifted out, the first bearing an injured soldier, his head swathed in bloodstained bandages. A doctor examined the second and I saw him shake his head before leaning to close the man's eyes with his fingers. The dead man wore a turban and I remembered what Maria and Simonetta had told me about the bravery of these Asian soldiers. The *fascisti* had tried to spread terror about these men through propaganda posters. On the walls of our little town of Corbello, the *fascisti* had posted graphic images of black men grasping Italian girls, doubtless designed to put the fear of rape into our hearts. And yet, it was my own countrymen who had tried to do this to me only a few days ago. Even when the war was almost over, there were other posters bordered in red, desperately calling for Italians to fight with the *tedeschi* for the freedom of Italy. No wonder so many ordinary people were confused and disillusioned.

I watched as at least two more doctors, white coats over their uniforms, moved amongst the many wounded waiting on the ground, some in the shade, others under the full glare of the sun. I'd brought Madre Caterina to be examined. She had lost weight, the starburst of wrinkles that used to light up her smiling face had disappeared, her skin was stretched taut across her cheekbones. 'These young men are in more need than I am, Fosca,' she told me, gazing at the injured soldiers. Even as she spoke, she started to cough, bending over as she tried to catch her breath and a nurse came to talk to us and Maurice translated again. There was a hospital set up and more suited to civilians in the village up the road, he said, and I realised the male nurse was talking about Corbello.

We said our goodbyes to Franco, who scribbled down that he promised to come back to Italy to find us when the war was over. There were tears in his eyes as he kissed little Tommaso goodbye and I prayed that Franco would be spared more suffering.

Corbello was almost unrecognisable. I wanted to weep as I surveyed the wreckage. The little town had only just finished repairing damage from the devastating earthquake of 1917 when the war broke out. Two buildings remained fairly intact: one was the school where I had taught for so many years, together with the apartment where I had lived with Silvio and given birth to Giampiero. The other was the church, fragments of its windows scattered over fallen masonry, sparkling in the sun like coloured raindrops. The rest of the place resembled a pile of abandoned toy bricks, with townspeople clambering over the ruins searching for what they could salvage. The eleventh century watchtower that had proudly soared from the entrance to the castle stronghold town in the Middle Ages and which had been the proudest heritage of Corbello was also gone.

My school had been turned into a field hospital. I sat in the corridor with Madre Caterina, my little boy on my lap. This was where my pupils had once lined up before lessons and I felt a yearning to return once more to the life I had known as schoolmistress of Corbello. There were other civilians waiting. An elderly man and a pregnant woman. An old woman entered and I didn't recognise her. She was rail-thin, dressed in rags, her cheekbones prominent in her face, like the features of a wooden puppet.

'How can you have the audacity to return to Corbello?' she croaked when she saw me and then I realised who it was. Aurelia stared at me with such hatred in her eyes that I had to turn away.

'I shall come back tomorrow, when I hope you will be gone,' she said.

There was no kindness in her voice. No asking how I was, no acknowledgement of my beautiful child on my knee. I understood then that she still blamed me for the death of her sons. After she had gone, Madre Caterina grasped my hand. 'Poor woman, she is eaten up with sorrow. Fosca. Don't stay in this place, my child. Come back home with us to Sansepolcro as soon as the *tedeschi* abandon the city. There will be plenty of work for us to do down there.'

The doctors were all busy in the operating theatre and, while we waited, I recognised one of the stretcher-bearers as he carried in the latest casualty. It was Pasquale, the town's big blacksmith, and he raised his hand in greeting. He had helped me with odd jobs when I worked at the school, mending locks on the shutters or repairing the old metal stove we used in the classroom. I hoped I would get a chance to talk to him again; there was so much I wanted to ask, but we were called soon by a young *inglese* medical orderly who spoke a few old-fashioned words of Italian, as if he had consulted an antiquated travel guide. He was gentle with Giampiero and gave him a biscuit. These Englishmen were very different from the *tedeschi* who had marched in and plundered from us. The war wasn't over yet, but there was already a sense in the air that life might become easier. Madre Caterina was given penicillin for her chest infection and I took our straggling band of refugees to shelter down in the tobacco house. By that time our ears had grown used to the pounding of cannon fire from the big guns directed at Sansepolcro and we wondered if there would be anything left of that city. Half deaf, we grew used to shouting at each other over the sounds of battle, our ears ringing from the din, but we were safe enough where we were.

Days later, Pasquale rounded the bend, sounding the horn over and over on the tractor and trailer he'd unearthed from a farmer's barn. He brought welcome news.

'Sansepolcro is liberated!' he shouted. 'Gather your belongings, sisters. It's time to return. Your carriage awaits.'

As we chugged away from Corbello, avoiding bomb craters in the main road, I averted the children's eyes from gutted army lorries and bombed houses by telling them stories. My mouth came out with all manner of ideas, to distract them from broken bodies lying in ditches or beneath crushed vehicles. Flies buzzed everywhere.

'Look at the fiery sycamores. And those puffy clouds. What pictures can you see in them, children? Maybe dragons or ice cream?' I said.

As we entered the city, at each side of the gate, the American and British flags fluttered a victory welcome. In the streets, British tanks were draped with their own flags, and children clambered up to sit on the bodywork, joining with *partigiani* come down from the mountains to celebrate. I strained my eyes to see if Simonetta was amongst them, but she was nowhere to be seen. Lupo waved at us and we waved back. People lined the streets, waving and shouting at the troops, who returned the greetings. *'Evviva gli inglesi,'* they shouted and we joined in. I think we believed the war was at an end. But there was more to come.

CHAPTER THIRTY-TWO

For those few weeks that the *inglesi* occupied Sansepolcro, life in our little city became almost bearable. There were times when I felt guilty and I thought of the *partigiani* who had returned to fight for us in the mountains. Still clinging to the hope that he was alive, I wondered in which camp Silvio might be. Was he perhaps in Germany? There were reports about the terrible conditions in the labour camps over there. Gobbi had spun me rubbish about him being in the camp near Corbello, using me to gain access to Simonetta and the others. I would never forgive him for leading me down that path.

Occasionally, dances were laid on at the Dante Theatre. The *inglesi* soldiers were starved of female company. Sansepolcro began to be nicknamed by the locals as the *'nido d'amore'* – the nest of love, and many local girls fell for *inglesi*. I was invited more than once to come along. Even Madre Caterina tried to encourage me. 'You're young, Fosca. You don't need to spend your evenings with nuns and children. We will take care of Giampiero – go out and enjoy yourself.' But I didn't want to. I missed Silvio. One day, I told myself, he will turn up out of the blue and life will return to normal. His image smiled at me from his frame on my bedside table in the nun's cell that Giampiero and I shared, lying top to tail in our narrow bed.

One Saturday afternoon, just before the *inglesi* pulled out of Sansepolcro, I stood with Giampiero and the children to watch a football match. The *biturgense* team, as the citizens of Sansepolcro call themselves, was doing better than usual against the *inglesi*.

They had a new striker. I didn't recognise him at first. Lupo's long hair was shorter and, dressed in his football kit of shorts and shirt, he was more presentable than the scruffy partisan leader I knew. Roberto and Ria jumped up and down, urging their uncle on: '*Zio, zio. Forza zio,*' whenever he gained possession. When he scored the winning goal, hats were thrown in the air, people hugged each other and we had to stop the children from running onto the pitch. Lupo stayed until evening, sharing supper with us instead of celebrating with his fellow players and helped settle the twins at bedtime.

The nuns always retired early but I sat up with Piero in the convent kitchen. I kept wanting to call him Lupo – his real name was alien to me – but I knew this was dangerous. The war was not yet over; he was still working with the *partigiani*, and scouting for the *inglesi*. The *tedeschi* were occupying the Gothic Line, holding back the advance of the allies on the mountains above Sansepolcro and the *partigiani* were indispensable for local knowledge: information about the geography, footpaths, contacts. But there were still fascist sympathisers in the city, ready to report the whereabouts of army deserters as they were described, despite the fact that most young Italians had long since abandoned loyalty to Mussolini.

The brief interlude of happiness on the football pitch forgotten, Lupo was tetchy. He asked me to prepare strong coffee, handing over a bag of real coffee grains from his knapsack. 'Keep the rest,' he said when I accepted it, my eyes rounding in surprise at the rare sight.

'I can't remember the last time I *saw* real coffee, let alone tasted it,' I said, sniffing the intoxicating aroma. 'Where did you find this?'

'Let's just say it was a favour extracted from somebody who didn't deserve it in his house.'

'Should you be drinking strong coffee?' I asked him. 'You're already very *nervoso*. It will make your mood worse.'

He smiled at me. 'You sound like a wife, Fosca.'

I was embarrassed at this comment and turned to compact grains into the Moka coffee pot with the back of a spoon, to hide my blush.

'General Alexander has ordered the *partigiani* to stand down over the coming winter, but we are not listening to him,' Lupo said, his voice raised as he continued. 'We have done so much for the allies, but they continue not to trust us. They are afraid communism will take a hold in our country. We've noticed a steady decline in the air drops and less willingness to engage with us.'

'Why should the allies tell us what to do in our own country?' I asked.

'*Esatto*. They treat us as their tools instead of proper fighters. They are more interested in beating the *tedeschi* than in what Italia needs. When we win this war' – he looked at me, his eyes piercing – 'I repeat *when*, Fosca, then the allies will depart and if we are not careful, *fascismo* will creep back into our lives. The *bastardi* are like bacteria that never dies. Many powerful industrialists and bigwigs who favoured Mussolini are waiting to pounce when the time comes.'

He drew his fingers through his hair and I felt sorry for him. He and other young men and women had sacrificed so much over the past months to help liberate our country. I leant from my chair to squeeze his hand and he held on to it while he continued to speak. 'But we will show them what we are made of. We are far more organised than the *alleati* give us credit. Without our help, the war will drag on longer. Mark my words.'

The coffee started to bubble over onto the stove and I pulled my hand away, busying myself with pouring the delicious liquid into two cups. I didn't mind if the coffee kept me awake. I had missed the company of Simonetta and the others since I'd been closeted in the convent, cushioned from what was happening in the real world. It was good to be with Lupo again.

'Why don't you take me to the post-match dance in the Teatro Dante?' I said, surprising myself at my spontaneity. 'The *inglesi* invite me often, but I never accept. I reckon you would move better on the dance floor.'

As I dressed for the dance, tutting at my scrawny appearance in the only dress I owned, Giampiero tugged at my hand. 'You look *bella*, Mamma. What shall I wear to the party?'

I crouched down beside him and hugged him close. 'This is a dance for grown-ups, *tesoro*. There won't be other children there tonight.'

His little mouth turned down and I scooped him up into my arms and twirled round and round, humming a tune. 'But we can dance together now, my little one.'

He clung on to me as we spun round, the dimples in his cheeks deep as he smiled, his laughter like music in our little room. I loved him so much and longed for Silvio to see him before he grew out of babyhood. Giampiero's foot caught the framed photo as I waltzed and it crashed to the floor, the glass smashing into pieces.

'Stay there,' I told him, as I put him down on the bed. 'I don't want you to cut yourself.'

A splinter pierced my finger as I picked the pieces up, and blood spotted my dress.

The theatre was packed with *inglesi*, cigarette and pipe smoke clouding the space where chairs had been pushed away. Women were outnumbered by at least three to one, and as Lupo and I entered, a soldier caught hold of me and whisked me into a dance. As I moved in time to the music, trying to keep my distance from the keen soldier, I looked over to Lupo and pulled a face, hoping he would get the message and rescue me by tapping on the young man's shoulder for the next number, but he winked and moved towards a line of men. In one corner, a trestle table had been erected and men clustered around large flasks of wine. On the stage, a band of half a dozen *inglesi* and a blonde performed a pacey tune. The *inglese* I was dancing with stepped on my feet more than once as he flung me about and I was relieved when it was over, and moved away to search for Lupo.

'I don't think the pair of you will win any competitions,' he said, when I found him. He handed me a tumbler of wine, his face lit up in a cheeky grin, his deep brown eyes flashing with mischief. The wine was unpleasantly bitter but I was thirsty and I drank the sour liquid.

The band left the stage for a break and an Italian couple took over. I recognised their song from the first bars. It had come out when Silvio and I were together.

'If you think you can dance better than that *inglese*, then show me,' I said to Lupo, the wine making me bold. We left our beakers on a table and he pulled me onto the floor. The song was a light-hearted rock and roll, saucy and poignant at the same time, and Lupo sang to me as we spun around. *'Baciami, piccina,'* he crooned, a grin on his face as he repeated the chorus line, 'kiss me, little one.'

He was a good dancer and singer and I was enjoying myself. I had never known him outside of a war situation but he was a good-looking man and while we danced, we became two breathless, ordinary young people intent on enjoying ourselves, the war in the distance. By the time the song finished, we were the only couple left on the dance floor, everybody else standing back to watch us. The carefree moments while we danced had taken me back to the weeks before Silvio had disappeared. There was a round of applause from the other dancers and when I understood that it was for us, I buried my face in Lupo's shoulder out of embarrassment.

But there were to be no more dances that evening. Instead of the band striking up again, a wail of sirens sounded like the savage cries of wounded animals. The whole theatre had to be vacated. Once we were outside, Lupo took my hand and we ran to the nearest place of shelter in the cloisters beside the cathedral.

Hunched together against the clammy walls, the frescoes gloomy in the subdued light of a flickering candle, I worried about Giampiero.

'The nuns will look after him. They will be sheltering in the cellars with the *inglesi*,' Lupo reassured me. 'They'll be serving their tea and sandwiches to everybody. Don't worry, *piccina*.' He had adopted the endearment of little one from the song and alarm bells sounded in my head. There was no way I wanted to lead him on. It was the moment I had enjoyed, I told myself: not dancing in his arms.

The noise of artillery fire distracted me from my concerns and I held my breath, waiting for the sounds of explosions. I began to tremble and Lupo took hold of my hand again, squeezing it hard. Although I had given up on prayer, I asked God to protect my son, promising I would do anything He asked of me, anything at all – if only Giampiero could be spared.

The brain-juddering crash told of a fallen missile. The sound of stones tumbling, a draught and then the candle flickering beneath the statue of Saint Benedict blew out. We stayed in darkness until the gunfire ceased and then we picked our way back to the convent through fires and rubble. The sky was like the mottled peel of a blood orange as we joined in a human chain, passing buckets of water to douse flames. I knelt to help a desperate woman pulling bricks and sticks of furniture from the ruins of a house. 'My baby, my baby,' she cried over and over.

An elderly man whispered that her baby could not possibly be underneath. '*Povera donna*, poor woman. She lost her baby last year. Leave the stones, *signori*. Leave them. I will take care of her.' We watched as he pulled her up, supporting her as they stumbled away from the devastation.

Back at the convent, we found the children safe in the cellar just as Lupo had said, tucked up with the nuns and a handful of convalescing *inglesi* soldiers drinking hot tea. I gathered Giampiero into my arms and kissed his soft head.

Lupo left not long afterwards and hugged me when he said goodbye. '*Arrivederci*, Fosca, I have work to do,' he whispered. I wondered if we would see each other again.

That winter of 1944 was harsh. The *inglesi* pulled out of town to advance up the mountains. Food was in short supply, but we improvised. Chickpeas were ground to make a coffee drink, people swapped favours: if you had extra oil, you exchanged it with somebody who had too much flour. But even that stopped as time went on. When you are hungry, all you can think about is food. There was no time to wonder where Silvio was as I concentrated on our survival. One day, we were amazed to be presented with half a dozen withered oranges by a rich relative of one of the nuns. We peeled the rind, shared the segments, so that each of us enjoyed the taste and then the children, still hungry, ate the peel. Some of the younger ones had never tasted an orange before and didn't know any better.

Deep snow closed mountain roads where *partigiani* and the *alleati* were holed up, waiting to forge through the defensive line held by the *tedeschi*. We tried to make a game of the snow at first, throwing snowballs with the children, building snowmen in the cloister gardens but the children were listless through hunger and it was too cold to enjoy these pastimes. Our clothes were patched and thin; there was little or no fuel to light the stoves to warm their skinny bodies. All the beautiful plane trees in the piazza had been felled for timber and any precious fuel we could scavenge was needed for the cooking stove. We began to chop up chairs and tables in the disused rooms for firewood. The landscape beyond the town walls was desolate: dead animals, tree stumps and trenches in the fields punctuated a scene haunted by death.

A plane fell from the sky a couple of weeks before Christmas and, despite warnings from the militia to keep clear of the wreck, the carcass was picked clean of anything useful: leather from the seats was cut off to patch boots, the crew's bomber jackets were fought over by a pack of desperate women, the fleecy linings highly prized against the cold.

And then the hunters, the young men and women who had fought against the *fascisti*, became the hunted. Anybody wearing red was immediately arrested by the militia on suspicion of being a communist and nobody knew whom to trust. The nuns took in more orphans, and our already small portions were shared out. Madre Caterina was in charge of the kitchen and I knew she continued to deny herself, dishing out watery soup to the children and sharing thin slices of black bread. The plump figure from my childhood was unrecognisable, her face gaunt, her hip bones protruding beneath her habit. Her cough had still not cleared up but not once did she complain. I made sure to keep her company when I could and started to give lessons in the relative warmth of the kitchen. Despite her spectral appearance, the children loved her and presented her with all kinds of gifts: the remains of a bird's nest, a bunch of ivy flowers, or the seeds of capers that grew on the bombed city walls. Giampiero drew picture after picture of houses for her. His pictures were of ruins where people slept under roofs patched with tarpaulins. But there was always food on the table, sketched in detail: bowls of shining red apples, cakes, whole cheeses, jugs of milk. 'Show me how to draw a dish of roast chicken, Mamma,' he asked me one afternoon. 'And what colour are sausages? Are they delicious?' I bit my lip to stop my tears and wondered how much longer this hell would continue.

On 25 April 1945 it was my twenty-fifth birthday. The blossom would normally have covered the fruit trees that had been cut down for firewood in the winter. That morning, the bells in the city started to ring. At first, we thought this was another warning and, once again, we moved to the cellars. But then we heard shouting. It wasn't the usual shouting of fear. We heard people shout, '*Evviva, evviva, la guerra è finita.*' We stayed there for a while, still not trusting our ears. Was it a trick? Could the war really be over? The sounds of footsteps and laughter preceded the arrival down the cellar steps of a pair of shapely female legs, their owner wearing a white dress. She stood at the bottom calling to us to bring the children out into the fresh air. A red belt and green hat finished off her patriotic outfit, but it was the boots of her companion that I noticed first: boots tied with odd laces. Lupo followed her down into the cellar. 'It's over,' he shouted, as his niece and nephew flung their arms around his legs. He tousled the children's hair and smiled at me. 'It really is over, Fosca.' I flung myself into his arms and we climbed together up to the watery sunshine.

Sansepolcro was a dazzle of light and noise that evening. We had lived in gloom for years, windows blacked against bomb raids, carrying out tasks under the dim glow of candles and paraffin lamps. Now as celebrations continued until deep in the night, it seemed that every light that ever existed blazed out to expel darkness. Impromptu gatherings sprung up in all quarters of the city, tables were dragged out, bottles of hidden wine and grappa unearthed and on each street corner there was a party. A melee of music lifted above the damaged buildings, causing dogs to howl as accordion players enticed couples to dance. A singer performed arias from his balcony; children chased each other in the tangles of dancers in the little *piazze* round the town. Not everyone was happy. There were the old, the confused, the bereaved, those who couldn't trust that peace had finally arrived, those who were too weary and had little energy to be joyful. But most people grabbed this moment with hungry hearts.

And this time when Madre Caterina urged me to go and dance, and promised that Giampiero would be safe with her, I accepted. I danced with anybody who asked me: with old women and men, the years dropping from them as they remembered steps danced since they were small. I danced with young men who pulled me too close, with girls who were waiting to be asked by boys, with a priest whose soutane flapped against my legs as he spun me round in a polka. I danced on my own as the stars came out to prick the sky. I twirled and twirled, my arms hugged around me when the world grew dizzy. I grew drunk from dancing, so that when I heard a familiar voice call, and his arms crept around me, I clutched on as I fell against Lupo and he guided me giddily round the streets.

Everywhere was thronged with crowds, men and women packed close and so it was only natural that we should hold each other too. He smelled of sweat and courage, his clothes were filthy and he told me he'd come straight from the mountains to celebrate. We danced until we could dance no more. In the hour before dawn, we walked arm in arm like old friends to the convent.

'I'm exhausted,' I told him, 'but I'm afraid if I go to sleep, when I wake up it will all have been a dream and tomorrow the war will continue.'

'Well, spend the rest of the night awake with me,' he said, pulling me down beside him.

We sat on the convent steps, dipped and worn from the tread of hundreds of feet, our backs against huge chestnut doors, their surfaces pitted and stained with age. There were notches on the frame left by tramps: symbols left by vagrants for each other, a signal that this place welcomed strangers. I ran my finger along the grooves.

'I was left here as a baby,' I told Lupo, who was yawning now, his eyes threatening to close with fatigue.

'And will you stay here for the rest of your life, Fosca?'

'Of course not.'

He turned to me and took my hands. 'We could be good together, you and I. With our ready-made family. My niece and nephew and your son. Three children who need a mother and a father. What do you say, *cara* Fosca?'

I frowned and gently withdrew my hands. 'Such a strange thing to say. I already have a husband. Silvio.'

He shrugged and rubbed the stubble on his chin. 'Why are you kidding yourself that he is still alive?' he asked eventually.

And as he spoke those words, I knew that he was right. He had been right all along. Simonetta had told me Silvio was dead and I had believed her at the time, but Gobbi had cruelly made me hope otherwise. I leant back on the steps, my tears falling.

'I'm sorry, Fosca.'

I shook my head, angrily wiping my face. 'If I could have only seen his body, Lupo, then maybe I wouldn't have clung on to my dream. And when Gobbi told me that he was alive…'

'What are you talking about?'

'He warned me not to say anything to anyone. That it would jeopardise my chances of seeing Silvio again if I spoke about it.'

'I don't understand.'

I sighed. 'He told me that Silvio was up at the camp near Corbello and I hoped when the German major and Gennaro were released, Silvio would be freed with them. But he wasn't there. All that time he wasn't there.'

He took my hand again and I let him hold it. 'Silvio died before my own eyes,' he told me. 'I thought you knew that. They hung his body up afterwards.'

I spoke through my sobs. 'Deep down, I think I knew it too. But I didn't want it to be true. And when somebody throws you a possibility, then you believe what you want to believe.'

There was silence between us. It was a relief to finally admit it: Silvio was not coming back. Giampiero was all that mattered now.

'Now is the time to rebuild your life, Fosca.' Lupo moved nearer, his arm around my shoulder and I leant into him. 'You're a beautiful woman. An excellent mother. You're a good person, and I'm not such a bad fellow when push comes to shove. We could build something together for these three children. Am I such a bad man that you think my offer of marriage is a ridiculous idea?'

'Where is love in all this, Lupo?' I pulled away from him.

He made a derisory noise. 'Pah! Love! Tell me what love is.'

'If you can't tell me what love is, then you haven't experienced it. My husband would have climbed to fetch the moon from the sky for me if he'd thought it would make me happy. That is what a woman wants to know about her man, Lupo; that he loves her to distraction.'

I started to rise as I said this and he jumped to his feet to help pull me up. 'At least consider my idea, Fosca.'

'Good night, Lupo. We're both over-tired. Maybe you will see things differently when you wake up.' I pushed open the doors to the convent. 'Thanks for dancing with me.' I paused. 'And thanks for your honesty.'

'When can I see you again?' he asked.

'Leave it for a while, Lupo. Let things settle down.'

I needed hot coffee to face the new day, so I went to the kitchen. Madre Caterina was already up, a spotless white apron tied around her thin waist. She took one look at my tear-streaked face and opened her arms to me as I sobbed my heart out.

'Silvio is dead,' I said. 'I know that now. How I wish we could have celebrated this day together.'

I stayed in her arms until I was calmer. Then we sat at the kitchen table, drinking coffee.

'What a night,' I said. 'And to top it all, I had the strangest of proposals.' I was hungry and cut another slice from the fresh rye loaf that she had baked. 'Lupo thinks we should marry.'

She smiled. 'And what do you think?'

'I think a couple of dances is not the same as spending a lifetime together.'

'You could do worse. He's a good man.'

'I don't want another husband,' I told her. 'Nobody can ever replace Silvio. And I won't marry simply to provide a father for Giampiero. We'll manage on our own.'

'And do you plan to stay here in the convent with him for the rest of your life?'

'That is exactly what Lupo asked me.'

'And?'

'And nothing. I'm not sure yet. I would love to get back my teaching job in Corbello but if you will have us a little while longer, then I'd be happy to stay. And now that the war is finished, I intend to pay my way. You've all been too kind for far too long.'

'You can't keep running away, Fosca,' Madre Caterina said. 'By rights that teaching job you studied so hard to attain, it should be yours. You should fight to get it back.'

She started to cough, turning to brace herself by hanging on to the stone sink and I watched her in concern, her shoulder blades obvious through the thinning material of her habit. When she was at last able to speak, she grasped my hands in her own, her veins showing blue through papery skin. 'It's not good for you to stay cloistered here. And it's not good for Giampiero either. He needs to be out in the world, learning about life. Don't waste these years.'

I vowed there and then that I would prove to myself as well as Madre Caterina that I was not a coward. But thinking about a situation and rustling up the courage to return to an atmosphere of hatred, where nobody wanted me, was quite another thing.

CHAPTER THIRTY-THREE

1947

'And so that was that,' Fosca told Richard. 'The war officially ended on 2 May. Giampiero and I stayed on with the nuns, while I helped provide schooling for our orphans, but it was never my intention to stay there forever. Before I knew it, nearly two years had passed. I'd spun out our return journey to Corbello, dreading my reception. I was hoping the tobacco house would still be empty so that I could prepare myself. When I felt the time was right and I was stronger, I would present myself in the little town. But you know how it was. You were here to greet me, Richard.'

Before Richard could comment, Giampiero ran into the kitchen, rubbing sleep from his eyes and Fosca pulled him onto her lap.

'I'm honoured that you shared your story with me, Fosca,' Richard said, leaning forward, his elbows resting on his knees. 'You've been through so much.'

'Others experienced worse. But I have to say, finding Simonetta and the gold has brought it all back again.' She sighed. 'Out of sight, out of mind, I suppose. I'm ashamed to say that I have pushed it all to the back of my mind. It was too painful. But now, with Simonetta being found, I can't avoid it any longer.' She hoisted Giampiero onto her hip. 'It's very late. I've taken up so much of your time. I'm sorry. I'd better get this little scamp back into bed.'

An owl hooted nearby and Richard looked up at mother and child. 'We'll talk again in the morning. *Buona notte*, Fosca. I hope you can manage to sleep.'

'*Buona notte*, Richard.'

Richard watched them enter the little house and he pulled out his pipe for the final smoke of the day. He saw her in a completely different light from the timid, bedraggled young woman who had turned up a few weeks earlier. He felt protective of this brave young woman, and, if he was honest with himself, he was beginning to feel a whole lot more besides. She reminded him a little of himself in the way she tried to present a courageous face to the world. An idea occurred to him to help Fosca in her quest to find out about Simonetta. He tore a fresh sheet from his notebook that was always at his side and started to draft a letter.

They shared a late breakfast, Richard introducing the English way of toasting *toscano* bread over the fire. Rosa had sent down a couple of jars of her peach jam and it went down well with a pot of strong coffee.

'I didn't sleep immediately,' he told her after Giampiero had got down and scampered outside to play on the smaller hammock that Richard had erected next to his. 'My mind was racing with everything you told me.'

'Me too. There are so many missing pieces to my story and I won't rest until I find out what happened to my friend. I don't know where to begin. But I do know that whatever happened, I owe it to her to find out. She told me she wanted revenge. She's gone. It's up to me now.'

'Let's think, Fosca, and try to formulate a plan of action. Will you let me help you?' He poured more coffee for himself but Fosca declined. 'I think we should first try to find out the whereabouts of this German major,' Richard continued. 'Thinking aloud: the last time you saw Simonetta was after the attack on the train when the gold was taken, wasn't it?'

Fosca nodded.

'Your German major and Gobbi were heavily involved in taking that gold from the train and to me it all hinges around that central point. These three elements, the gold found here near Simonetta's corpse and what we know about those two men, they're all too much of a coincidence to ignore. For some reason, the major spared you when you were caught spying up at the camp. He seems a soft touch to me. And it shouldn't be too difficult to track him down, I wouldn't think. Gobbi's wife, Magdalena, she told me about an English captain she had worked with back when I was buying this place. It was he who took charge of prisoners and resettlement at the end of the war. There will have been a record kept of the German prisoners rounded up, where and when they were shipped back. I'll see what I can do. For starters, I've drafted a letter to one of my pacifist friends in England and asked him to do some investigating for us. What was the major's full name? Can you remember?'

'Hansen,' she said, pronouncing the h with difficulty like all Italians, and he checked with her, writing the name in his notebook and holding it up for her to see.

She nodded. '*Grazie*, Richard. Our wonderful Mayor Gobbi,' she said with sarcasm, 'is somebody I could confront. He and the major were like this.' Fosca held up two fingers, one on top of each other. 'Who will believe that the mayor of Corbello is a thief and a murderer?' Fosca said.

'We have to prove that first, Fosca. Aren't you jumping to conclusions? Hold off with that.'

'But I feel it in here…' she said, punching her heart. 'I can at least try to contact Lupo to see if he has any ideas about what might have happened to Simonetta. He's an elusive man but I'm sure Pasquale will know how to get hold of him. If we all put our heads together, maybe we can come up with a plan.'

'Gorilla is a mine of information.'

When she looked puzzled, he laughed. 'It's the name I gave Pasquale when I met him during the war.'

She laughed too. 'And of course Lupo is really Piero but I still call him Lupo. All these disguises we hid behind! My only nickname was Tosca, because I *couldn't* sing. What about you?'

Richard shook his head. It was too complicated to explain what Dickhead meant in Italian and it was nothing he particularly wanted to share. Some things didn't translate well.

A few days later Pasquale brought Lupo down to the tobacco house. Richard had popped up to Corbello for groceries when the two men arrived.

'This is almost like old times,' Lupo said, leaning back in his chair, his legs stretched beneath the kitchen table. 'So, can we trust this *inglese*?' he asked.

'What do you mean trust? Why should we have to trust him?' Fosca said.

'I mean, how much should we tell him of what happened in the past?'

'I have told him everything I know already. And Richard was the one who found the gold in the well. Naturally I told him about the attack on the train too. I couldn't avoid telling him. The gold was found on his own property. It was his right to know.'

'He's a good man, Lupo,' Pasquale said. 'I knew him during the war when I helped at the *ospedale* for the *inglesi*. He's not a troublemaker. Richard is a pacifist.'

Lupo made a sucking noise with his teeth. 'One of those who can't make up their minds. Conveniently sitting on the fence.'

'I think it takes courage to refuse to fight for something you don't believe in and to go against the herd,' Fosca said, wiping the table, sweeping Lupo's hands away with her wet cloth.

'If nobody fought, if we hadn't "gone against the herd", as you put it, then right now we would be living under *tedeschi* rule in our own country,' Lupo retorted. 'And the *inglesi* weren't much help in the end either, as it happens. They told us what to do in our own country. *Porca miseria!* We were far more organised than they gave us credit for. We do not need help from this *inglese* now either.'

'This is indeed like old times,' Pasquale said. 'Squabbling. I hoped we had moved on.'

'I know what you mean, Pasquale,' Fosca said. 'We all know the war has ended. But I can't settle until I find out what happened to Simonetta. I need to find out why she died. We surely owe her that much.'

The roar of Richard's motorbike interrupted their discussion, and Lupo mumbled, 'I still don't see why we have to involve this *inglese*.'

'I told you, he's involved already,' Fosca answered. 'He wants to help and maybe he will have more perspective than us. Listen to him before you make up your mind.'

Richard took off his helmet before removing the groceries he had picked up from Corbello. In addition to fresh bread and pecorino cheese, there were jars of olives and home-bottled artichoke hearts that Rosa had given him from her larder. Giampiero had gone along for the ride and fallen asleep in the sidecar on the way back, despite being bumped up and down, and Richard wheeled the bike under the dappled shade of the olive tree to protect the child from the sun.

Fosca came over. 'They're here, Richard. Come and meet Piero, otherwise known as Lupo.' She took the shopping and followed him into the house after checking on Giampiero in the sidecar. Her heart missed a beat as she saw how he was losing his chubby baby looks. His features were beginning to resemble Silvio's, especially his little nose.

Back in the house she was conscious of Lupo's scrutiny of Richard as the *inglese* greeted Pasquale with a hearty handshake. Lupo didn't extend his hand but nodded a brief '*Buongiorno.*'

'So, you found gold in your well,' Pasquale said.

'Indeed. Fosca told me about the attack on the train too. It's the stuff of adventure stories.'

Lupo made a disparaging noise. 'It is the stuff of war.'

'We know where the gold most likely came from,' Pasquale begun.

'But exactly how it ended up in the well is another matter,' Lupo said.

'And whether Simonetta knew about it, is what I need to find out,' Fosca said.

'If that will ever be possible, Fosca.' There was warning in Lupo's voice.

'But as the gold was found on your property, you have a right to know more too, signor Richard,' Fosca said, glaring at Lupo.

'Well, let's share this food and wine while we discuss how to proceed,' Richard said as he fetched glasses. Fosca sliced the fresh ciabatta while Pasquale and Lupo waited, the latter watching with a grim look on his face at the scene of domesticity in this old building that had once served as a *partigiani* meeting place.

'I told Richard what went on here and he has offered to help us trace the *tedesco* major by writing a letter to a friend in England,' Fosca said. She retrieved the gold bar from its hiding place behind a small sack of salt in the niche in the hearth. The former *partigiani* handled it in turn, murmuring at its weight.

'No way should Gobbi get wind you have found it until we've done some more sleuthing,' Lupo said. 'He's a greedy *bastardo*. I put him in the category of all the other *bastardi* who escaped justice at the end of the war. All those *nazifascisti* who were let off to protect the country because the authorities feared a Soviet coup d'état.'

Richard had sympathy for this. 'Like Kesselring's punishment, which was reverted from a death sentence. The argument that he was a good soldier was sickening. He instigated many massacres here. But war is never just, in my opinion.'

'Don't forget that Gobbi helped us acquire guns from the train and turned a blind eye more than once on our meetings as well as helping us on several occasions to acquire false documents,' Pasquale, ever the peacemaker, said.

'Pah!' was Lupo's response. 'The man infiltrated us in order to save his own skin because he knew the war was coming to an end and he quickly changed his politics. He's a greasy *bastardo*.'

'What's a *bastardo*, Mamma?' Giampiero asked. He had slipped in during the talk and was chewing on a heel of loaf.

'You'll find out sooner or later, *ragazzo*,' Lupo said, his chair scraping against the flagstones as he got up to leave. 'You'll let me know what you find out, *inglese*? From this letter you plan to send about the major?' He pulled his cap on and lifted his hand in a farewell. '*Alla prossima!* Until the next time.'

Fosca walked out with him to his truck, Giampiero clinging to her hand.

'When will I see Roberto and Ria again?' the little boy asked.

'Whenever your mamma invites us,' Lupo said, looking pointedly at Fosca.

'As soon as we have a place of our own, you will all be welcome,' she said.

'You know that you could have a place of your own with me tomorrow.'

'Please, Mamma,' Giampiero said, tugging on her hand. 'I miss them so much. I want them to come and play.'

'I'll keep you informed, Lupo. *Arrivederci.* Come on, Giampiero. I have to clear up and then we'll go up to Corbello to visit Angelina and Rosa.'

'Informed about coming to stay with me, or what the *inglese* finds out?' Lupo said as he tipped his cap, his gaze lingering on Fosca a little while longer than she wanted before he turned to stride away. She noticed that, despite the new trousers and shirt he wore, he was still wearing the boots with odd laces and she shook her head.

Clearing up did not take long and Pasquale offered to drive Fosca and Giampiero to visit Rosa, but she declined. 'We will walk. It will do us both good and Giampiero slept most of the afternoon. He needs tiring out if he is ever going to get to bed tonight. *Grazie.* I'll see you later. Tell Rosa I'm willing to help in the dining room if she needs me.'

After he'd gone, Giampiero asked to play for a while on the hammock and Fosca sat on the poetry seat, as she had begun to call it, deep in thought as she watched him.

'Penny for them,' Richard said, from where he was digging a new bed. 'Although I think I know what's going on in your head. Simonetta, right?'

She nodded. 'It's her funeral next week, but it will be unfinished business until I find out how she died.'

'I will do what I can to help, Fosca, but…' he said, before pausing. 'Have you thought, as Lupo said, that you might never find out? That closure could be a problem? When my grandfather died, my mother was distraught. He had brought her up on his own when her mother died young. Somebody told her, "Grieve not that he is gone, only rejoice that he was." She embroidered those words on a sampler and kept it in a frame above our living room mantlepiece. I've never forgotten the wisdom of those words.'

'Words,' she said. 'At the moment I need more than words, Richard.'

He said nothing and then she apologised. 'I'm sorry. You mean well. And… I know that words are important to you. You love to write.'

'Yes. Writing helps me make sense of the world. Seeing words on paper is a kind of affirmation. My father wanted me to concentrate on teaching. He thought I was wasting my time writing, that I was an idler. Some people paint or take photographs, but I write.'

They watched Giampiero swing beneath the olives, sunlight dancing and dappling on his little head as the hammock moved the branches of silvery leaves.

'You should prune those trees before winter,' she said.

'You have such good ideas about the land, Fosca. I can learn from you. And… I would like to learn more Italian. One day I should like to be able to read those Italian poems we picked up in Arezzo.'

'Certainly I can help you with your Italian. You already speak it quite well.'

'Maybe we can read some poems together?'

'We can try.'

'By the way, I sent the letter to that pacifist friend of mine this morning. I remembered the name of the man that Gobbi's wife mentioned, the one who resettled prisoners at the end of the war: Captain William Graham. I had to wrack my brains to remember but then it came to me. Fingers crossed I didn't get it wrong and that it wasn't Captain Graham William. Anyway, this pal of mine is a bright chap and should hopefully be able to do some digging around for us. Maybe we'll be able to track down this Major Hansen and ask him if there's anything he remembers about Simonetta.'

'*Grazie*, Richard. Any piece of information that helps is good.'

Richard was a kind man, Fosca thought as she sat watching him work. After their discussion with Pasquale and Lupo, she felt that together, they were on the brink of something.

Simonetta's funeral was a sorry affair, with a handful of mourners: herself, Lupo, Pasquale, and the acrobats Primo and Secondo. Fosca hardly recognised them in their neat suits. They placed knotted red kerchiefs over her coffin next to a spray of white roses that Fosca had picked. The priest rushed through the service. He didn't know Simonetta and nothing in his words bore any relevance to her, Fosca thought. Simonetta wasn't even Simonetta. She was a Jewish Italian with the real name of Natalia. Maria would have known that. The nuns would have said that the two women were together now and Fosca thought it would be comforting to cling to such a belief.

She blocked out the words intoned by the little priest and in her head, she offered silent thoughts for the girl she'd known during the war. It was a conversation rather than a prayer and she pictured herself sitting cross-legged, talking to Simonetta in the hayloft in the house at the edge of Sansepolcro. Her friend wore her ragtag of garments and her unruly hair was tied back in two thick plaits. Fosca thought about the way she was so dainty with her tiny feet and pretty features – and yet so tomboyish with her scarred hands and the way she stood when she was adamant about something: her legs akimbo, her arms folded against her skinny chest. She pictured her leaping across the roofs of Anghiari like a young boy, scaling ladders and trees, or crouched down in the undergrowth to spy on the enemy. She remembered her courage, her kindness, the little gifts she produced on her visits. And she vowed with all her heart to Simonetta that her story would not end here in this church, propped up by scaffolding and metal poles, the cracks in the walls secured with tie-bars, like sticking plaster over wounds.

At the last minute, the door to the church creaked open on its old hinges and she turned to see Bruno enter and sit at the back. For this she was grateful, but at the end of the service, when she would have approached him to talk, he had already disappeared. There was no wake and Fosca, Lupo and the acrobats stood alone as Simonetta's body was interred afterwards in the cemetery down the hill. As the last sod of earth was thrown on top of the mound, Lupo stood to attention and pulled a revolver from his pocket to fire three shots in the air, scattering ravens who were perched on the walls of the cemetery like vultures, the flapping of their wings and the *kraa kraa* of their calls a ghastly chorus-ending to the event.

CHAPTER THIRTY-FOUR

Fosca had still received no word about the teaching post and when she went to knock on the door of Gobbi's office in the *comune*, there was a notice saying that he was away, at a conference in Arezzo.

'He won't be back until the end of next week,' his secretary told her, trying to conceal a *Grazia* magazine beneath a pile of envelopes. 'Can I take a message, signora?'

'No, *grazie*. I will speak to him personally.'

Annoyed that she would have to wait to talk to the elusive Gobbi, she decided to pay a long overdue visit to Madre Caterina.

Richard offered to drop her and Giampiero at the bus stop for the journey into the city. She had baked the nun's favourite *cantuccini* and soft almond *amaretti* and Giampiero had drawn a picture of the tobacco house where they were living. It was a sign of progress, Fosca thought, that the image was child-like, free of gaping holes in the roof or possessions strewn amidst bleeding bodies on the ground. He had scribbled in a dog sitting at the door at the last minute and looked up with determination at his mother, saying, 'Because one day we shall have one, won't we, Mamma?'

'We'll see,' was her answer. Although she felt more settled, this was Richard's house, not theirs. The future was uncertain and acquiring a dog was not on her list.

Mother and child clambered out of Richard's sidecar as the Sansepolcro *corriere* lumbered towards them where they had pulled in by the bus stop.

'It would be so easy for me to run you into the city,' Richard said. 'Are you sure you want to take the bus?'

'*Certissima*. Really sure. It will be Giampiero's first ride and you have plenty to do. We'll see you later.'

Richard was at long last busily renovating the inside of the tower. The openings for the new windows had been strengthened, ready for their frames and Pasquale was fitting a temporary stairway so that work could start on the upper mezzanine area. The sounds of sawing and hammering were an everyday happening, together with the sight of Richard, bare-chested and wearing a pair of khaki army shorts tied at the waist with an old belt, mixing cement in the yard or patching up rotten doors. Giampiero 'helped' him when allowed, concocting potions with cement in an old enamel chamber pot, keeping up a steady chatter as he stirred the mix with twigs. The child had been in the company of women nearly all his young life, and enjoyed being with men who didn't fuss about getting grubby.

The little blue *corriere* was almost full, the only empty seat next to a woman busy with her knitting needles. She moved a basket of lettuces and potatoes so that Fosca and Giampiero could squeeze in beside her. Rummaging through the vegetables, she pulled out a little bag of dried sunflower seeds, offering them to Giampiero.

'I don't think he will like them,' Fosca said, thanking the woman, remembering how she and Silvio used to enjoy sharing these in the backseat of the cinema, leaving piles of shells beneath their feet.

'Try this instead,' the woman said, handing him a slice of *torta del pane*. 'Made from apples grown on my land and dried in the sun.'

The woman put away her knitting and she and Giampiero kept up a stream of conversation, Giampiero telling her that they were going to visit the convent where his mamma had lived since she was a tiny baby and that he'd drawn a picture for his favourite nun in the whole world and he hoped that there would be a cake, even though it wasn't a birthday because nuns didn't celebrate their birthdays, only their saint's days and just in case there wasn't a cake, he would only nibble a little from the lady's cake and save the rest to share and how he was wearing his best clothes and had been warned not to get them dirty but he didn't like his new trousers because they were too tight and useless for climbing trees.

The woman smiled at Fosca over Giampiero's head. 'You have a little chatterbox and quite a charmer here, signora. *Complimenti.*' And when the bus stopped on the edge of the city, she leant over to kiss Giampiero and handed him the rest of the simple fruit bread and told him not to eat it all at once and to be sure to share it with his beautiful mamma as well as Madre Caterina (because by now Giampiero had provided the kindly woman with further details).

Mother and child walked along the alleys where washing hung from windows to dry and cats curled on doorsteps in the sun. It was almost midday and the aroma of cooking seeped through shutter slats, together with sounds of dishes clattering and mothers commanding their families to do this and that. Once again, Fosca was moved by these noises, so beautifully and comfortingly extraordinary in their ordinariness. And she pushed away sad, fearful memories of occupation. The sounds in the town today were sounds of freedom.

A black crepe bow hung from the front door of the convent and she tried to think which of the elderly sisters might have passed away. She would pay her respects later in the tiny cemetery at the back of the cloister garden with its simple wooden crosses, the final resting place for the Mothers of Mercy.

The door was opened by Mother Superior and, drawing mother and son inside, she clasped both Fosca's hands in her own. 'My poor child. I am so sorry. You are too late.'

Fosca bit her lip, willing away the taste of sorrow. 'When?' she asked.

'Last night. The end was peaceful.'

'Mamma, you're hurting me,' Giampiero said, pulling at Fosca's hand that was too tightly gripping his.

She bent down to him, 'I'm sorry, *tesoro*.' She looked up at the nun and asked if Giampiero could go and play with the kitchen cat for half an hour.

'*Certo*,' the nun said. 'I will call one of the novices to stay with him.' She picked up a handbell from the shelf by the door and rang six long chimes. Each nun knew their own call – a code known to each individual, who would present themselves to the Mother Superior's office as soon as they recognised their own peal.

Madre Caterina was laid out in a coffin resting on a stand at the foot of the altar steps. The familiar cloying scent of incense, candlewax and lilies took Fosca back to the many occasions when she had knelt to pray in this chapel, repeating words that she didn't understand. Long words like perpetuity, eucharistic, novena, consecration, transubstantiation, the letters tangling into one big mystery. When she had been instructed to confess her sins before taking her First Holy Communion, she couldn't think of anything she had done wrong, and so she'd invented any old thing to whisper to the priest who sat behind the grid in his gloomy confessional box. She had done as she was told whilst she was small but as the years passed, the dogma became more incomprehensible until she had eventually worked out her own way of talking to a higher being.

Her old friend in the lined coffin, roses at her head and feet, had shrunk from the stout figure of Fosca's childhood, but her hands were the same. They had been arranged with the wooden beads of her rosary threaded between the strong fingers that Fosca remembered pummelling dough for the bread that the community ate each day, or rolling pasta to make ribbons of tagliatelle or little ravioli shapes; hands that had applied ointment to Fosca's scratched arms when she had teased the convent cat too far; hands that had braided her hair and even delivered an occasional smack to her legs when she had been up to mischief. Fosca extended her own hand to Madre Caterina's and recoiled at the coldness. She brushed away a tear and silently said her farewell.

The sunlight was glaring after the shadowy chapel and it was a minute before her eyes readjusted. Giampiero was sitting on the ground with a young novice dressed in white, a simple veil covering some of her thick, chestnut-brown hair and Fosca thought what a shame it was that when this girl eventually took her vows, her curls would be shaved off and her head and part of her face totally covered by the heavily starched wimple of the order's habit. The pair were laughing at the antics of a litter of kittens that patted and pounced at a piece of string dangled above them by Giampiero.

'Mammina,' he shouted. '*Guarda!* Look at them. Can we take one home to Richard? Clara says they need a home. *Per favore!*' he pleaded.

Fosca knelt down to peer at the squirming balls of fur, reasoning that cats were easier creatures to care for than a dog. 'They are very sweet, my darling, but we have to check first with Richard. And we can't take them all that way home on the bus.'

'We can look after them for you until it is time,' the young novice called Clara told Giampiero.

'When are you due to take your vows?' Fosca asked.

The girl sighed. 'I'm not sure, signora. Mother Superior says I'm not ready.' She reached out a hand to stroke one of the kittens. 'To tell the truth, I didn't want to enter the order in the first place. But there are too many of us at home to feed and my father arranged it. I have six sisters and four brothers – two of them died in Germany. It's easier for my parents to send me away.'

Fosca bit her lip, uncertain if it was wise to add to the poor girl's confusion. 'Think carefully, Clara, before shutting yourself away here. Maybe you could find work. Try something else before you make up your mind.'

'Where would I find work, signora? I can't read or write. There's little work in the area with the men returned from war.'

'Can you cook?'

'Of course, signora. And I know how to make a meal from nothing. My family is very poor.'

Fosca squeezed her hand, an idea fermenting. But she would think it through before promising anything.

She made arrangements to return again on the following day to attend Madre Caterina's funeral and had a quick word about Clara with the Mother Superior. 'Would you consider letting her have a trial time away from the convent if I found work for her at our local *osteria* with a good family, Madre?' she asked. 'I can keep an eye on her.'

'I believe God would approve of such an idea,' the tall, austere nun answered, her hands folded together, hidden by the long, grey sleeves of her tunic.

'Don't say anything to Clara, but I hope to have an answer tomorrow and' – Fosca paused – 'I will take two of the kittens if you could find me a strong box.' She hoped Richard wouldn't mind a journey down to the city, but she rather thought he wouldn't as he had offered today anyway.

On the following day she left Giampiero with Rosa and Pasquale again. There would be no room for him in the sidecar with the extra passenger she planned to bring back to Corbello. The *osteria* was becoming like a second home for the little boy and Rosa was pleased with the idea of Clara coming to work with her in the kitchen for a trial period. 'And she could help me with Angelina, and maybe the laundry. We can turn one of the store rooms into a little bedroom for her.'

'I'm sure that she'd be more than delighted with that,' Fosca said. 'Back home she told me she shared a bed with two of her sisters. A room of her own will be luxury.'

Richard was only too happy to accompany Fosca down to Sansepolcro but insisted they stop for a coffee *granita* on the way, at the newly opened bar at the top of Anghiari. They sat under a pergola covered with a trail of flaming red trumpet vine, enjoying the view that extended towards the city and the mountains. Fosca was dressed in black, but she had brought her hat from Arezzo market with the silk roses instead of a veil. 'I think Madre Caterina would approve,' she said, peeping under the rim at Richard. 'She was a happy soul and I often thought she must have found it difficult adhering to convent rules, although she never once complained.' A little frown furrowed her brow as she turned to Richard. 'I loved her, you know. She was my whole world when I was little. I knew nothing else, you see.' She sighed and pushed away the half-finished glass of icy coffee granules. 'I can't finish this.'

'Do you want me to come to the funeral? I'm quite good at church. My Sundays were spent at the Meeting House when I was a boy. I won't be able to join in with your prayers, but I'm good at silence.'

She smiled. 'No, Richard. I'll be fine. Will you find something to occupy yourself?'

'Plenty. Don't worry about me.' As they walked back to the motorbike, he told her that he was intent on viewing Piero della Francesca's famous painting of the resurrection. 'It was rescued from the allies bombing it to smithereens,' he said, 'by a British lieutenant. He'd been ordered to obliterate the centre of Sansepolcro to drive the Germans out. At the last minute, apparently, he had a light bulb moment and remembered reading about the painting in an essay. Aldous Huxley had described it as the "best in the world." So, he ignored orders and the painting was saved. As it happened, the Germans had already vacated the city hours earlier.'

'Thank heavens for renegades,' she said.

'Indeed.'

Her mind filled again with her renegade friend, Simonetta. 'By the way, have you heard anything from Inghilterra yet?'

'Not a dicky bird. If I don't hear soon, I'll send another letter to my friend. Maybe the Italian postal system is not so reliable.'

They agreed to meet up in the afternoon and Fosca made her way into the chapel convent, pulling her hat down on her head and slipping into a back pew. She was the only lay person in the congregation and she let herself be carried away by the Latin chanting, perfect for thinking back to dear Madre Caterina. She even joined in with the singing in her out-of-tune voice, remembering how the pair of them used to sing together in the kitchen, teased later by the gardener for likely causing rain to fall as a result of their terrible caterwauling. Later, at the graveside, she threw in a handful of wild rose petals that she had collected earlier that morning from the hedgerows.

'Come to my office, my dear,' the Mother Superior said afterwards as the file of nuns drifted back to their duties. 'I have something for you.'

The nun handed her a battered suitcase made from cardboard, with a label, *Per Fosca*, written in Madre Caterina's untidy scrawl. She had once told Fosca she'd had to leave school at the age of seven to help tend the family's sheep. 'Make sure you study well, Fosca,' had been one of her many pieces of advice. 'You are lucky to have the opportunity, unlike me. Barely had I started my schooling when I had to finish. Learn to write and read for me.' And Fosca had paid heed and passed her exams to become a *maestra*, qualified to teach at primary level.

'This was found in Madre Caterina's cell,' the nun explained. 'It's the case she brought with her to the convent.'

'*Grazie*,' Fosca said, wondering what on earth the contents could be. Generally, the nuns gave away the clothes they arrived in to the poor.

A knock on the door and Clara entered, devoid of her novice's habit, wearing a plain cotton dress and stout lace-ups. Her beautiful thick hair was tidied away beneath a cotton scarf patterned with daisies, a few curls escaping. But it was the smile that lit up her face that immediately struck Fosca. She seemed a different girl already. In her arms was a small box, its lid perforated, and Fosca smiled when she heard the protest of mewing and scratching within. 'Giampiero will be pleased,' Fosca said. 'And these little creatures can earn their way by catching mice.'

In the bustle of sorting out Clara, carrying the kittens and making her farewells to the nuns, she left the suitcase behind and would have forgotten about it totally had not Mother Superior hurried outside with it to where Richard was helping the two women arrange themselves in the sidecar.

'Looks like you'll have to hang on to me again,' Richard said with a grin, placing Madre Caterina's suitcase next to the box of kittens. '*Che peccato!* What a pity!'

Clara set to immediately at Rosa's, rolling up her sleeves and wiping down surfaces in the kitchen until they gleamed. In no time at all, she had mixed pasta using a dozen eggs she collected from the *osteria*'s hen coop and set Angelina to help her arrange ribbons of tagliatelle to dry in little nests on a clean cloth.

'She's an angel,' Rosa told Fosca when the two women drank coffee together later in the yard. 'Thank you for bringing her to me. Angelina already follows her like a puppy. I fear she'll get little time to herself, but for the moment, she doesn't seem to mind.'

'I'm so pleased. It was only a hunch, but something told me she would not achieve her potential as a nun.'

'Well, you would know all about that, having been brought up in the convent.'

'Exactly. I could always tell the women who had a true vocation from those who ended up accepting it to help out their families.' The two women sat in silence, enjoying a rare moment to themselves. The sound of children's laughter drifted over from the rope that Angelina and Giampiero were taking in turns to swing from. 'And thank you for looking after Giampiero yet again,' Fosca said, getting to her feet. 'He loves being here. It's sometimes lonely for him down at the tobacco house when I'm busy.'

'And what about for you? Are you lonely? Alone with the *inglese.*'

Fosca found herself blushing. It was irrational. There was no reason to be coy but she admitted quietly to herself that she enjoyed Richard's company. He was a patient man and she felt easy in his company.

'As soon as I get my teaching job back, we'll move to Corbello. I'm going to check again with Mayor Gobbi about what is happening.'

'He is never around these days. Since his wife left him, he's hopeless,' Rosa said, collecting the coffee cups. 'People are beginning to wonder what exactly he does for the town. He is a *sindaco* only in name. He says he goes away to attend conferences to improve the town, but he's most likely enjoying himself somewhere with a woman. He's always been one for the ladies, that one. No wonder his wife left him.'

*

That evening, after she had settled Giampiero for the night, she sat at the kitchen table in the tobacco house and opened the battered suitcase that Mother Superior had given her. She used a kitchen knife to prise open the rusted clasps. As she picked out each item, arranging them on the scrubbed tabletop, she saw it was a box containing memories. A pair of tiny white woollen bootees, faded yellow at the toes. An envelope containing a curl of black hair as fine as gosling down. Drawings on scraps of paper and cardboard of stick people, their arms and legs protruding from round bodies. A handful of dried rose petals. A tiny, pearly tooth wrapped in cotton wool stored in a matchbox. But it was the dress that made her heart stop beating for a second.

The material was faded, with sprigs of tiny acorns printed on green cotton that had bleached to grey on the patched sleeves and hem. It was identical to the scrap of material Fosca had pinned under the frame with Silvio's photograph. She examined the dress and there, cut into the neck facing, was a square gap that matched Fosca's scrap of fabric. Underneath the dress she found an envelope bearing her name and even before opening it, she knew what she was about to discover.

The writing was almost illegible, written mostly in capital letters, the words misspelled. Her hand to her mouth, she deciphered the heart-wrenching message that Madre Caterina should have revealed to her many years earlier.

Fosca, my darling,

You will read this when I am gone.
  Please forgive me.

When I was fifteen years old, the man who had raped me was dead, killed in a brawl.

My mother and father threw me out of our home on the hills above Arezzo where we had eked out a living. I had kept my growing stomach concealed for as long as possible but they showed no pity on me when they discovered I was pregnant. With nowhere to go, I walked for three days until I reached the city of Sansepolcro. I looked for work, but nobody would take on a heavily pregnant girl. On a dark night in April at the back of a derelict building, I gave birth and, not knowing what else to do, I left my baby girl on the steps of a nearby convent.

I was very sick after the birth and began to beg on the streets. I resigned myself to selling my body to put food in my mouth. One night, a priest found me sheltering in the porch outside his church and took me to the Convent of the Mothers of Mercy, the very place where I had left my baby. When I had abandoned her on that night one month earlier, I'd steeled myself to forget. I had given her up. She was premature. She probably would not survive.

The nuns took me in without question. They cared for me and nursed me back to health. For the first time in my life I felt loved and I took it as a sign from God. In gratitude for my salvation, I believed that I should take vows and join their order.

When you are fifteen, you are a child. You reason like a child.

As soon as I was strong enough, they set me to work. My first task was helping with the orphans. A baby was crying in the nursery and they told me to pick her up and check if the napkin was soiled. It was you, Fosca. You were alive. The most beautiful baby that ever lived. I knew it was you as soon as I held you tight and felt your little heart beat next to mine. I kissed your velvety brow as you stared at me with your deep brown eyes. You fell asleep in my arms and I fell in love. It was a further sign from God.

In time, I grew to accept that taking my vows was what God had ordained. It was not a bad life and I could see you each day. You grew up to be a beautiful young woman. I lost you for a while when you met your young man, but imagine my joy when you returned with my grandson.

This suitcase contains memories from your young life. I told myself I was preserving them for you but in reality, they were for me, your mother.

Do not blame me for what I did, Fosca. I did what I thought was best for us both. But, be sure to nurture your little son, love him each and every single day and be open with him always. For I have not done the same with you.

Remember me in your prayers and know that I loved you very much.

Your madre, Caterina

Fosca sat at the table, a confusion of anger, shock and grief weighing on her heart. A mother herself, she found it impossible to imagine the lie that her own newly discovered mother had felt forced to live. It must have been daily torture for her to deny maternal feelings and to keep her secret for so many years. Fosca had loved this woman who had always offered her comfort and guidance but not once had she suspected her true identity. She lit a candle and took it over to the cracked mirror above the washstand and stared at her reflection. Did she look like Madre Caterina? Would she look like her when she was older? Her mother was only fifteen years older than her. With her free hand, she traced around her eyes and over her high cheekbones, trying to find a resemblance to the plump woman she remembered before illness had changed her into a shadow.

She was fiercely angry at the fate that Caterina had been dealt: a desperate young girl who believed she had to take vows of chastity, poverty and obedience in exchange for shelter. Yet, she had never seemed bitter. Fosca had never experienced a call to vocation for herself, so how was she to judge, she thought, if Caterina's had been true?

And Fosca was angry that yet again it seemed to be women who bore the brunt of hardship in this world. It was women who picked up the pieces. If there could be one change, one positive outcome to this war, it would be the recognition that the small virtues of women be considered big, and that their skills at caring for others, the way they instantly responded in times of difficulty, be recognised.

Clara's story could so easily have been Caterina's and Fosca felt even more justified in her rescue of the young girl. And once again, she thought of Simonetta and Maria and their courage and spirit. There and then, she hardened her resolve to find out what had happened to Simonetta and stand up to Mayor Gobbi. Above all, she resolved to be open and honest with her precious son through his life. She tiptoed into the little storeroom that she had scrubbed and painted for Giampiero and held up the candle, the soft, flickering light showing him asleep on top of the covers, his dimpled arms and legs splayed like a little starfish, his features still babylike in repose. The kittens were curled next to him on the pillow and she picked them up gently and took them outside.

She stood for a few moments, gazing up at the inky sky pierced with stars. A light was burning in the tower and she suddenly felt the need of company.

Richard opened to her knock, a towel held round his waist and she turned to leave, muttering an embarrassed apology.

'Don't go,' he said. 'It won't take me a jiffy to change. I was covered in dust from the beams I've been scraping so I sluiced myself down at the pump outside. The sooner I can install a bathroom in this place, the better.'

She moved over to his poetry bench while she waited, the kittens trailing behind her, jumping at the hem of her three-quarter-length skirt. A nightingale was doing its utmost to attract all the females in the area with his lilting melodies and she leant her head back against the stone wall and listened to the song.

Richard came towards her. In one hand he carried a paraffin lamp that swung light back and forth across the shadows. In the other hand he held the remainder of a bottle of wine. He set the lamp down and sat next to her. 'My favourite bird is singing again,' he said. 'Apparently, the nightingale is the metaphor for love, beauty and poetry, so… everything I most appreciate in life.'

She smiled, but said nothing.

'It's been a difficult day for you,' he said, picking up on her mood. 'In England, we usually drink a farewell to the person we bury and reminisce about their life.' He pulled the cork from the bottle with his teeth and produced two glasses from the pocket of his wide trousers.

'They buried my mother today.'

He stopped pouring, a frown on his face. 'I don't understand.'

'Neither do I, really.' She turned to face him, tilting her face upwards to the stars to contain the tears she hadn't shed. 'Madre Caterina was my mother. And I never knew.'

He pulled her close and she sank into him, letting her sorrow out. Her shoulders heaved as she sobbed and his touch on her was gentle and soothing as he rubbed her arms and back and waited for her crying to ebb.

Afterwards, she stayed leaning against him, her head against his shoulder.

Eventually she pulled away and wiped the tears from her cheeks with the backs of her hands. He offered her his none-too-clean handkerchief and she took it and blew her nose. 'I'll wash it for you,' she said. '*Grazie*. Sorry about that outburst, Richard. Thank you for listening.'

'What a shock it must have been. I am always here if you need someone to talk to.'

'It's such a waste of opportunities,' she said, folding and unfolding the damp handkerchief. 'If I'd known, I would have shared Giampiero with her more, maybe stayed at the convent to help her in her old age.'

'It seems to me she didn't want that for you. Didn't she encourage you to return to Corbello to get back your job? Forgive me…' He paused, most likely searching for the right words. 'Being shut off from life, in a convent, could also be considered a waste for a young woman and a little boy. Best to be out in the world. Living.'

'I think you're right, but I'm still angry she had to keep the secret of her being my mother. She robbed me of my birthright, in a sense. And I feel so stupid that I never for one moment realised.'

He took her hand and she didn't pull away. 'We all make mistakes, Fosca. She did what she thought was best.'

They were quiet for a few moments. The nightingale was still chirruping away in the still air, the three-quarter moon casting a delicate light, turning the tower in front of them into a grey-blue cut-out.

'I almost forgot,' Richard said, breaking the silence and giving her hand a little shake in his eagerness to tell her. 'I dropped in to have a beer with Pasquale this morning and he gave me this.'

He pulled an envelope from his pocket addressed for the attention of signorina Fosca, c/o Osteria da Bruno. The handwriting was neat and Fosca turned it over to see the addressee but there was no name on the back. She opened it carefully. Written in stilted Italian, it read briefly.

Signorina Fosca,

I write to you because I believe you are a woman of conscience.

   I need to talk about events that occurred whilst I was in your town. I do not have much time left and so I am unable to return to Corbello. Please come to find me in Venice at Scalon del Doge, 3.

Sincerely,
Manfred Hansen

Fosca handed the note to Richard. 'How strange that this should turn up now, when we have just started searching for him… What do you make of it?'

'It can't possibly be anything to do with the letter I sent to England. I only posted that a couple of days ago. Let me see, Fosca.' He took the note and scanned the lines, pulling a face as he did so.

'Mysterious. Cloak and dagger. Is he saying that he has some kind of fatal illness? Could he want to pass on information about the rest of the gold? Maybe he'll lead us to the truth about Simonetta.'

She took the note from him and read it again. 'Who knows? But I do remember he told me he'd studied music in Venice and longed to return. Maybe he *is* telling the truth and he's very sick and needs to clear his conscience, or something?' She looked up at Richard. 'What should I do?'

'Fosca, how do you fancy a trip to the floating city? I've never been. Let's broaden our horizons. And if we find out what our Major Hansen wants to tell us, then we'll kill two birds with one stone. No way can I let you go alone. What do you say?'

She smiled at him broadly. 'I say *sì*. Anything that helps me find out about Simonetta's death, then, *sì*.'

Richard poured two glasses of wine and raised his to the stars.

'To Venezia,' he said. 'But most of all: to Madre Caterina.'

'To Mamma,' Fosca replied, clinking her glass against his.

CHAPTER THIRTY-FIVE

The tongues will be wagging at Corbello's washing fountain so much that they will drop off, Fosca thought. Two nights with a man in romantic Venice, without her child! The news would be all round the little town.

Fosca woke early in the floating city, unable to sleep, her mind churning with questions she would put to the German major. She and Richard had arrived late last night after a long train journey and made their way through the back alleys, following a map that the ferry captain had scribbled on the back of a bill when they'd docked at Riva degli Schiavoni. 'You'll be looked after well in my sister's *pensione*,' he'd assured them. 'And it'll cost you less than a tourist hotel.'

He'd enquired whether they were on their honeymoon and Fosca had quickly butted in. 'No, no. We're not a couple. I'm teaching this Englishman Italian.'

His response was raised eyebrows and when Richard put in his version, 'And we're looking for a German she used to know,' the man had guffawed. 'It will turn into quite an international celebration, I'm sure. You'll have to let me know how you all get on. *Buona fortuna!*' the cheery ferryman cried as he started up the engine, waving and winking at them both, which had made Fosca blush and Richard grin.

Fortunately, there were two single rooms vacant in the Pensione Vecio, both overlooking the Rio della Panada in the mediaeval, eastern part of the city. Fosca had fallen asleep to the sound of water lapping against the building and as the first rays of sunlight filtered through the shutters, she jumped out of bed to fling them wide. Instead of a green Tuscan valley from where the Apennines soared blue and misty, opposite her a tangerine-pink palazzo rose from the water, its windows framed in white, the architectural style Arabian and exotic, like nothing she'd ever seen.

Pots of white geraniums cascaded from the upper windows and a red and gold banner flapped lazily in the early morning breeze. Three gondolas bobbed up and down in the gentle current and a lone gull perched as still as a stone sculpture on the striped post where boats were tethered. The sounds of shutters opening nearby interrupted her daydreaming and Fosca turned to see Richard.

'*Buongiorno*, signorina,' he said, leaning out to wave at her from the next window. His hair was bed-tousled, his chin dark with morning stubble. Silvio had sometimes teased her in the mornings, rubbing his bristly chin against her breasts to wake her as she drowsed. She shook the image from her mind and waved back. 'Good morning,' she said in English and he beamed back at her. She pushed back the hair from her face and sighed. 'I have such mixed feelings this morning. What does Major Hansen want to tell me? I couldn't sleep properly through worrying,' she said.

'Well, my remedy is a special breakfast in St Mark's Square before we meet him. My treat.'

As they walked, her eyes grew drunk from the sights of the magical city. Stepping along the narrow alleys, Richard explained to her that Venice had been spared devastation during the war, its architectural and artistic treasures recognised by all sides.

It was still early with hardly anybody about in St Mark's Square and Fosca pivoted in a slow circle, trying to take it all in. The cathedral resembled an illustration from the *Arabian Nights* with its domes and gold minarets, its crosses glinting in the sunshine. The soaring bell tower with its sharp pinnacle was like a child's drawing coloured with red crayons.

Richard started to read from his little blue guidebook about the arcades on the three sides of the square. 'The *procuratia* are three connected buildings along the perimeter of St Mark's Square—' but Fosca interrupted him.

'Let's drink in the sights, Riccardo, and walk about. Let history speak for itself.'

He snapped the guide shut and smiled. '*Perfetto!* Exactly what I prefer to do.' He linked arms with her. 'But breakfast first.'

'Not in this square,' she said. '*Troppo caro.* Tourist prices.' She led him down a side street, a *calletta*, where the aroma of fresh coffee enticed them into a bar.

They sat at a table in its garden planted with palms and fig trees offering a tantalising glimpse of the Grand Canal beyond. 'I feel as if I've landed on another continent,' Fosca said, sugar round her mouth from the *cannoli* that she had chosen. Richard had gone savoury, enjoying a couple of little *pizzette*, bubbling with warm mozzarella cheese.

'I never imagined anywhere like this. *Grazie*, Riccardo.' She didn't know why an Italian version of his name tumbled out of her mouth, but from his smile he seemed to like it. 'But we mustn't forget why we came here. We need to meet our man and hear what he has to say.'

He nodded and opened a tourist map of the city. 'The address he gave us – the Scalon del Doge – is located near the Rialto Bridge,' he said, pointing. 'It won't take us long to get there.'

As they strolled, the palette of colours and elegant Moorish-style *palazzi* melting into reflections in the murky canal waters took Fosca's breath away. The archways and little humpbacked bridges they crossed, the songs of the gondoliers echoing in the narrow *rios* as they guided their crafts were scenes she wanted to fix forever in her mind. Gulls fluttered in Piazza San Marco like daytime ghosts. She laughed as a small boy scattered them, scampering into their midst when they squabbled for breadcrumbs. The sound of the child's delight echoed round the square and she wondered what Giampiero was up to and that brought her down to earth again.

'Richard, the next time you see me gazing with my mouth open at this amazing city, remind me why we have come. We need to get on with our search but I am so distracted.'

It took them a while to locate Hansen's address, but eventually they found the dark alleyway littered with pigeon droppings that emerged to the daylight of Scalon del Doge. At the end of the tiny *piazzetta*, the Grand Canal's waters lapped at two rowing boats moored in the small inlet. Number three was halfway up a wide flight of steps. Fosca lagged behind Richard as they climbed, fear taking over her resolve. 'What am I going to say to him?' she said. 'What if it's a trick?'

'I won't let anything happen to you, Fosca.'

Nobody answered when they knocked and they stood waiting. They knocked louder a second time and a woman leant from a window at the top of the narrow building. 'If you're looking for a foreign gentleman,' she shouted, 'he's moved, signori.'

Fosca felt her shoulders slump. 'Do you know where to, signora?'

She shrugged and leant out further. 'If only I did. *Magari!* He did a flit. Owing me rent. If you see him, tell him my husband is looking for him.' She slammed the window and Fosca and Richard looked at each other in dismay.

'What next?' Fosca said.

'We find somewhere to eat a delicious lunch and decide on a plan B.'

As they crossed Piazza San Marco again, Fosca stopped in her tracks as music from a violin and piano drifted to them from a *caffè* under the ancient arcade.

'Caffè Florian,' Richard said. 'For the rich and famous. Dickens, Byron, Proust…'

She interrupted. 'That pianist. He's good. Could it be him?'

They moved closer but the oily-haired man in the white tuxedo at the piano was not Hansen. He was stout, his features rounder than the blond major's and when he started to sing in perfect Italian, she shook her head with a sigh. 'It's definitely not him.'

They walked the city all day, stopping wherever they heard strains of piano music. As night fell, light spilled from lanterns and travelled across the water, turning the city into a theatre set. Footsore, they entered yet another bar. Fosca walked through to the cloakroom at the back, scrutinising customers as she passed. But there was no man resembling the German major in this place either.

'We're never going to find him,' Fosca said, as they sat afterwards on the steps of a church. 'It's like looking for a woman called Maria.' She sighed.

Richard looked at her quizzically. 'What do you mean?'

'Such a vast city. How will we ever find him?'

He smiled. 'We say like looking for a needle in a haystack. Don't give up, Fosca. At least we're having a good time while we look, aren't we?'

He stopped at a stall selling carnival masks. 'Maybe we should be wearing a disguise when we find him?' he suggested.

'You do know that it's the wrong time of year for Carnevale masks,' she said, 'when Venetians go mad with celebrations in the streets before the start of Lent?'

'I don't need an excuse to make merry,' he replied, pulling her by the hand and running down narrow alleyways until they returned to San Marco, scattering pigeons and gulls and causing people to turn and stare as they sped by.

'Stop, stop,' she cried, 'I have a stitch. You're mad, *pazzo*.' She pulled away and bent down, hands on her knees, laughter bubbling out with each breath. She felt like a child, uninhibited and free, Venice casting its spell on her. And when she looked up at Richard, he could even have been Silvio. 'Where are you taking me now?' she asked.

'A haunt of many famous people,' he replied. 'It's around the corner. I bet we find our German pianist in there.'

'But no more running,' she said, feeling uncomfortably hot. 'Behave, Richard!'

'This place makes it hard to behave, don't you think?' he said, taking her hands and spinning her round. 'With no reminders of war, no bombed buildings. It's like stepping back in time... or into the future. It's what your beautiful country will look like again when everything has been restored.'

His mood was contagious. When he kept hold of her hand, it felt to Fosca like the most natural thing in the world to leave hers there.

Harry's Bar was a drab unassuming place and as she peered at the menu on the wall outside, she was shocked again at the prices. 'We can't go in here, Richard. It's far too expensive.'

'You only live once. My treat again.' He pulled her in and made for a table in the far corner.

'What do you recommend?' Richard asked the waiter.

He suggested they try the Bellinis, a drink that the owner signor Cipriani had invented in 1934. 'It is named after the colour in a painting by Bellini,' the young man explained.

'*Due, per favore*,' Richard said, and Fosca smiled.

'*Bravo!*' she said, congratulating him, but then she turned to the waiter. '*Ma, uno solo*. Just one.'

When Richard grimaced at her as the waiter walked away muttering, she told him under her breath that for that money she could buy meals for one whole week. Nevertheless, she managed a sip from the bubbly pink drink of peach juice and sparkling white wine.

'I think you're right after all,' he said, wrinkling his nose as he finished it. 'Sickly! Give me a strong country wine any day.'

When he went to pay the bill, Fosca heard him ask the same questions that he had put to countless bar owners that day. Pointing to the piano, he said, 'I'm looking for a German friend. He's an excellent pianist. Does he by any chance play here?'

The owner counted out the change, with a grimace. 'If his name is Hansen, then I've lost patience with that one, signore. Your friend is a slave to drink. It will be the death of him and he's driving my customers away.'

'Do you know where he lives?'

'Somewhere in Cannaregio, I think. When you see him, tell him not to come back.'

'*Grazie*, signore,' Richard said. 'Keep the change. You've been most helpful.'

'I can't believe we might find him,' Fosca said when they were outside. They moved to a bench and pulled out the map to locate the district.

'Here it is,' Fosca said, peering at the small writing.

'It's quite a walk from here and it's late. Better to go first thing tomorrow morning, Fosca. And if he's been drinking, we won't get much sense out of him tonight anyway.'

She sighed. 'I won't be able to sleep again thinking about it.'

'Nightcap?' he asked. 'Something to help you sleep?'

They dawdled back towards Pensione Vecio and as they mounted a humpback bridge, music drifted to them over the water. Half a dozen couples were dancing outside a modest-looking bar, candles flickering on outside tables, light bouncing off the narrow canal like musical notes. The pianist played a medley of popular songs and they leant against the railings to watch the dancers.

'Dance with me in this city of candlelight and music?' Fosca asked, pulling him with her down the steps.

'You'll regret it, I'm warning you. I have two left feet.'

'*Non importa*,' she said. 'It doesn't matter.'

She started to hum along to the song and he winced and laughed. 'If you stop singing, Fosca, I will dance.'

Fosca punched him playfully and they slow waltzed, merging with the other dancers.

Richard was an awkward mover, Fosca thought. Rigid, not quite matching the rhythm of the music and when the pianist switched to a livelier folk tune, and they were both at arm's length, it began to feel easier. But at one point, when they were twirling and he was supposed to keep tight hold of her, he lost his grip and if she had not collided with another dancing pair, she might have ended in the canal. They dissolved into laughter and decided it was safer to listen, seated at a table outside the bar, and to share a bottle of Valpolicella.

The music stopped and the dancers dispersed. There was still half a bottle of wine on the table and Fosca lingered, sure that Richard was also reluctant to return to the pensione even though it was late.

'I'm sorry about my awful dancing,' he said, pouring her more wine.

'I'm sorry about my awful singing. It's something I seem to have inherited from… my mother,' she said, sadness in her voice.

'Not many Quakers see the point in dancing, so that's my excuse,' Richard said.

'Cicero believed only mad drunkards danced, you know. So your Quakers are not alone in their thinking. The nuns loved to feed us with his quotations.'

'We are both products of our upbringings.'

'I don't stick to everything I was taught.' She paused and lifted her glass to her lips. 'The war changed my beliefs. People refer to me as signora, Richard. But I never married in a church. Legally, I am still a signorina. Silvio and I, we made up our vows and recited them in a meadow. I felt married, but the nuns who brought me up wouldn't have approved. So...' She took a long sip of her wine. 'You know one of my secrets now.'

'So do you have lots of secrets?'

'Who knows?' she said enigmatically, thinking what fun it was to flirt again, but not ready to reveal everything to him yet about her past.

They were quiet on their stroll back to the pensione. The streets were almost deserted, strips of light peeping from shutters in houses where inhabitants were still up. Water lapping against wharves and their footsteps echoing in the *calli* were the only sounds as Venice settled for the night. Back at the Pensione Vecio, at two o'clock in the morning, they whispered their good nights outside their rooms.

'Last breakfast in Piazza San Marco tomorrow?' he asked. 'Before we finally track down Hansen and see what he has to say?'

'*Perché no?* Why not? These two days have been such fun, Riccardo, but we have to finish what we came here to do. *Grazie.*'

She reached up to kiss him on the cheek and their lips collided. For a moment, she leant into him, the touch of his warm lips on hers lighting a flame and then she came to her senses and pushed away. What had she been thinking? Her fingers fumbled with the key in the lock and he stepped in to help and for half a moment she wanted him to take her in his arms and finish the kiss properly. In her room, she leant her back against the door, steadying her breathing, thinking how life could change like the wind. Venice was playing tricks with her emotions tonight but tomorrow they would confront the major. Then, after he revealed what he had to say, they would leave and her life would return to normal. She steadied her heartbeat by picturing her son's smiling face and she concentrated on how she would soon hold him in her arms.

In the room next door, Richard listened through the flimsy walls as Fosca prepared for the night. He heard the splash of water as she poured water into a basin, and the sag of the bedsprings as she climbed under the covers. He wondered if she wore a nightdress and what it would look like against her smooth, olive-brown skin. He put his hand to the wall and the thought of sharing her bed continued into his dreams.

Their walk in the morning took them to a quieter district of Venice, seldom visited by tourists, where washing was strung across the waterways and the faded buildings had crumbling façades. They stopped by a couple of fishermen mending their nets in a square dominated by a fine Gothic church and Fosca asked them if they knew whether a German signore lived nearby.

'He's tall, blond. And he speaks good Italian,' she told them.

The men exchanged looks and laughed, one of them gesturing with his thumb to his mouth. 'You're the second stranger to ask about him today,' the younger man said. He pointed to a building further down the walkway. 'Number 154,' he said. 'But he's no doubt sleeping it off. Knock hard, I would.'

The paintwork on the door was peeling, the window frames rotten. On the sill, thick with pigeon droppings, a potted geranium had given up on life.

'Can this be the right address?' Fosca asked.

'Only one way to find out,' Richard said as he knocked at the door. It fell open immediately as he struck his knuckles against the wood and a cat streaked out, making Fosca jump.

'Major Hansen?' Richard called in English but there was no reply.

'Maybe he's asleep, like the fisherman said.'

'Let's go inside and wake him with a coffee.'

'Should we?' Fosca said.

'Having come all this way, I'd prefer not to leave without talking to him.'

'Absolutely,' Fosca said, steeling herself.

The room they entered was the kitchen where a shabby table and four cane chairs dominated the space. She moved over to the stove, but the ashes were cold. 'No coffee then,' she said. 'What a pigsty.' She tutted at the pile of unwashed dishes in the sink, a cluster of flies feeding on smears of food. 'If you could have seen how he lived during the war. What a come-down, Richard,' she whispered.

'Major Hansen?' Richard called up the staircase.

Still no reply.

'Wait down here, Fosca. I'll take a look upstairs. I'll wake him up if I have to.'

Fosca stood in the centre of the kitchen, listening to Richard's footsteps as he climbed the narrow stairs. The floorboards above her head creaked as he moved about. Something dripped onto her face and she wiped it away with her finger at the same moment as Richard uttered a cry.

'Oh good God. Fosca, go and ask those fishermen to fetch a doctor. Hurry!'

She ran to the men and it was then that she noticed the fingers on her right hand where she had wiped her face were stained red.

'Signora,' the younger fisherman said. 'Are you hurt? You have blood on your face.'

*

'We told you over and over,' Richard said to the inspector seated opposite. 'The man was already dead when we arrived, a revolver in his hand. The door was ajar. I went upstairs. I thought he was asleep. He was on top of the covers, his back to me. But then I heard the flies.' Richard lowered his voice. 'And the covers I thought were red, were his sheets stained with blood. His body was still warm.'

'Signorina, tell me your version again.'

'Richard wouldn't let me go upstairs. I was waiting for him in the kitchen when he shouted that I should fetch a doctor. Later I realised it must be bad because blood had dripped through the ceiling.'

'I told her to run for help, but I knew it was too late. I worked as an orderly during the war, *ispettore*. I know a dead man when I see one,' Richard said.

'Talk to those fishermen,' Fosca said. 'They'll confirm we weren't in the major's house for long.'

'Major? How do you know that he was a major?' the inspector asked.

'I knew him during the war,' Fosca explained. 'He was stationed in our village. We came to see him because he sent me a letter. He wanted to tell us something. How many times do I have to tell you?'

'The fishermen told us we weren't his first visitors that day. You need to ask them for a description of whoever came before us,' Richard said.

'Do not worry, signore. I have that under control.'

'We have a train to catch,' Fosca said. 'I have a young son to get back to.'

'Once we have gone through more formalities and taken your details, you will be allowed to go. But do not leave Tuscany, signore,' the inspector told Richard. 'I will contact the *questura* in… Corbello, you say,' the police officer said, checking his notes, 'to make sure they know your whereabouts. You will have to register at the *questura* each morning and evening.'

'Don't worry, *ispettore*,' Richard said. 'I am not going anywhere.'

They caught the late train back to Tuscany.

'We found him,' Fosca said, leaning back wearily against the seat. 'But, too late. Now we shall never know what he wanted to tell me.'

'Whatever his message, somebody thought it too important for you to hear.'

'What do you mean?'

'I believe his death was made to look like suicide. The gun in his hand didn't look right. It wouldn't have remained in his hand if he'd fired it himself. There was something staged about the angle of his arm and the way his fingers were wrapped around the grip panel.'

'But who and why?' Fosca wanted to scream with frustration. 'Whoever finished him off, do you really think they knew Hansen wanted to speak to me? How did they know?'

'Maybe whoever it was received a letter too and was invited to come and talk? Hansen cleaning up his conscience before he died?' Richard suggested.

She blew out a huge sigh. 'What next?' she asked. 'I believed we were so near to finding out what happened to Simonetta and, probably, the rest of the gold.'

'Fosca, I don't want to frighten you, but I think you're in great danger. That attack was vicious. There were bruises and cuts to his face that he couldn't have inflicted himself. Whoever killed Hansen wanted to make sure he was dead. Maybe he was dead before he was shot – to make it look like suicide? I'm moving in to the tobacco house for a while. But we are not giving up on Simonetta. You can be sure of that.'

Fosca liked that he'd used 'we'. It strengthened her and made her feel less alone. Over these past two days, whenever she'd tried to visualise Silvio, Richard's features had superimposed on his face. Today and yesterday, until they had discovered Hansen's body, were two of the best days of her life. She felt a twinge of guilt. These new emotions were probably due to the special atmosphere of Venice, she told herself. On the remainder of the journey back to Tuscany she sat quietly in the train, closing her eyes to avoid looking at Richard sitting opposite her.

CHAPTER THIRTY-SIX

Fosca woke too early for the third night in a row, her mind weary from thoughts that would not lie still. Before dawn, she picked up the photo of Silvio and lit the candle at the side of her bed.

'What should I do, *amore mio*?' she whispered. His face stared back at her, expressionless, even more faded since the glass in the frame had shattered, and she sighed. She and Richard had come so close to the truth in Venice, she was sure of that, but now she felt frustrated and guilty. In the end, those two days had been nothing but a pleasant interlude and Silvio, her own husband, had hardly been on her mind.

She crept from the house to climb into Richard's hammock and settled down, gazing up at the full moon caught like a silver pearl in the lattice of olive branches. Madre Caterina had always organised her planting according to the phases of the moon: carrots, onions and potatoes when it was full and at its waning, tomatoes, corn and watermelon. Her mother had always been busy but Fosca felt restless on this early morning: idle and frustrated that she was no nearer to finding out how Simonetta had died and, to her mind, doing too little for her friend.

When the cockerels began to crow, heralding daylight, she resolved to confront Gobbi on her own. Hansen was gone, so the mayor was now top of her list. When she and Richard had filled in Pasquale about Hansen's fate on their return from Venice, and Fosca had been all set to rush in and quiz Gobbi, everybody had warned her to hold fire. 'Be patient, don't rush things, Fosca,'

Pasquale had said. 'Wait until the police have finished their investigations. Wait until we have all come up with a good plan.'

Fosca was tired of waiting. It was time to carry out her own plan. Once she had her job back as schoolteacher of Corbello, she reasoned, then she would gain back the respect of the townspeople. She knew that most of them thought of her as the girl who had been too friendly with the *tedeschi* in Bruno's *osteria*. But when she was back in the classroom, helping their children, they would start to listen to her. She knew she was good at her job. And when the time was ready, she would reveal everything she knew about their mayor and explain what had happened during the war. That required a strong dose of *pazienza*, and first of all she needed that job.

Later that morning, after she had left Giampiero with Rosa, she stood, weary but determined, in the mayor's office.

'I have come to see when I can start teaching.'

She refused Gobbi's invitation to sit and remained standing, her feet planted firmly apart on the rug, her chin jutted forward, fists clenched at her sides, trying hard to contain her anger.

Gobbi fiddled with his fountain pen, his gold signet ring catching light from the sun beaming through the open window. 'It is complicated,' he said. 'There is the small matter of having a teacher already in this post. I cannot simply dismiss him.'

'I have heard that he wants to leave. That he will be handing in his resignation very soon. I should step into his role smoothly. So, I suggest I assist him now in his classes so that the handover is easier for my pupils.'

The mayor looked at her, his eyes narrowing. 'You do not tell me how I should run my *comune*, signora,' he said.

In her weary state, she saw red, forgetting completely her advice to herself about treading softly and she blurted out, 'You are not in a position to dictate to me either, signor Gobbi. I suggest I start next Monday, unless you want the whole of Corbello to know about your cruel lies about my dead husband being alive.'

And, like a wild boar thrashing about in a mud hole, she continued in full swing. 'And what's more, your townspeople might also be interested to hear of your dealings with a certain *tedesco* officer. And how you stole gold, pretending to be a supporter of the *partigiani* when all the time you were rubbing your greedy hands together. That gold, plundered from the Italian state, should rightfully have been returned as soon as the war was over. And while we are on the subject of ownership, please make sure that my brooch is returned to me as soon as possible.'

Before he could reply, she swung out of his office and descended the stairs of the town hall, her legs threatening to collapse beneath her after the confrontation. Shaky but simultaneously annoyed and proud of herself, she couldn't wait to tell Richard that she had started the ball rolling by threatening Gobbi. Maybe he would not consider it the wisest move but she was done with pussyfooting. At the moment there was no definite proof that he had been involved in Hansen's death, but she was sure he would let his guard down sooner or later and let something slip. She slowed her pace, trying to calm herself, thinking that once she was back in the little school apartment, she would be out from under Richard's feet. Her stay at the tobacco house had been fun while it lasted, but it was time to exact vengeance for Simonetta's death and after that she would resume normal life.

Fosca collected Giampiero from Rosa, her mind still a giddy helter-skelter from her confrontation in the mayor's office. She forced herself to concentrate on Rosa's news.

'Guess what?' Rosa said. 'I think there will be a wedding soon in the village. And, unfortunately, I might lose my new assistant.'

Fosca raised eyebrows. 'Clara? She's not…'

Rosa shook her head. 'No, she's not pregnant. But she's in love.'

'Who is the lucky man?'

'A certain somebody you know. One who set his cap at you!'

'Not Lupo?'

'Yes. Lupo. Except we all call him Piero now.'

'Well, I wish them both all the happiness in the world. Lord knows, they both deserve it.'

'So, you don't mind?'

'Of course I don't. I never had romantic feelings for him and, in truth, I think he was only looking for a mother for his niece and nephew. If he's found love, then that's wonderful. He's a good man. Maybe Clara will calm him down.'

They chatted for a while longer while Fosca helped Rosa lay tables in the dining room. Fosca suggested that it was Angelina's turn to come and play at the tobacco house for a couple of hours and after hugging her friend goodbye, she followed the children as they skipped hand in hand down the path, stopping every now and again to pick up a treasure to show her: a pheasant's feather and a dandelion clock.

Voices drifted to them as they approached the tower, the tinkling sound of a woman's laughter, joined by guffaws from Richard. A beautiful young blonde, her trim figure encased in tight, striped pedal pushers, cinched at the waist with a wide belt, was leaning against Richard's sidecar. Puffing on a cigarette in a long holder, she looked like a fashion model, her bright lipstick accentuating full lips as she and Richard engaged in animated conversation. Fosca felt a pang of envy, which she quickly quashed. She and Richard were good friends, that was all. When the children ran over to him and Giampiero flung his arms around his legs, he beckoned Fosca forward.

'Come and meet Barbara,' he called. 'She's paid me a surprise visit from England.'

Barbara smiled and looked Fosca up and down before proceeding to talk to her in English. Fosca shrugged her shoulders and held up her hands. 'I speak very little English,' she said, apologetically.

There followed an awkward, drawn-out, three-way conversation with Richard interpreting until eventually Fosca excused herself to prepare lunch for the children. 'If you would like to join us, I can prepare more pasta.'

'I've promised to take Bar into Anghiari. So, no, thank you. We'll have something to eat there and catch you later.'

Fosca watched as he took Barbara's hand, helping her as she climbed gracefully into the sidecar with her long legs, the two *inglesi* looking like a couple of film stars. With more exchanges in English, the pair disappeared with cheery waves and a roar of the motorbike's engine. Barbara attempted an '*arrivederci*', which made Richard laugh. 'Your accent is *terribile*, Bar,' Fosca heard him shout as they disappeared in a cloud of dust, leaving her feeling strangely alone.

Fosca spent the afternoon tidying and sorting her few belongings for her move up to the school. She was confident that Gobbi would not put obstacles in her way now that she had issued her threats. Later that afternoon, the *postino* arrived with letters for Richard and she let herself into the tower and placed the letters where he would see them on his return. Two smart leather suitcases sat in the middle of the floor and she wondered where Barbara was staying. There was only one bed in the tobacco tower: a mattress on the new mezzanine floor, and she forced herself to banish images of Richard and Barbara sleeping together. She had no right to feel resentful. It was only normal, she told herself, that a handsome man like Richard should want to spend time with his English girlfriend. They were beautiful people who doubtless had known each other for a long time. Her time spent with Richard in Venice had been a fleeting weekend and it was the charm of the city that had worked its way into her heart and not the man, she told herself. She closed the door to the tower firmly and called to Angelina and Giampiero that it was time for lunch.

'I far prefer riding in a motor car to this crate,' Barbara shouted above the roar of the bike as they bumped along the dusty road. 'I shall look a wreck when we arrive.'

'You will look fine,' he answered. 'You can powder your nose or whatever you need to do when we get there. It's only a little town. Nobody will care what you look like. Are you hungry?'

'*I* shall care,' she said, holding on to the silk headscarf tied under her chin. 'Do they do salad dishes in this restaurant?'

Richard laughed. 'Yes. As sides. I think you'd better leave me to order the food, Bar. They might be insulted if you ordered nothing but salad.'

As he parked in the little market square a gaggle of children surrounded the bike. One of the little ragamuffins offered to clean it. Richard told them that they could all help but that he would be keeping a watchful eye on them so that they didn't scratch the paintwork. 'I'll pay you when you're finished if you do a good job,' he added and, pointing at the restaurant opposite, he warned that he would be watching from there.

'Very impressive. You sound like a native,' Barbara said, as she touched up her lipstick, bending to check in the motorbike's mirror, much to the amusement of the little boys, who pointed and giggled, making smacking noises with their lips. '*Bella, bella,*' one of them said and the others dissolved into fits of laughter.

'These Italians certainly start young with their lovemaking,' she said, smiling at Richard. 'I hope some of their technique has rubbed off on you.'

'Bar—' he started, concerned that she still had a yen for him, but she interrupted, smiling at his discomfort.

'Don't worry, darling. I haven't come over here to pursue you. I simply fancied a little holiday. I wanted to make sure you were all right and to understand why you'd been lured away to this out-of-the-way place. You did leave Blighty rather suddenly.'

She linked arms with him as they strolled over to the tables arranged outside the restaurant. Men who were playing cards at a table outside the bar stopped their game to ogle at the *bella signorina* on his arm. It had always been so, Richard thought. Wherever they had been, Barbara always attracted attention, like a peacock opening a fan of ostentatious feathers.

'I love it here,' he said. 'And it's beginning to feel like home.'

'I can see that. You seem to have a ready-made family too. Pretty little thing. Bit dowdy, but with a makeover, she'd be absolutely stunning.'

He frowned. 'Are you talking about Fosca?'

'Yes! What did you think I meant? Your old house or your motorbike? Honestly, Richard, you can be so dense sometimes.' She inserted another cigarette into her holder and asked him for a light, and he caught her familiar scent of Chanel No. 5 as he leant in to flick his lighter. She had once told him that a woman wore perfume whenever she hoped to be kissed, and he truly hoped the message that it was over had got through and that she wasn't on some mission to win him back.

Richard ordered a dish of three different types of home-made pasta and a bottle of Chianti and he watched the young waiter blush to his roots as Barbara peered over the top of her sunglasses at the poor chap, teasing him with one of her sexy looks.

'They're all so beautiful, aren't they?' she commented as the young man scurried back to the kitchen. 'No wonder there are so many *bambini* around.' Her gaze fell on the little ragamuffins who were busy on the other side of the piazza, spitting on their rags and polishing Richard's motorbike. 'Mind you, I can't imagine ever producing one,' she said, exhaling smoke into the Tuscan air.

She picked at her pasta, telling him that although it was delicious, it would play havoc with her waistline. Richard couldn't help comparing her picky appetite with Fosca's healthy appreciation of food. Fosca ate well, but she worked hard too. Her figure was shapely and firm. The enjoyment of food was one of the many aspects that endeared him to this country. As he watched Barbara toy with her pasta, he felt mildly irritated.

'What are your plans, Barbara?'

'Are your bored with my company already?' she asked, placing her knife and fork on top of the pasta left on her dish.

'I can take you to visit one or two places in the next few days, but I am fairly busy. I'm anxious to get my place watertight and ready before the autumn rains.'

'Please don't worry on my account, Richard.' She lit another cigarette and leant back in the chair, crossing her legs. 'I'm not stopping long. I'm on my way to Rome after seeing you. Sorelle Botti have asked me to model their new wedding gowns. They like my long legs and blonde looks, apparently. So, I shall love you and leave you in two days' time.' She leant her chin on her free hand and pouted at him. 'Aren't you the teeniest bit disappointed, darling?'

He smiled at her. 'Barbara, I wish you all the luck in the world. If it all goes horribly wrong in Rome, you know where to find me.'

'You always were such a sweetie.' She pouted her lips at him in a kiss, her laughter like the tinkling of breaking glass.

The young waiter came to clear their plates, expressing dismay at Barbara's half-finished portion. 'Was the pasta not to the signorina's satisfaction?' he asked and it took a while for Richard to explain that the signorina *inglese* did not have a big appetite but it was all *squisito* and to make sure to compliment the chef on the delicious food.

'They almost take it personally,' he told Barbara.

'Goodness. What a palaver!'

It was useless to explain to this girl who had such a different temperament and who came from a culture so unlike the Italian. In one of their casual language lessons, Fosca had taught him an expression that summed it up perfectly: '*Si vive per mangiare*', we live to eat, rather than eat to live. Mealtimes in Italy could be long, drawn-out affairs. Every aspect of the food – its origins, the way it had been cooked, down to the exact quantities and timing of the addition of a pinch of herbs or salt, the way the vegetables were chopped and prepared, how they were grown, where the meat was sourced – all these things were endlessly discussed, compared and argued over with enthusiasm. He remembered Fosca's telling comment about how she had shared an orange during the war, eating the peel afterwards because their hunger was so desperate. No wonder Fosca and his Italian friends now relished their food. They had every right to do so. Richard ordered two coffees and the bill and when the tiny cups of espresso arrived, Barbara wrinkled up her nose and commented that she would rather have a cuppa any day.

Giampiero had settled easily that evening, tired from playing with Angelina and the walks back and forth to Corbello. Fosca sat outside enjoying the golden warmth of dusk and embroidered a row of lazy daisies around the collar of an old dress. For a while she'd listened to the murmur of Richard's and the Englishwoman's voices drifting from the tower, until the roar of the motorbike disappearing up the hill to Corbello told her that they had gone out. The resident nightingale was singing again and she stopped to soak in the beauty of its song, setting her work down on her lap, feeling lazy, her eyes closing as she listened.

A girl called to her from the tower, her hands beseeching her from the newly installed window. Fosca couldn't move from the bench, her feet hindered by brambles bound round her legs. When she tried to call back to the girl, she couldn't open her mouth.

A tap on her shoulder jolted her awake. Night had fallen and she jumped in alarm when she opened her eyes and made out the dark shape of a man looming over her.

'Hey! *Scusami* – it's only me,' Richard said, sitting down beside her on the bench. 'What's up, Fosca? You look as if you've seen a ghost.'

'You woke me from a nightmare,' she said, breathing deeply to calm herself. 'I dreamt of a girl like Simonetta. She was up there.' Fosca pointed to the tobacco tower. 'And I couldn't reach her.'

'Shall I get you a glass of water?'

'*Sì, grazie.*'

When he returned, her heart had stopped its fluttering and she felt calmer. 'Ridiculous what the mind does to your subconscious,' she said, shaking her head. 'The girl in the dream, Richard. I absolutely need to find out how she died.'

'Simonetta is playing on your mind.'

'Of course.' She drank the water and turned to him. 'Where is Barbara?'

'I've taken her up to Corbello to rent a room from Rosa. She refused to stay the night in what she described as a dirty, rat-infested hole crawling with spiders.'

Fosca laughed. 'There are plenty of mice but I've never seen rats.' She sighed. 'Simonetta was so brave, but absolutely terrified of the tiniest of mice.' She bit her lip. 'We are no further on with finding out what happened to her, Richard, are we?'

He pulled a letter from his shirt pocket and waved it at her. 'I finally received an answer today from my friend back in England. But the plot thickens, as they say. Do you remember I told you about Gobbi's wife, Magdalena, working with an English captain at the end of the war – an Oxford tutor in charge of the relief services in this area? Magdalena told me she was leaving Gobbi and going to Oxford on the advice of this captain. At the time, I imagined they were having an affair. I asked my friend to track down this fellow, in case he could lead us to Hansen. Of course, Hansen found us himself first, but what my friend has to say has added another dimension to the puzzle.'

She was puzzled. 'But, Richard, what has this to do with Simonetta?'

'Well, neither the university nor the Release and Resettlement Services have ever heard of this army captain, apparently. My friend went beyond my brief, even checking for an Italian woman called Magdalena Camarlengo in Oxford to see if anyone of that name had enrolled on any English language courses at the colleges, but not a dicky bird did he uncover.'

'So, where is she?'

Richard shrugged his shoulders. 'I wonder if Magdalena and Gobbi cooked up some sort of ruse between them, and this English captain never existed in the first place. We should try to find out where Magdalena has gone. Perhaps she has the gold stashed somewhere and her husband will be joining her at some stage. He disappeared the other week, didn't he? For a conference or to be with his wife in some secret destination where the gold is? I think we need to turn the heat up with Mayor Gobbi.

Maybe we should get your friends together for another meeting to decide what to do.'

Fosca bit her lip. 'I hope I haven't blown it already. I went to see him this morning and demanded my job back and threatened to tell the whole of Corbello about his part in the gold theft if he didn't do so.' She sighed. 'I'm afraid I rushed in but that man does something to me and I was tired of getting nowhere.'

There was a pause and Richard frowned. 'Maybe you were a little hasty with your blackmailing… but his citizens definitely have a right to know about the theft. Who wants a *sindaco* at the helm with a shady past?'

He stood up and stretched his arms above his head, yawning. 'Oh well. No use crying over spilt milk, as we say in England. I'm turning in now. Barbara has worn me out and she hasn't even been here twenty-four hours. *Buona notte*, Fosca. Let's talk again in the morning when we have clearer heads.'

'*Buona notte*,' she replied, not liking to think about the reasons why Richard might be tired. She herself was so exhausted she felt she could fall asleep standing up.

CHAPTER THIRTY-SEVEN

On the following morning, Fosca was enjoying time to herself at her sewing machine. Richard had taken Barbara to Arezzo to catch the train to Rome. He'd suggested they had a powwow on his return to talk through what to do about Gobbi. Before she'd left in a cloud of perfume, Barbara had given Fosca two blouses with fashionable roses and stripes that didn't fit and Fosca was altering them for herself, letting out the darts on the bust, enjoying the feel of good quality cotton under her fingers as she worked. At the last minute, Giampiero had begged to tag along with Richard, so Fosca was alone, relishing rare solitude.

During the week after the trip to Venice, Pasquale had set up a screen in the little piazza outside the *osteria* and shown the film *Gilda* to his customers, and Fosca had been entranced by the theme tune, 'Amado mio'. As she stitched, she belted out her own lyrics, wiggling her hips to the rumba beat, drawing parallels with the time she'd spent away with Richard. She sang on tunelessly at the top of her voice, inventing her own lines, nobody around to interrupt her. '*The night is shining, with a thousand lights,*' she trilled, when she was interrupted by a loud cough. She jumped, turning in embarrassment to see Gobbi standing behind her. He had let himself into the tobacco house without knocking.

'*Buongiorno*, signora Fosca,' he said. 'I have been considering your request about the teaching post and would like to discuss arrangements. The apartment next to the school is in need of repair, but I have alternative lodgings to show you.' He glanced around the kitchen. 'What I have in mind for you and your son is something more modern. Come with me and I will show you.'

Pleased that he had climbed down and her confrontation had not been in vain, without thinking twice, Fosca stood up to follow Gobbi as he led her to his Lancia, opening the door and gesturing her into the front passenger seat.

'The house I am showing you is beyond Corbello,' he said, as he turned the key in the ignition. 'But it lies along the route of the *corriere* and the *comune* will provide you with a new bicycle.'

Fosca kept her reservations about riding a bike to herself. It was a giant step forward to be told that the job was hers. She would see this accommodation first and then discuss details. After twenty minutes and as the track ascended steeply, she grew concerned. 'It seems a long way to me,' she said, the thick forest on either side of the track showing no sign of human habitation.

'We are nearer to the town than you think, signorina. After the next bend, we shall arrive. You will see for yourself that Corbello is visible from the windows at the back of the house.'

He stopped the car by a gate and came round to open her door. 'After you,' he said and as she stepped out of the car, she felt a sharp blow, and stars burst in her head before she sank to the ground.

Fosca came to in darkness, her mouth dry, her head pounding, her feet and hands bound tight. She winced at the pain at the back of her head, the taste of blood in her mouth. When she moved, dizziness engulfed her and the feeling in her stomach was like the nausea of morning sickness when she had carried Giampiero. She breathed deeply, trying to still her panic, willing the sickness away, but when she attempted to pull herself to a sitting position, her head spun and she had to lie down again and shut her eyes.

Some time later, when she felt able to open her eyes, she saw that she was inside a building with a slit in the stonework high above. Through this gap, Fosca concentrated her gaze on a bright star. It gave her a connection with the world, proving that she was still alive. Furious for letting herself be duped again by Gobbi, she screamed, '*Aiuto, aiuto*, help, help.' There was no reply, not even the bark of a dog. She must be somewhere isolated in the countryside, in a shepherd's hut perhaps, or a small barn. There was no response when she shouted again.

An owl hooted and she jumped at the anguished shriek of a hunted animal. Cold and frightened, she began to shiver. She willed herself to remain calm, telling herself that Gobbi would return sooner or later. When she tried to bring Silvio's face to mind for comfort, it was Richard's kind features that came to her instead: his blue, blue eyes that crinkled at the corners, the way he threw his head back when he laughed. She squeezed her eyes tight shut. 'I am so sorry, Silvio. Please forgive me,' she whispered, apologising for her fickle thoughts, and then she urged her imagination into play to stop herself from falling into a vortex of panic and she pretended that Giampiero was cuddled in her arms, keeping her warm.

She wasn't aware of having slept but she must have done, because the sound of a chain banging loose against stone, and daylight flooding through the open door jolted her awake. Fosca struggled to a sitting position, leaning her back against the rough wall of the building and noticed for the first time, dried hay piled in one corner. If she had explored the space better before, the hay would have provided warmth during the night. She was in a farm building, no bigger than three metres square, and propped against the end wall were a scythe, a hoe and a worn pair of rubber boots.

A man barged in, blocking daylight as he stood at the doorway and she shivered as she recognised Gobbi's stubble-covered face, his eyes squinting at her in the semi-darkness of the building. 'I have brought you something to eat and drink,' he said, dumping bread and a bottle of coffee at her side.

She lunged at the food with her bound feet, spilling the drink, wanting to throw the offerings at him. 'I don't need this. I need to be with my son. Let me out.' She tried to hobble to her feet but he pushed her down again.

'Where is the gold, you bitch?' he asked her. 'If you tell me where you've hidden it, then I'll let you go.'

'I don't know what you're talking about. Let me out of here. They'll come looking for me soon. I've told the Englishman about our talk yesterday. He'll put two and two together and go to the police.'

He pulled out a revolver and pointed it at her and she flinched before recovering herself, her voice shaking as she said, 'If you shoot me, then what will you have gained? And as for the gold, we found one single bar concealed in the well of the tobacco house, that is all.'

'I don't believe you. There were more than three-dozen gold bars on that train and my share disappeared from its hiding place. I want to know where it is. What did Hansen tell you in Venice?'

Her heart missed a beat when she heard that. 'What do you mean? I don't know what—' And then realisation dawned. 'How did you know I was in Venice?'

'The women at the fountain are like a local newspaper,' he jeered. 'I hear them through my office windows. And, anyway, Hansen told me I wasn't the only one he'd sent letters to. You were on his list as well as my wife – God damn her, wherever she is. The man was riddled with cancer… what was the point of gold to him?'

And then Fosca felt terror slide up and down her body like a snake. *The stranger who visited Hansen must have been Gobbi.*

Gobbi is the visitor who killed Hansen, and Gobbi must think that Richard and I got to him first.

Fosca willed herself to keep calm and use her wits.

'The German major told us many things,' she said, praying Gobbi would fall for her lies. 'He gave us a map showing where the gold is buried.'

His eyes lit up. 'Give it to me.'

'Do you think I carry such a thing on me? It's in a safe place. Let me out of here and I'll show you. We can sort this together.'

He waved the revolver at her. 'Stop telling me what to do again,' he shouted. 'You women are all the same. The war has not helped. You think you don't need men anymore, but you think wrong.' He moved to kick her in the ribs and she yelped in pain, hunching her legs up to her body to fend off further blows.

She battled to keep her voice steady. 'Look, Edoardo,' she said, using his Christian name in an effort to approach him on an equal footing. 'This will get us nowhere. Work with us; we can share the gold.'

He pushed his free hand through his hair while he considered her words and then he shook his head. 'I don't need to be lumbered with amateurs. Hansen wanted to collaborate with me too. He had some crazy idea about returning the gold to the people. But I shut him up and the same will happen to you if I run out of patience. It's too late for collaboration.'

'It is never too late. We can work together,' Fosca continued to lie, desperately trying to still the panic in her heart.

Her torso smarted from his kicks. Her head wound throbbed. It was hard to focus on this vile man and his crazy ambitions for lost gold. All she had wanted was to find out the truth about Simonetta. 'I need water, Edoardo,' she said.

'You can wait until you are begging me for water,' he said. 'Maybe then you will reveal where the gold is hidden, because so far I don't believe a word you have told me. Hansen wouldn't tell me either. You will end up like him when I've finished with you.'

He backed away from her and she heard the door chain being secured.

'I'll be back,' Gobbi shouted, his footsteps retreating from where she crouched in agony on the floor. The sound of a car revving and disappearing was replaced by birdsong and the gentle whoosh of branches in the morning breeze.

When she was as sure as she could be that Gobbi was really gone, Fosca shuffled on her bottom to the far side of the space, wincing with each move, the uneven dirt floor digging into her bottom and thighs as she dragged herself towards the tools in the corner. Gobbi had not thought his kidnapping plan through properly. Anybody in their right mind would have checked the building first and bound and gagged their prisoner more securely. It was a dangerous sign to Fosca, the sign of a deranged, desperate man, and she knew she had to act fast if she was to escape. She wondered who was looking after Giampiero now that she'd been missing for a night. Richard would have raised the alarm but she couldn't sit back and wait to be rescued. She had to get away before he returned.

The light from the high opening was good enough to make out the scythe and she shuffled nearer to rub the ropes round her wrists against the blade. In her clumsy haste, she nicked her arm and blood trickled down her hands. Willing herself to slow down, she continued to grate the rope against the farm tool until she freed both hands. Once the feeling returned to her fingers, she slashed through the ropes that bound her feet. Tying her handkerchief around her bleeding wrist, she stood up, nausea hitting her again so that she had to steady herself for a few precious moments against the building. Fosca breathed in and out until the room stopped tilting. She moved to the door and pushed but it wouldn't budge. The wood was thick but if she hacked at it with the scythe, maybe she could make a hole. The panels were flimsier along the bottom edge, uneven from where they had scraped against the stone threshold and animals had gnawed.

Fosca slashed at the wood. As she worked, each blow was filled with hatred for Gobbi. As she swung the scythe, her head swam with pain but she willed herself on, summoning strength from deep within. Finally, she lay on her back, pushing her legs against the planks with all her might and with a splintering crack, the lower half of the door gave way. She thrust the scythe through the opening before squeezing through on her stomach, the uneven edges scratching her back as she pushed out of the gap. Picking up the scythe as a weapon, perspiration streaming down her, she ran for the shelter of the woods, putting distance between herself and the farm building, crashing through the undergrowth as fast as she could, fearful that Gobbi would be back soon to check on her.

She had no idea where she was, so she made for higher ground, hoping the view would help fathom which direction to take. It was impossible to move quietly through the undergrowth. Dry twigs crackled beneath her feet as she panted her way to the top and she dispelled thoughts of mines and booby traps abandoned by the retreating *tedeschi*. The sounds of leaves and pine cones crushing beneath her feet were magnified in her ears with each step, but she pressed on, her lungs bursting, her ribs aching as she reached the summit.

Up here she was grateful to at last come upon a smooth animal track. The trees danced in a refreshing breeze and she leant for a moment against a pine to catch her breath. Beneath her in a shimmering heat haze lay the sprawl of Sansepolcro, the bell tower of San Giovanni Evangelista encased in scaffolding. Bells rang out, reminding her that normal life existed somewhere beyond this nightmare. Just over a kilometre below, she made out a cluster of squat stone buildings and she aimed for these. Summoning all her strength and determination, the scythe clutched in her left hand like a gruesome pirate's hook, she slithered down the other side of the mountain. It was half an hour later, though it felt like hours, when Fosca pulled on the entrance bell wire. The friar who opened the door of the monastery of St Francis at Montecasale caught Fosca before she fell to the ground in a faint.

Richard borrowed Pasquale's truck to take her home. The friars had contacted the *carabinieri* in Sansepolcro after Fosca had related her story and they, in turn, had notified the *carabinieri* in Corbello, who then notified Pasquale. Gobbi was arrested on his way back to the shepherd's hut and was now in the *questura* waiting to be charged with violent assault and kidnapping.

'They will want to question you too, Fosca,' Richard said as he carried her to the truck, 'but you need to be properly examined by a doctor first.'

'There is no need for that,' she said, her arm around his shoulders as he tenderly placed her in the passenger seat. 'The friar in the monastery dispensary is a doctor. He stitched the wound in my head and gave me herbal ointments for my bruises. Please don't make a fuss, Richard. I want to get back to see Giampiero.'

'He's safe with Rosa, Fosca.'

'*Grazie*,' she said, relaxing back into the seat.

If she was honest, she liked Richard fussing over her. She had been about to reach up to hug him when he walked into the monastery, but then she'd remembered Barbara and had stopped herself.

'I can't wait to wear my own clothes again,' she said, pulling at the rough wool tunic that the friars had lent her. 'I seem to be destined forever to dress in monastic garments.' Her skirt and blouse had been torn to shreds by brambles and thorns by the time she arrived at the monastery and the friars had lent her what they could to cover her modesty.

'Oh, I don't know.' He grinned, taking in the voluminous outfit, the sleeves rolled up to fit her arms and the thick belt hoisting up the length. 'You might even start a new fashion.'

She smiled, feeling suddenly weak after her ordeal.

'What will happen to Gobbi?'

'He will face a very hefty sentence, I should imagine. Apart from the murder of Hansen, he'll be charged with war crimes,' Richard said, pulling out the throttle on the truck and starting the engine after a second attempt. The vehicle shuddered as he set off, the engine noisy and he had to shout to be heard, but it was a more comfortable ride for Fosca than it would have been travelling in Richard's sidecar.

'What do you mean?'

'Once word got out that Gobbi was under arrest, an elderly relation of the butcher came forward. He had been too intimidated to tell his story whilst Gobbi was in office, but he revealed how, on the day the boys and the priest were shot in Corbello, he had been hiding upstairs in his house, too terrified to come out. From his window, he witnessed Gobbi shoot the two boys in cold blood.'

Fosca gasped. 'You mean Ennio and Gennaro? *Dio mio.* I hope that he is sentenced to death. Those poor boys. What their parents have gone through… it was bad enough when we thought they'd been shot by the *tedeschi*, but to know it was one of our own. *Madonna Santa*. That man is even worse than I feared.'

'Pasquale had to restrain Bruno when he found out. He'd armed himself with a hunting rifle and was all set to march into the *questura* to blow Gobbi's brains out.'

'I wouldn't have blamed him. I always believed that Hansen had shot the boys.' Fosca stared out of the window at the countryside, wondering when the effects of war would stop trailing its sorrow.

'It will all come out in the trial.'

'Maybe we will finally find out about Simonetta too.'

'I think you should stay at Rosa's tonight. She can look after you better than I can,' Richard said, overtaking a tractor on a straight run.

She shook her head, clutching hold of his arm as he drove. 'Please, no, Richard. I want to be down at the tobacco house. With Giampiero. Like normal.' She paused before adding, 'That is, if I won't be in the way.'

'Of course you won't.' He turned to her. 'Never.'

He smiled his eye-crinkling smile and her heart did a flutter of the nicest kind.

'Is Giampiero all right? Was he worried when I wasn't there to put him to bed?'

'He's absolutely fine. After I'd raised the alarm, I went up to Rosa's with him and entertained him with stories that my mother used to tell me. I quite enjoyed it, actually. But he'll be so happy to see his mother again.'

Richard helped Fosca put Giampiero to bed again that evening, this time reading him two chapters of *Pinocchio*, the little boy laughing at the way he pronounced the Italian words and correcting him, Richard telling him that he would made an excellent teacher, like his mother.

Fosca and Richard sat together for a while in the kitchen, sharing a bottle of sparkling white wine to celebrate her homecoming and when she began to yawn, he took his leave. He handed her a little handbell he'd found in the tower and urged her to ring it during the night if she needed anything. Fosca fell asleep straight away, listening to the breathing of her son in his little bed they'd pushed beside hers, thinking that it was one of the most beautiful sounds she had ever heard.

The next morning, Rosa came to see if anything needed doing, bringing a basket of pasta and tomato sauce and pieces of chicken roasted in rosemary and garlic. Seeing how pale and exhausted Fosca looked, she insisted she wanted to take Giampiero up to the village with her to stay the night and give Fosca a break to recover. But although the events of the previous day had taken more out of her than she realised, Fosca wanted Giampiero nearby. She spent a lazy couple of hours on a chair in the shade, her legs up on a stool and a cushion that Richard had arranged for her. For once her hands were idle and she watched him digging all morning, Giampiero helping. Richard was bare-chested and wore the old army shorts that she'd patched for him in the early days of her stay at the tobacco house. His skin was bronzed after the hot summer and, with all the hard work he'd put in on the renovations, his body was lean and toned.

At midday, he asked her if she wanted to help him plant something. 'I thought it was time,' he said, scooping her up in his arms again, although she protested that she was strong enough to walk. He carried her over to where he had been digging. In truth, she was already feeling much stronger and rested but she was enjoying the closeness, resting next to Richard's bare torso warm from the sun.

He'd dug a hole in the spot where Simonetta's body had been found and Giampiero had helped him fill it with water with a little watering can. 'Let's plant this peach tree here,' he said. 'We may never find out exactly what happened to your friend, but this is one way she can live on.'

When she answered, her voice was thick with emotion. 'I shall never forget her, Richard. And this is such a beautiful idea.' She picked up a handful of earth and dropped it in the hole while he infilled with more soil and compost. 'I pray that the truth comes out about everything that happened when the lawyers interrogate Gobbi.'

Neither of them spoke as Richard added more soil and compost round the tree, the sound of the spade filling the silence.

'We can plant more fruit trees here and turn it into... a living place,' he said. 'When we go to market next time, we can choose.'

'More peaches, apricots. Plums and apples. Oh, and a pear too,' she said. 'Simonetta loved pears.'

'A proper orchard.'

'With chickens scratching about. And maybe geese to keep unwanted visitors away,' she added.

She'd been near to death at the hands of Gobbi, she was certain of that. Now was the time for thinking about the future. It was good to make plans together.

Ten days later, Fosca felt normal again. Wearing a head scarf to keep her head wound clean, she showed Richard how to arrange old sheets around the bases of the silvery, gnarled trees to catch the ripe olives and she instructed Giampiero and Richard to stand underneath the branches. Then, with a huge grin, she shook the first tree vigorously, the little black fruits raining down on their heads like stones.

'Mamma,' her little boy wailed, rubbing his head, and Richard laughed.

'So that's your trick, is it?' He grabbed a pail of water and threw it over her, little Giampiero squealing with delight and joining in with the water fight.

'You can fetch more water from the well now,' she shouted, holding up her hands to stop the water going in her eyes. 'I'd collected that for the pile of washing I have to do.' She called for a truce and emerged from behind the thickest olive tree, its ancient branches twisted like the sinews on the arms of an old man. Fosca caught Richard looking at her, his eyes lingering on her top and, glancing down, she realised that the water had made her blouse transparent, her nipples showing through the thin material and she crossed her arms over her breasts and turned to retreat to the house.

'Tell you what,' he called after her. 'You can cook me a meal tonight to say how sorry you are.'

'*I'm* sorry,' she shouted back, turning at the door. '*You're* the one who started the water fight—' And then she caught him gazing at her again and hurried inside to change.

Giampiero was tired after the fun and games and by six o'clock he was tucked up in his bed fast asleep. She stood for a few moments looking down at him, the shape of his little ears like seashells, his nose and the tiny strawberry-shaped birthmark on his neck, identical to Silvio's.

Downstairs she pulled down the drying rack lined with porcini mushrooms she'd harvested earlier in the month and soaked them in water. Then she arranged a mound of flour on the scrubbed table and broke two eggs into the middle, adding a generous pinch of salt, mixing the pasta dough with her hands for tagliatelle, Richard's favourite pasta. After the summer months she'd lived in the tobacco house and cooked for him, she'd learned his preference was for simple dishes.

Richard arrived just as she finished laying the pasta out to dry on a clean cloth. He had washed and shaved, his hair still wet and combed back from his face. He held up a bottle of wine. 'Montepulciano,' he said. 'Gorilla recommended it. He's bought a barrel for the *osteria* and asked me to try it out.'

'The meal's not quite ready. The pasta needs to dry a little longer before I boil it.'

'Then fetch two glasses and we'll walk to the end of the garden to drink to the sunset. We call it sundowner in English.'

As well as placing glasses on a tray, she added a dozen small squares of *parmigiano* cheese to go with the wine. Wine was apt to go to her head if she drank on an empty stomach.

There was a slight rise in the land at the end of the tobacco house garden and Richard had built a small pergola and placed a table and chairs beneath. In a couple of years, Fosca told him, the vine cuttings would provide shade but in the meantime he had draped it with rolls of raffia. In the distance the town of Corbello was bathed in evening sunshine, its walls and roof tiles golden pink. Even the shapes of the scaffolding and the ladders leaning against the bombed houses looked picturesque in the soft light, like pieces of modern sculpture.

He poured a measure of ruby-red wine into the glasses and raised his to hers. '*Cin cin*, Fosca.'

'*Alla salute*. Good health,' she replied.

They sat quietly, listening to the sounds drifting down from Corbello: the braying of a mule, the barking of dogs, a woman shouting a man's name and his churlish response, the chimes of the church bell for evening prayer. Absent was the thunder of war and the booms of cannons that had drowned out normal life in the last months of 1945. The landscape was slowly turning to how it used to be: ragged tree stumps were already sprouting green shoots, the fields were ploughed, revealing the rich brown of the fertile soil that produced harvests of grapes and tobacco plants. But the healing of people's fractured minds would take longer.

Fosca wondered if she would ever stop thinking about Simonetta. Both Richard and Lupo had warned her that she might never find out how she came to die. But she had the feeling that she was giving up on her friend. She shivered in the cooler air. Richard moved over to her and rubbed her arms and she looked at him in surprise, rising from her chair, flustered as she said, 'The pasta will be dry enough now to boil. And if Giampiero wakes up and doesn't find me in the house, he'll worry.'

'Will he? We're not far away, Fosca. He'll see us from the house. Maybe you worry too much—'

She snapped a reply. 'Don't tell me not to worry about him. I've done nothing else since he was born.'

He lifted both his hands in the air and she relented. Turning to him, she raised herself up, her soft lips meeting his before she murmured, 'I'm sorry, Riccardo. When I am with you, I grow confused, I don't know why, I know you mean well.'

That was all she could say before he pulled her closer and they kissed – tentatively at first, but with increasing passion until she pulled away. She shivered again, but not because of the freshness of the air, and he turned her round, pulling her into his body, wrapping his arms around her and she leant back against his chest, enjoying his strength, feeling safe.

'I've wanted to do that for a long time,' he said. 'But I wasn't sure you wanted me to.'

'I thought you were with Barbara,' she said, turning to him again.

He shook his head, cupping her face in his hands, tracing his thumbs down her cheeks. 'That was over a long time ago. It's you I want, Fosca. If you will have me.' He kissed her forehead. 'I love the way you are. You are so brave. Far braver than you believe.' He dropped a kiss on her nose. 'I love it when you smile. I want to make you smile for the rest of your life.' He kissed both her cheeks. 'I love the way you love your son and I love the way you are so kind to others. I want to be kind and loving to you. You give so much. You need somebody to love you back.'

And then he kissed her long and hard on her lips and she found herself sinking against him, letting go. Being in Richard's arms was like coming home.

'Mamma, I can't sleep.' Giampiero tugged at her skirt and Fosca and Richard broke away from each other.

Richard smiled at her ruefully. 'Perfect timing,' he said.

The three of them walked slowly back to the tobacco house, hand in hand, Giampiero in the middle as they swung him into the air and he squealed with delight. 'Are you two going to get married?' the little boy asked, when they stopped.

'If your mamma will have me,' Richard said, without a pause, glancing over his head at Fosca.

'So, when you get married, can we have a big party and invite Angelina and all the children from the village? And drink Coca-Cola?'

Fosca smiled at Richard. 'I have to consider my answer first. Come on, Giampiero. Back to bed.' She lifted him onto her hip and murmured to Richard, 'I won't be long and then we'll eat.'

Fosca sat for a while on the bed, watching her little boy fall asleep. She traced her fingers round her lips where Richard had kissed her. The way he had made her feel was how Silvio had made her feel, and yet it was different. Silvio's had been a gradual courtship: shy glances at first, a hand brushing a hand until one day he'd asked permission to kiss her. She'd been a young, innocent girl back then but Richard made her feel… she placed her hand beneath the swell of her breast… Richard made her feel like a woman.

When she returned from Giampiero, Richard was sitting on his poetry bench, looking nervous. He held a small box, which he thrust into her hands.

'Open it,' he said. 'I hope you like it. I bought it in Venice but there's never been a right moment to give it to you until now.'

She lifted the lid and undid a package wrapped in a thin sheet of notepaper covered with his handwriting. Inside was an exquisite piece of Murano glass, shaped like an acorn.

'It's beautiful,' she said, holding it up. 'When did you buy this?'

'I saw it when we were in Venice and managed to pop out one morning while you were getting ready for the day.'

She laughed in delight. 'When you said you were going out to smoke your pipe.'

Her eyes glistened with unshed tears. 'It's truly beautiful. Exactly the same as the acorns on my mother's dress.'

'That's why I chose it.'

She kissed him again.

She straightened out the creases on his note and started to read Richard's words to herself while he moved away, hands in his pockets, scuffing the dirt at his feet. Richard had written in Italian. There were mistakes in the grammar but there was no mistaking the sentiments behind the lines. His poem described the first time he'd seen the most beautiful Italian girl at his well. The world had stopped turning for him when she'd looked up like a startled doe, her brown eyes reflecting panic. From that moment he had vowed to chase away her fears. Like the lightning that forked in summer storms, she had pierced his heart that day and filled him with life. He had watched her in the shadows, in the daylight and admired her warlike spirit. Her heart was gentle and brave; she was strong like the olive trees that grew in his garden. She did not know her strength.

He turned round when he heard her approaching. 'Tear it up, Fosca. I'm embarrassed. You're better than lines on that scrap of paper. I wanted to try to write something beautiful... I just wanted to tell you...'

She stopped his words, placing a finger on his lips. 'I love you, Richard,' she whispered. 'Nobody has ever said such beautiful things about me.'

'I want to know you more, Fosca,' Richard said. 'And one day I shall write the poem you deserve. This is only the beginning for both of us.'

The pasta was forgotten as he took her in his arms again and they kissed. When they came up for air, she leant against him and for the first time in a long time, she was at peace with herself. For now, it was all that mattered. Simonetta was gone but she, Fosca, was alive and so was her beautiful son. And with Richard next to her, she felt she could confront the world again, a step at a time. The future was no longer a bleak place.

CHAPTER THIRTY-EIGHT

A woman sits by Lake Garda in the shade of an umbrella pine, an unlit cigarillo in her hand. The surgeon has warned her that the new tissue on her face will die if she smokes, but for the time being, feeling the slim brown cylinder in her fingers is sufficient. Eventually she will give up nicotine, just as she has given up other pastimes and partners. Her future is full of plans and time is on her side.

The magazine on her lap is closed, her head brimming with ideas. The woman has her eyes on the art deco house on the island, its mustard-yellow stucco façade reflected in the rippling water. The garish bougainvillea climbing the walls will have to go. Instead, there will be ornate terracotta pots of white roses and a wall of misty lavender planted on the terrace where guests will dine al fresco. A yacht sails by and voices float to her over the water and she hears the clink of glass against glass and jazz from a wind-up gramophone typical of the sounds of exclusive holidays, the market that the woman is planning to tap into.

It was a shame in some ways to cut loose from Manfred, her German major. The woman shivers as she remembers how Manfred's hands deliciously played her body on their afternoons in the Arezzo hotel, coaxing pleasure the way he coaxed notes from his beloved piano. But that is over and done with now, lost to the past. She hated that he showed more commitment to alcohol than her and the last time they were together she decided he was no longer a part of her plan. It was the easiest thing in the world to wait for the right time to remove the gold stashed in the well near the ruined tobacco tower and to disappear, leaving a false trail in her wake. For a while the woman toyed with the idea of starting a new life in Argentina. There are many Italians living there. She's heard there are plenty of *tedeschi* too, a safe haven for Nazi war criminals. But the woman will never leave her native land. Italy is in her blood and she is convinced one day her country will rise again in the glory that Mussolini conjured – until power consumed his vain head.

The bruising and swelling on her face will eventually go down. For the time being the woman wears large, dark sunglasses and spends her days resting and planning. Her plastic surgeon has described the recovery process as a journey, not a race. She stretches her arms, careful not to strain, the gold bangles falling down her arms with a pleasing jangle. Then she begins to flick through the hairstyle pages at the back of *Vogue*. A short gamine style with a high fringe might suit her face well, totally different from the long wavy hair that her husband used to admire. She will keep her own colour. The constant battle with roots will be too tedious and too much like a disguise.

A toned young man, his white shirt unbuttoned at the neck, leans down to her with a silver tray containing a small bowl of stuffed olives and a tall glass of Prosecco, the bubbles catching the setting sun. 'Your *aperitivo*, signora Elda.' For a split second she does not register the name, the letters she extracted and rearranged from her real name, Magdalena. The hesitation goes unnoticed and she thanks him, takes the glass and sips at the cool drink. She watches the movement of his pert bottom in his tight black trousers as he walks back to the kitchen to prepare her dinner. Despite his prowess between the sheets, Elda will not be hiring Domenico when she opens her hotel on the island. There is nothing much between his ears to stimulate her. No way will she allow any man to wheedle his way into the new life she is mapping out for herself.

This morning Elda signed the sale contract for Villa Borghese and soon she will leave Domenico and this rented house behind. The pale blue Alfa Romeo Cabriolet is paid for and waiting in the showroom for her to pick up when she is ready. She will not employ a chauffeur. She will drive herself along the winding lakeside roads. Brescia, Verona, Venice and Milan are all conveniently near and if she feels the need to disappear for a weekend to visit the opera, or pick up a handsome man for the night, then a chauffeur will only be an encumbrance. A short enough drive away is the border with Switzerland, where she has deposited her prize in a Geneva account under yet another name. Elda enjoys the thrill of speed; she has even toyed with the idea of driving in the first Mille Miglia race since the war but has decided against it for the time being. It will be prudent to lie low for a couple more years. She tosses the cigarillo into the lake. It floats for a few seconds and then sinks without trace beneath the water.

It is growing chilly and Elda rises from her recliner, pulling her cashmere shawl around her shoulders, careful not to stretch her neck muscles. After dinner she will retire early. The only blight on her life at the moment is her need for powerful sleeping draughts. The little red Seconal Sodium barbiturates are her only defence between nightmares and sleep. These nightmares are filled with images of a young partisan girl. The girl they called Simonetta, who had been in the tobacco house where Elda had made love with her German boyfriend. The little bitch had witnessed them concealing the gold bars they had stolen from her husband's share in the well.

*

Simonetta had been in the wrong place at the wrong time. She had been searching that day for a new hiding place for the *partigiani*. The tobacco house was no longer safe. She hoped that Fosca had followed her advice and would leave as soon as possible. Later on, after dark, Simonetta planned to visit to bid her farewell. On one of the occasions that Maria had walked with her from Anghiari, they'd caught a glimpse of the corner of a stone building through the bare trees and this was Simonetta's destination today.

The group were trying to be kind to her since the death of Maria, making sure she ate, and drank copious amounts of red wine. For food, she had little appetite, but drink was her medicine. After the first couple of beakers, Maria was closer to her. Memories of the first time they'd kissed filled Simonetta's head with bursts of colour and she saw again her beautiful face, the way she twisted her dark hair around her middle finger when she was concentrating, Maria weaving stories while they lazed by the fire – stories filled with the life they'd share when the war was over, Maria taking her hand and telling her that that there was no need to be shameful or apologetic for the feelings they had for one another.

'I don't deserve to be so happy,' Simonetta had whispered and Maria sat up on their mattress, propped herself on one elbow, her finger slowly tracing her lover's mouth.

'That is nonsense, *cara mia*. Everybody deserves to be happy.' And then she had kissed her inhibitions away, until Simonetta felt true to herself.

The two women had to be ultra-careful and discreet. Not only was Simonetta Jewish, but she was committing the dual sin, in the eyes of the Italian state and Catholic Church, of being in love with another woman. Her parents had been conservative, and would never have tolerated her coming out. It was impossible for such a relationship to exist in a Fascist regime, where it was considered sick and a sexual aberration. Gay men, known derogatorily in slang Italian as *femminèlle*, were shipped off in shackles to islands round the coast and treated as a danger to public health. Maria was Simonetta's saviour.

But none of her friends were letting her grieve properly. She'd told them she was hunting out a new place for them to hide and plan their missions, and this was partly true, but in reality, she craved a night on her own to yowl and howl at the moon. Three nights previously, she'd stolen from the shepherd's hut where she and the others had been hiding and made her way to the spot where Maria had fallen. She'd picked wild snowdrops from the hillside and made a nosegay to place on the grass. But the gesture had done nothing to calm her distress. The stars above where she knelt, that she and Maria had loved to watch, lying on their backs counting them as they slid down the sky, were like daggers scratching the blackness. She'd jumped up, crushing the snowdrops underfoot, grinding them into the rocky hillside where Maria had been blown into fragments.

Now, away from the path she'd followed, she'd pushed through the undergrowth and made her way back to the tobacco house. There was nobody there that night. Fosca was working up at Bruno's *osteria*. As she walked the forest paths, she imagined Maria close by her, shadowing her, keeping a careful lookout for the enemy. Nobody was safe to wander freely at this time with mines, gun points positioned where least expected and troops on reconnaissance. Her heart was leaden. All she wanted to do was curl up like a wounded animal and find a lair that no other creature would discover. The tobacco house was the last place they had lain together, Maria holding her tight, her heavy breasts warm against Simonetta's back, one hand resting on her hip as they murmured their goodnights.

Simonetta had been asleep for a couple of hours on the mattress in the kitchen where she and Maria used to sleep, when she was woken by voices. She peered through the window and recognised the couple immediately, her eyes rounding in surprise. The wife of Gobbi and the German major they called Hansen were by the well, a box beside them on the ground. She watched as the *tedesco* climbed down the ladder a short way and Magdalena passed him one after another of what Simonetta was sure were the bars of gold from the train.

When there were no more, the couple embraced. They could not keep their hands off each other as they kissed passionately, tearing at each other's clothes, their groans intensifying. She watched in dismay as they hurried towards the house and she moved fast to scale the ladder to the space above the kitchen where grain was stored. The murmurs from the couple grew louder as they writhed on the floor beneath where she perched and she wanted to stop the sounds with her fingers in her ears but she dared not make a movement. After their coupling, they talked quietly, then there was silence.

Simonetta peeped through the boards. For about fifteen minutes she remained where she was, her knees numb from crouching, her teeth chattering with the draught that blew through the ventilation gaps beside her. They were asleep when she checked again, their legs entwined, the woman's blouse open, the German's arm stretched over her naked breasts. Gently rising to her feet, desperately wanting to be out of this place to inform the others, pins and needles attacking her as she unfolded her legs, she moved towards the ladder.

The top rung disintegrated as her foot met the worm-riddled wood and she yelped as she began to slip. Strong hands yanked her down the rest of the way and she turned to spit in Hansen's face. He grabbed her from behind, his hands crushing her as he held her fast, and as hard as she kicked and wriggled, she couldn't escape.

'Spying on us, were you, signorina?'

'We all know what happens to spies, don't we?' Magdalena said.

'*You*—' Simonetta started to say, before the full force of something hard impacted with her jaw and she lost consciousness.

Simonetta would never know for how long she remained on the floor but she could hear the couple quarrelling when consciousness returned, the pain in her mouth and head excruciating as she tried to focus.

'It's the only possible solution. We have to get rid of her,' she heard Gobbi's wife say.

'There must be another way. Can't we simply frighten her? Bribe her or something?'

'You understand nothing about the *partigiani. Nothing* frightens them. They are young and foolhardy. Their idealism makes them fight to the death. She won't go away with her tail between her legs. If *you* don't kill her, I will. Otherwise all our plans come to nothing.'

Blood trickled from Simonetta's mouth and she ran her tongue over her smashed teeth. The pain in her head drummed like a hundred horses' galloping hooves and she felt sick. But concentration and remaining awake were essential. Simonetta started to inch her way towards the back door, her head pounding as she dragged herself along.

The couple continued to argue over by the hearth as she lifted herself on all fours in the shadows, fumbling to raise the latch, her head spinning. Slipping through the door, groping her way along the stone walls of the building, Simonetta forced one foot after the other. There was no way she could travel far, disoriented, woozy, her legs not obeying her head. Sinking behind a tangle of wild roses, the thorns scratched her arm through the material as she slumped on her stomach and she felt blood seeping through her sleeve. Fosca's brooch dug into her breastbone on its chain and an idea came to her. Unhooking the brooch, she wound her handkerchief round and round her right hand and snapped a branch from the dog rose to scratch a letter on the silver casing. If she could somehow leave the brooch in their agreed hiding place, then maybe Fosca might get the message. But that would mean returning inside, which was impossible for the time being. When Simonetta had finished her crude scratching of the letter M, she slipped the brooch into her pocket and began to crawl away from the buildings in search of a better hiding place.

The back door was flung wide and torchlight strobed the ground until it located Simonetta prostrate in the longer grass. Shouting filled the night air: 'The bitch is over there. Quick before she gets away.'

Shots cracked open the night.

Simonetta struggled to her feet, Maria beckoning and smiling to her with open arms from where she waited, mist swirling in the background.

In Corbello, dogs barked as Simonetta's body crumpled to the ground.

*

Elda's nightly dreams are consumed by the scene with the dead girl. The only way to stop the partisan bitch was to pull the trigger herself. Hansen had been ineffectual, trying to convince her of some other way, so Elda had taken over, grabbed his gun and fired. The torment that will not leave Elda's head is the shock of bony hands as they break through the earth and stones that she and Hansen heaped later on the girl's body. Elda cannot count how often she has woken screaming from those nails clawing at her throat. She hopes that in time she will forget and that the nightmares will dwindle but for now she is dependent on her little red helpers. It is a small price to pay for a life of luxury.

Domenico has prepared a delicate starter this evening of quail's eggs nestled on a bed of rocket, sprinkled with shavings of her favourite Parmesan cheese. She has ordered a bottle of white Verdicchio and lake trout for the main course and he presents it to her on a delicate porcelain platter, bowing low as he sets the food down. Later, as Elda starts to choke and clutch her throat, she will regret dismissing him for the rest of the evening. Perhaps he might have called for help. She slumps to the floor, her mouth foaming poisonous white spittle onto the expensive Aubusson rug.

Domenico is the only mourner in the church besides the priest who plucks a homily from the air. It has not been possible to track down any living relatives of Signora Elda Lombardo. In searching her rented house, a will was found, bequeathing everything to Elda's faithful servant, Domenico di Gasperi. Forging a will had been a small matter to a man who, during the war, for exorbitant prices, successfully modified documents for countless desperate refugees.

If you happen to visit Lake Garda in high season, you might see Domenico cruising the lakeside roads in a smart pale blue Alfa Romeo Cabriolet. Sometimes he escorts ladies who come to stay at his exclusive *albergo* on the island and takes them to dine at restaurants nestled in the coves of Lake Garda or accompanies them to pamper their ageing bodies in the spas along the water.

And in the meantime, the bars of gold stolen from the Italian state by the *tedeschi* and Gobbi, aided by the courageous *partigiani*, lie out of reach, locked in a dormant account in a Swiss bank. Gold stolen during a destructive war, locked away where nobody will ever see it glisten or know a thing about the lives it changed.

AFTERWORD

There was a kind of gold rush in Italy after war's end.

Much stolen treasure and gold had been hidden near borders, in lakes, in cellars and even forests. Gold was stolen by the Nazis from the vaults of the Bank of Italy and stashed in impregnable bunkers like in the vast subterranean city commissioned by Mussolini and built deep within the mountains near Sant'Oreste, in the region of Lazio.

Valuables were hastily hidden by fleeing Jews and seized by dodgy partisans, Germans on the run, the Wehrmacht and crooks.

From 1945 onwards, much German gold ended up in Switzerland, including fillings from the mouths of Jewish victims and valuables taken from concentration camp prisoners.

Half a century later, attention was drawn to this scandal of Nazi gold tucked away in Swiss vaults during World War II. Less attention has been paid to Italian fascist gold. In 2000, the Swiss weekly paper, *L'Hebdo*, issued an article with the title: 'Treasure Hunt: Who's Sleeping on Mussolini's Gold?'

To this day, Nazi gold stashed away in Swiss bank vaults is still a contentious topic. In 1996, Swiss banks were forced to pay $1.25bn to Jewish victims for the Jewish gold still dormant in Swiss banks.

Some argue that Switzerland complied with the allies' demands in 1945 to hand over all valuables deposited by Germans during World War II in Swiss banks.

Truth or speculation, questions linger to this day.

A LETTER FROM ANGELA

Dear reader,

I want to say a huge thank you for choosing to read *The Tuscan House*. If you did enjoy it, and want to keep up to date with all my latest releases, just sign up at the following link. Your email address will never be shared and you can unsubscribe at any time.

www.bookouture.com/angela-petch

I hope you loved *The Tuscan House* and if you did, I would be very grateful if you could write a review. I'd love to hear what you think, and it makes such a difference helping new readers to discover one of my books for the first time.

I love hearing from my readers – you can get in touch on my Facebook page, through Twitter, Goodreads or my website.

Thanks or *mille grazie*,
Angela Petch

 AngelaJaneClarePetch

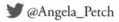 @Angela_Petch

🌐 angelapetchsblogsite.wordpress.com

Ⓖ Angela Petch Author Page

QUESTIONS
FOR READING GROUPS

1. What role do the tobacco buildings play in the story?
2. Richard, Fosca and Simonetta are all courageous in their own ways. Do you agree?
3. In writing this book, I was greatly inspired by Ada Gobetti, one of the most renowned anti-fascists in Italian history. She once said that there would have been no *resistenza* without the input of women in World War II. Do you agree?
4. What do you think about Richard's pacifist beliefs and had you heard of the Friends Ambulance Unit before reading?
5. How important a figure is Madre Caterina to the story?
6. Do you think Fosca's character changes and develops over each time period of the novel?
7. Do you think Fosca should have confided to the partisans about Gobbi's promise to her about her missing husband? In what way might that have changed the outcome?
8. How do you imagine Fosca and Richard's futures will play out in post-war Italy?
9. Who is your favourite character, and why?

BIBLIOGRAPHY

A Few Days Leave in London by Kenneth Sutor

A House in the Mountains by Caroline Moorehead

BBC WW2 People's War

Blitz by Jane Waller and Michael Vaughan-Rees

È passata la rovina a Sansepolcro by Giovanni Ugolini

Friends Ambulance Unit (FAU) in WW2 by A. Tegla Davies

From Oasis into Italy: War Poems and Diaries from Africa and Italy 1940–1946, written by men serving in the armed forces in the Second World War (Editors: Victor Selwyn, Dan Davin, Erik de Mauny, Ian Fletcher and Advisers: Field Marshal Lord Carver and General Sir John Hackett)

Guerra e resistenza nell'Alta Valle del Tevere (1943–1944) by Alvaro Tacchini

In Love and War: A Letter to My Parents by Maria Corelli and Jason Goodwin

Primo Levi's Resistance by Sergio Luzzatto

Scenari di guerra, parole di donne by Patrizia Gabrielli

The Voice of War, edited by James Owen and Guy Walters

Voices Against War by Lyn Smith

ACKNOWLEDGEMENTS

History for me is about people and how they react to events. When I was at school, I had a very boring teacher who wrote copious notes on the blackboard and failed to bring history alive. Older now, I have a hunger to dig up stories about our past. Sadly, our elderly relatives and friends who lived through the Second World War are slowly disappearing from our lives. I attended my aunt's funeral recently and her daughter had managed to talk to her about her experiences as a Land Girl and taken notes a few months earlier. This year, I lost my elderly one-hundred-year-old Italian friend, Bruno, and, fortunately, he had made recordings of his experiences as a POW during World War Two. These memories are very precious and they help us to understand not only our past, but also our future. My parents died far too young. If they were still here, I know I would be prompting stories from them. During the Second World War, my father was in North Africa and Italy – where my hero was located. It would have been useful to pick his brains. Not everybody of his generation was happy to reveal what went on in their war. This is understandable – it was a painful time. But chunks of history are lost in this way. In writing *The Tuscan House* I came across my father's handwritten account of walking through London during the Blitz in 1940, as a young man of twenty. I have borrowed some of his descriptions. I don't think he will mind them living on in my story.

I often ask myself how I would have behaved during the war years. I wrote a great part of this book during the Covid-19 epidemic. Some describe it as living in a war but I don't think we have suffered anywhere near to what our parents and grandparents experienced. The courage that I have read about, told by those who lived through it, is simply mind-numbing. It is said that unless you actually go through something, you cannot foretell how you would react. Would I have had the courage to put my life on the line each and every day like Fosca, Simonetta and so many others? How desperate would I have felt and what would I have done to save the lives of my children? What if I simply couldn't bring myself to fight – not through cowardice, but because of my beliefs, like my pacifist character, Richard? I have tried to examine these questions through the characters in *The Tuscan House* and to present a slice of ordinary people's history through their eyes.

For my research, as well as speaking to Italian friends and visiting locations, I read many books. I mention them in the bibliography, but particular thanks and admiration go to Caroline Moorehead and her wonderful book *A House in the Mountains*, chiefly about the women who liberated Italy from fascism. My characters are entirely fictitious, a blend of many accounts and people who inspired me, and I hope that I have put over the hopes and fears of ordinary people in my story.

Similarly, another fascinating source was the collection of memoirs *Scenari di Guerra, parole di donne*, compiled by Patrizia Gabrielli from women's diaries stored in the National Archive Museum of Pieve Santo Stefano, near where I live in Tuscany. Italian women were encouraged to keep the home fires burning and Mussolini was keen to build up a mythical image of the woman by the hearth, producing baby after baby for the good of the nation. However, their important contribution to the resistance, their enormous bravery, their spirit of adventure and desire for liberation from tyranny, brought huge changes to their futures. In 1946, Italian women were allowed to vote for the first time in the national election but they have had to fight for recognition of their efforts in the resistance ever since. Lidia Menapace, who was an active member of the resistance in northern Italy and who died aged ninety-six on 7 December 2020 from complications with Covid, is purported to have said that without women, there would not have been any *resistenza*.

Wherever possible, I have tried to keep true to historical events. However, the town of Corbello exists only in my imagination, as a combination of the two Tuscan hilltop towns of Citerna and Monterchi that actually exist in the Tiber Valley near to the city of Sansepolcro. There are plaques on their town walls commemorating the courage of young partisans and Gurkha soldiers who lost their lives in combat and they remind the visitor of those who helped liberate Italy. Various anecdotes, including that of Tony Clarke, a British army captain who disobeyed orders and saved a famous Piero della Francesca painting from being bombed in Sansepolcro, are true. Huge thanks to Italian World War Two historian and friend, Alvaro Tacchini, a fount of local knowledge.

I have so many people to thank for help in writing this book. First of all, patient and encouraging Ellen Gleeson, who guides me down the rocky path of edits that always sends me into a spin with the initial structural changes. Huge thanks to the Bookouture family, as this wonderful publishing team describe themselves, and my author friends on Twitter and Facebook. You all understand what efforts are needed for writing a book from start to finish and you are wonderfully supportive. For helping me blow up a train, thanks go to Steve Musson! *Mille grazie* to my little team, Noi di Rofelle, my dear Italian friends Silvia, Antonella and Marcello, who help me when I have questions about slightly strange Italian sayings. I was inspired by an out-of-print collection of war poems and diaries, *From Oasis into Italy*, published by Shepheard-Walwyn, to create Richard, the poet. The verses and literary pieces in that book were written by men serving in the armed forces during the Second World War, including in Italy. As I read the collection, I was very moved, imagining those men writing lines during a lull, under canvas, in a field hospital or at the edge of a battlefield. Their achievements should not be forgotten.

Finally, infinite thanks to my wonderful, supportive husband, Maurice.

Made in the USA
Monee, IL
21 April 2021